ALICIA ALLEN INVESTIGATES 2

WILFUL MURDER

D1385927

ALICIA ALLEN INVESTIGATES...

A CRIME TRILOGY
by
CELIA CONRAD

ALICIA ALLEN INVESTIGATES 2

WILFUL MURDER

Celia Conrad

Barcham Books

First published in Great Britain in 2011 by Barcham Books, an imprint of
Creative Communications, Suite 327, 28 Old Brompton Road, London, SW7 3SS
barchambooks@btconnect.com
creativecom@btconnect.com

ISBN 978 09546233 3 3 (0 9546233 3 9)

Designed by Andrew Dorman
www.andrewdorman.co.uk

Printed and bound by CPI Group (UK) Ltd, Croydon, CR0 4YY

For Gavin

Chapter 1

January 2007

I was absolutely incredulous. Michael Seaton was dead; murdered by his own son...

'Alicia, I thought it must be you; although I couldn't quite be sure until you turned around,' she said excitedly, edging forward and tapping me on the shoulder, causing me to start. I was on the tube and it was particularly crowded. Talk about a face from the past. It was Sally Hamilton, and we had been at university together. I recognised her at once, although she now wore her sandy-red hair long and straight and not in the layered bob she donned as a student. The last thing I heard was that she intended to spend a gap year travelling before taking up her place at Law school.

'Sally, you have a very good memory for faces,' I replied wearily, forcing a smile.

'So do you! But you've hardly changed. You always were quite distinctive. What's the book? You seemed totally engrossed,' she added with giddy enthusiasm as she glanced down at the well-thumbed paperback I was clutching.

'Just a thriller I've been reading. So how are you? I haven't seen you since our graduation ceremony.'

'I know. I can't believe how many years it must be. I'm fine, thanks. How are you? Not married yet then?' she continued, without pausing for breath nor waiting for me to reply to her first question as she glanced down at the ringless third finger of my left hand. 'Me neither.' She shrugged her shoulders.

'I'm well, thank you.'

'Do you work near here?'

'No. I've been to an interview in Southampton Row.'

'So where's work for now?'

'I've been working on and off as a locum since last summer.'

'Why?'

'Long story. Put it this way, my last job didn't work out.'

'That's a shame. How did the interview go today? Who was it with?'

'Darlington & Lowndes.' She furrowed her brow and her honey brown eyes glazed over for a moment.

'They deal with landed estates, don't they?'

'Yes.'

'So?'

'All I can say is that I felt no rapport with either of my interviewers and by the end of the interview I was totally indifferent about the position.'

'Oh, that's tough. What is it you specialize in anyway?' she asked, screwing up her forehead and looking at me quizzically.

'Tax, Wills and Trusts, so Private Client. I also do Family work. You?'

'Commercial litigation. I'm at Knight & Bailey. We're based near Liverpool Street. We call it "Night and Daily" as we're expected to work incredibly long hours, although I did manage to escape early tonight.' At this point the train pulled into Hyde Park Corner tube station, two seats directly behind us became free and we sat down. 'That's better. Now I can talk to you properly,' she said, turning towards me and smiling broadly.

'Are you on your way home?' I wondered whether she lived anywhere near me considering we were heading in the same direction.

'No. I live at Swiss Cottage, but I'm meeting a friend in

Knightsbridge. We're going for a drink in Harvey Nichols and then on to dinner. I'm a bit late actually,' she said, glancing at her watch. 'The tubes are awful tonight.'

'Yes. There were signal problems with the Piccadilly Line earlier.'

'*We* should catch up, too, you know,' she said, touching my arm. 'Sounds like you need a fun night out. Are you still in touch with Jo du Plessis? I remember you two were always such good friends. What did she end up doing?'

'She joined the police. She's Mrs Brook now. She married Will a few years ago.'

'Oh. I see. What does her husband do?' she asked, unzipping her handbag and taking a business card from an inside pocket. She wrote her mobile number on the back before handing it to me.

'He's ex-CID. He has his own detective agency. Jo works with him.'

'Sounds a more exciting job than mine. May I have your number?' she asked as I slipped her card into the depths of my overcoat pocket.

'If you have a spare card I'll write it on the back for you.'

'Great,' she said, pulling another card out of her bag and giving me a black biro. I scribbled it down. 'Now I come to think of it, I may have some work to pass your way. I know you're not working right now, but a friend of mine needs some advice.'

'What kind of advice?'

'She wasn't specific, but she's getting married in a few months time and is about to inherit a ton of money from her grandfather. She told me that she wants to sort out her affairs before her marriage, and probably wants a Will or something, so that'd be right up your street. She's not a run of the mill client, that's for sure.'

'From a monetary point of view?'

'Well, that, and also her unusual family circumstances. Virtually all her close family are dead.'

'What exactly are you saying?'

'Too many deaths in the family for my liking. Sorry, but I have to go,' she said, standing up and taking the card from me. The train pulled into Knightsbridge tube station. 'I'll ring you and we can talk about it then. Enjoy your evening,' she called out, turning back as she stepped from the train. 'Bye, Alicia. I'll be in touch.' The doors closed and, as the train pulled off, I watched her waving to me from the platform.

I continued on to South Kensington and walked home in the bitter January cold. I stopped off at the mini-mart and bought some Black Pepper Pringle Dippers. I wanted Smokin' Bacon flavour, but they were out of stock. It was now too late to call Jane Edwards at Legal Beagles recruitment agency for a post-interview discussion. She would probably call me the next morning anyway.

After soaking in a hot foam-filled bath, I felt refreshed and relaxed. I opened the tube of Pringle Dippers, took a salsa dip out of the fridge and sat on the sofa munching them. While I mulled over the events of the day and read the *Evening Standard* I consumed nearly half the tube.

In the scheme of things my day had turned out better than expected. The interview at Darlington & Lowndes had been an unmitigated disaster, but the unexpected meeting with Sally Hamilton had lifted my spirits. I was curious about this friend of hers and the comments Sally had made. I hoped to hear more from her soon.

As anticipated, I received a call from Jane Edwards asking for my feedback on the interview.

'It was a complete waste of time. When I tried to explain why I've been working as a locum they weren't interested.'

'You wouldn't want to go back for a second interview then?'

'No. Although I suspect that a second interview won't be forth-coming anyway. But I would like to know what they have to say, if only for future reference. So, could you find out for me?'

'Of course. I'll put a call in to them now.'

I went downstairs to put out my rubbish. I could hear the 'phone ringing as I sprinted back upstairs. In that short space of time someone had put my post on the mat. I picked it up and let myself back into the flat. Jane was on the line.

'Alicia?'

'Speaking.' I sifted through the post. There was a cream envelope with an Australian postmark on it. It was addressed by hand in black ink and I recognised the handwriting at once to be that of my friend Kim. I would not mistake those thick looped 'L's anywhere.

'I've just spoken to Rosemary Whiteman at Darlington & Lowndes,' said Jane. Rosemary was the firm's personnel manager. I put the rest of the post down, picked up the silver paper knife my sister Antonia had given me for my thirtieth birthday, opened the cream envelope and pulled out the contents. It was indeed from Kim; in fact, an invitation to her wedding in Brisbane. She and her fiancé Rob were getting married on Saturday, 10 March 2007.

'And?' I scanned Kim's invitation.

'She told me she and Charlotte Melrose enjoyed meeting you. She also said they were very impressed with you personally and with your experience, but on balance feel they cannot take your application further because you are not quite the right fit for their firm and…' I interrupted her.

'How many times have I heard that phrase?' Firms used that expression frequently. I had always wondered what it really meant, and thought that it was probably the one they relied upon when they could find no reasonable excuse *not* to employ someone.

'I know. It's disappointing, but I'm sure you'll find the right niche soon. I'll keep an eye out for you and be in touch if anything comes up that's suitable.'

In truth I did not feel the least bit disheartened because I had already concluded that Darlington & Lowndes was not the firm for me. Besides, with no work commitments to hold me back, there was nothing to prevent me from going to Australia. Clouds do sometimes have silver linings after all.

11

I logged on to the internet to check out the cost of flights to Brisbane and trawled through several sites looking for a reasonable deal. I had intended to e-mail Kim but decided to 'phone her as I had not spoken to her since before Christmas. I had missed her desperately after she had moved back to Australia the previous August.

'Guess who?' I said, trying to disguise my voice.

'Hi, Alicia. I'd recognise that voice anywhere. What a great surprise! How are you?' She sounded bright and cheerful as always.

'I'm fine. I received your invitation today.'

'You did? Are you coming?'

'Of course I am. I couldn't miss your wedding.'

'Well, that's fantastic. I thought maybe you might have started a new job and wouldn't be able to take the time off?'

'Not yet. No.'

'Good. I mean, I'm sorry you're not sorted on the work front, but I'm glad you can make it.'

'I know what you meant. How's Rob?'

'He's good. He'll be really chuffed you're coming over. I can't wait to see you. I know you'll have a fabulous time. Have you booked your flight?'

'No. I was looking on the internet for deals.'

'Well, e-mail me the details when you have. I'll make sure that someone comes to collect you at the airport and you must stay with Mum and Dad. OK?'

'I don't want to impose.'

'You won't be. It'd be a pleasure to have you.'

'That's very kind. Let me think about it. You know how I like to be independent.'

'OK. But you're most welcome.'

'Thank you. How are all the preparations going?'

'Really well. It's been a bit hectic, but we'll be right. I think I'm almost ready but I keep finding something else to do. I guess you'll want to travel around Australia while you're here. I mean you might as well. How long are you staying for?' I could not help smiling to myself. I had forgotten how bubbly and chatty Kim could be. It was sometimes difficult to get a word in edgeways.

'I'll stay for as long as I can. I'd like to spend some time in Melbourne and Sydney as well.'

'Jeremy Brown lives in Melbourne, doesn't he?' Jeremy was the father of my sister Antonia's boyfriend Tom.

'Yes; he said I'm always welcome there.'

'Did you know Tom's going to be Rob's best man?'

'No.'

'Hasn't Antonia told you?'

'You know what my sister's like about telling me things,' I replied. 'In fairness she started a new job a couple of weeks ago and she's been under a lot of pressure. She probably forgot.'

'Hmm… How's your mother?'

'She's well.'

'And Dorothy?' She was referring to my neighbour Dorothy Hammond who was eighty-three and lived in the garden flat downstairs.

'Very frail, but as sharp as ever.'

'Oh, bless her. She's such a sweetie. And what about Cesare? Do you ever hear from him?' Cesare Castelli used to live in the flat on the floor above mine but had moved to New York.

'You must miss him.'

'I do actually. He'll always be a good friend.'

'What's the new neighbour like?'

'Her name's Catherine Caldecott and she's rapidly becoming the neighbour from hell. She's completely refurbishing the place and in the process has flooded my flat twice. The constant noise of banging and drilling has almost driven me mad.'

'I wondered what that noise was in the background. Poor Ally. It sounds like you need a break from that place. Maybe this trip will be a good opportunity for you to take stock and think about where you go from here.' There was a slight pause at the end of the line.

'Oh, I know what I was going to ask you. How's Jo?'

'She's staying in the South of France with her mother's family. I think the time in France is doing her the world of good. She's planning to come back after Easter.'

'Oh, I'm glad to hear she's doing well. Listen, Ally, I'll let you go. I've kept you talking for far too long already. Send my love to your mother, Dorothy and Jo, and you take care. Don't forget to e-mail me your flight details. OK?'

'I promise. And you send my love to Rob.'

'Will do. Bye for now then, Ally.'

'Bye, Kim.'

I went back online to double-check available flights to Brisbane and printed off a few details, but decided not to book anything until after I had spoken with Antonia and found out what her plans were.

'You didn't tell me that Tom was going to be Rob's best man,' I chided.

'You didn't ask,' she snapped.

'*Mamma mia*, Antonia. Don't be peevish. I was a little surprised when Kim told me, that's all. Usually if you know something that I don't, you can't wait to tell me! Is everything OK? *Tutto bene? Che passa?*' It was not like her to be so defensive and I wondered if something was wrong. I suspected that adjusting to her new job at the advertising agency was proving to be more of a challenge than she had initially thought, and I was concerned.

'*Mi dispiace*, Ally. I didn't mean to be sharp. I'm a bit hard-pressed at work. I'm not even sure I'll make it to the wedding, to be honest, because it's going to be difficult to get time off work when I only just started and I've a lot of projects on at the moment. It's probably better if you book your flight rather than wait for me.'

'*Non è problema, carina mia*. That's fine. I only called because I thought it would be fun for us to go together, unless of course you're travelling with Tom.'

'It would have been great for all three of us to make a trip of it, but Tom's actually flying out next month which puts paid to that. I'm sorry, Ally. Listen, I don't mean to push you off the 'phone, but I have to get on. I've a presentation this afternoon and I really need to go through it all.' She sounded agitated and not her usual calm, confident self.

'OK, *carina.* I'll speak to you soon. *Buona fortuna!*' I said, but she had put down the receiver at the other end before I had finished uttering the words.

I decided to drop in on Dorothy to tell her about Kim and enquire how she was. I was not sure how much longer Dorothy would be able to manage living alone in her flat. She was determinedly independent and had told me that provided she was able to cope and had Smoky, her Persian cat, for company she would remain there. She was very stubborn and there was no point in arguing with her. Dorothy's niece, Anne Mullen, had repeatedly asked her to go and live with her in Suffolk, but she had refused all requests, and Anne had become a frequent visitor to the flat. Anne and I had an agreement that I would keep an eye on Dorothy for her and I made a point of popping in to see her most days to check that all was well and whether she needed anything. Dorothy had given me a key to the flat as a precautionary measure.

'You're sounding very chirpy today,' I said to her as she opened the door.

'Well, one of Miss Caldecott's workmen has just sorted out my dripping kitchen tap,' she replied, walking slowly but steadily through to the kitchen. 'I met him as he was coming in this morning and asked him if he wouldn't mind having a look at it for me. What a kind man. He fixed it there and then. From what he said I don't think he's very happy working for Miss C.' I nodded in agreement. 'Do you want a cup of tea, dear?' she asked, opening her kitchen store cupboard and taking out a packet of Palmiers.

'That would be lovely,' I said, filling the kettle for her.

'Could you open those and put some on the tray over there. I'll finish making the tea. You're looking rather perky yourself,' she said knowingly. 'What's happened?'

'You'll never guess who I heard from this morning.' Dorothy poured the tea.

'I have no idea. Let's go and sit down and you can tell me.' I picked up the tray of tea and biscuits and carried it through to her reception room. Smoky was sitting under Dorothy's chair. As I walked into the room he moved forward and sidled up to me. I placed the tray on the table. Dorothy followed me in.

'Do you remember Kimberley Davies?'

'Of course I do, dear,' she said, easing herself down in her armchair. I pulled the cushion up to support her back and handed her the cup of tea. Smoky came and sat by her side and started to preen himself.

'And you knew she'd moved back to Australia after she and Rob got engaged?'

'Yes.'

'They're getting married in six weeks time and she's invited me to the wedding.'

'Oh, how lovely. I take it you are going?'

'Yes.'

'How long for?'

'Not sure, but I haven't booked my flight so nothing is definite. Will you be OK here? Don't you think you should go and stay with your niece?' I asked with a concerned squeeze of her arm.

'If I didn't know you better, I'd think you and she were in league, and conspiring for me to move to Suffolk!'

'I only have your best interests at heart, Dorothy.'

'I know you do, dear,' she replied, patting my hand. 'Have a biscuit,' she said, changing the subject. She was better at that than I am.

'I suppose you'll be the next to walk up the aisle.'

'I don't think so; bearing in mind I don't have a boyfriend.'

'Hmm...' She paused for a moment, rested her head against the chair and closed her eyes as if she was thinking very hard. 'What happened to that charming young man who came looking for you just after you returned to London last year?' she said, opening her eyes and fixing them on me steadily. I looked at her quizzically.

'Which young man?'

'The tall, good-looking, blond one. His name is on the tip of my tongue.'

'Alex Waterford?'

'Yes. That's him.'

'He moved abroad.'

'Oh, now that *is* a shame. He seemed such a lovely young man and very suitable too.'

'Well, appearances can sometimes be deceptive, Dorothy, but somehow I don't think I'll be seeing him again.'

Chapter 2

Alex had left for Singapore and I had not seen him for nearly six months. He was offered a job in a legal practice there and said it was a great opportunity for him to make a fresh start, but we agreed to stay in touch. He told me that I was welcome to come out for a holiday at any time. When he first moved to Singapore he e-mailed me regularly, but I had not heard from him for several months, although *I* had continued to e-mail *him*. I began to feel I was wasting my time trying to maintain his friendship.

Dorothy's remarks, however, caused me to reflect upon the situation and, although I was disappointed that he had not been in touch, there could be any number of reasons for that. I decided to take the direct approach and 'phone him; then I would have my answer.

'How lovely to hear from you, Alicia. How are you?' He was absolutely disarming and I was wrong-footed, although I suppose I should have known better than for Alex to react as I expected.

'I'm fine, Alex. I was wondering how *you* were as I haven't heard from *you* since well before Christmas.'

'That long. It can't be. I've been so busy. I don't know where the days have gone.' He was very casual about it and this began to irritate me.

'Well, the reason why I'm calling is to take you up on your offer…if it still stands that is.'

'My offer? I'm not with you.' He seemed slightly confused or was pretending to be.

'To come out for a holiday. You said that any time I fancied a trip I should just call.'

'Oh yes, I remember.' There was a slight pause. 'When were you thinking of?'

'I'm going to Kim Davies' wedding at the beginning of March, and I thought I might stop over in Singapore for a few days on my way to Brisbane and visit *you*.'

'When exactly?'

'The end of February.' This time there was a longer silence at the end of the 'phone before Alex replied.

'The thing is, Alicia, you're more than welcome to come and stay at my apartment, but I actually won't be in Singapore then. And I'm going to be away for most of March. I'm so sorry. It's very unfortunate as I'd love to see you and to show you around. I think you'd really like it here.' He sounded blasé about it.

'Oh, well, never mind. These things can't be helped,' I replied, trying to conceal my annoyance, for although Alex was being friendly I sensed he was giving me the brush off, albeit politely. 'Maybe I'll see you sometime then?' I continued, stifling my irritation.

'You will. I don't mean to be rude, Alicia, but I've a client waiting. So we'll catch up soon, yes?'

'OK,' I replied rather flatly.

'Bye, Alicia.'

'Goodbye, Alex,' I said, somewhat perplexed by the tone of the whole conversation.

Nevertheless, I was glad that I had made the call and spoken to him. I decided to erase all further thoughts of Alex from my mind, walk to the travel agents and book my plane ticket. I would not be stopping over in Singapore after all; well, not this time anyway. The likelihood of ever seeing Alex again seemed an increasingly remote possibility.

It was late afternoon when I returned home. I checked the answer-phone for messages and there were two missed calls whose numbers were withheld but no messages. I sat down at my desk with a huge mug of hot chocolate and a packet of plain chocolate biscuits and logged on to the internet. I e-mailed Kim with my travel details and then Jeremy Brown to ask him if his offer to stay with him in Melbourne still stood. While I was online I thought I might as well carry out a quick search for any suitable job vacancies. I was trawling through one of the recruitment agency websites when my 'phone rang. I was so deep in thought that it startled me.

'Hello.'

'Alicia. Is that you?'

'Speaking.'

'Good. Alicia, it's Graham Ffoulkes. I'm glad I caught you in. I tried a couple of times before but there was no answer.' I was more than a little surprised to hear his voice at the other end of the line. He had been the Partner for whom I had primarily worked at my previous firm.

'Yes, I was out.'

'Are you OK? You sound a bit withdrawn?'

'No. I'm fine. I didn't expect to hear from you, that's all.'

'Well, I thought it was about time I gave you a call to see how things were. Have you found another job yet?'

'I've been working as a locum for a while to keep up to speed with everything and I've had a few interviews, but no permanent job, no.'

'Oh, I'm very sorry to hear that. Who were the interviews with if you don't mind me asking?'

'Not at all. Farrow & Co. and Darlington & Lowndes.'

'What happened?'

'Oh, I wasn't the right fit or something. It's just something I have to deal with.'

'I understand what you're saying.' He paused. 'Listen, if you're interested I might be in a position to help you.'

'*You?*' I wondered how exactly.

'Yes. I know it's short notice but are you free for a drink this evening?'

'I could be. Why?'

'There's something I'd like to discuss with you.'

'Oh, OK.'

· 'Do you know Jimmy's Wine Bar?'

'I do. That's the one just off Buckingham Palace Road, isn't it?'

'Yes. Could you make it around six-thirty?' I looked at my watch. It was now after five.

'OK. Yes. I'll see you there then.'

'Excellent. I look forward to it. Bye, Alicia.'

Graham was standing at the bar chatting with the bartender when I walked in. He had his back to me so was unaware I was behind him. I tapped him lightly on the shoulder and he turned around and beamed at me. He looked well and a tad thinner than when I last saw him. His hair was cut in a more modern style and this new look suited him.

'Great to see you, Alicia,' he said, shaking my hand with vigour. 'A glass of wine? Red or white?'

'Red, please.'

'Is Chianti OK for you?'

'Fine.' He ordered a bottle and we sat down at a table in a quiet corner.

'I wanted to have a chat with you first, before the others arrive,' he said as he poured me a glass of wine.

'Others?' I picked up the glass.

'Yes. You remember Peter Crawford, a former matrimonial colleague of ours?' I nodded, taking a sip of wine. 'Well, he, Rachel Piper and I have set up our own firm, CFP & Co. in Belgravia. You won't know Rachel, but she and I used to work together at Merrydew Williams about ten years ago. She's an international tax specialist and property lawyer. I won't beat around the bush, Alicia. The reason why I asked you here is because Peter, Rachel and I would like you to join our firm, if you're interested, that is.'

'Oh,' I replied, probably sounding rather flat, although unintentionally so.

'You don't sound very enthusiastic.' He seemed genuinely disappointed.

'Oh, no, it isn't that. I'm very interested. It's just come as a big surprise, that's all. Unexpected, but not unpleasant.'

'I understand you might have reservations about working at CFP after your previous experiences, but I firmly believe that if you join us you won't regret it. And we are prepared to make you a very good offer.'

'That's very generous of you, and it isn't that, believe me.'

'Peter's assistant, Angela Pritchard, is joining us, and our secretaries Danielle and Carrie. Ella's also coming across.' Ella MacDonald was the feisty no-nonsense legal executive I had worked with formerly and I liked her immensely. 'I think it will be a very friendly team and we'd be delighted if you'd join too,' he said, looking at me expectantly.

'If I were to come on board, when would you want me to start?'

'The beginning of February.'

'Oh.'

'You look anxious, Alicia. Is there a problem?' He obviously detected my slight hesitancy.

'No; at least, I hope not. You remember Kimberley Davies, Alex Waterford's secretary?'

'Yes, of course.'

'Well, she moved back to Brisbane and she's getting married on 10 March and I've planned to go out there for the wedding and to stay on for a few weeks. I booked my ticket today actually. I would feel bad about starting at the firm and then taking time off immediately.'

'We can work around that. I'm quite happy for you to start at the firm, settle in, take your holiday and come back.'

'Really? That's very kind of you to accommodate me. But are you sure?'

'In the circumstances, it's probably the least I can do.'

'Why? What do you mean?'

'We all feel bad about what happened before and what you've been through since but we wouldn't be offering you this position unless we felt you were the best person for it.'

'Thank you. I appreciate that.' My judgment of the legal profession had been somewhat coloured recently and I had forgotten that, very occasionally, gems of lawyers like Graham and Peter Crawford existed.

'That's settled then. Now come and meet Rachel. She and Peter have just walked in,' he said, waving over to the two people who had appeared in the doorway of the wine bar. Rachel was willowy and almost as tall as Peter. She reminded me of a more mature version of Jo, except her nut-brown hair was curly and she wore it short.

I warmed to Rachel immediately. I think it was her unpretentiousness that drew me to her and the fact that she was on the same wavelength as Graham and Peter. For the first time in ages my feelings of disillusionment with the Law began to dissipate and I felt genuinely excited about the opportunity which was being handed to me. Graham indicated he would e-mail their offer letter to me the next day and, if everything was agreed, I would join the firm. It is amazing how quickly things can change sometimes. In the space of twenty-four hours my whole life had taken a dramatic turn. I wondered what else could be around the corner.

I had been working at CFP & Co. for a couple weeks when early one morning I received a call on my mobile from Sally Hamilton.

'Can you talk?' she asked.

'Yes. But just hang on a sec. I'll close the door,' I said, putting down the receiver, standing up, walking to the door and shutting it. Danielle and Carrie's desks were outside my office and they had a habit of listening in. As much as I was fond of them, I did not want them to overhear my private conversation. 'That's better,' I said, returning to my desk and picking up the 'phone. 'It's good to hear from you, Sally. How are you?'

'I'm good thanks. I really must apologise. I've been meaning to call you for several weeks but things have been manic here. Do you remember I mentioned that a friend of mine needs some advice?'

'Yes.'

'I spoke to her last night. I told her about you and she wants to meet you as soon as possible. I don't know whether you're working yet otherwise I'd have given her your work number. For obvious reasons, I didn't like to give her your mobile number without speaking to you first.'

'No, of course. I am working as it happens.'

'Did you get that job you'd just been to the interview for the day we met?'

'No. I'm working at Crawford Ffoulkes Piper & Co. It's a new firm based in Belgravia. I've been here two weeks.'

'Oh, I am pleased for you. How's it going?'

'Well.'

'Good. Why don't you e-mail me all your firm's details and I'll pass them on to my friend.'

'OK. I'll do that now.'

'Great. Expect to receive a call from someone called Isabelle Parker.'

'And what else should I expect?'

'You've lost me.'

'The last time we spoke you commented that there were too many deaths in her family for your liking. I wondered what you meant by that remark. Has there been some family tragedy or something?'

'It's an ongoing one. Most of her close family have died off, but no doubt she'll tell you. I'm sure Isabelle will call you soon because she's very reliable. 'Phone me sometime and let me know when you're free. I'd love to catch up if you have the time. Anyway, I'd better get back to work and put some chargeable time on my

timesheet. Speak to you soon.'
    'Thanks for the recommendation. I really appreciate it.'
    'My pleasure. Bye, Alicia.'
    'Bye.'

I e-mailed Sally the details she had requested and thought nothing more about it. As I was preparing to leave that evening a rather crimson-cheeked Danielle popped her head around the door to my office.

    'I'm very sorry, Alicia, but I forgot to tell you that I had a call for you this afternoon. You were on the 'phone at the time,' she said as she came into my office.

    'Oh, well these things happen. Who was it from?' I asked, taking my black overcoat off the hanger on the back of the door and putting it on.

    'A new client. Somebody called Isabelle Parker. She said you come highly recommended. She wanted to see you as soon as possible, so I've made an appointment for her to come in tomorrow morning at ten. Is that OK?'

    'That's fine. I was hoping to hear from her, but I didn't reckon on her calling just yet,' I replied, picking up my purple scarf and wrapping it snugly around my neck.

    'Oh, and Alicia, she sounds Australian, so you're bound to get on with her! Maybe she can give you some tips for your trip.'

    'Goodnight, Danielle,' I said, ushering her out of my office and then switching off the light and closing the door.

Chapter 3

Isabelle arrived exactly on time. As I walked towards the diminutive fair-haired young woman sitting in reception, I was immediately struck by how immaculate she looked. She was dressed in a simple chocolate brown wool trouser suit but the cut was superb. She wore a cream cashmere pashmina loosely draped about her neck. There was a camel coat placed on the chair beside her, the material of which looked exceptionally fine. I noticed that her dark brown suede handbag matched her ankle boots. She also had a soft brown kid leather briefcase with her. She was flicking through one of the copies of *Country Life* left on the table in reception for the perusal of visitors.

'Miss Parker?'

'Yes,' she replied, looking up and smiling broadly as she pushed a wayward strand of her shoulder-length honey blonde hair behind her left ear. She had a dewy complexion and a healthy glow that I associate with an outdoor lifestyle. She picked up her coat, briefcase and bag and stood up to shake my hand. We were about the same height.

'I'm Alicia Allen,' I said, taking her hand. 'Do you want to leave your coat and scarf in reception?' I asked, beckoning over to Susannah, our young but very efficient receptionist, to come and assist.

'Yes, that would be good,' she replied, smiling at me and handing her coat to Susannah. She took off her scarf and passed that to her as well. Danielle had been right. She had a slight but unmistakable Australian accent.

'Would you like something to drink? Tea, coffee or water?'

'Coffee, please.'

'Could you arrange that please, Susannah?' I asked, addressing her. I led Isabelle through to my office and indicated that she should sit down in the comfy chair in front of my desk. I walked around to the other side of the desk and sat down in my swivel chair.

'It's very good of you to see me at such short notice,' she began. 'Sally Hamilton recommended you. She's a friend of one of Drew's cousins. That's how we met, but she's a good friend of mine now.'

'Drew?'

'My fiancé. He's the reason I'm here,' she said, looking down for a moment and toying with the sizeable diamond solitaire engagement ring on her left hand. 'We're getting married in June and I want to sort out all my affairs. One of the things I need to do is make a Will. I want to make sure that Drew is protected should anything happen to me. I think it's only sensible.'

'Yes, it is. Unfortunately, not enough people think that way. They don't like to make a Will because they think it tempts providence, but it's much better to protect those you leave behind.'

'Well, in my case it's probably more essential than in others.' There was a sense of irony in the way she said it.

'Why?' Knowing what Sally had told me I was curious.

'Most of my immediate family are dead. My paternal grandmother is all I have left. If I was a superstitious person I'd think we'd been cursed.' Although she laughed, I could see she was being deadly serious.

'What do you mean?'

'It's a long story and I don't want to take up too much of your time.'

'You're not. I'm interested. What makes you say that?'

'As you've probably gathered from my accent, I'm Australian.' I nodded. 'I was actually born here, but to all intents and purposes I'm Australian because I went to live in Melbourne when I was three. My father was Australian and my mother was English and they lived in England but, after they were both killed in a motor boat accident in Sardinia, my brother Michael and I went to Australia where we were brought up by our paternal grandparents.'

'What about your maternal grandparents in England?' There was a knock at the door and Susannah entered with the tray of coffee and a plate of assorted chocolate biscuits. She put it down on my desk. 'Thanks, Susannah.' She left the room. 'Black or white?' I asked.

'Just a dash of milk for me.'

'Sugar?'

'No. You're all right.' I handed her the coffee.

'Help yourself to biscuits. Everybody's always far too polite to take any and I end up eating them all.'

'Thanks. I will.' She leant forward and picked up a Bourbon. 'What were you asking?'

'About your maternal grandparents.'

'Oh, yes,' she replied as she chewed a mouthful of biscuit and cleared her throat. 'My maternal grandmother Elizabeth died giving birth to my uncle Patrick in 1953. He was premature and only survived a few days. It was really quite tragic. Grandpa Jam was left with a tiny daughter aged two, my mother, to bring up.' She took a sip of coffee.

'Grandpa Jam?'

'His name was James, but Michael couldn't say James when he was very little and used to call him Jam and it stuck. No pun intended! We always called him that. Grandma Edie, that's my paternal grandmother, says Grandpa Jam went off the rails after Elizabeth died and a few years later married again to someone much younger than him. They also had a daughter but, according to Grandma Edie, his second wife ran off with the child and they were both killed in a car accident. Apparently Grandpa Jam was devastated and blamed himself for what had happened. He never talked about it. My mother became his whole existence after that. My father didn't stand a chance really because no man that came along was ever going to be good enough for his daughter.'

'How did your parents meet?'

'My mother was studying art history and went to Venice as part of her course. My father was on holiday. He was a medical student at the time. Grandpa never approved of the match and he opposed their marriage. I guess he didn't want my mother to move to Australia. I'm sure he resented my father for taking away the most precious thing he had left. He blamed my father for the motor boat accident in which both my parents were killed. He wasn't interested in Michael or me and so my paternal grandparents stepped in.' She finished her biscuit and put her coffee cup down.

'That's terribly sad.'

'Not so sad as it happens. True, he had nothing to do with us for five years, but then he came out to Australia for a few months and after that we'd spend alternate Christmases with him in England. It was good because that was our summer holiday and he used to take us skiing in Switzerland. When Michael decided to come over to London after university, Grandpa Jam was delighted. Michael studied economics and law and wanted to go into banking. He was always crazy about motorbikes and Grandpa bought him one for his twenty-first birthday. He was on his way to Devon on the very bike that Grandpa bought him when he was killed.'

'So your brother's dead as well? How long ago was that?' I could barely contain my astonishment. I now understood the significance of Sally's comment about Isabelle's family.

'Two years ago. It was another devastating blow for Grandpa Jam. He blamed himself. He started to go down hill after that. He developed heart problems, which made him quite weak, and then there was a break-in at the house. Grandpa was all alone at the time. The police said he must have disturbed whoever it was, but we'll never know. He was found at the bottom of the stairs with a broken neck.' I could detect the emotion in her voice. She paused for a second and looked down momentarily. When she looked up I noticed her eyes were brimming with tears. 'I'm sorry,' she said, blinking hard.

'For what? I think you have good reason to feel the way you do. Did the police catch whoever did this to your grandfather?'

'Murdered him, you mean,' she replied vehemently. 'No. And the irony is nothing was taken from the house, at least not as far as we could tell, so he was murdered for no reason at all. The police said it was an accident and he must have stumbled. But he wouldn't have had an accident had it not been for the burglary, so whoever it was, was responsible for his death. The pathologist's report said the shock brought on a heart attack.'

'Oh, I see. How dreadful. When did this happen?'

'Last September. The thing is Grandpa was very wealthy and I'm about to come into a significant amount of money,' she said, opening her briefcase and taking out a small plastic file full of papers, pulling out a letter and handing it to me. It was a letter addressed to her from a firm of solicitors called Holmwood & Hitchins and referring to the estate of her grandfather, the late James Latham. I had not had any dealings with the firm, although I knew of them. They were based in St James's and handled large and landed estates. The letter was from someone called Jonathan Masterton, one of her trustees. I quickly scanned the letter. It explained that under the terms of Grandpa Jam's Will she was the sole beneficiary to his estate and would inherit on her twenty-fifth birthday. She was to make an appointment to attend at their offices to talk through Probate matters with them.

'Do you have a copy of the Will?'

'No, but I can get one if you need it. Why?'

'I'd like to see what the exact terms are.'

'I can help you there. Grandpa made his Will years ago. I think it was in 1969, but definitely before Michael and I were born. Our mother was still alive then, and my understanding is that he left everything to her, with the proviso that should she predecease him her inheritance would pass to any grandchildren living at the time of his death. However, we wouldn't get the money until we were twenty-five, and until then the money was to be held on trust. I'm sure that's correct.'

'It's probably worded along the lines of "to my grandchildren as shall attain the age of twenty-five" because when your grandfather made his Will he did not have any grandchildren and could not refer to you by name. From what you tell me, and as Holmwood & Hitchins state in their letter, you are the only potential beneficiary, so when you are twenty-five you will become absolutely entitled to everything.'

'OK. I follow that. But what if I die?'

'Well, if you die before you're twenty-five that would mean there are currently no potential beneficiaries to inherit, but legally the trust would remain open for a term of years until such time as it is deemed that there are no other possible beneficiaries who can claim. After you reach twenty-five the money is yours and you can Will it to whomsoever you like. When will you be twenty-five?'

'6 June.'

'And what date are you getting married?'

'The same day.'

'And do you have an idea of the size of the inheritance to which you'll become entitled?'

'About two hundred and fifty million,' she said casually with barely the blink of an eyelid.

'OK,' I replied, swallowing, 'so we really do need to sort out a Will for you. Did you know that marriage revokes a Will?'

'No. Do you mean that if I make a Will now it won't be valid the day I marry?'

'Well, you can make a Will in contemplation of marriage to Drew and declare that the Will is conditional upon your intended marriage taking place by such and such a date, and for the Will not to be revoked by the marriage. So, if the marriage didn't take place for any reason, then the Will wouldn't stand up, but if it does, it would. Does that make sense?'

'Yes, it does.'

'Tell me, have you considered a pre-nuptial agreement at all? I don't know how you feel about such agreements but someone in your position might...'

'No. I don't want one,' she said, interrupting me. 'I thought you might ask me but it isn't necessary.'

'OK, well that is of course entirely your decision, but I'm more than happy to talk through that side of things with you should you decide that it is something you wish to pursue. In relation to your Will, I do need to take your instructions and some details to enable me to prepare a draft for you. I also think that in view of your financial position we need to consider some serious financial planning advice before finalizing anything. With your agreement, I would like to run this by Rachel Piper, one of the Partners here, as she specializes in international tax planning, and see what input she can give us. It may be that she will suggest a meeting. Is that OK with you?'

'Whatever you think is best.'

She told me her fiancé was Andrew Hyde-Dowler and that he was an up-and-coming artist having obtained a number of important commissions. She was actually an artist herself. She had studied at the Victorian College of Art, part of the University of Melbourne, where she obtained a Bachelor of Fine Art. Her *métier* was sculpture. She told me that she and some of her fellow students had exhibited at the Melbourne International Arts Festival. She was hoping for a solo exhibition of her work at the Sutton Gallery in Fitzroy, Melbourne, at some point. I supposed that she had inherited her artistic ability from her mother and grandmother.

She and Drew were living in her house in Hampstead, near his studio, which overlooked the Vale of Health. She handed me a portfolio setting out her complete financial position so that I had full details of her current financial worth.

We discussed whom she wanted to appoint as Executors of her Will and she decided she would appoint Drew and my firm. The only person – apart from Drew – that she wanted to bequeath anything to was her best friend, Lucy Winters, whom she had met at university. She said that Lucy had become like a twin sister to her as they were the same age and she had helped her cope with the death of her brother. Lucy was going to be her bridesmaid. She wished to leave her the sum of one million pounds free of tax and for Lucy to have her diamond necklace which had belonged to her maternal grandmother. She also wanted to make a number of bequests to charities. The whole of her residuary estate was to pass to Drew. If for some reason he died before her and they had no children then the residue would be divided equally between the charities to which she had left bequests. If they had children then the money would be held on trust for them until they came of age. She confirmed that she would update her Will as events changed.

I explained the firm's terms of business to her, showed her our client care letter and took her through the clauses. I told her I would prepare a draft Will, run it past Graham and Rachel, and then send it to her for her to review. If she had any queries we would then arrange another meeting to discuss it further.

'How soon can you get the draft to me?' she asked as I handed her back the letter from Holmwood & Hitchins with the portfolio. 'Oh, you can keep those. I had copies made for you.'

'Thank you. I'll send the draft to you in the next few days. I'm actually going away myself in a couple of week's time so I'd like to sort this out for you before I go if possible.'

'How long are you away for?'

'I'm planning to be away for about three weeks, all being well.'

'Where are you going, if you don't mind me asking?'

'To Brisbane, for a friend's wedding, and then I hope to go on to Melbourne. I'll to try to get to Sydney as well. We'll see.'

'Have you been to Australia before?'

'No. First trip.'

'It's a shame I won't be in Melbourne. I could have given you a guided tour. Take my grandmother's address. Grandma Edie loves having visitors. She lives in Glen Iris. It's not far out. She has a place in Brighton as well because she has so many friends there.'

'Oh, I couldn't. You're my client.'

'That's nonsense. Take her address. Think of it as a point of contact.' She took one of the yellow Post-it notes off my desk and a pencil from the pot, scribbled the address down for me and handed it to me.

'Thank you,' I replied, taking it.

'Actually, come to think of it, Lucy and I have a mutual friend working in Brisbane. I know you've got friends out there but it never does any harm to have more,' she said, flipping open her mobile phone and trawling through the contacts list for the number. 'Her name's Luisa Bruneschi. She's a Melbourne girl, but she's been working in Brisbane for a few years now.' She took another Post-it note off my desk and transcribed Luisa's contact details. 'These are her mobile and office numbers. The 04 number is her mobile.'

'Thank you, but you shouldn't have. Before you go, there is just one other thing I wanted to ask you.'

'Yes?'

'Why did you not ask Jonathan Masterton to make a Will for you, bearing in mind he's one of your trustees and dealing with your grandfather's estate?'

'I never really cared for the firm. Any dealings I've ever had with the lawyers there have been fraught, particularly after Michael was killed. I think Grandpa only stayed with them because they've been our family solicitors since the year dot. I have nothing against Jonathan Masterton. In fact, my understanding is that Grandpa actually recommended him to the firm when he returned home from Australia.'

'Really?'

'Yes. I think he knew his father or something. Jonathan's children used to come to the house to play with Michael and me. I know both his sons very well. But I think now is the time to break with the past and make a fresh start.' She shrugged her shoulders. 'So that's what I intend to do.'

'Well, that's your prerogative.'

'Anyway, I very much appreciate you seeing me at such short notice and for your time today. Thank you for listening to me.'

'I'm pleased to be of assistance. You'll hear from me shortly.' She stood up and I went out into reception with her. 'I don't suppose you could get a copy of your grandfather's Will to me today?'

'Yes. Of course I can. I'll send one over by courier this afternoon.'

'Thank you.'

'I feel much happier now I've seen you.' Susannah fetched Isabelle's cashmere coat and pashmina and I helped her on with the coat. She folded her pashmina, placed it around her neck and looped it through. 'Thank you again,' she said, extending her hand to me. 'Goodbye, for now.'

I liked her. She was natural and unspoilt, despite all that wealth, which was very much to her credit. And no-one could dispute that she had certainly had more than her fair share of tragedy.

'How did your meeting go with Miss Parker?' asked Graham, popping his head around the door. I looked up from my desk.

'I was just going to come and talk to you about her. Have you heard of James Latham?'

'Well, I've heard of the Latham family. They were big industrialists and I think they were in the cloth trade in Victorian times. That's how they made their money. Why?'

'Isabelle Parker is James Latham's sole heir, apparently. She's about to come in to two hundred and fifty million pounds.'

'Only two hundred and fifty million?' Graham replied with a whimsical smile. 'So what does she want you to do for her?'

'She's getting married and wants me to make her a Will. She's given me a copy of her portfolio, but I haven't seen her grandfather's Will yet, although she roughly told me the terms. I've asked her for a copy urgently. I want to make sure that I'm clear as to what her financial position is going to be. If you don't mind I'd like to have a chat with you to discuss what financial planning advice she needs and I'll definitely need expert tax advice from Rachel.'

'Of course. It sounds like she needs it. Who's dealing with her grandfather's estate?'

'Holmwood & Hitchins; but she doesn't care for the firm.'

'Oh well, their loss is our gain,' he replied, winking at me.

I received a copy of Grandpa Jam's Will that afternoon. The Will was quite straightforward, although lengthy. It surprised me that he had not updated his Will, particularly after his daughter died in 1985, but I did not read anything untoward into that. Upon reviewing the terms I noted that everything Isabelle had told me was correct. The first point to note was that the Partners of Holmwood & Hitchins or their successors were to be executors and trustees of his Will.

There were a few legacies, one of which was for £20,000 free of tax to "my housekeeper". There was no other reference to the house-keeper in the Will and she had not been referred to by name, so that meant whoever his housekeeper was at the time the Will was made would be the one entitled to the legacy. She must have been a good housekeeper as in 1969 £20,000 would have been a great deal of money, and it is certainly not a sum to be sniffed at today. There was also a legacy of £100,000 to the Richmond Rosemont Art Foundation in memory of his beloved first wife Elizabeth Latham. That fitted in with what Isabelle had said about her grandmother's passion for art.

A few days later I received a call from Sally Hamilton.

'Isabelle rang me after your meeting. She liked you enormously.'

'Oh, I'm flattered.'

'You should be. She was full of praise for you. Anyway, the reason why I'm calling is that I wondered if you were free tonight.'

'Why?'

'I'll be totally honest with you. I've got two tickets to go and see

Sleeping Beauty at the Royal Opera House and I was supposed to be going with a friend of mine but he's blown me out. Says he has to work late. I don't want to waste the ticket. Please say you'll come.'

'Hmm...'

'Please. You'd be doing me a great favour and it'd give us a chance to catch up.'

'Oh, go on then. I'd love to. Where shall we meet?'

'Do you know Patisserie Valerie just off the Piazza?'

'Yes.'

'OK. I'll meet you there as near to six as you can make it. We can have a quick bite to eat before the performance starts.'

'Sounds good. I'll meet you inside.'

'Great. I look forward to it.'

Sally was already there when I arrived. I saw her waving to me from the far corner at the back of the café. I made my way over to her and up the steps to where she was sitting.

'This place is always so busy. I was lucky to get a table. Theatre crowd I guess. It's lovely to see you,' she said, squeezing my arm. 'What do you want to eat?' she asked, scanning the menu and then passing it to me. 'I'm going to have the Croque Madame.'

'I'll have the Croque Monsieur. I'm starving this evening,' I replied, looking avidly at the menu and espying the offering of a toasted cheese and ham sandwich with chips and salad. A rather harassed waitress came to take our orders.

'One Croque Monsieur and one Croque Madame, please. Oh, and a large cappuccino for me,' asked Sally. 'What do you want to drink, Alicia?'

'A bottle of mineral water, please.'

'Sparkling or still,' asked the waitress, her pen poised.

'Sparkling, please.' I turned to Sally. 'I'm curious. How did you come to be so friendly with Isabelle Parker?'

'I met her at the private view of an art exhibition a few years ago and we really hit it off. Isabelle was there, supporting her fiancé. It was his exhibition you see.'

'He must be very successful then.'

'He's making a good name for himself. He's a qualified architect but his heart wasn't really in it and so he turned to his real vocation. From what I hear he has been acclaimed for his artistic ability and his work has been very well received. He found himself a studio, had a couple of fairly sizeable commissions painting country houses, was recommended, and carried on from there. His reputation is building. Actually, he had an exhibition a few months ago and there's an exhibition of his latest work in Mayfair in a month or so's time. I'm sure you'd be able to get a ticket to the private view if you asked.' The waitress arrived at our table with my bottle of mineral water and Sally's cappuccino.

'I *am* interested in seeing his work, but I'd like to know how you wangled a ticket for the private view where you met Isabelle,' I said as I poured some water into my glass.

'It wasn't really a chance meeting. I was actually there because I was accompanying a cousin of mine who happens to be a good friend of Drew. They went to the same school.'

'Oh, I see. So was it your cousin you were going to the ballet with tonight?'

'No.'

'Boyfriend then?'

'Sort of. I think he's working up to finish it. Things haven't been going well. This evening was planned ages ago otherwise I don't think he'd have agreed to go at all. You know, Alicia, I don't seem to have much luck on the man front,' she said, shrugging her shoulders. 'What can you do?' she asked, picking up her cappuccino and swallowing a large mouthful. I was not sure whether that was a rhetorical question, but if not, the benefit of my own experiences would take her no further in answering it.

'Isabelle seems very smitten with her beau,' I replied, changing the subject.

'Yes, I think he can hardly believe his luck to have got her.'

'What makes you say that? The main thing is that he loves her.'
'Oh, come on, Alicia, if you were him wouldn't you love her too? He has a lot to gain by marrying her. People would kill to be in his shoes. Even Chris, my cousin, said he could kill him for getting her.' I wondered whether Sally's scepticism had something to do with the fact that she was going through a rocky relationship. This was becoming a rather bizarre conversation.

'Oh, that's a very cynical attitude, Sally. People say things like that all the time. It doesn't mean they're actually going to kill someone. Antonia and I are always threatening to kill each other. Food for thought though,' I said with an impish look, 'talking of which, where is our food?' The waitress appeared with it. 'Oh, thank goodness,' I said as she put it down. 'I'm so hungry,' I added, picking up my knife and fork and tucking in to the toasted cheese and ham sandwich. 'No more talk of murder. *Buon appetito, amica mia!*'

Chapter 4

It was almost the end of February, only a few days before I was due to leave for Australia, and I had not heard from Isabelle Parker despite leaving several messages for her. Although she had not returned my calls, I was not particularly concerned. I knew that, in my absence, Graham would be on hand to deal with any queries that she might have in relation to her Will and ongoing financial planning.

I was very excited about my forthcoming trip. To give me total flexibility with my holiday plans I chose not to stay with Kim's family. I had booked myself into a serviced apartment on Wickham Terrace in Spring Hill, fairly near Brisbane's Central Business District and all the amenities. After the wedding I had arranged to stay with Jeremy Brown in Melbourne, then to travel on to Sydney and explore that city too.

Tom had flown to Brisbane a couple of weeks earlier. Due to her work commitments, Antonia could only manage to take just over a week's holiday and was not expected until the day before the wedding. It seemed a long way to fly for a week but at least she would be there. I decided to arrive the previous weekend so that I had a few days to explore Brisbane.

One evening while I was relaxing at home after a workout at the gym, I started to think about Isabelle. I wondered if there was any information about the Latham family on the internet, so I carried out a search. I was intrigued by what Isabelle had told me about Grandpa Jam's second wife running off with their daughter and dying in a car accident and interested in discovering any detail relating to it.

My initial search brought up several entries, one of which was an article relating to the Latham family history. It seemed Graham was right and that originally the family were cloth manufacturers. The founder of the family business, Edward Latham, came from the West Country. He was born in 1762 near the historic mill town of Buckfastleigh in Devon, and made his money from the woollen trade but diversified into cotton when it supplanted wool. The family had amassed their fortune from the cotton industry in the eighteenth and nineteenth centuries. In fact they owned cotton factories in Lancashire, predominantly Oldham, up until the 1960s when the mills in Lancashire closed at a rapid rate. Everything in Lancashire was sold off by James Latham, Isabelle's grandfather. He was an investment banker by profession and although the industry declined he retained some interest in the business in Devon. There was a photograph of the family seat, Stowick House, which was about three miles out of Buckfastleigh. The house was presumably part of Isabelle's inheritance. It was a beautiful pale yellow stucco-fronted Regency country house and had been featured in *Country Life*.

I then came across a biographical article about James Latham and skimmed through it. As well as being a descendent of Edward Latham, one of the most successful factory owners in Lancashire, he was a financier and great patron of the arts who had campaigned actively to raise funds for the preservation of works of art. The article went on to say that he was tragically widowed when his first wife Elizabeth died in childbirth in 1953 and that he remarried in 1955 only to suffer further tragedy when his twenty-nine year old wife Diane and their two year old daughter Frances were killed in a car accident in May 1960.

I scanned down the page and there was a photograph of Diane at a charity gala in 1957. The caption underneath the photograph read: *'Mrs Diane Latham wearing a design by Norman Hartnell'*. The exquisite 1950's ball gown was set off by a magnificent diamond pendant necklace. It reminded me of one of the fabulous evening dresses Audrey Hepburn wore in the film *Sabrina*. From the photograph I could see that Diane was also tall, elegant and dark-haired and it appeared almost as if she had modelled herself on the gamine Hollywood star, an all-time favourite of mine. I wondered whether Dorothy would know who Diane Latham was, because this would be the era when she worked as a seamstress for Hartnell. If Dorothy had met Diane Latham she would remember. I printed off the article and decided to ask her when I next saw her.

The following morning I finally received a call from Isabelle Parker.

'Thanks so much for sending me the draft Will. I've read it through and I'm very pleased with it. It all looks pretty clear and I'm very happy to sign it.'

'Good. I'll send the engrossment out to you together with instructions on how the Will should be signed and witnessed, and you can just send it back to me in the stamped addressed envelope included. We can then put the Will into our deeds room for safe-keeping.'

'Actually, there *is* something else I'd like to run by you, and I was hoping I could drop in to see you on Friday. I might as well sign the Will when I'm with you. Are you free then?'

'Friday's my last day. I'm only here in the morning because I leave for Australia in the evening, so if you could make it fairly early that would be better for both of us.'

'Oh, of course. I forgot. Would ten-thirty be OK?'

'That would be fine. I'll see you then.'

'Thanks, Alicia. Bye.'

That evening I went to see Dorothy armed with the article about the Lathams which I was keen to show her.

'Won't you stay and have some dinner, dear?' she asked as I followed her into the kitchen.

'Oh, Dorothy that's really sweet but I don't want to impose. I only popped down for a chat and to check that you're OK *and* to try and persuade you to stay with Anne, at least until I get back.'

'You're not imposing and I'm absolutely fine. You're such a worrier. Now, are you staying to dinner?'

'I'd love to but I've a million and one things to do before Friday. I am tempted though. It smells delicious.'

'Well, it's steak and kidney pie and, chores or no chores, you still need to eat. Nobody can survive on just Pringles!'

'I do eat other things.'

'Don't worry, dear. I'm rather fond of them too,' she replied, tapping me on the arm. 'I particularly like the Cheese & Onion ones,' she said, giving me a knowing glance. There was simply no point in arguing with Dorothy, so I let the subject drop.

'OK. I'll stay.' She walked slowly through to her living room and I followed her in and she settled into her chair. 'There's something I want to ask you about or should I say 'somebody'. When you were at Hartnell's did you ever come across anyone by the name of Diane Latham?'

'Why? What makes you ask?'

'The thing is I'm dealing with a matter for James Latham's granddaughter and Diane's name came up in conversation. I was looking on the internet, which is where I found this article,' I said, handing it to Dorothy. 'Do you recognise her?' I pointed to the photograph.

'I might do, dear, if I had my glasses,' she quipped. I espied them on her bureau and fetched them for her.

'Here they are,' I said, passing them to her.

'Thank you. Now let me think. Her name does sound familiar but it was a long time ago and my memory isn't what it was.' She paused for a few moments and I sensed that she was thinking hard. I watched as she scrutinised the photograph. 'I do remember her,' she said, taking off her glasses and resting them on her lap and looking up at me. 'She was his second wife and a fair bit younger than him. They had a daughter and she and her daughter were killed.'

'There doesn't seem to be much wrong with your memory. The article refers to them being killed in a tragic car accident after Diane lost control of the car driving around a hair-pin bend.' Dorothy slipped her glasses back on and I waited while she read the relevant section.

'Yes. It was a terrible tragedy. There were all sorts of rumours at the time.'

'What rumours?'

'All the rumours that are spread when a young and beautiful woman estranged from her older and exceptionally wealthy husband dies.'

'Estranged? I didn't know there were marital problems. You're not saying that he had anything to do with her death, are you?'

'Well, that's not for me to say. I think it was in the papers. I'm sure you could look it up. There must have been an inquest too.'

'Yes, of course. Did you know Diane Latham, Dorothy?'

'Not to speak to. But I know someone who may have done.'

'Who?'

'Emily Middleton. She was a dear friend; still is. Mind you, I haven't seen her for years, although we've always kept in touch. She was widowed last year and moved up to Skipton to be near her daughter. She wrote me a lovely letter last Christmas when she sent me her new address. She moved last summer you see. You'll find it in the top drawer of the bureau,' she said, indicating for me to take it out. 'It's the blue envelope.' I found it and handed it to her. 'I realize you can't talk to me about your clients, Alicia, because of solicitor/client confidentiality, but I know you well enough to spot when you have concerns over something. I've seen that look on your face before. Is something worrying you?'

'It's nothing.'

'Hmm... Well, it's time I responded to Emily's letter. Maybe she can help you find what you're looking for.'

'I don't want to put you to any trouble.'

'You're not. That's settled then. Now, by the smell of it, that pie is cooked. You can tell me about all your holiday plans over dinner!'

Later that night I reflected on what Dorothy had said. From what she had told me there might be a question mark over James Latham's involvement in the death of Diane and their daughter. I was probably reading more into it than there was but either way I had to find out. Apart from Grandma Edie, all of Isabelle's immediate family were now dead. Isabelle had joked about the family being cursed. Although I did not believe that, with this family tragedy seemed to strike far more often than could be regarded as usual, even by the greatest stretch of the imagination.

On the other hand, all the deaths Isabelle had described could be explained, but then a rather disturbing thought came to mind. What if somebody was trying to murder members of Isabelle's family one by one and she was next in line? From our last conversation I knew that something was troubling her and I was not imagining it. Although what Dorothy had told me placed concerns in my mind, I had a preternatural feeling that something was amiss.

I woke up early on Friday morning and finished packing. I was determined to travel light so packing a suitcase had become rather a challenge. I called Mamma before I left for work to let her know that all was well and not to worry about me.

'*Ciao, tesorina. Stai bene?*'

'*Sì, mamma. Non preoccuparti! Sono quasi pronta. Ho ancora qualcosa da mettere in valigie.*'

'*Mi manchi. Tieni sana e salva!*'

'*Sì mamma. Ti amo.*'

'*E ti amo, mia carina. Baci. Baci.*'

'*Ciao, mamma.*'

'*Ciao, carina.*'

I intended to text her when I reached Singapore because I knew she would not have a moment's peace until she had heard from me.

Isabelle arrived punctually at ten-thirty and I went to greet her in reception. She looked as if she had been crying because her eyelids were slightly pink and puffy.

'Thanks for seeing me today.'

'Oh, no problem at all. Danielle has printed out the engrossment of your Will. If you'd just like to read it through and check it, I'll arrange for two of the secretaries to witness your signature,' I said, handing her the document. 'Would you like a cup of tea or coffee?'

'Actually, could I have a glass of water?'

'Of course. Susannah will see to that for you. Tell her when you've been through the Will and she'll give me a call.'

When she was ready I took Isabelle into my office to sign her Will. Carrie and Danielle witnessed her signature and the two secretaries then left the room. 'I'll arrange for you to be sent a copy for your own file,' I said.

'Thanks. That would be great.'

'Is there anything else I can help you with?' I watched her shift uncomfortably in her seat.

'There was something I thought of running by you, but it's really nothing.'

'Don't take this the wrong way,' I said gently, 'but you look upset. If something is worrying you, then please tell me. I'd really like to help and I can't if you don't tell me.'

'No, you're all right. As I said, it's nothing. Everything's fine,' she said, smiling at me – but it was one of those strained smiles and I was not convinced in the slightest. 'Anyway, I have to make a move. Thanks again for all your help, Alicia. Have a great time in Australia.' She stood up and extended her hand.

'Thank you. I intend to,' I replied, shaking it and observing her expression closely.

And so she left. I sensed that something was wrong but if she would not confide in me there was nothing I could do. At least I could leave for my holiday knowing I had done my best. I did not really believe that anything bad would happen to her, or rather I hoped not.

Chapter 5

I resolved to arrive early at Heathrow Airport for my ten o'clock night flight to Brisbane. There had been so many delays on the Piccadilly Line in recent weeks that I was worried I would be late. Fortunately, there were no glitches and my journey from South Kensington to Heathrow was a speedy one. I was grateful that I did not have an enormous suitcase to lug around which I would find impossible to carry.

I made my way from the tube up to Departures, checked the monitor screens, and then located the Club World check-in for my British Airways flight. By transferring all my membership rewards points from my American Express card to the frequent flyer programme, I had been able to make up the balance and purchase a Club class ticket. This was my little indulgence.

Check-in proceeded smoothly and swiftly and, having dispensed with my bag, I elected to pass through the security checks straightaway. There were still a couple of hours to kill before the flight so I had plenty of time for shopping, to check out the Molton Brown Spa, and to relax in the executive lounge. Suddenly, long haul travel had taken on a whole new meaning.

My purchases included a pair of sunglasses, a sun hat, a tankini and a refill for my perfume. The sales assistant at the fragrance counter popped a few samples into my bag including a couple of men's fragrances. As I walked away I opened one of the men's samples and sniffed it – but it was too overpowering for my taste. I then opened a second one and recognized the scent straightaway. It was Ralph Lauren Romance. It is strange how a certain fragrance can remind you of somebody. I always associated Alex with the smell of that aftershave and naturally I began to think of him. I started to feel a combination of frustration and irritation over my relationship with Alex, and I berated myself for allowing myself to be bothered by negative thoughts.

I wandered into the executive lounge for a pre-flight drink. Armed with a Campari and soda and a copy of *The Daily Telegraph* I found myself a comfortable sofa in a secluded corner and waited for my flight to be called. When I boarded the plane I was feeling more than a little weary, and I was looking forward to my dinner, a sleep and a completely stress-free flight. I was not in the mood to engage in any form of meaningful conversation and just wanted to be left alone. Unfortunately, the middle-aged man who had the seat adjacent to mine was keen to chat. I did not wish to be impolite, especially as he seemed friendly enough. Besides, I had the consolation of knowing that if he started to bore me I could escape from him via sleep.

'Hectic day?' he asked as I sighed heavily. I nodded. I was struggling to put my hand-luggage in the overhead locker and being vertically challenged I could not quite manage to push it in. 'Let me help you with that,' he said as he stood up, re-arranged the locker, put my bag inside and clicked it shut.

'Thanks,' I replied as I sat down and fastened my seat belt.

'I had a pretty tough day myself,' he continued, running his hand back through his thinning grey hair and grinning at me to reveal exceptionally white teeth. I could not fail to notice the scar on his chin as it was very prominent. 'Are you going to Brisbane?'

'Yes. Are you?'

'No. Only as far as Singapore. I have some business to attend to there and then I'm flying on to Melbourne. John MacFadzean, by the way,' he said, turning to me and extending his hand.

'Alicia Allen,' I replied, taking it.

Our conversation was interrupted because the air stewardess came to offer us each a newspaper and while his attention was diverted I took the opportunity to read more of my *Daily Telegraph*. John MacFadzean did not speak to me again until half way through dinner.

'How's your meal?'

'Fine, thanks.' I replied, putting down my knife and fork. I had opted for the chicken. 'Yours?'

'Good. So what takes you out to Brisbane?'

'I'm going to a friend's wedding there, and then on to Melbourne to visit another friend. Do you come from Melbourne?'

'No. I'm actually from Wellington, but I lived in Sydney for ten years before I moved to London where I now live and work.' That explained his accent. When he first spoke to me I could not ascertain whether he was an Australian or a Kiwi.

'So what do you do?'

'I'm a lawyer. You?'

'Me too.'

'Really? What area?'

'Tax, Wills and Trusts.' He started to chortle. I wondered what was so funny. 'Have I missed something?' I asked, slightly perplexed.

'No. It's remarkable. That's my area of law, too, although I deal mostly with trusts and tax.'

'Which firm?' I was curious.

'Holmwood & Hitchins. I've been a Partner there for some years now.' I had just put a piece of chicken in my mouth and I nearly choked on it. It seemed an incredible coincidence to be on a plane with a Partner from the firm dealing with Isabelle Parker's grandfather's estate. I wondered what the odds on that happening were. Maybe he was one of her trustees? Isabelle had only mentioned Jonathan Masterton. 'You OK?'

'Yes,' I replied, trying to conceal my amazement. 'My food just went down the wrong way,' I added, taking a drink of water and swallowing hard. 'What made you decide to make your practice in London then?'

'I suppose I fell into it. I happened to be in the right place at the right time. It was through a lawyer friend of mine that I ended up in London. We'd worked together in Australia; he'd moved back to the UK and when an opportunity arose for me to go to the UK, we met up, chatted and he told me there was a chance of a job. I'd already looked into getting dually qualified so it wasn't a problem.'

'Would you ever return to Australia permanently?'

'No. I get to come back a fair bit and I still go home to Wellington from time to time, but I have a good life in England. I've lived there for over twenty years now and regard it as home.' He did not mention a wife or partner and he was not wearing a wedding ring.

'Has your family settled in as well as you?'

'I don't have family back in the UK. My mother came over from Wellington about eight years ago but she died last year.'

'Oh, I'm sorry. You must miss her.'

'Well, yes of course. I was an only child and we were close.' He paused for a second and then changed the subject. 'So are you looking forward to your trip?'

'I am. I originally intended to stop over in Singapore but the friend I was hoping to stay with is away. I hope to make it there another time. Are you there long?'

'Only for one night, this time. It's a great place. Great nightlife,' he said, yawning. 'I don't know about you, but I'm bushed. I could do with some sleep.'

'Yes. Me too. Goodnight then.'

The benefits of having a flat bed were that I was actually able to sleep, pass the time and avoid the tedium of the thirteen-hour flight. I slept really well and, amazingly, woke up only a couple of hours before the end of the flight. John McFadzean was awake and watching a film, but after flicking through all eighteen movie and TV channels, I decided to listen to some music instead and read the magazines I had picked up at Heathrow. Eventually we arrived in

Singapore. Because of the time difference it was now early evening and my ongoing flight to Brisbane was not for several hours.

'Good flight?' asked John McFadzean after we landed.

'Yes, thanks. It helps to sleep. I just crashed.'

'I noticed.' He chortled again. 'Let me help you with that,' he said, fetching my bag down for me. 'Take my card.' He pulled his wallet out of the back pocket of his cream chinos, opened it, and fumbled inside for a business card which he then handed to me. 'If you ever think about changing jobs give me a call. Have a good trip,' he said, picking up his bag. 'I really enjoyed meeting you, Alicia. Goodbye.'

'Goodbye.' I sensed he was in a hurry and, since I did not particularly want to chat further to him, I held back to let him get off the plane first.

I took advantage of the executive lounge facilities to shower and change into lighter clothes. I waited in the lounge until the plane was boarding and turned on my mobile to send a text message to my mother saying that I had arrived safely in Singapore. I had bought her a mobile for Christmas and trained her up on how to send and receive texts. Mine beeped as soon as I switched it on. I had two new voice mail messages, but before I accessed them I sent the short text message to my mother.

The voice messages were from Sally Hamilton who sounded very agitated. In the first message she said that she was desperately trying to get hold of me and wondered where I was. She had clearly forgotten that I had left for Australia. She must have called around the time the plane was taking off. Sally said I should call her as soon as I received her message because she needed to speak to me urgently. The second message had been left the following morning. Wherever I was or whatever I was doing, could I please return her call. She did not say what was wrong, but I had an awful sense of foreboding as I called her number from my contacts list and pressed the dial button.

'Sally, it's Alicia. What's the matter?'

'Oh. Alicia. Thank goodness. Where have you been? I've been trying to get hold of you.' Her voice was strained.

'Yes, I know. I just picked up your messages. I was on the plane. I'm in Singapore.'

'Oh. I'm sorry. Of course you are.' She hesitated for a moment. 'I had to call you Alicia. Something terrible has happened.'

'What?' I asked with my heart in my mouth.

'There's been an accident. It's Drew.' Again she paused for a second. 'He's dead.'

Chapter 6

'What sort of accident?' I was stunned by the news that Isabelle's fiancé was dead. 'When did this happen exactly?' I had seen Isabelle less than twenty-four hours previously and it was only lunchtime on Saturday in London now.

'Early yesterday evening. I don't know the full facts, but Drew was working in his studio and there was some kind of explosion. Lucy rang me. Isabelle isn't in a fit state to talk to anyone right now.' I did not suppose she would be. Presumably Lucy was the best friend called Lucy Winters to whom Isabelle had left one million pounds in her Will.

'I'm not surprised. Did the police give any indication as to what caused the explosion? I mean, do they think it was an accident or are they treating it as suspicious?' My mind was already working overtime.

'I don't know any more than I've told you, Alicia. I felt I ought to tell you, as Isabelle's now your client, and I thought you'd want to know. I'm sorry to be the bearer of bad news, especially at the start of your holiday. You probably think it ridiculous of me to ring you. It's not as if you can do anything.' My flight was being called in the background.

'No, I'm glad you 'phoned me. But I have to run 'cos the plane's boarding. I'll speak to you when I get to Brisbane. Is that OK?'

'Yes. That's fine. Have a good flight.'

'Thanks. You take care. I promise I'll ring you. *Ciao*. Bye.'

'Bye.'

The plane from Singapore to Brisbane was smaller, a Boeing 767, and there were no flat beds, but I had had a good sleep on the longer leg of the journey so I was not overly bothered.

I was thinking very deeply about Drew and Isabelle and was oblivious to the people around me. I did not pay attention to any of the passengers but sat back in my window seat, closed my eyes and mulled over recent events. It was only the smell of the aftershave from the passenger who was settling into the seat next to mine that made me open my eyes. I turned my head and looked at the man in the adjacent seat.

'Good evening, Alicia,' he said, beaming at me. I just stared at him. I could not believe my eyes and looked back at him in disbelief, totally lost for words. He was the last person I expected to see. 'Well you could say something or look a little bit happy to see me.'

'Alex. What are *you* doing here?'

'The same as you. I'm flying to Brisbane. I thought I'd surprise you.'

'Yes. You certainly did that. But then you're always full of surprises,' I replied sarcastically.

'I thought you'd be pleased.' Secretly I *was* pleased, but I was not going to let Alex off the hook that easily after he had given me the run-around these past few months.

'Pleased? What makes you think that?' I said, feigning outrage. 'The last time I spoke to you, you gave me the brush off and made every excuse under the sun for me *not* to come out to Singapore. And I hadn't heard from you for weeks before that. Now you just turn up and expect me to be pleased!'

'Oh, come on, Alicia. Don't be like this. Let me explain. You always think the worst of me.'

'Perhaps it has something to do with your erratic behaviour.' I paused for a moment and looked at him. 'What are you really doing on this flight? And how did you know that I was going to be on it? That's too much of a coincidence, even for you. I thought you said you weren't going to be in Singapore,' I continued without giving him a chance to get a word in edgeways. He was smiling at me as if my remarks were washing over him, and that did annoy me. He was so infuriating. 'What are you grinning at now?'

'You. I'd forgotten how endearing you are when you're like this. You're looking fantastic by the way.' So was he, but I was not going to tell him that. 'Great haircut.'

'Flattery will get you absolutely nowhere,' I replied, crossing my arms defensively. 'Go on then, explain yourself.'

'I have a confession to make.'

'Shouldn't you see a priest then?' I turned away from him.

'Alicia. Look at me. Please. Kim and I arranged this. She told me which flight you'd be on and we thought it would be fun to surprise you. I never meant to upset you and I'm really sorry if I have,' he said, squeezing my hand. 'Don't be cross.'

'Hmm… I'm not cross with Kim,' I replied, pulling my hand away. 'It's typical of her to do something like this. It's *you* I'm upset with,' I said, avoiding his gaze as I knew that if I looked at him I would melt. 'I'm not sure whether I've forgiven you yet for not keeping in contact with me. You didn't have to be so convincing on the 'phone either!'

'I am sorry. Truly I am. I have something for you.'

'To ease your conscience?'

'Alicia!'

'What is it anyway?' I asked, curiosity getting the better of me and taking a peek at the box he was holding.

'Open it and you'll find out,' he responded, handing it to me. I sensed he was observing me closely as I opened the box. It was a Baume Mercier watch. It had an interchangeable stainless steel bracelet with an integrated folding clasp, and blue mother of pearl dial set with twelve diamonds.

'Oh, it's lovely,' I said, turning it over. 'But it must have cost a fortune and I'm not sure I can accept it.'

'Why don't you try it on,' he said, ignoring my response. 'Here let me help you,' he added, leaning over and undoing the bracelet and slipping it on my left wrist.

'It's a really beautiful watch, Alex. But I really can't accept it in the circumstances.' I went to take it off. 'It's too much.'

'Keep it,' he said, putting his hand over mine and looking at me with a whimsical expression. 'I thought that since you're always running late a watch might come in handy. Think of it as my way of saying sorry. Accept it as...a peace-offering.'

'It *is* exceptionally generous of you. Thank you very much.' I turned to him. 'I guess life's too short to argue anyway.'

'My sentiments exactly.'

'But that doesn't mean you're completely forgiven.'

'I didn't imagine that I would be,' he replied with a wry smile, and patting my knee.

That was the irony about Alex. It was impossible for me to be annoyed with him for very long. He would always do or say something to make me feel incredibly guilty for thinking badly of him. Besides, the news from Sally had put my squabbles with him into perspective and suddenly they seemed rather insignificant.

After dinner Alex fell asleep, but although I felt tired I could not settle and I wriggled around restlessly in my seat. My thoughts turned to Isabelle and how devastated she must be to lose Drew and in such shocking circumstances. Was it an accident or did someone murder him? If it was murder, what was the motive? Drew was the one who would have benefited by Isabelle's death, but what about his death? Maybe somebody wanted him out the way to clear the path to Isabelle. Nothing made sense. I must have drifted off to sleep at some point because I was awakened by Alex calling my name.

'Are we nearly there?' I asked, taking off my eyeshade, opening my eyes, pushing down my blanket and sitting up.

'Yes. Did you sleep well?'

'Not really,' I responded, running my hands back through my now dishevelled hair. 'You?'

'Yes. I can sleep anywhere.'

'Hmm... I can imagine.'

'How about I treat you to breakfast on your first morning in Australia?'

'I'd like that. Does that mean I've passed the test?'

'What test?' He looked bemused.

'Don't you remember, when I came to dinner at your flat you said that the true test was the breakfast test?' He did not answer me but just continued to gaze at me. 'You know, whether we would have anything to talk about in the morning.'

'Yes. I remember *that* test.'

'You said we would have plenty to talk about.'

'Yes, but there was a condition as I'm sure you recall: spending the night together and...' I interrupted him before he could continue.

'But we just did,' I said mischievously.

'Not in quite the way I had imagined. But you're right, and we're still talking. Any thoughts on where you'd like to go for breakfast?'

'Why don't you surprise me? You're good at that,' I added, raising my eyebrows. 'Then you can tell me what you've really been up to since I last saw you.'

'There's very little to tell, Alicia. I lead a sheltered existence.' He leaned back against the headrest and turned to look at me sideways.

'Like I believe that for one second.'

I had expected to walk out into brilliant summer sunshine, but instead it was pouring with rain. Not quite the weather I had anticipated for my debut arrival in Australia. It was incredibly humid and even the rain was hot.

Alex suggested that we take a cab from the airport to his hotel in the city. He was staying at the Marriott Hotel, only a short walk to the Central Business District and therefore a perfect location for him. While he checked in I sat in the lobby and studied the map of Brisbane in my guidebook. To hit the main shopping area in Queen Street Mall I needed to walk from the Marriott Hotel at the top end of Queen Street down the length of Queen Street.

I glanced at my new watch. It was just after nine and I was actually feeling quite awake and not at all jet-lagged. I supposed that would catch up with me later. I thought that after breakfast I would settle into my apartment in Spring Hill and relax. It was very late back home and I decided not to call Sally but send her a text message confirming that I would speak to her in the morning (her time). I had just finished when Alex returned.

'Everything OK?'

'Yes. Fine. Why?'

'You look perturbed that's all. Anything I can help with?'

'I had some sad news yesterday from a friend. I was just sending her a text to let her know I'll 'phone later.'

'Oh, I'm sorry to hear that. You sure there isn't anything I can do?' I shook my head. 'I just need to pop up to my room for a minute. I have to make a call. Actually, why don't you come up with me? The executive lounge is on the floor above my room. You can sit and have a cup of coffee if you want. I won't be long. Then we can grab some breakfast.'

'OK.'

Alex and I took the lift up to the executive lounge.

'Great view of the river, isn't it?' he said as he walked me across to a table by the window. Alex was referring to the Brisbane River which the Marriott Hotel overlooks.

'Yes. Pity it's raining though.'

'I'll only be a few minutes. What do you want to do? Stay here, go downstairs to Petries Bar, or go out?'

'I'm quite happy to stay here,' I replied. 'I'll read the newspaper while I'm waiting.'

'OK. I'll be back in two ticks.'

'So what was this sad news then?' asked Alex across the table as he broke off a piece of raisin toast, popped it in his mouth and stirred his coffee. 'You seem preoccupied since you sent that text. Are you OK?'

'I'm fine. It's one of my clients. Her fiancé was killed in an accident yesterday.' I swallowed a mouthful of paw-paw.

'Oh, that's awful, but there isn't really much you can do about it, is there? You can't make this your problem, Alicia.' He leant back in his chair, picked up his cup and sipped his coffee.

'I'm not. She's my client.'

'Yes, and your duty doesn't extend beyond that. This is also your holiday. Don't take this the wrong way, but I think you should take a step back. It doesn't pay to get involved with your clients.'

'I don't.' I retorted, stabbing at the paw-paw with my fork in irritation. It nearly flew off the plate. 'What gives you the right to criticise me?'

'I'm not criticising you. Quite the opposite, in fact. You're one of the most caring people I know. That's a fantastic quality and I admire you for it. I couldn't practise the area of law you do. I think clients are inclined to lean on you, that's all.'

'It isn't like that. You don't understand. This is a really strange case.' I retrieved the paw-paw.

'Why? What were you doing for her anyway?' Alex leaned forward and put his elbows on the table.

'It's not what I was doing for her that's strange. I've just made her a Will. It's her circumstances that make this case odd.'

'I don't follow.' He furrowed his brow.

'In her life she's had one tragedy after another. All her immediate family are dead. Her parents were killed in a motor boat accident when she was three and her brother in a motorbike accident two years ago. Her grandfather's second wife and daughter were killed in a car accident, her grandfather died after a break-in last year and now, as she's about to come into a huge inheritance and marry her fiancé, he too gets murdered.' I swallowed a mouthful of lukewarm caffè latte.

'OK, I agree there are a lot of tragic incidents but these things sometimes happen.'

'Stretching a point, don't you think, Alex?'

'All right. But we both know that fact can be stranger than fiction. Anyway, I thought you said her fiancé was killed in an accident, only you said murdered.'

'Slip of the tongue.'

'No. I know you, Alicia. You don't make mistakes like that. You must have a reason for saying he was murdered.'

'It's just a feeling. Sally, that's the friend who called me to tell me about his death, said that he was working in his studio and there had been some kind of explosion. I asked if the police were treating it as suspicious, but she didn't know.'

'Your client's friend or your friend?'

'Both. I went to university with her and she met my client a few years ago at an exhibition. She introduced the client to me.'

'Oh, I see. Is that why you feel obligated?'

'No. It's more complicated than that.'

'These things always are. But even if it does turn out to be murder, Alicia, what can *you* do about it? If I were you I'd keep well out of it. I would have thought that the least you're involved the better.' Alex had a point but I was not going to concede it. However, I did not wish to fall out with him over this, so I decided it was preferable to have no further conversation on the matter and changed the subject.

'Will you be working this week?'

'Yes. I have to. That's the only way I could wangle a trip here. I've got meetings all day tomorrow and then a work dinner. I leave for Sydney early Tuesday morning but I should be back on Friday afternoon.'

'I suppose you're heading straight back to Singapore after the wedding?'

'No. I'm taking a holiday. I thought I'd catch some surf up on the Sunshine Coast. Why don't you come with me? You're more than welcome. It'd be fun; and give you a chance to see some more of Australia too.'

'Hmm...well...I...' I hesitated because the offer was totally unexpected and I was also thinking how I would co-ordinate that trip with Melbourne and Sydney, my time being slightly limited.

'It was just an idea. You don't have to if you don't want to. Are you upset with me over what I said about your client?' Alex clearly took my vacillation as reluctance.

'No. Well a bit, yes. But that has nothing to do with this.' I knew I sounded as if I was unwilling.

'You're still annoyed with me for not keeping in touch?'

'No. Not any more, although I probably should be.'

'What is it then? If you don't want to come with me just say so.'

'Believe me, Alex, I would. No. It isn't that either.'

'What then?' He sounded slightly exasperated.

'You remember Jeremy Brown?'

'Of course I do. His son's dating your sister, isn't he?'

'Yes. He's going to be at the wedding but afterwards I've arranged to visit him in Melbourne and...'

'Oh, right. So what you're saying is you've already planned something else. No problem. I understand.'

'No. We haven't finalized the dates yet. I'd like to come if I can.'

'I'll leave it up to you. The offer is there. Just let me know what you decide.'

'I will. You don't mind if I head off now, do you? I'm feeling really tired all of a sudden. I think I'd like to have a shower and sleep for a few hours.'

'You do look a bit whacked. But don't sleep too long or else you'll be jet lagged for longer.'

'I just need a nap.'

'You're welcome to crash here you know.'

'Thanks, but I'd like to get settled in.'

'Fair enough. How about I take you out for dinner tonight?'

'I'm sorry, I can't.'

'Oh.' He sounded disappointed.

'It's not that I don't want to, only I'm seeing Kim tonight. I'm going to meet her family. Which reminds me; I haven't called her yet. She'll be wondering what has happened to me.'

'Don't worry. I've spoken to her.'

'When?'

'I called her when I went to my room.'

'So that's what you went off to do. Did you tell her your little surprise went according to plan?' I chided.

'I told her you weren't impressed by our surprise. She said she'll 'phone you later. How about you have dinner with me on Friday instead?'

'OK.'

'Great. I look forward to it. I'll ask reception to call you a taxi. Where is it you're staying?'

'Wickham Terrace. I don't think it's far from here. I could probably walk,' I said, taking out my map from my handbag.

'It isn't,' he said, showing me the route on the map. 'But you're tired; and it's pouring with rain. Take a taxi. Actually, I thought you might be staying with Kim's family.'

'She did offer, but they're in Bardon and I want to be in the city. Also I prefer to be independent.'

'Hmm... Don't I know it!'

Chapter 7

I must have fallen asleep as soon as my head touched the pillow. Had it not been for the sound of the 'phone ringing, I probably would have carried on sleeping for several more hours. So much for taking Alex's advice. I glanced at my watch; it was five o'clock. I had only intended to take a short nap but as it happened I had slept away most of my first day in Australia.

'Hello,' I said, answering the call in a rather sleepy voice.

'Did I wake you? I'm sorry.' It was Kim.

'Don't be. It's just as well you did or else I'll never sleep tonight, and I've slept too long as it is. Now I won't get anything done,' I said, sitting up on the bed. I wanted to make that call to Sally and find out if she had gleaned any other information about Drew's 'accident'.

'Well, I hope those things you have to do aren't work-related. I know you. You *are* still coming to dinner tonight? You're not too tired?'

'I'm fine,' I replied, yawning as I glanced at myself in the mirrored door of the wardrobe opposite the bed and toying with my hair which was sticking up on one side. 'I'm looking forward to seeing you and meeting your family. How do I get to you?'

'Oh, don't worry about that. Rob and I'll come and collect you about seven. It's a shame you're not staying with my parents here in Bardon especially since Jeremy, Tom and Antonia will be nearby. We'd love to have you. Are you sure you're OK alone?'

'Yes, perfectly OK.' The apartment where I had chosen to stay was more than adequate for my needs both in terms of location and facilities. It was situated amongst picturesque parkland but close to the city centre and kitted out with all mod cons. I also had my own balcony boasting a fantastic view of the city.

'Well, if you change your mind you only have to ask.'

'I know.'

'See you at seven.'

'Yes.'

There was no reply on either Sally's mobile or landline, so I sent her a text message to say I had tried to call and to give her the number where I was staying. I supposed that she would return my call if she had anything to report. I called Mamma for a brief chat and reassured her that all was well, the flights were excellent, the apartment was great and I had had a long sleep and was in good form. I unpacked my clothes and had just stepped into the shower when the 'phone rang. Were it not for the fact that I had left my shampoo on the basin and leaned out of the shower to retrieve it, I would not have heard it. I grabbed a towel and ran to answer the call, dripping water everywhere.

'Hello,' I said slightly breathlessly.

'Alicia?' I recognised her voice at once.

'Hi, Sally. How are things?'

'OK. I'm sorry I missed your call. You OK? Is this a bad time?'

'No. Not at all. What's happened?'

'I spoke to Chris.'

'Chris?'

'My cousin. The one I told you about. He was a school friend of Drew's.'

'Oh, of course. And?'

'It was no accident. Drew was murdered. Someone planted a device in his studio and that's what caused the explosion.' Although I had suspected foul play the news that he had been murdered certainly put a different spin on matters.

'What sort of device?' My head was buzzing.

'Chris didn't say. He was with Drew's parents when he rang and was a bit monosyllabic to be honest. But I don't suppose he knows anyway.'

'How's Isabelle bearing up?'

'Remarkably calm, considering. Lucy's with her. I'm sorry to be the bearer of such bad news. The last thing you need is to be disturbed on your holiday. How's Australia?'

'Hot! To be honest, I've slept for most of the day so I haven't seen much of it yet. But I'm going out shortly.'

'Oh, I hope I haven't held you up by calling.'

'No. Not at all.'

'Well, I'll let you go.'

'Thanks, Sally. I'll speak to you soon, but please ring me if there's any news.'

'Yes, of course I will. Have a lovely evening.'

Kim sent me a text soon after seven to say she and Rob were waiting outside in the car. I stepped out onto the balcony and looked down. It had stopped raining, but it was very close and there was not even the hint of a breeze. I could see Kim leaning nonchalantly against the driver's side of the car. She had partially kicked off her left shoe and was toying with it as she stood chatting to Rob through the open car window. I picked up my bag and key and made my way downstairs as quickly as possible. When I arrived Rob was also standing outside the car.

'Ally,' exclaimed Kim, extending her arms to give me a big bear hug. 'You don't get any fatter do you?' she said, laughing, 'and I bet you're still eating Pringles too. Life just isn't fair.'

'Oh, I don't know. It has its compensations,' I whispered to her. 'You're the one getting married.'

'Hi, Alicia, how are you?' asked Rob, kissing me on the cheek and then giving me a hug. 'It's good to see you. Kim's really rapt you could make it. We both are.'

'How far is it to Bardon from here?' I asked, settling myself into the back of the car.

'Not far. It's about a fifteen-minute drive. But we thought we'd give you a quick tour.'

'I hope you're hungry, Alicia. We're having a big barbie tonight,' said Kim.

'We have to live up to your expectation of the Australian outdoor image you see,' said Rob, turning and grinning at me.

Rob drove up to the lookout at Mount Coot-tha to give me a panoramic view of the city. Unfortunately, it was a bit misty, so the views were a little disappointing.

'Are you OK?' Kim asked as we stood at the railing overlooking the city waiting for Rob who had gone back to the car to fetch Kim's jacket.

'Yes. I'm fine. Why?'

'You seem preoccupied. I know you must be tired. You're not mad with me over Alex, are you?' I shook my head.

'No, of course not,' I replied taking her arm. 'Although he was the last person I expected to see. No, I had some bad news earlier and it's on my mind.'

'Not your family?' I shook my head. 'Anything I can help with?'

'No. It's to do with one of my clients. Her fiancé was killed on Friday night. I can't stop thinking about it.'

'That's awful. What happened to him?'

'He was murdered. Blown up in an explosion, apparently.'

'What? I mean, no wonder it's on your mind. But you're not involved though, are you? My advice is to steer well clear of any involvement. You don't need this, Ally.'

'That's what Alex said.'

'He's right. The last thing you want is to become embroiled in a murder investigation. Goodness knows what it might lead to. I know I don't have to spell it out to you.'

Chapter 8

Early in the morning on my first full day in Brisbane I decided to check out the shops. I needed to buy a present for Daniel, my Godson, as it was his first birthday in a few weeks time, and thought I would take an initial look in David Jones and then wander around the Myer Centre. From my apartment it was a pleasant walk into the city and, as it was still relatively cool, I ambled down the hill into Queen Street and along to the Mall. However, it soon became scorching hot and by the time I returned to the apartment late in the afternoon, having walked back up the hill with my purchases, I was frazzled. I did think of taking a tour on the City Sights bus as one of its stops is Spring Hill, but I discovered I was too late to catch the last bus tour of the day. As I traipsed back to Wickham Terrace all I wanted were copious supplies of ice-cold water and a long cool shower.

The concierge stopped me to give me an envelope on my way to the lift. It was a hand-written note from Luisa Bruneschi, whose number Isabelle had given me in the office. It read:

Alicia, I'm a friend of Isabelle Parker. She mentioned you to me. I was working in the area and dropped in on the off chance of seeing you. Perhaps you'd like to give me a call while you're here as I'd like to meet you. In case you don't have my details I've enclosed my card. Hope to hear. Regards. Luisa Bruneschi

I felt somewhat perplexed by this latest turn of events. I was bewildered that she knew where I was staying and seemed keen to meet me; nonetheless, I resolved to call her the next morning. I had my shower, changed into some fresh clothes and settled down to write some post cards before I went out to meet Tom with whom I had arranged to have dinner. I was on my third postcard when I received another call from Sally.

'What's that noise?' I could hear a thudding sound in the background.

'Driving rain pelting against the window of the office. It's absolutely pouring outside.'

'Proper English weather then?' I laughed.

'Don't get me started! I take it you're enjoying blissful blue skies where you are.'

'It was pretty stormy yesterday, but it's simply sweltering today,' I replied, opening the balcony door and stepping outside. The intensity of the heat struck me. I quickly shut the balcony door and retreated inside to the comfort of my air-conditioned apartment. 'It must only be about eight o'clock there. What are you doing in the office so early?'

'I've got a big case on this week. The reason why I'm calling is to let you know Isabelle 'phoned me at six-thirty this morning asking for your number. Obviously, I didn't give it to her. I wouldn't do that without speaking to you first. She was quite insistent though and said she *must* speak with you.'

'Is that all she said?'

'Yes. I tried to put her off as I'm sure you can do without any of this. I told her that you were on holiday for at least three weeks, probably couldn't help her anyway, and that I was sure the police were doing their best with the investigation. But she was persistent and I said I'd ring you. She left another contact number where you can reach her. Sorry, Alicia.'

'Don't be. What's the number?' I asked, reaching for a pen. She read the number out to me but the biro I grabbed did not work. 'Hang on a sec. I need to get another pen,' I said, reaching over to pick up a pencil off the coffee table. 'OK. Give it to me again.' She repeated the number and I wrote it down on the back of a Queensland beaches postcard. 'Thanks, Sally.'

'That's OK. Are you going to call her? Only, if she rings again, what do you want me to tell her?'

'Just that you've passed on her message.'

'OK. Speak to you soon.'

'Bye.'

I strolled down to Anzac Square. Tom was waiting for me at the Shrine of Remembrance.

'Perfect timing,' he said, looking at his watch and stepping forward to give me a kiss on the cheek.

'Well, you did say seven-thirty,' I replied, glancing at my own watch.

'Nice watch.'

'Alex gave it to me.'

'Did he now? I heard you saw him.' He raised his eyebrows.

'Kim?'

'Of course. Have you eaten today, only I thought you might like a stroll around first – unless you're absolutely starving?'

'Moderately. I had a sandwich at 'Subs and Sandwiches' in the Myer Centre. A walk would be good.'

'Cool. Let's head down to the river and walk through the Botanic Gardens,' he said, leading the way. 'I spoke to Dad today. He's arriving on Friday afternoon. He's looking forward to you going to Melbourne.'

'I'm looking forward to it too.'

'So what did you get up to today?'

'Shopping primarily. I bought some clothes for my Godson in David Jones and then went to the Myer Centre. I wanted to get that City Sights Tour bus, but I was too late so I may do that tomorrow.'

'It's not a bad way of orientating yourself. Kim said we must stop you thinking about work. She told me about your client.'

'Yes. It's all very bizarre.'

'And not something you want to get involved in.'
'So you all keep telling me.'

Later that evening when I returned to the apartment I toyed with the postcard and weighed up whether to ring Isabelle or not. I did not relish the thought of becoming involved and I wondered whether I could really do anything to help her. Nonetheless I was intrigued by what had motivated her to call me; I was more convinced than ever that she had had something serious on her mind the morning she came into the office to sign her Will. However, since my curiosity had landed me in some scrapes in the past, it was probably better to let sleeping dogs lie, and so I resolved not to 'phone her; well, not immediately.

As for Luisa, I wondered whether she knew about Drew's death. Lucy could have told her, but even if she did, she could not possibly want to meet me about that. After all, the only connection I had with Isabelle was that I had made her Will. It was very peculiar.

Fate, however, has a bizarre way of dictating events regardless of the decisions we make. The following morning I was fast asleep and was awakened by my mobile phone ringing. It was on my bedside table and in my stupor I reluctantly reached over to pick it up and answer it.

'Hello,' I said sleepily as I sank back into my pillow.
'Alicia. Thank goodness.' The voice was quite breathless.
'Who is this?'
'It's Isabelle…Isabelle Parker.' I sat bolt upright. 'I'm sorry to call you so early, but I don't know who else to turn to. They won't believe me. You've got to help me. I wouldn't ask, but I'm desperate.' She sounded strange and her voice was quavering. This was a conversation for which I was completely unprepared, not least because I believed Isabelle did not have my mobile number. Perhaps Sally had given her it after all.

'Isabelle. I'm sorry about Drew,' I said softly.

'Thank you. I really can't take it in.' There was a pause. I wanted to ask her what the explosion was, but in her stricken state I felt it inappropriate to press her for those details. 'Did you get my message?'

'That you wanted to speak to me? Yes. Last night. I...' I felt a momentary tinge of conscience that I had elected not to call her, but she interrupted me before I had a chance to respond, so the awkward moment passed.

'I couldn't wait. I had to ring. You're probably the only one who can help me. Please promise me you will,' she asked in such a plaintive voice that I felt myself coming out in a cold sweat at the prospect of what that request might entail.

'I'll help you if I can,' I replied cautiously, feeling my back stiffen with the tension, 'but what about the police? Can't you speak to them?'

'I've tried but they won't listen to me. They think I'm hysterical, and I probably am, but that's because they won't take any notice of what I'm saying.' She sounded increasingly distraught.

'Isabelle, I'm struggling to follow what you're telling me,' I replied, getting out of bed and padding through to the kitchen to fetch myself a drink of water. 'What do you mean they won't believe you? Believe what?' I asked, opening the fridge door and taking out a bottle of Summit Mountain pure natural spring water.

'That whoever murdered Drew intended to kill me. And what's more, I think that whoever did it murdered Grandpa Jam and Michael as well. I'm convinced that Drew's murder is connected with the other two.'

When I first met Isabelle she had struck me as a realistic young woman with her feet firmly on the ground. So, although she was demonstrably distressed and traumatised by recent events, I felt that she would not make such a statement unless she had strong reasons, or proof, in support of her assertions. Nevertheless, I felt slightly overwhelmed by what Isabelle had said and struggled to make sense of it.

'You're losing me, Isabelle. I thought you said that Michael was killed two years ago in a motorbike accident and, in the case of your grandfather, wasn't murder ruled out?' I opened the bottle of water as I balanced my mobile between ear and chin and poured some into a glass.

'It's very complicated.' I began to imagine all sorts of scenarios. 'Will you help me?' I walked through to the sitting room area.

'What exactly do you want from me?' I asked warily.

'To help me find the murderer. I barely know you, but I feel I can trust you.' Notwithstanding her flattering comment I was still reluctant to become involved.

'Isabelle, I'm a private client lawyer, not a private detective. I fail to see what I can do...'

'Oh, please, Alicia. I have nobody else,' she implored. There was probably a ten second time lag at my end of the line before I responded as I needed to collect my thoughts.

'OK. I'll help if I can, provided you're straight with me and tell me everything. But I still don't know what I could possibly do.'

'Oh, thank you. You don't know how grateful I am.' I detected a distinct sense of relief in her voice. 'I'll come out to Melbourne to see Grandma Edie this week if the police say I can leave and I'll be in touch then. I really have to go. Thank you again, Alicia. You don't know what your help means to me. Bye.' And she was gone.

My conversation with Isabelle had been a strange one from which I gleaned almost nothing. She had not told me why she believed Drew was murdered and I was both baffled and fascinated as to how she connected the three deaths because there was no similarity in the way they had died. This was the last thing I had expected to happen when I was on holiday. Fate certainly has a lot to answer for.

Since I was completely taken off guard by Isabelle's call I had not mentioned to her that Luisa Bruneschi had contacted me. I had no intention of telling Luisa that I had spoken to Isabelle. In any case, Isabelle was speaking to me in confidence. I decided to err on the side of caution and to say nothing when I called Luisa later that morning.

'Hello. Luisa Bruneschi speaking.' I presumed she was working in an office as I could hear the sound of tapping on a keyboard.

'It's Alicia Allen. You left a note at my apartment yesterday afternoon.' The tapping stopped.

'Oh yes. Hello. Thanks for calling me. I saw Isabelle a few weeks back when I was in London and she mentioned you. She told me you were coming out to Brisbane and I thought you might want to hook up. I was just passing your way and dropped in on the off chance.' She did not allude to Drew, but then she might not know about his death or, if she did, thought better than to discuss what had happened over the 'phone.

'That's very thoughtful. But how did you find me?'

'I'm an investigative journalist. It's what I do.'

'You're likely to be short of copy if you go around investigating people like me!'

'You'd be surprised. I bet there's more to you than meets the eye.'

'You'll have to tell me when we meet. That *is* what you want, isn't it?'

'Yes. I'd like that very much. Are you free for lunch today?'

'I could be.'

'Great. Do you know the South Bank Parklands?'

'I know how to get there on a map. I was intending to go to the Art Gallery at some point.'

'Cool. I'll meet you there then. Say twelve-thirty.'

'Fine, but how will I find you?'

'There are benches directly in front of the main entrance. Call me when you get there. Have to run. Bye, Alicia.'

'Bye.'

I made my way over to the South Bank early as I decided to spend the morning there. As I strolled across Victoria Bridge which spans the river to the South Bank, I could see the Performing Arts Centre to the left of it and the Art Gallery and Museum to the right. The concrete buildings reminded me of the Royal Festival Hall and Hayward Gallery of the South Bank Centre in London.

I had heard that the South Bank Parklands were really picturesque and well worth a visit. After a brief exploration, I retraced my steps along the walkway between the Performing Arts Centre and the Museum and Art Gallery. I passed the entrance to the Museum and wandered down the concrete passageway towards the Courtyard Café at the far end. Before I reached it I followed the path around and came out at the entrance to the State Library in front of which there are some 'infozone' benches. A little further ahead and to my right was the Art Gallery and the benches to which Luisa had referred. It was still only eleven o'clock so I thought I would take a look around the Gallery.

I kept an eye on the time and was waiting for Luisa at twelve-thirty on the dot. I glanced around but apart from the man lying on one of the benches and a young couple hovering on the steps there was nobody to be seen. I called Luisa's mobile and stood, with my 'phone to my ear, waiting for her to answer.

'Hi, Alicia. I can see you. I'll be with you in two ticks. I'm coming across the bridge. I'm sorry I'm a bit late.' She clicked her mobile off. I swivelled around and saw a leggy brunette with wavy shoulder length hair gesticulating wildly as she strode confidently towards me. She was wearing navy blue palazzo pants and a crisp white linen sleeveless shirt and strappy navy shoes. Although she was naturally dark-skinned she was also tanned and the whiteness of the shirt made her look even more so. 'Alicia, great to meet you,' she said, sweeping her sunglasses back and up into her hair revealing deep brown eyes. She shook my hand firmly. She stared very hard at me for a split second before smiling broadly. I did not quite know what to make of her and wondered what I might glean over lunch.

'I have to say I was very surprised when I received your note. Isabelle gave me your contact details, but I never expected that *you* might contact *me*.'

'She spoke very highly of you. I was curious to meet you. I hope you don't mind.'

'No. Not at all. But I'm amazed you went to so much trouble to find me just to satisfy your curiosity.'

'Oh, it was easy. Thanks for agreeing to meet for lunch. Unfortunately, I'm a bit pressed for time. Do you mind if we grab a snack from the Café and eat it out here? Is that OK?'

'No problem at all.' As we wandered along to the Café we made small talk.

'How did you like the Art Gallery?'

'I enjoyed it.'

'You saw the nineteenth century stained glass window depicting a kangaroo hunt?'

'Yes, I did.'

'How are you enjoying your stay?'

'It's good. I've only been here a couple of days but I'm getting the feel of the place.' I ordered a ham salad baguette and she opted for the same and insisting on paying. We meandered back to where we met and sat down on one of the benches.

'I suppose as Isabelle's lawyer you're aware of what happened to her fiancé. I heard about his death from Lucy.' She did know after all.

'Is that a statement or a question?' I took a bite of my baguette.

'It's just that I thought that as her lawyer…'

'I'd be privy to certain information?' I said, finishing her sentence. 'She came to me for a Will. I've only met her twice.'

'Is that all?' She was looking at me very intently over the top of her baguette.

'What do you mean? In terms of what she asked me to do for her or how many times we've met?'

'I meant, is that all you did for her? Just make a Will?'

'Well, that's *all* she asked me to do. Now tell me, how did you come to be friends with Isabelle?' I asked, swallowing another mouthful and changing the subject.

'We met at the Melbourne International Arts Festival a few years back. I was there doing a story. I spilt a glass of red wine over her dress. I was very apologetic and we got talking and hit it off. She was there with Lucy Winters. We're all good friends.' She wiped some crumbs from her lap.

'How fascinating…do you enjoy working as a journalist?'

'I do. I get to meet a lot of very interesting people. It's amazing what you can find out if you do your research thoroughly.' I sensed she was scrutinizing my every move and it made me slightly uncomfortable.

'Very true. Where do you work?'

'The *Courier Mail*. Take my card,' she said, delving into her handbag. It was one of those little bucket bags where everything falls to the bottom. 'It's in here somewhere,' she said, extracting a simple white card with her contact details on it and handing it to me. As she did so she glanced up and beamed.

'Thanks,' I replied, taking it and putting it in my bag. 'Isabelle told me you were from Melbourne. With a name like yours you must be of Italian extraction?'

'I am. My grandparents came over from Sicily after the war.'

'You speak Italian then?'

'No, unfortunately. Everybody always thinks because of my name that I must be bilingual, but I'm not.'

'That's a shame.'

'Do you speak any languages?'

'My mother's Italian. Her family's from Grassina. My sister and I are both bilingual. My father was English, hence the surname 'Allen'.'

'You'll really like Melbourne then, with its strong Italian influence.'

'So everybody tells me.'

'What's going to happen with Isabelle?' she asked, changing the subject back.

'What do you mean?'

'Now that Drew is dead.'

'I'm sorry. I don't follow what you're asking me.'

'Legally speaking?'

'Well, the status quo remains unchanged.'

'Right. Do you mind if I make a move?' she said, glancing at her watch. 'Only, I really should be heading back now.' I noticed that she had only eaten half her baguette.

'You carry on. I'm going to stay and finish my lunch. It's cooler here and I can't face the blazing heat quite yet.'

'Oh, OK,' she replied, standing up and throwing the remains of her baguette into a nearby bin. 'What are your plans for the rest of the day?'

'I think I'll head back across the bridge and walk around the older parts of the city.'

'Have a look at the Casino. It's the former Treasury building and heritage listed, and if you walk along George Street and Margaret Street you'll find the Mansions, a row of restored old terraced houses.'

'Yes. They're on my list of things to see.'

'If you walk in that direction you can wander down to the Botanic Gardens via the Queensland Club and Parliament House. Have you been to the Gardens yet?'

'Only at night.'

'Well, they're worth going to in the day. It's a pity that you weren't here a few months ago. The jacaranda trees were magnificent then with their lilac-blue blossom. It's a shame I have to go as I'd love to stay and chat. I really enjoyed meeting you. If you need anything while you're in Brisbane let me know.'

'Thanks. I will. And thanks for lunch.' I stood up to shake her hand and then she left.

Although Luisa asked a number of questions about Isabelle and seemed very interested in her affairs, I supposed that this could merely be down to her being a journalist. As Isabelle's friend I expected her to be concerned about her welfare, but it still struck me as rather odd for her to have contacted *me*.

Chapter 9

On Friday morning I strolled over to the South Bank again to visit the Maritime Museum. I thought I would walk down through the Botanic Gardens and across the Goodwill Bridge. Antonia was due to arrive that morning and said she would call me, but I had not heard from her and I was a little concerned. When I 'phoned her mobile it went straight to voice mail so I left a message to let her know where I would be.

I switched my mobile off while I was in the Museum, but when I turned it back on there was a voice mail message from Antonia to say that all was well, Tom had met her at the airport and Jeremy was expected shortly. Apparently she had made arrangements for the four of us to go out to dinner at a restaurant in Duncan Street. I did not catch the name of the restaurant, but she told me she would pick me up at eight.

It was typical of her to organize something without consulting me first and, although I am sure she did it with the best of intentions, she really should have asked me if I had made any alternative arrangements. Since Alex had asked me to go to dinner with him on Friday night, before I returned her call I sent him a text message to find out if his invitation was still open. I wandered along to Little Stanley Street, found a charming café and ordered myself an Appletini. I had only been there a few minutes when my mobile rang. I hoped it was Alex responding to my text, but it was Antonia.

'Did you get my message?'

'Yes.'

'Where are you? There's a lot of background noise.'

'I'm on the South Bank. I left a voice mail message on your mobile earlier.'

'I got it. I didn't think you'd still be there. Is everything OK?'

'Yes. How was the flight? Did you sleep?'

'Oh, fine. I took some Melatonin. I slept like a log. Now about dinner tonight, I thought Asian but if you don't fancy it we can go somewhere else.'

'Actually, Antonia can we take a rain check on dinner. I...' She interrupted me before I had the chance to finish my sentence.

'But I've arranged it now and Jeremy's really looking forward to seeing you again. What's the problem? Don't you want to go?'

'Well, I would come only...' Again she interrupted me.

'I'm not listening to any excuses. *Mamma mia.* I'll see you at eight.' She hung up. I was really annoyed with her. She was such a bossy boots at times and could be quite exasperating. I rang her back but she was engaged on another call. The waiter appeared with my Appletini. I took a sip, my mobile rang again and thinking it was Antonia I answered it abruptly.

'Alicia? It's me. I'm back.' It was Alex.

'So I hear. Good trip?'

'Yes. Everything's OK. I got your text, thanks. Where are you? I can hardly hear you.'

'I'm over on the South Bank.'

'Oh, have you been to the Art Gallery?'

'Yes. I went there the other day. I've just been to the Maritime Museum.'

'Good. So long as you're making the most of your holiday and not worrying about your clients.' I felt he was checking up on me. 'My dinner invitation is still open, but I'll have to get back to you once I've sorted out all the carnage here. I'm not sure whether I'll be able to make it. I meant to call you earlier but I've been so busy dealing with my clients.'

'They just can't do without you, Alex,' I said flatly. There was a slight pause at the end of the 'phone.

'Nobody can.'

'Really? *I* seem to have managed without you for the past few months,' I was annoyed with Antonia and was taking out my frustration on him.

'Well in that case I'll leave you alone then…if that's what you want.'

'No. I don't recall asking you to do that,' I responded, back-pedalling. 'Listen,' I said softly, 'please don't feel bad about dinner as Antonia arrived today and to be honest I've been roped into spending this evening with her. She's already arranged for a group of us to go out to dinner and…'

'Oh, that's a shame. I was really looking forward to it.'

'I could always put Antonia off.'

'No. It's fine. You wouldn't want to disappoint her. Anyway, as I said, I wouldn't be able to get back to you until much later and I don't want to mess you about. You enjoy your evening with your sister.'

'Are you sure? I feel bad about letting you down.' Now I felt guilty.

'You're not. Don't worry. Frankly I've been feeling a bit off colour these past few days. I could probably do with an early night. How about I escort you to the wedding tomorrow? I could come and collect you about five. Is that OK?'

'Yes. I'd really like that.'

'Good. I'll see you then.'

Antonia arrived at my apartment at seven-thirty.

'I thought I'd come earlier because I wanted to have a chat and catch up before we meet Tom and Jeremy,' she said, wandering around the apartment. 'You're looking really well,' she said, peering at me hard. 'You've caught the sun. What have you been up to these past few days?' she continued as she popped her head around the bedroom door. 'Have you had a chance to have a proper look around Brisbane?'

'Yes. Kim and Rob drove me up to Mount Coot-tha on Sunday before going on to dinner at her parents' house. I've seen Tom quite a lot. I met him for dinner at the beginning of the week and he came with me on the City Cat the other day. We took a river cruise from New Farm to Bulimba. Then he took me to the Queensland rugby league Suncorp Stadium, and to the XXXX Brewery, and on to Park Road in Milton. I think I've wandered around most of the city myself as well and looked at all the shops.'

'You've had a good time?' asked Antonia as she walked out on to the balcony. I nodded. 'Tom said he'd been keeping you company. So you weren't lonely then?'

'No. I've met Kim for lunch a couple of times as well. One of my client's has a friend who's working over her and I met up with her for lunch on Tuesday. You know me. I enjoy other people's company, but I don't mind my own either.'

'I don't know how you can stand to be alone. I mean it's really lovely around here and this apartment is great but being on your own can't be any fun. I'd hate it.'

'This is the perfect location for me. I'm so close to Roma Street Parkland. Did you go there when you came here before?' Antonia shook her head. 'It's very pleasant to go and sit there or have a wander around.'

'And I suppose being here makes it so much easier to see Alex,' she teased.

'On the basis that Alex has been in Sydney all week, not exactly, no. But you'll get to meet him at the wedding tomorrow so you'll see him for yourself.'

'Yes. Finally. We should go. We're meeting Tom and Jeremy at eight-thirty.'

'Are we going to that restaurant in Duncan Street?'

'No. There's been a change of plan. We're going to the Spanish Garden at the Breakfast Creek Hotel. We pass Newstead House on the way, so you'll get a preview of Kim's reception venue.'

'I've already seen it on the way in from the airport.'
'Oh, of course.'

When Antonia and I arrived at the restaurant Tom and Jeremy were waiting for us.

'How have you enjoyed your past week in Brisbane?' asked Jeremy as we sat down at our table.

'I've had a great time. I think I've pretty much walked the whole city. I was surprised how easy it is to get around.'

'Well, it's very compact and easy to explore on foot,' said Tom. 'On Sunday, if it's a good day, we could go to the Mount Coot-tha Botanic Gardens for a picnic. I thought that in the evening we could take the river tour on the Kookaburra Queen and have dinner. Would you like that?'

'The wooden paddle steamer?' He nodded. 'That sounds great, but I'm not sure what my plans are. May I let you know tomorrow?'

'No problem.'

'What plans?' quizzed Antonia.

'I thought I might go up the coast for a few days.'

'Alone?' asked Antonia. I did not respond.

'Sounds like you're making the most of your trip to Australia,' interjected Jeremy. 'I'm very pleased to hear that you've enjoyed your stay in Brisbane, Alicia. I hope you'll find Melbourne as entertaining.'

'Oh, I'm sure she will,' said Tom. 'With all that Italian influence she won't be disappointed.' I laughed.

'You're welcome at any time. Just give me a call and let me know when to expect you,' said Jeremy.

'Thank you. It'll probably be in a week or so's time.'

'I thought you said you were only going up the coast for a few days?' asked Antonia. 'What else do you have to do here?' Antonia was probing, but I was not going to be drawn and ignored her comment.

'She can come and stay any time she likes. It isn't a problem,' said

Jeremy, addressing Antonia. 'As I said, you're very welcome, Alicia, you know that.'

'Thank you. It may be sooner than a week. It's just that I haven't quite decided what to do and I wanted to keep my options open in case things change. The one thing I've learned is that life's unpredictable and you can never guarantee what's going to happen.'

'But that's what makes it exciting, don't you think?' said Jeremy with a glint in his eye.

Chapter 10

I was unable to raise my head off the pillow, I felt as sick as a parrot and all I could hope was that I might sleep off whatever it was before the wedding. Goodness knows why I had such an upset stomach, but unfortunately I did and it was not going away fast. Eventually, I managed to keep down half a glass of water and several painkillers and, at some point, drifted into drug-induced sleep. Suddenly, I was conscious of someone knocking on the door to the apartment. I dragged myself up off the bed, grabbed the white towelling robe from the bathroom and staggered to the door. I opened it to a beaming Alex immaculately attired in evening dress. I felt extremely self-conscious at my own dishevelled appearance.

'What will people think?' he said, smiling warmly and raising his eyebrows. Then he must have realized that I was unwell. 'You look dreadful. What's the matter?'

'I've been really ill,' I replied, leaning back against the open door and running my hand back through my rather unkempt hair.

'I thought there must be something wrong as I've been knocking for ages.' I gestured for him to come into the apartment and closed the door.

'I feel awful.' I sank down onto the sofa. He slipped off his dinner jacket, put it neatly on the chair opposite and sat down next to me.

'You feel quite hot,' he said, turning to me and touching my forehead.

'I did manage to get some sleep, but I still feel bilious. Can you pass me that water please?' I pointed to the glass on the side table next to him. He stretched over and handed it to me and I caught a waft of his aftershave. I took a couple of sips.

'I have to say I've been feeling queasy myself these past few days. There must be a bug going round. I was really quite sick earlier in the week and I wasn't feeling at all well last night.'

'I know. You told me when we spoke yesterday.'

'Do you think you can make it?'

'I didn't come all this way to miss it, but it's too late for me to be ready in time for the ceremony now. I'll have to join you at the reception.'

'It isn't too late. Knowing that you have a habit of running late,' he said whimsically and dropping his voice, 'I took the liberty of arriving early. I did call to let you know that I was on my way but your mobile went straight to voice mail and so I decided to surprise you instead.'

'Nothing new there then,' I replied with hardly veiled sarcasm.

'The concierge downstairs gave me your room number. He said you were in.'

'You mean you didn't persuade him to give you a key?'

'I would have done if you hadn't answered. Does it not occur to you that I might actually be worried about you?'

'But that would mean you would have to care about me, Alex,' I said, staring at him hard for some sign of emotion.

'I'm just a sucker for a pretty girl in distress,' was his swift riposte. He swivelled around to face me. 'Now listen,' he said, putting his arm around me, 'we still have bags of time. Why don't you take a shower and get ready. I can come back in thirty minutes. Is that long enough?' I nodded. I could manage that if I made an effort.

'I didn't notice what time it was.' I scanned the room for the watch Alex had given me. I was sure it was there somewhere. 'You told me you would come and collect me at five, so I presumed when you arrived that that was the time.'

'Well, that will teach you not to presume anything about me without checking,' he said, picking up his jacket and walking to the door. I stood up and followed him. 'Oh, and Alicia,' he added, turning around and pausing for a second after he had opened it, 'don't forget to lock the door.' He mimed the turning of a key with his hand. 'You wouldn't want anyone walking in on you unexpectedly while you're in the shower! See you in half an hour then.'

Alex was always punctual and I knew he would return on time so I rushed and felt flustered. I was finishing dressing when I heard him knock on the door, but in my haste to do up the zip of my dress I yanked at it and the zip stuck.

'Oh, good. You're ready,' he said as I opened the door. 'And you look much better. It's amazing what you can do in thirty minutes. That dress is lovely. Blue really suits you.'

'Thank you. It isn't new. I bought it last year. It's the dress I wore on my thirtieth birthday. But I'm not quite ready as it happens. This zip is stuck. Look, it just won't budge,' I said, tugging at it.

'Don't pull it. You'll break it. Do you have a pencil?'

'Yes. By my note pad, over there.' I pointed to the pencil on the coffee table. 'Why?'

'Because the graphite works as a lubricant. It will help to ease the zip.' I handed him the pencil and he rubbed the zip with it. 'There,' he said, releasing the zip and sliding it up, 'Problem solved. Don't say I never do anything for you,' he added, gently resting his arm on my shoulder and then handing me back the pencil.

'It's strange, isn't it, Alex,' I said, toying with the pencil, 'to think that if each carbon atom were bonded to four others instead of three that I would be holding a sparkling diamond in my hand and not a dull piece of graphite? It's amazing what difference the absence or presence of one little carbon atom can make.'

'Yes, the difference between your zip being stuck and unstuck,' he replied with a mischievous smile. 'How do you feel now?' He passed me my handbag.

'OK'ish. But still a bit nauseous.'

'Oh, that reminds me,' he said, fumbling in his jacket pocket. 'I picked this up while I was waiting for you to get ready.' He held up a small packet.

'What's that?' I asked.

'Anti-emetic powders. If you have one now it should help settle your stomach.' He walked to the sink, picked up a clean glass off the draining board, and filled it with water from the tap. I watched him as he ripped open one of the sachets and whisked its contents into the glass of water with a fork. 'Here,' he said, handing the glass to me. 'Drink this.'

'Thanks,' I replied, taking the rather suspicious looking potion from him. 'It looks and smells absolutely disgusting, but I'll take your word for it that it works and that you're not trying to poison me.' I gulped it down.

'Trust me. You'll thank me when you feel better. Come on. We had better get going,' he said, glancing at his watch. 'You can tell me what's been happening this week on the way to the church.'

'So how far is it to Mitchelton?' I asked as we set off for St Matthew's Church in Alex's Holden hire car.

'Not far. Just a little further on from Bardon. We have plenty of time. Feeling any better yet?'

'A little. Your miracle potion seems to be working.'

'Good. Told you to trust me. Now what was I going to say…oh, yes, I was wondering if you'd given any further thought to coming up to the Sunshine Coast with me.'

'I have. If the offer's still open, I'd love to tag along.'

'Really? I mean great. I thought maybe you might be going straight to Melbourne, that's all.' Alex seemed slightly taken aback that I had taken him up on his invitation and it amused me.

'No,' I replied, shaking my head. 'Jeremy's quite flexible about when I go so it isn't a problem.'

'If it's all right with you I'm planning to head up there tomorrow. How about I pick you up round about two?'

'Fine. I'll be ready.'

'That'll be a first.'

'Oh ye of little faith! I will surprise you…yet.' I nudged him with my elbow. 'Anyway, it's a woman's prerogative to be late.'

'So, what's been happening with that client of yours, the one you told me about?' he asked casually, looking at me sideways.

'Now who was it that said I shouldn't get involved with my clients or be thinking about them on holiday?'

'OK. I deserved that. Satisfy my curiosity then. Was her fiancé murdered?'

'He *was*.'

'Then you *were* right. Even more reason for you to keep out of it.'

'I can't. I've made a promise to help.'

'Alicia. This is madness. I can't believe you did that after everything I said.'

'Don't tell me what to do, Alex.'

'And incur your wrath? Oh, come on. Don't be so defensive. I wish you'd think of me as your ally and not your enemy. I'm on your side. I thought we'd already established that.' We had pulled up outside the church and in my irritation with him I flung open the car door and scrambled out as quickly as I could. In a flash he leapt out of his driver's side and sprinted around to my side of the car. 'Alicia,' he said, catching hold of my arm. 'Look at me, please. I'm sorry. OK. I just worry about you getting involved, that's all. You don't know what it might lead to.'

'Leave it, Alex. I'm not going to argue with you over this.' I replied, wrenching my arm away from him and storming off.

The church was in a stunning location built at the top of the hill and I could understand why Kim and Rob had chosen to marry there. It was a quaint mid-Victorian church, big enough to hold all Kim and Rob's guests, but small enough to make the ceremony more of an intimate personal gathering, which meant that I would be in close proximity to Alex. Although I had ignored him since we arrived at the church I was actually cross with myself for snapping at him and losing my temper. We sat on the same pew but at either end and even though I tried hard not to look at him, I could not help myself from stealing a few icy glances. Now I supposed the trip to the Sunshine Coast was off and it was my own fault. I was just going to have to put that stubborn pride of mine behind me and apologize to him.

Kim looked a picture of elegance in an ivory off-the-shoulder dress. The bodice was fitted, but the skirt floated from her waist and trailed gently to the floor. She wore an ivory chiffon stole draped loosely across her shoulders and had flowers pinned in her hair. The ceremony was lovely and as she and Rob exchanged vows I felt very privileged to be able to share her special moment.

I was one of the first guests to arrive at Newstead House for the reception. This was because Kim's parents had insisted I accompany them in their car. I did not see Alex after we left the church, nor while the photographs were being taken. I hoped that he would come to the reception as I wanted to make it up with him. I paced around anticipating his arrival like a cat on hot bricks.

'Waiting for me?' he whispered in my ear. He was standing behind me. I nearly jumped out of my skin and turned to face him.

'Alex!' I exclaimed, catching my breath. 'Where did *you* spring from?'

'It's amazing I'm still alive after all those deathly looks you were giving me in the church. Where did you learn that look, or does it come naturally to you?'

'I *am* sorry. I guess I do have a rather fiery temperament. It's the Italian in me I suppose! It gets the better of me sometimes.'

'Hmm... Not that I've noticed,' he replied, tongue-in-cheek.

'Alex, I...'

'So this is where you both are,' said Antonia, interrupting our conversation and cutting me short. She must have crept up on us without either of us noticing. 'Tom and I have been looking all over for you, Alicia.' She was addressing me but observing Alex – which hardly surprised me as this was the first time she had seen him and I was aware that she must be very curious about him. I hoped that she would keep her observations to herself.

'Alex, let me introduce you to my sister Antonia.'

'How do *you* do?' He extended his hand.

'How do you do? I'm very well, thank you.' She shook it firmly without taking her eyes off him for a second. 'I feel as if I know you already.' Alex looked slightly perplexed. 'Kim has mentioned you in conversation and I've heard a good deal about you.' He glanced at me. He was probably wondering what I had told her. 'I'm very pleased to meet you…finally. I thought you must be Alex. I saw you at the church and I would have spoken to you, but you weren't with Alicia so I presumed you must be someone else,' she said, giving me a searching look.

'You have to be careful about doing that.'

'Doing what?' Antonia looked bemused.

'Presuming things about me. You're liable to get the completely wrong end of the stick. People always do. Come on, I'll escort you two in.'

After the speeches and the ritual cutting of the cake I resolved to go outside for some fresh air. I looked for Alex as he had vanished halfway through dinner and nobody seemed to know where he was. I scanned the room and searched around but I did not find him. I wandered down through Newstead Park towards the river. He might have gone for a walk. In any event, the light was just starting to fade and it seemed an admirable idea to sit in the riverside rotunda and watch the setting of the sun.

'Are you having a good time?' asked the young man who had appeared from the shadows. He startled me and I took a sudden sharp intake of breath.

'I didn't see you standing there,' I said, putting my hand up to my chest and looking at him. I vaguely recalled seeing him at the church. 'I was just watching the sun go down. Isn't it a beautiful sight?'

'Yes it is. Are you OK? I really didn't mean to give you a fright.'

'I'm fine,' I replied, regaining my composure.

'It's a great place to hold a reception, don't you think?'

'Yes, it's a fantastic location.'

'I don't suppose you have a light, do you?' he asked, taking out a packet of Peter Jackson cigarettes from his jacket pocket. I guessed they must be an Australian brand.

'Sorry, I don't smoke.'

'Just as well. It's a vile habit. I really should give it up.' He put the packet back into his pocket. 'You don't mind?' he said, looking at the seat next to me as if asking my permission to sit down.

'Oh, please.' I beckoned for him to take a seat.

'You're Alicia, aren't you? Kim's lawyer friend from London?'

'I am. But I'm afraid you have the advantage on me. You are?' I could see him more distinctly now but I could not say I had seen him at the reception.

'Paul Heddington. I'm a friend of Rob and Tom's. We've known each other for years.'

'Do you work and live in Brisbane?'

'For now. I'm a freelance writer. Here, take my card,' he said, removing his wallet from the inside pocket of his jacket, opening it and pulling out a card from one of the compartments. Give me a call if you ever feel like meeting up.'

'Thanks,' I replied, taking it. 'I'm going to head back now.' I stood up. 'It's a bit cooler and I left my jacket back at the house.' I crossed my arms in front of my chest and rubbed my upper arms.

'Here, put my jacket on,' he said, taking it off.

'Oh no. I'll be fine honestly.'

'Please,' he said, putting it around my shoulders.

'Thank you.'

We walked back up through the park to the house. We chatted about Brisbane, Australia and the wedding. He was quite droll and he made me laugh. As we approached the house I saw Alex standing on the lawn. He must have seen me, too, as he started to stroll towards me, but he stopped short when he saw Paul and gave him such a withering look that I am surprised Paul did not shrivel up and disappear into the ground.

'Well, it was great talking to you,' Paul said, quickly picking up the vibes.

'You too, Paul.' I took off his jacket and handed it back to him. 'Hope you have a good time back here and thanks for the loan of the jacket. I really appreciated it.' Then turning to Alex I said, 'You didn't need to be so rude to him. He was only being friendly.' We started to walk across the lawn and up to the house.

'Did I say anything?'

'You didn't have to. The way you looked at him was enough. Talk about if looks could kill.'

'Well, you'd know all about that,' he retorted.

'What's got into you, Alex? Where have you been all evening and why are you behaving like a jealous teenager?'

'Who said I'm jealous?'

'Stop behaving like a teenager then.'

'He was coming on to you.'

'Now you really are being ridiculous. I'd think I'd know if he was.'

'You were wearing his jacket.'

'I was cold. He was just being a gentleman.'

'I'm only looking out for your best interests.'

'Since when?'

'Oh, what's the use,' he said, raising his hands in the air, turning his back on me and striding off.

'Alex!' I exclaimed. 'Wait. We need to sort this out.' He did not turn back. I could have kicked myself for letting my temper get the better of me yet again. I had to speak to him. Unfortunately, the wedding guests were gathering outside, my view was obliterated, I could not see which way he had gone and I was unable to run after him in my strappy high heels.

'There you are, Alicia,' said Antonia, catching my arm. 'Are you OK? You disappeared for ages. I was worried you were sick again. I was thinking of sending a search party out for you and thought you might be cold,' she said, handing me my jacket. 'You left it behind when you rushed off.'

'What? I mean, no,' I replied as I continued to look into the distance trying to locate Alex. 'I'm feeling much better on that front.' I turned to her. 'I went for a walk. I needed some fresh air as it was a bit stifling inside. I went down to the rotunda but it is a bit cooler now. Thanks for this,' I said, putting on my jacket.

'You do look a bit flustered. Are you OK? Where's Alex?'

'I'm fine and I don't know.'

'Well, as long as you're OK. Kim and Rob are about to leave. I didn't think you'd want to miss giving them a proper send-off,' she added, leading me by the elbow to where all the activity was about to take place.

The guests were milling around chatting while they waited for the newly-weds to emerge. After a few minutes Kim and Rob appeared on the steps. Kim had changed into a pale pink dress and had the dreaded bouquet with her. I knew what that meant.

'Come on, Ally,' said Antonia, dragging me by the hand. 'She's going to throw the bouquet any minute now. We had better get in place.'

'You don't want any competition from me, not if you're hoping to get Tom to propose!' I teased.

'It's only a bit of fun. We both know that nobody ever takes it seriously. Anyway, I hope you don't think *I* need some silly bouquet to get him to propose.'

'Most unlikely if *you* have anything to do with it,' I replied slightly waggishly.

'OK,' said Kim, calling down to everybody from the steps above, 'all the single women step forward.' She waited while a group of us positioned ourselves within throwing distance of her bouquet. 'Get ready. On a count of three,' she said, turning her back to us. 'One...two...three!' She tossed her bouquet backwards and then quickly swivelled around to see who was going to catch it. There seemed to be a mad surge and whoever it was in front of me lunged forward to grab it but in so doing toppled forward and the bouquet hurtled straight into my stomach.

'Looks like it's your lucky day!' said Kim's friend Emma, who was standing next to me as she put her arm around me. 'Anyone in your sights?' she asked, just at the moment I saw Alex walking across the lawn. I presumed he must have seen the spectacle from afar. I sensed my cheeks were burning and turning a deep shade of crimson. I hoped she did not notice. By the time the 'bouquet throwing' throng disbursed, Alex was well out of sight and I wondered where he had disappeared to this time. We waved off Kim and Rob with confetti, tin cans and all, and I meandered back up to the house looking for him.

I sat down on the step and dropped the bouquet by my side and put my head in my hands.

'You OK?' It was Tom. He sat down on the step next to me.

'I'm really tired,' I said, looking up. 'I feel a bit faint actually.'

'Oh, that's probably because you haven't had copious supplies of Pringles today,' he said teasingly.

'I haven't eaten anything at all. I couldn't. I felt too ill.'

'I noticed. I'm pulling your leg. Come on. Chill!' he said, nudging me. 'Anyway, you're not the only one who's feeling rough.'

'What do you mean? I mean, who are you talking about? Are you OK? You're not ill or anything?'

'I'm fine. Never better. I was referring to Alex. You should have seen him earlier. Sick as a dog. I thought he looked positively green to be honest.'

'Where is he now?' I was concerned and felt slightly guilty for berating him.

'He's gone back to the hotel.'

'Oh, poor Alex. I hope it isn't anything serious. He told me he's been feeling off colour these past few days. He seemed OK the last time I saw him but he must be feeling bad to leave. I'll call him when I get back to the apartment and see if I can do anything for him.'

'I'm sure that will perk him up,' he said playfully. 'We should get you back. You look done in. I'll give you a lift. A full night's sleep will do you the world of good.'

In the car on my way back to Wickham Terrace I sent Alex a text message:

Hope all is well. Are you OK? Please call me. I'm worried about you!

I did not receive a response and I hoped that this was because he was asleep and not too ill to reply. Mind you, after our latest spats I could not blame him if he was ignoring me. I decided not to switch off my mobile just in case he called. Tom and Antonia dropped me back at the apartment despite Antonia's protestations that I should stay the night with them.

As I was unlocking the door my mobile beeped indicating I had received a text message and I immediately thought that it must be from Alex. In fact it was from Sally Hamilton. It simply said:

Alicia, please call. I need to speak to you urgently. Isabelle's in hospital – suspected suicide attempt. Sally

Chapter 11

I was shocked, and sat and stared at the message for a few moments. That was definitely not news I expected to receive. When Isabelle called me the previous Tuesday she did not strike me as someone who was contemplating suicide. Yes, she sounded desperate, but for me to help her find Drew's killer not to kill herself. Then again, that was almost six days ago, I had not heard from her since and I had not been privy to the events of the past week. Any number of factors could have tipped the balance, if indeed it was an attempted suicide. Who was to say that it was? After all, she was convinced that she was the intended murder victim, not Drew. And, if she was correct, it was more than possible the murderer might make a further attempt on her life, in which case she was in grave danger.

I returned Sally's call immediately hoping to glean some information which would shed light on this latest development. Her 'phone diverted straight to voice mail and I left a message asking her to text me when it was convenient to call. I kept my mobile on in case Alex or Sally responded to me.

As it happened, I heard from neither Alex nor Sally during the night and so was not disturbed. Nonetheless I was quite wakeful, up at six and dressed and packed by seven. If I had not heard from Alex by ten I would call him because I was worried that he might still be ill. Waiting until two o'clock to see if he came to collect me was not an option. It was nine-fifteen when I received the expected text from Sally:

Please call me when you're up. I'm at home.

'Sally, it's Alicia. What's the news on Isabelle?'

'She's still in hospital. We thought she'd tried to commit suicide, hence my message.'

'What do you mean, you thought? Are you saying that isn't what happened?'

'Well, you know that Lucy Winters is staying with her, don't you?'

'I think you told me that, yes.'

'Lucy had a long-standing arrangement to go and see some family friends down in Hampshire but said she wouldn't go because she didn't want to leave Isabelle, but Isabelle insisted that she should. Although Isabelle told her she would be OK, Lucy said that she felt anxious about her and came back early. Anyway, she found her collapsed on the bedroom floor. When she couldn't rouse her and saw some pills on the bedside table, her immediate thought was that Isabelle had taken an overdose.'

'That must have been such a shock for Lucy. To find her like that, I mean. Was it an overdose?'

'So I understand. They gave the pills to the paramedics.'

'They?'

'Timothy was with her. He brought her home apparently.'

'Who's Timothy?'

'He's a good friend of hers, but I've only met him briefly and I don't know him really. She says he's been very supportive.'

'Lucky he was with her then. How's Isabelle doing?'

'She's in the high dependency unit. I don't think she's out of the woods yet. She went into respiratory failure. She's lucky they could bring her back. She nearly died.' Her speech was quite staccato.

'I don't know what to say. It's just too awful for words. How did you hear about this?'

'Lucy called me.'

'Do you know how long Isabelle will be in hospital?' From the sound of it Isabelle would not be in a fit state to come to Australia for some time. I did not mention to Sally that Isabelle had 'phoned me at the beginning of the week, and she did not ask me if I had called Isabelle. I felt it was more prudent to wait and see what the prognosis on Isabelle's health was before deciding what to do.

'I'm not sure. They're closely monitoring her. I'll let you know when I hear more.'

'Are the police involved?'

'I don't think so. I didn't get the impression that they were treating what happened to her as suspicious. Why?'

'No reason.' In fact I thought there were a number of reasons why the police should be treating this 'suicide attempt' as such, bearing in mind what had just happened to Isabelle's fiancé and what she had told them. If the police had thought that these were simply the rantings of a demented fiancée then, if nothing else, this latest development should focus their minds. I hoped that one of the investigating officers would now give credence to what she had told them. It was possible that they were making enquiries but keeping a low profile so as not to alert the murderer.

'Anyway, how are you? How was the wedding?'

'I'm good.' My sick episode hardly seemed worth mentioning after hearing the dreadful news about Isabelle. 'The wedding was absolutely lovely.'

'How are you going to spend the rest of your holiday?'

'I may go up to the Sunshine Coast for a few days and then over to Melbourne.'

'Aren't you going to Sydney? It would be a shame to go all that way and not to make it there.'

'I intend to. I have to see how things pan out. But if I don't make it this time I'll just have to come back!'

'Well, that's as good a reason as any for another trip. Talking of which, I'm really sorry to keep calling you with bad news when you're on holiday. I'm sure the last things you want to hear about are work-related matters.'

'It can't be helped. Anyway, this is exceptional. Please call me if you have any more news.'

'OK.'

'Thanks, Sally. Take care.'

'You too!'

Isabelle's 'suicide attempt' struck me as rather odd, but theorizing over the facts was pointless. I needed to speak to Isabelle. A few minutes after speaking to Sally I received the long-awaited text message from Alex which diverted my attention. It read as follows:

Good morning. I'm much better thanks. Look out of your window… A

I stepped out onto the balcony and espied him leaning casually against the side of his hire car. He was wearing stone-coloured chinos and a pale blue cotton shirt the sleeves of which he had rolled up. He had pushed his Persol sunglasses on to the top of his head.

'Are you coming down or am I coming up?' he called out, looking up at me and shielding his eyes from the glare of the sun with the back of his hand.

'I'll be with you in five minutes.'

'I hope so. You know how I hate waiting.'

I locked the balcony door and quickly checked the room to make sure I had not left anything behind, picked up my bags and key and closed the door. I called the lift but I waited ages before it arrived. When it did and the door opened Alex was standing inside.

'I thought I'd come and give you a hand with your bags,' he said, taking them from me. 'Aagh!' He clutched the side of his stomach and winced.

'Alex, are you in pain? Are you sure it's a stomach bug. You really should see a doctor.'

'Don't worry, I'm fine. It's just a bit of cramp. It'll pass in a minute. Let's get these bags into the car and go for a coffee.'

'You would tell me if you weren't well, wouldn't you?'

'Of course I would. You worry too much.'

We drove down to Park Road at Milton where we had our pick of cafés to choose from. We chose to stop at the same one where Tom and I had lunch the previous week. Alex ordered a doppio espresso for me, a glass of water for himself and some pastries.

'They don't sell Pringles here, I'm afraid,' he said with a twinkle as the waitress served us.

'Even *I* don't eat Pringles for breakfast...' I paused for a second and watched him take a sip of water. 'Alex...'

'Yes,' he said, glancing up at me and smiling warmly. I noticed that he was rather pallid and a bit hollow-eyed. To me he looked far from well, although he made light of it.

'I *am* sorry about yesterday. Don't hold it against me.' He leaned back in his chair.

'That depends what you had in mind,' he replied, offering me the plate of pastries and raising his eyebrows.

'Stop it. I'm trying to apologise,' I picked up a pain au chocolat and put it on my plate.

'You have nothing to apologise for. Besides life's far too short to hold grudges. Just forget it. I already have. I'm looking forward to our trip. How's your pastry?'

'I haven't tried it yet. Aren't you eating?'

'I think I'll pass on the pastry. You enjoy it. But are you OK, Alicia? You seem a bit distracted.'

'I need to ask you something.' I said, methodically cutting the pain au chocolat into four pieces.

'Well, ask it then.'

'And you won't get mad at me?'

'You have my word.'

'You remember that client I told you about, the one whose fiancé was murdered...' I popped a piece of the pain au chocolat into my mouth.

'The one you promised to help?' I swallowed the remainder of the piece of pastry and cleared my throat.

'Yes. She thinks that the death of her grandfather, brother and fiancé are all connected and that the murderer actually intended to kill her and not her fiancé. She sounded so desperate and that's why...'

'You agreed to help. Oh, Alicia!' He shook his head and put his hands over his face in total dismay.

'Don't say it, Alex. I know. But there's something else.'

'Now why doesn't that surprise me?'

'She plans to come out to Melbourne to see her grandmother next week and wants to see me. I guess she'll explain more when she does.'

'Is she Australian then?' asked Alex, slightly digressing from the main thrust of the conversation.

'Her father's family is, yes, but her mother's side is English. What makes you ask?'

'Maybe there's some distant relative she doesn't even know about who's trying to kill her off to get her money.'

'Hmm... Anything is possible I suppose, although there doesn't seem to be anyone apart from her paternal grandmother, but who knows. The thing is there's been another development.'

'Which is?'

'She was rushed into hospital the other night.'

'Why? What's wrong with her?'

'An overdose. Everyone seems to think that she was attempting to commit suicide, except...'

'You?' I nodded.

'I don't think that she wanted to kill herself. If what she told me is correct then it makes sense that the murderer might have made another attempt on her life.'

'True, but how long ago was it that you spoke to her?'

'At the beginning of last week.'

'Things could have changed, Alicia. I know that's not what you want me to say, but I can't believe the thought hasn't crossed your mind either.'

'Of course it has, but instinct tells me that she didn't attempt to kill herself and somebody else wants her dead. And someone *is* responsible for her fiancé's murder!'

'I'm not disputing that. Maybe she killed him and then was overcome with such remorse that she decided to kill herself.'

'Now you *are* being ridiculous.'

'Just playing devil's advocate! Help me out here. Give me some background details. Who is she and why would anyone want to kill her?'

'Isabelle Latham. She's about to inherit millions of pounds from her grandfather James Latham. She came to me to make a Will because she was getting married.'

'Wanted you to tie up all her millions so that her prospective husband couldn't get his hands on it, did she?' he said flippantly.

'Can't you be serious for one minute, Alex? This is important.' I gave him a withering look.

'OK. OK,' he said, holding up his hands. 'So was her fiancé loaded too?'

'I don't know. Drew was an artist. He painted country houses and he had an exhibition in Mayfair coming up in a few months time. I wonder what they'll do about selling his work. Maybe the Hyde-Dowler family will hold a posthumous exhibition.'

'Hang on a minute. Are you talking about Andrew Hyde-Dowler?'

'Yes. Why? Did you know him?' I was aware that Alex had a very wide circle of friends, but it would be unbelievable if he had known Drew.

'Not personally. But I've seen some of his work. I'm a great fan of his father Dominic Hyde-Dowler, the art historian. He worked closely with J. G. Links and is an acknowledged expert on Canaletto and you know how I love Canaletto.'

'Hmm… I do recall your enthusiasm for his paintings, but when did you see Andrew's work?'

'I went to one of his exhibitions. I wanted to meet his father and I managed to wangle an invitation through a friend. You know how it is, a friend of a friend and all that?'

'No, I don't know. Female was she, this friend of a friend?'

'And the relevance of your question is?'

'When was this exhibition you went to?' I asked, suitably chastened.

'Last year, and, yes, before you ask, well before I left for Singapore.'

'Did I say anything?'

'You don't need to, Alicia. It's just the way you look at me sometimes. Do you want me to see if I can find out anything about Drew's past? It might help shed light on what happened to him. You never know what I might be able to dig up.'

'If you can, I'd appreciate that.' I ate another piece of pain au chocolat.

'Good,' he said, looking at his watch. 'Now tell me, what have you learned of the circumstances surrounding all these deaths in Isabelle's family? I'm quite intrigued.'

'Does that mean you want to help me?'

'I could be persuaded,' he teased. 'But seriously, I do, yes. I wouldn't be offering otherwise.'

'That's a start, and I appreciate it. All I know about the death of her grandfather, and that of her brother, is what she herself told me – which at this stage takes me precisely nowhere. As for the car accident of her grandfather's second wife, the information I have gleaned doesn't emanate from Isabelle.'

'What do you mean?'

'Well, I was curious about her grandfather and decided to research him on the internet. I came across an interesting article about his work. There was a photograph of his second wife, Diane, at some charity gala wearing a dress designed by Hartnell. It turns out that Dorothy has a friend from Hartnell's who would have known Diane well. She's going to write to her on my behalf. Dorothy recalls the case being reported in the press at the time; and there would have been a coroner's verdict.'

'We could look that up,' said Alex enthusiastically.

'Yes. I also had the impression from what Dorothy said that there was a possibility that Isabelle's grandfather had something to do with Diane's death.'

'Ah...the plot thickens. Maybe these are revenge killings by someone who was closely connected to Diane.'

'Her Nemesis you mean? But why kill the whole family and not just James Latham, and why wait forty-odd years to do it?'

'Hmm...' Alex paused for a moment. 'I don't know, Alicia. But there's a fortune at stake here. I reckon we need to research Isabelle's family tree.'

'To find that distant relative you think is bumping everyone off?'

'Any better ideas?'

'Not currently.'

'Dorothy's pretty amazing, isn't she?'

'Yes. She speaks very highly of you, too, and she isn't one to throw away a compliment.'

'Really? I only met her once.'

'I think you made a lasting impression.'

'Maybe her good will towards me will brush off on you...*eventually*. Come on. We'd better get going. I'll go and a pay and then we can head off. You can fill me in on your murder theories in the car.'

Chapter 12

While I waited for Alex outside the café I sent Tom a text message to confirm that I could not make his Sunday outing after all because I was travelling up to the Sunshine Coast. I told him that all was well, I was feeling considerably better, and would speak to Antonia later.

'Everything OK?' asked Alex as he reappeared.

'Yes. I was just sending a text to Tom.'

'Why?'

'At dinner the other night Tom asked me if I wanted to go for a picnic at Mount Coot-tha today and to let him know my plans. You didn't touch your pastry,' I said, changing the subject. 'Are you sure you're feeling OK. Only you don't look at all well.' He was deathly pale.

'I couldn't stomach it. But believe me I'm tons better than I was yesterday evening. You're not trying to find a reason to back out on me are you?'

'No. I'm worried about you. You're not your usual self.'

'I'll be fine when whatever it is has worked its way out of my system. I just need a break. Work has been manic lately.'

'Burning the candle at both ends finally catching up with you?' I teased, nudging his elbow. We walked back to the car.

'You know me.'

'Hmm… How long does it take to get to the Sunshine Coast from here?'

'A couple of hours, depending on the traffic.'

'Do you want me to drive? If you're not feeling well I'd be happy to, but you'd have to direct me.'

'No. I can manage,' he replied, taking the car keys out of his trouser pocket, unlocking the car with the remote and holding open the door for me. 'Hop in.'

Alex turned off the main highway and on to the coastal road at Caloundra. I had followed the towns on the map as we headed out to the north of Brisbane, passing places such as the dairy town of Caboolture and the Glass House Mountains. As we drove we discussed Isabelle and the numerous deaths in her family, but as much as we debated the matter we came to no satisfactory conclusion.

'You just don't have enough information,' said Alex. 'Clearly you need to talk to Isabelle, and it's probably worth a chat with her paternal grandmother because she might know about Diane Latham and the family background.'

'Well, yes, I have thought of that. Isabelle gave me her details but I don't want to contact her until I know how Isabelle is. Imagine if she doesn't know what has happened to Isabelle or Isabelle dies? The last thing she would need is me turning up on her doorstep asking questions.'

'I take your point; but since you're going to Melbourne anyway, you'd be perfectly placed to see her. She might be able to shed light on Isabelle's friends and associates.'

'Talking of which, one of her friends, Luisa, who's a journalist at the *Courier Mail*, contacted me last week. It was rather bizarre really.'

'In what way?'

'When Isabelle came to see me in the office, she insisted that I take Luisa's contact details. Anyway, last Monday when I returned to the apartment there was a note from her saying that she wanted to meet me. What immediately struck me as odd was how she knew where to find me in the first place. I have the note here in my bag,' I said, rummaging in my handbag for it and holding it up.

'What does it say?'

'I'll read it to you.' I could tell that Alex was listening very intently as I did so.

'I would have thought the same as you had I received that note. 'Did you meet her?'

'Yes. I was curious about what she wanted.'

'And what did she want? Only I have the distinct impression that you didn't take to her.'

'No. Don't get me wrong. She's very pleasant and possibly I'm just paranoid, but I felt that she was only interested in finding out what I had done for Isabelle and the legal status of things.'

'I think you're right to be cautious. And in any case you're not permitted to discuss Isabelle's legal affairs with her for professional reasons. She isn't a solicitor, unlike me, and there is the question of client confidentiality to consider.'

'Quite. When I talk to Isabelle I will ask her about Luisa. It's probably all fine and I'm reading too much into it.'

'Perhaps. How does she know Isabelle anyway?'

'They bumped into one another at the Melbourne International Arts Festival. Let's talk about something else. You've probably had enough sleuthing for one day. I know I have. You seem to know your way around Australia well.'

'Fairly well. I lived here for two years.'

'When?'

'About five years ago. I was working out here.'

'I suppose you've been to both the Sunshine Coast and Gold Coast?'

'Yes. Why?

'I just wondered if you had any preference between the two.'

'The Gold Coast is fantastic, but the beaches get very crowded. I've stayed at Coolangatta a couple of times. It's the southernmost town on the Gold Coast,' he said, leaning across and pointing to the name on the map. 'The beaches are emptier but it has fantastic waves if you like the surf. This area here,' he said, pointing to the spot on the map between Point Danger and Kirra Point, 'has the best surfing. But the Sunshine Coast is quieter and also has superb beaches. I think you'll love it. We're staying at Alexandra Headland. Noosa's just a little further north and if you like sand then you'll love Laguna Bay. You might also want to take a look at the Cooloola National Park.'

'You seem to have it all worked out.'

'Not really. I've just been here before and thought you'd like Alexandra Headland.'

Alex had reserved a fully self-contained apartment with a deck over-looking the Pacific Ocean, a living room opening on to a balcony with ocean views that was only metres away from Alexandra Headland's patrolled surf beach.

'Is this OK for you?' he asked as I pushed open a sliding door and stepped outside onto the deck.

'It's perfect. I love it,' I replied, looking at the very white fine sand and inviting sea. 'It's a stunning location. You couldn't have chosen anywhere better.'

'Good. I'm pleased you like it,' he called out. From the corner of my eye I watched him lie down awkwardly on the bed as if he was in discomfort. 'It's very comfortable. Come and try it,' he said, extending his arm across the other side of the bed and inclining himself towards me. I spun around to face him and he smiled at me. I stepped back into the room, slipped off my shoes, sat down on the bed and then swivelled around so that I was sitting back on my haunches facing him. He looked really pale and drawn and feverish. I could see beads of perspiration on his forehead. I leaned forward to touch his cheek with the back of my hand.

'You're burning up. I think you have a high temperature. You're getting worse. I'm going to call for a doctor.' I reached across him for the 'phone.

'You could administer to me. That would make me feel much better,' he said, catching my arm. He tried to pull himself up, but as he did so grimaced with pain and rolled away from me clutching his right side.

'Alex,' I said, leaning over him and stroking his forehead. 'Have you ever had your appendix out, only your symptoms are exactly the same as my late brother's when he had appendicitis?' He shook his head. 'I know I'm not a doctor, but I think that's what it is. You can't leave this. You need urgent medical attention now.'

'That's ridiculous.'

'Why? You're really ill. I'd never forgive myself if something happened to you. Where's the nearest hospital?'

'Nambour, I think.'

'How far away is that?'

'About a twenty minute drive.'

'I'll call for an ambulance as it might be quicker. What's the number for the emergency service?'

'000.' He had doubled over with pain and pulled his right leg up in an attempt to ease his discomfort.

The ambulance arrived much sooner than I anticipated. The paramedics gave Alex a quick examination, told us that it was indeed a suspected case of appendicitis, put him on intravenous fluids and said that he needed to be admitted to Nambour General Hospital for an immediate operation.

'You can come in the ambulance if you like,' indicated Jan, the female paramedic, as she and her male colleague, Stuart, lifted Alex's stretcher into the ambulance.

'Thanks. I'd like to be with him to make sure he's OK.'

'How long have you two been together?' she asked as she jumped up into the back of the ambulance with us.

'Well, we're not…'

'We've known each other nearly fifteen months now,' said Alex, interrupting me before I could finish what I wanted to say. He reached out to take my hand. 'She's one in a million,' he added in a low voice. I was slightly taken aback by his comment, but in a pleasant way, and I did not remove my hand.

I sat and waited in A&E while a doctor examined Alex. I found a *Better Homes* magazine and flicked through it, but could not concentrate on what I was reading.

'Miss Allen?' I looked up. Standing in front of me was one of the doctors I had seen walking through the emergency department when Alex was first brought in. I could not fail to remember him as he was extremely tall, probably about 6 feet 4 inches and had a shock of curly black hair. He looked as if he had just come from one of the surf beaches. He was also very tanned, but then most of the people around here were.

'I'm Dr. Phillips. I've been assessing your boyfriend's condition.' I stood up and shook his hand.

'He's not...' I paused. I was going to say he was not my boyfriend, but it seemed ridiculous to worry about something like that now.

'He's not, what?' asked the doctor.

'He's not...going to die, is he?' I asked, quickly recovering myself.

'Your boyfriend has an acute form of appendicitis. He needs to have his appendix removed. We're getting him ready for theatre now.'

'He will be OK, won't he?'

'You did well to get him here. Don't worry. We'll look after him.'

'Can I see him?'

'Of course you can.' He led me through to Alex's cubicle and pushed open the curtains. 'I'll leave you two alone then,' he said, smiling at me, and then left, drawing the curtains behind him. I pulled up the chair as close to the bed as I could and sat down. Alex looked ashen.

'You're a fine one,' I said softly, stroking his hand. 'I don't know...talk about a let down,' I teased. 'What a fine time to fall ill! What am I going to do about you?'

'I'm sorry,' he replied in a faint voice. He sounded very weak. 'I wanted this to be a special trip. Now I've ruined it. I *will* make it up to you, I promise, *if* you'll let me.'

'It doesn't matter. What's most important is for you to get better quickly.' The nurse appeared.

'Time to go,' she said to him and smiling at me. 'He'll be fine,' she added, patting me on the shoulder. An orderly appeared and they wheeled the bed out into the corridor. 'You can walk with us down to the lift if you want,' said the nurse, so I did. As they were about to push the bed in Alex grabbed my hand and squeezed it. He mumbled something but what he said was scarcely audible so I moved closer.

'Don't worry. You'll be OK,' I said. He mouthed a few words but I could not make out what they were. Alex, bed and all disappeared before I had the chance to find out what it was he had said.

Chapter 13

I stayed at the hospital until Alex's operation was over. I wanted to make sure that he was all right and there seemed little point returning to the apartment as by the time I arrived there I would need to start heading back. The waiting seemed interminable, although actually it was no more than an hour or so. I felt reassured that Alex was in good hands and relieved we had sought medical attention in time; his condition might have deteriorated and become peritonitis. I stepped outside briefly for some fresh air, and when I came back inside I espied the nurse who had accompanied Alex to theatre, so I hotfooted it along the corridor to speak with her.

'Oh, excuse me, please,' I said, 'I was wondering whether Alex Waterford was out of theatre yet, and if so which ward he's in.'

'Wait there a moment and I'll find out for you,' she replied. I watched as she walked purposefully down the corridor and I stood for about five minutes before she returned. 'If you'd like to follow me,' she said, ushering me through the double doors. I felt my heart pounding.

'Is he OK?' I asked hesitantly as I walked along beside her.

'You can ask him yourself,' she said as she stopped in front of a door to her left. 'He's only just come out of recovery so he's still very sleepy, but the operation went well. He'll be a bit sore for a while though,' she said, with a wry smile. 'I'll just check his obs and then leave you in peace,' she added, opening the door. I followed her in and stood waiting at the end of his bed until she had finished.

The nurse left and I pulled up a chair beside the bed to sit with him. I thought he might appreciate seeing a friendly face when he came round. I had picked up a copy of the *Courier Mail* in one of the waiting areas and was turning the pages quietly to avoid disturbing him. I looked to see if there were any features by Luisa, but there were none.

'Hello.' I glanced sideways. Alex was now awake.

'How are you feeling?' I put down the paper.

'Sleepy. Have you been here all the time?'

'I didn't want to leave until you woke up. I'll head off soon and let you get some rest, but I'll come back tomorrow.'

'Is everything OK?'

'The nurse said the operation went well. You'll be in here for a few days though, and you're going to be sore for a while.'

'Thanks for being here.'

'You should thank the doctors and nurses.'

'No, I mean for looking out for me. Thanks for caring.'

'You know I care. I was really worried about you. Is there anything you need?' He just looked at me with a very strange expression.

'It's not going to be much fun for you with me stuck in here. Why don't you go and see Jeremy Brown in Melbourne.'

'We'll talk about that when you're feeling a little bit better. Get some sleep. I'll be back tomorrow.' I kissed him on the cheek and stood up to leave.

'OK.'

I took a taxi back to the apartment. It was now very late and I was really tired. I had no appetite, took a shower and went straight to bed. The next morning I thought of going for an early morning swim, but I was starving because I had not eaten dinner and went for an early breakfast instead. After breakfast I called Jeremy to find out when he was returning to Melbourne from Brisbane. I told him about Alex's emergency appendectomy.

'Oh, I'm very sorry to hear that,' he said, sounding concerned.

'I'm heading back to Melbourne later today so you can come down any time you like. Send my best wishes to Alex. Can you just hold on a sec?' I could hear Antonia talking in the background but not what she was saying to Jeremy. 'Alicia, Antonia wants a word. I'll pass you over to her. I'll see you soon. You take care.'

'Yes. OK. Thanks. Bye, Jeremy.'

'Hi, Ally. I couldn't help overhearing your conversation with Jeremy. Listen, Tom and I were chatting last night and we thought we might take a few days off and go up the coast ourselves, especially as I'm only here until the end of the week. So, if you want to go to Melbourne we don't mind looking in on Alex while you're away to check that he's all right and whether he needs anything.'

'I'm sure he'd appreciate that. I haven't decided what I'm doing yet and I haven't spoken to Alex, but thanks for the offer. I'll let you know.'

'Good. So...' she paused, 'is everything OK?'

'Yes. It's lovely up here. I have to go. Bye, Antonia. *Ciao, ciao, sorellina,*' I replied, pushing her off the 'phone.

'OK. *Ciao.* Bye.'

I had not wanted to disturb Alex too early but I thought he would now be awake. I called the hospital to find out how he was progressing but the 'phone to his room was engaged, so I left a message with reception that I would ring back. I took a stroll along the beach and sat and watched some seriously good surfers riding the waves. Watching them was the nearest I intended to go to a surfboard. It all looked rather too terrifying and ambitious for me and the most I might do would be to go out on a boogie board. I returned to the apartment and called the hospital again. This time I was put straight through to Alex.

'Hello.' He sounded much brighter.

'Alex, it's Alicia. How are you feeling?'

'Hello you! I'm not bad at all thanks. It only hurts when I laugh, as they say.'

'Oh, poor you. Did you sleep OK?'

'Sort of. I've had some pain relief so that helped. Did you try to ring me earlier?'

'Yes. Why?'

'Only, I've been talking to your sister.'

'Really? What was she calling you for?'

'Oh, to tell me all about you, or rather to warn me off you...'

'What?'

'Don't worry. I'm only teasing. Since she and Tom are coming up here there's no reason why you can't go to Melbourne. Think about it. Are you coming in today?'

'Yes. Can I bring you anything?'

'No. Just you. Listen, why don't you make the most of the day and come in this evening.'

'Are you sure?'

'Of course. If you're going to stay on, there's no reason why your trip should be completely ruined because of me.'

'It's not ruined. I'll see you later then.'

'I look forward to it. Enjoy your day.'

I arrived at the hospital at around seven o'clock. I had spent almost the whole day on the beach sunbathing, swimming and people watching and, although I could not fail to enjoy the beauty of my surroundings, I felt lonely without Alex. With the upheaval of the previous day superseding everything else I had forgotten to 'phone Sally to enquire after Isabelle's welfare. I was now anxious to make contact with her, but since it was the middle of the night in London my call to her would have to wait. If there was any change I felt sure she would call me.

When I opened the door to Alex's room he was sitting up in bed and watching the evening news. He must have been feeling better as I noticed that he had eaten all his dinner. I glanced at the television and I was transfixed by the image on the screen; it was of John MacFadzean, the Kiwi lawyer I had met on the plane. I barely comprehended what the newsreader was saying, something along the lines of *the police investigating the brutal murder of John MacFadzean whose body was found in Gertrude Street, Melbourne today.* And then the screen went blank; Alex had turned the television off.

'Turn it back on!' I snapped.

'All right. All right. What's the big deal? Lovely to see you, too, Alicia. Thanks for asking how I am,' he said sarcastically, but he did turn the television back on.

'Oh, I'm sorry, Alex,' I replied, turning to him. 'Of course I want to know how you are, but you've got to see this.' Unfortunately, the news broadcast had come to an end. I started to pace the floor.

'See what? You really are infuriating sometimes. What's going on?'

'That man on the telly just now, the Kiwi lawyer who's been murdered, I met him on the plane on the way to Singapore.'

'You're not serious.'

'Deadly serious.'

'You sure it's him?'

'Yes. He had a very distinctive scar on his chin. He worked for Holmwood & Hitchins. I've got his card somewhere. His murder must be significant.' I continued to pace the floor.

'Significant? You're losing me Alicia.' Alex sounded confused.

'I'm sorry Alex. I'm not explaining myself very well. Holmwood & Hitchins is the firm dealing with Isabelle's grandfather's estate and I'm pretty certain John MacFadzean was one of her trustees.'

'Can you stop pacing about? You're making me dizzy.' I sat down at the end of his bed. 'OK. That's better. So what are you saying?'

'Two people who are closely associated with Isabelle have been murdered within a week or so of each other. Coincidence is one thing, but I don't think there's anything coincidental here. There has to be a connection.'

'But aren't you forgetting something?' I looked at him quizzically. 'These two murders took place on either side of the world and the timing doesn't seem right.'

'Well, we'd need to find out when John MacFadzean was murdered, but don't forget, Drew was murdered ten days ago on the Friday I left, so that would give the murderer plenty of time to get out to Australia to do John MacFadzean in.'

'But what about Isabelle's brush with death on Saturday night? If it was attempted murder rather than attempted suicide, are you telling me the murderer got straight on a plane to Melbourne and murdered John MacFadzean? Bearing in mind it takes nearly twenty-four hours to get here and it's nearly half a day ahead in Melbourne, if the murderer had left on Saturday night he'd only have arrived this morning.'

'The timing of John MacFadzean's murder is the key. That news report said that his body had been *found* today not that he had been *murdered* today. What if he was murdered early last week or the murderer has an accomplice?'

'Hmm… There are a lot of "what ifs", Alicia!' Alex winced as he strained to pull himself up in the bed.

'Was there an earlier news report?'

'Yes. It was on this morning's news as well, but then the bulletin only referred to the body of a middle-aged man being found in Gertrude Street. A later one said that the man had been identified as John MacFadzean and the police were appealing for witnesses. They didn't give any indication as to when he was murdered though.'

'Did they say how he was murdered?'

'Repeatedly knifed. He died from multiple wounds. It's quite a rough area at night apparently. The police think it's a mugging turned nasty.'

'It could have been made to look like that.'

'How about you call Luisa? As a journalist she would be well placed to find out some details for us. Mind you, you probably don't need to contact her as she'll know where you are as we speak.'

'Don't. That's freaky.'

'I'm joking, Alicia!'

'Hmm… Glad you still have your sense of humour. Anyway, I'm

not one hundred per cent convinced about her, as you know. Before I forget, I've brought these in for you.' I reached for a bag of bananas, papaya, and a mango. 'Slightly different from grapes anyway,' I said, handing them to him.

'Thanks. That's very thoughtful of you.' He paused. 'I think you should go to Melbourne, Alicia.'

'Are you trying to get rid of me?'

'Not at all.'

'Why do you want me to go then?'

'It's obvious you're keen to find out more about this MacFadzean character, and you were going to Melbourne anyway before I even asked you up here. Let's face it, I'm not much use to you right now.'

'How are you feeling anyway?'

'Finally she asks me.' He rolled his eyes upwards. 'Sore.'

'You'll be out of action for a while.'

'It couldn't have happened at a more inopportune moment really.'

'You mean because you're going to miss out on the surfing.'

'I think you know what I meant, Alicia.' He fixed his gaze on me. 'Don't worry. I'll be fine. They'll let me out in a few days. They're only keeping me in because I can't go home! I'll just recuperate in the sunshine and if you can make it back I'd like that.'

'I'd like that too, but I'm going to have to return to London and then you'll be going back to Singapore so I probably won't see you. I'm not sure if I...' I bit my tongue because I sensed I was going to make a fool of myself.

'You're not sure if what?'

'If I can cope with all the comings and goings. First you're there and then you're not.'

'You don't have to.'

'What do you mean?' I replied defensively. I had a niggling feeling he was about to say he was leaving for good.

'I'm not going back to Singapore, Alicia.'

'You're not? Are you staying here then?' I asked, trying to conceal the disappointment in my voice.

'No. I'm coming back to London. A friend's staying at my flat but that can easily be sorted out on my return.'

'Really?' I was completely taken aback.

'And I was wondering...' He was interrupted by one of the orderly's coming in to collect his dinner tray followed by one of the nurses to check on him.

'Is he a good patient?' I asked as she raised the back of his bed and rearranged his pillows.

'Oh, he's not too bad,' she replied. 'You must be his girlfriend. He talks about you all the time.' I looked at Alex with a puzzled expression. Then turning to him she said, 'How's the pain? Can I bring you anything?'

'I'm OK for now, but I might need something a bit later to help me sleep.'

'Right. I'll come back and check on you in an hour or so. I'll leave you two to it,' she said, and left the room.

'Everyone here thinks I'm your girlfriend. It's embarrassing.'

'In what respect? That they think I'm your boyfriend or the thought of me being your boyfriend?'

'It's just a bit awkward.' I stood up and walked to the end of the bed.

'How so?'

'I can't do all this dancing around each other stuff anymore. I need to know how you really feel.' I felt my face reddening and looked away.

'Come here,' he said, indicating for me to sit on the bed. I sat down very gingerly. 'What's with the worried expression? Don't you believe anything I ever say to you? What I was going to say before the nurse interrupted us was that I wondered whether when I returned to London we could pick up where we left off. I wouldn't blame you if you didn't want to, but I meant what I said before I went into theatre. I love you.'

Chapter 14

Alex insisted that I go to Melbourne even though I was reluctant to leave. I hated the idea of doing so, especially now. Whilst I knew that he was recovering and Antonia and Tom would be along to visit him, I still felt bad about going. Alex suggested that they have use of the apartment for the few days they were staying up there. It was unlikely he would be discharged before then and so they might as well enjoy the benefit.

I slept fitfully that night as I repeatedly ran the revelations of the previous day over in my mind. Furthermore, Alex's declaration had set my head in a spin. The following morning I watched the breakfast news eagerly expecting further information on John MacFadzean's murder, but there was none. I managed to book myself on a plane to Melbourne that afternoon and called Jeremy to confirm my arrival. I then spoke to Alex to let him know my plans.

'How are you?' I asked.

'Bored! What time's your flight?'

'Keen to get rid of me?'

'Stop it!'

'I'm off this evening. Satisfied?'

'Yes. I think you should go, that's all.'

'Shall I call Antonia and tell her that she and Tom can stay at the apartment?'

'I'll do that. She left her number. Are you coming in before you go?'

'Of course. I'll come and see you on my way to the airport.'

'Oh, good.'
'Can I bring you anything?'
'Just yourself.'

I had not heard from Sally, although I had left a couple of messages, but I expected she was very hard-pressed at work. I was concerned about Isabelle and if she was out of hospital yet; I also wondered whether the news of John MacFadzean's murder had filtered back to her. I had so many questions to ask Isabelle and the list was growing ever longer. What possible motive could there be for John MacFadzean's murder? Despite what Alex had said, my instincts told me that there was a connection between what had happened to Drew, Isabelle and John MacFadzean.

I packed and went for a stroll along the sea front. There was a stand selling postcards and I bought one to send to Dorothy. I wrote that I hoped all was well and that she had received a reply from her friend Emily Middleton. I knew that Dorothy would have written because she was very reliable. Alex had planted a seed in my mind that some distant relative of Isabelle's was carrying out the recent murders to avenge Diane's death and I needed to find out as much about Diane as I could.

I left Alexandra Headland as soon as possible because I wanted to spend some time with Alex before making my way to the airport. He was sitting in the chair beside his bed when I walked in. He beamed at me.

'Hello,' I said, bending forward and pecking him on the cheek. He put his arms around me to give me hug and I hugged him back, but gently because I was conscious of his stitches and I did not want to hurt him.

'You smell gorgeous. It makes a change from the smell of disinfectant anyway!'

'Thanks, and there was me thinking you were paying me a compliment.'

'You know I find you irresistible. You're only safe because I'm incapacitated.'

'I see you haven't lost your charm. Are you flirting with me?'

'Me? Why don't you give me a kiss?'

'You've just had one. Don't be so demanding.'

'Oh, you're such a tease. Come here!' But as he tried to lunge forward he screwed up his eyes in pain, and fell back clutching his stomach. 'That hurt,' he said through gritted teeth.

'That'll teach you to keep your hands to yourself.'

'How can you be so cold-hearted when you know how much I'm suffering? You should be offering me TLC and sympathy,' he said in a plaintive voice and with a Little-Boy-Lost look.

'How's that?' I asked, kissing him on his forehead.

'Hmm... Not sure. You'll need to do it again. Here,' he said, pointing to his mouth. He closed his eyes and puckered up his lips and I sat back and laughed. 'What's the matter now?' he asked, opening one eye and then the other and observing me closely.

'Nothing. Nothing at all.' I sat on the edge of his bed opposite him with my feet dangling as they did not reach the floor.

'Spit it out. I know you. Something's on your mind. You're preoccupied. All this murder business is really getting to you, isn't it?' I shrugged my shoulders. 'Listen,' he said, tapping my right shoe with his left foot, 'I can't say I'm enthusiastic about you being involved in that Isabelle murder stuff but...'

'Alex. Don't start!' I interrupted with a huffy voice.

'Alicia, for once in your life don't jump down my throat!' he scolded. 'Stop being defensive and hear me out. What I was trying to say is that, since you're already involved by virtue of your promise to Isabelle and thus liable to become more embroiled, I will support you. I realize I'm not much use to you at the moment, but if there's anything I can do, tell me. I know you think that I'm not interested or think your notions are ridiculous, but that isn't the case at all. My only concern, and yes, it is a big one, is that you don't endanger yourself. I know you like to be independent, but you don't have to do this alone. Do we have a deal?'

'OK, but….'

'No buts.'

'All right.'

'Good. I'm glad we agree on something. Hopefully you'll have news of Isabelle by the time you get to Melbourne. 'Have you thought anymore about contacting her grandmother?'

'I have, especially with everything that's taken place, but I haven't heard from Sally. I thought I'd give her a call once I'm in Melbourne to find out how Isabelle is first, and then take it from there.'

'Yes. It's probably best to play things by ear. Where does her grandmother live?'

'Didn't I say?'

'No.'

'Glen Iris.'

'You will keep me posted, won't you?'

'Yes, and you'll call me when they let you out of here.'

'Will do.'

'Talking of which, I suppose I'd better start making tracks,' I said rather reluctantly, looking at my watch.

'I suppose you had. Come on give me that kiss,' he said, extending his arms towards me.

'You take care,' I said, moving forward, putting my arms around him and lightly brushing his lips with mine.

'That feels wonderfully good,' he said. 'I could get used to all this pampering.' I kissed him again.

'Well, we'll just have to see what we can do about that when I'm back. I'd better go,' I said, looking at my watch again and picking up my bag. *'Arrivederci, carino mio. Ti voglio bene. Mi manchi quando non sono con te. Non vedo l'ora che ci vediamo di nuovo. Ciao. Ciao!'* I blew him another kiss as I walked towards the door.

'Speak to me in English. You know I don't understand Italian.'

'You'd better start learning then. After all Italian *is* the language of love…'

When I arrived at Melbourne's Tullamarine Airport at around ten o'clock that night it was raining and pleasantly cool. Although I had told Alex I would call him when I arrived I did not want to disturb him in case he was asleep. While I was waiting for my luggage in the baggage hall I 'phoned the hospital and left a message for him that all was well and I would ring him in the morning. I felt exhausted and was very grateful to Jeremy for offering to pick me up at the airport.

'Alicia,' he called out as he strode towards me. 'Welcome to Melbourne,' he said, leaning forward to kiss me on the cheek and taking my bag. 'You travel light. Great to see you.'

'You too. Thanks for coming to fetch me. I really appreciate it.'

'No worries. You must be tired. Let's get you home.'

I was unable to make out my surroundings through the window of the car on the drive to Carlton because it was dark and rain was pelting against the windows. Finally, Jeremy turned into a tree-lined street of Victorian terraced houses, drove to the end of the road and pulled up on the left-hand side in front of the last but one house. He took my bag and we made a mad dash to the shelter of the front porch.

'Home Sweet Home,' said Jeremy as he unlocked the door and ushered me inside. 'This is your room,' he said, walking down the hallway and opening the second door on the right. I followed him into the bedroom. He put my bag at the bottom of the bed. 'Is that OK for you?'

'Oh, it's lovely,' I replied, glancing around the room. It had every-thing I needed: an inviting bed with a blue and white duvet and pillows to match, fitted wardrobes, chest of drawers and a television. Jeremy had even put a vase of fresh flowers in the room.

'The bathroom's down there,' he said, pointing to the door at the far end of the hallway, 'and there's a shower here,' he said, opening the next door along the hall. 'Make yourself at home. If you need anything just ask.'

'That's really kind, thank you.'

'No problem. You're very welcome. I did ask Tom and Antonia if they wanted to come and stay, but Tom said they were going up the Sunshine Coast for a few days as Antonia has to go back at the weekend.'

'Yes. That's right. They'll be there tomorrow.'

'I was very sorry to hear about Alex. How's he doing?'

'Well. He should be out of hospital by the end of the week. It was he who persuaded me to come to Melbourne rather than stay with him.'

'He was right. You can go back to the Sunshine Coast another time. Are you hungry? I don't suppose you had more than a snack on the plane. I could fix you something in seconds.'

'Oh, I'm fine thanks. I've eaten heaps today. I'm really not at all hungry.'

'How about a cup of tea and a chat then?'

'Sounds perfect.'

'So, is there anything particular you want to do or see while you're here? Have you made any plans? You've just missed the Formula One Grand Prix in Albert Park. I don't know if you're interested in motor racing. I've been a couple of times.'

'I wouldn't have minded going for the experience!'

'I can take you for a drive along the track if you like,' he said, reaching for the kettle. 'And if you're interested I'm more than happy to give you a tour of the city. We may not have a fantastic harbour setting like Sydney, but I think Melbourne has plenty else going for it.'

'Well, I haven't been to Sydney yet, but I imagine it must be a pretty stunning sight to fly in over the Opera House and the Harbour Bridge. I'm hoping to make it there.'

'Yes it is, and you should. As for Melbourne, I think it's a city you need to live in. I didn't like it at all when I first moved here but its subtle charms have grown on me and now I wouldn't want to live anywhere else in Australia. So, what I'm saying is that I hope you're here long enough to get to like it.' Jeremy filled the kettle with water, placed it back on the base and pressed the switch. He took a small teapot and two mugs out of an overhead cupboard. I watched him as he put three teaspoons of leaf tea into the teapot – presumably one for each of us and one for the pot.

'Oh, I'm sure I will. It's quite a funky area around here, isn't it, with the University on your doorstep and all that Italian café culture?'

'Yes. You should feel right at home here. Lygon Street is the centre of the action and you definitely need to explore around there, but you should also go to Drummond Street, Carlton Gardens and the two streets which flank the gardens; Rathdowne and Nicholson streets,' he said, rummaging through a pile of papers on the work surface next to the oven and pulling out a well-used map of Melbourne. 'Look,' he said, opening the map up and smoothing it out across the kitchen table. 'It's this area here.' He pointed to Carlton Gardens and circled the area with his finger. I noticed that Gertrude Street ran from Nicholson Street and across some major streets, Brunswick Street and Smith Street, into the Fitzroy area. The kettle boiled and he poured the boiling water onto the tea-leaves. 'We'll just leave that to brew for a few minutes,' he said as he walked to the fridge to fetch some milk. 'I presume you do take milk with your tea?' he asked, holding up a carton. I nodded.

'Gertrude Street is where that Kiwi lawyer was murdered, wasn't it?'

'You heard about that then?' He poured some milk into a small jug.

'Oh, yes. I saw it on the news. The thing is Jeremy I'm probably more curious than most to find out what happened to him.'

'How so?' He looked slightly perplexed. He poured the tea through a tea strainer and handed me the cup and the jug of milk.

'Thanks,' I said, taking it from him. 'I met him on the plane on the way over to Singapore and we had a long chat.' I poured the milk into the tea.

'Have you told the police?' He came and sat down at the table and pushed the biscuit tin, which was already on the table, towards me. 'Help yourself,' he said, taking off the lid.

'I did consider it, but then I thought that all I could really tell the police is that I was on the plane with him on such-and-such a date and they'd know that from the plane records anyway. And I have been a little distracted by recent events,' I replied, delving into the biscuit tin and taking out a bite-sized Cherry Ripe.

'No, of course. I understand that. But it might be worth contacting them. After all, they don't know what you talked about. Did he say anything at all that could help with the murder enquiry? Think really hard, Alicia.'

'I don't need to, Jeremy.' I replied, tearing open the wrapper of the Cherry Ripe. 'I remember exactly what he said to me. But there's a lot more to it. Let me explain.' I took a bite of the Cherry Ripe. I savoured the coconut, cherry and plain chocolate combination.

'I wish you would.' I cleared my throat and took a sip of tea.

'As you know I recently changed jobs. Well, a client was recommended to me, but this client is *not* your usual type of client you understand. She's about to inherit two hundred and fifty million pounds.'

'Not an insubstantial amount then?' he said, with a hint of sarcasm as he leaned forward and put his elbows on the table.

'Exactly. Anyway, what is really weird about her case is that most of her family members are dead and not from what one would term completely natural causes either.' I proceeded to tell him something of Isabelle's tragic background.

'I follow what you say, Alicia, but how is any of this connected to what has happened here in Melbourne?'

'Oh, I'm coming to that.' I relayed to him the extraordinary events of the past few weeks.

'But you still haven't explained where John MacFadzean fits in.'

'The firm of solicitors dealing with my client's grandfather's estate is called Holmwood & Hitchins. You'll know from all the press on John MacFadzean's murder that he was a lawyer?'

'Yes.'

'He told me that he was a trust lawyer and a Partner in that firm. You see my point?'

'Yes. Talk about coincidence.'

'I know. As you can imagine, after hearing about the murder of my client's fiancé, the 'alleged' attempt on her life, and then this, you'll see why I began to think they are connected in some way. Alex joked that the killings are the work of some distant relative from over here.'

'Why from over here? Is your client an Aussie girl then?'

'Her paternal family's from Melbourne. After her parents were killed she and her brother were brought up here by their grandparents.'

'I see. Do you really think there might be an Australian connection?'

'I can't be 100 percent certain yet, but I see no point in speaking to the police here until I've discussed the matter with my client and found out what she knows.' I wanted to ask Isabelle about Luisa as well as John MacFadzean.

'I can understand your motives. Some holiday this is turning out to be for you.'

'Oh, I'm having a great time despite everything. Do *you* think that John MacFadzean was the victim of a brutal mugging?'

'Well, it is a possibility, but that's something for the police investigation. There have been a spate of killings in Gertrude Street in recent months, but I don't think this one is connected. In the other cases the victims were shot.'

'Is it a rough area?'

'Not really, but it depends which part of Gertrude Street you're talking about. The end nearest Carlton Gardens, that is the Nicholson Street side, is safe, and the whole street is pretty much OK during the day. Admittedly, the street does become seedier as you walk further down it. Look,' he said, pointing on the map to the junction where Gertrude Street meets Brunswick Street. 'There used to be an old man's drinking pub on the corner. Not the sort of place for a young woman like you to go on your own, for example. This area of Gertrude Street down here,' he said, pointing now to the area between Brunswick Street and Napier Street, 'is where you'll find Menzies Mansions. That's where John MacFadzean's body was found.'

'What's Menzies Mansions?'

'Housing Commission tower blocks.'

'Hmm… Why do you think someone like him would go to that area?'

'Fitzroy itself has a tremendous amount going for it. You just have to keep your wits about you in Gertrude Street and, as I said, it's not somewhere a woman should go alone at night.'

'Nor a man, judging by what happened to John MacFadzean.'

'In all major cities in the world there are areas which are more salubrious than others, Alicia, and Melbourne is no different. If you go to Sydney I wouldn't advise you to go to certain streets in the Rocks late at night either. I'll take you down Gertrude Street and you'll see what I mean. Fitzroy is a pretty colourful place and very trendy. It has quite an arty and funky ambiance. It's really the home to the Bohemian culture of Melbourne. You'll see cafés full of students, artists, musicians and writers. There are some great bars and ethnic restaurants. Brunswick Street is the main street. It's well worth a visit.'

'Sounds like it.'

'On the subject of John MacFadzean, there was a piece about his murder in *The Melbourne Age* yesterday and the problems with gangs down there. It appears there has also been a crack cocaine problem in the Gertrude Street/Smith Street area. Here,' he said, picking the newspaper up off the surface next to the oven and handing it to me, 'have a read of that. I'm off to bed. You sleep well,' he said, squeezing my shoulder.

'Thanks. I will.'

'This trip to Australia is turning out to be a rather eventful one for you, isn't it?' he said as he turned and hovered in the doorway.

'Hmm… You could say that.'

'Goodnight, Alicia.'

'Goodnight, Jeremy.'

Chapter 15

The newspaper article was really about all the killings that had taken place in Gertrude Street. John MacFadzean's death was mentioned, but only as the latest in a series of brutal murders highlighting problems in the area. Few actual details of the murder were provided and in fact I learned no more from reading the article than I had from watching the news. Jeremy had made an interesting point when he said that he did not think that MacFadzean's murder had any connection with recent events there, and this supported my theory that somebody else killed him. Maybe MacFadzean had a rendezvous in the vicinity of Gertrude Street, and had been lured to the area near Menzies Mansions where he was stabbed to death and the killing made to look like a mugging? My murder theories were all very well but I was not exactly in a position to prove any of them. What I needed to obtain was some substantive evidence.

As for the murders in Isabelle's family, when I returned to London I intended to pay a visit to the Family Records Office in Islington to check any records relating to Diane Latham's birth, marriage to Isabelle's grandfather and her death. I would also make a trip to the British Library Newspaper Collections at Colindale in north London to see what had been reported in the press, if anything, on the divorce case and her subsequent death. For this I might need to enlist Alex's help if he was back in London and well enough to assist.

If John MacFadzean was a trustee of Grandpa Jam's estate this did not automatically mean that he was murdered because of it. I did have to concede Alex's point that it could be coincidental. On the other hand, there was no reason to suggest that he was not murdered because of his possible connection to the estate. I did appreciate, however, that he was murdered on the other side of the world, whereas the other murders had taken place in England. A motive for his killing might well be that he knew something or discovered something in the course of his work that someone else did not want him to know, but all this was pure conjecture.

I was awoken by the rich aroma of freshly ground coffee and the smell of toast. I pushed back the bedclothes, pulled on my dressing-gown and padded out to the hall.

'Good morning,' I said, popping my head around the kitchen door. Jeremy was sitting at the table drinking coffee and eating toast and marmalade.

'Good morning, Alicia. Did you sleep well?'

'Yes, thanks.'

'Help yourself to anything you like for breakfast. I'm really sorry I can't stay and chat but I'm going to have to dash. I've got an early start this morning. Here's a set of keys for you so you can come and go as you please,' he said, handing them to me. 'I forgot to give them to you last night. The gold one's for the top and the larger silver one's for the bottom. The small silver one is for the screen door. The bottom one's a bit stiff but I'm sure you'll work it out. OK?'

'Yes. Thanks,' I replied, placing the bunch on the table.

'Have you decided what you're going to do today?' he asked, taking his navy suit jacket off the back of the chair and putting it on.

'I thought I might wander around here and venture down to the City Circle if I have time.'

'Not going to Gertrude Street today then?' he teased.

'I might. If I'm in the area.'

'Are you OK with finding your way around?'

'Oh yes. I have a guidebook and a map. I'm sure I'll be fine.'

'Well, you've got my mobile if you need me. OK, see you later then. Enjoy your day.'

'Thanks, Jeremy. *Ciao.*'

I thought that since Carlton was the heart of café culture I must experience it for myself and decided to have breakfast out. Jeremy lived really close to Lygon Street and I could walk there in no time. While I dressed I peeked out the window and was pleased that the rain had cleared and there was not a trace of a cloud in the sky. Equipped with sunscreen and sunglasses, I ventured out into the sunshine in search of Melbourne's Little Italy. I stopped at one of the pavement cafés for a caffè latte and a pastry, and watched the passing parade. To an Italian drinking coffee is an occasion, and people watching is one of my favourite pastimes. I waited for my order to arrive and called Alex.

'How's the patient this morning?'

'I'm good. I should be out of here soon. Where are you? It sounds like you're out and about.'

'In Lygon Street, having breakfast.'

'You've settled in then? Everything OK with Jeremy?'

'Oh, yes.'

'Good. How's the research going?'

'If you mean John MacFadzean, I was chatting to Jeremy about him last night and the latest fix in which I find myself.'

'You told him then?'

'Yes. Well, the gist of everything, yes. I was hoping he might be able to help me. It's not as if I have any other contacts here, is it? I'll know more when I've spoken to Isabelle.' The waiter arrived with my coffee and pastry.

'Have you heard how she is?'

'No,' I replied, stirring my coffee. 'I'll text Sally after we've finished talking, but I don't expect to hear from her until this evening because of the time difference. Jeremy seems to think that I should tell the Victorian State Police that I met John MacFadzean on the plane to Singapore, and that he was probably one of Isabelle's trustees. I guess he has a point. If there is a possible connection it should be checked. I just don't want to say anything yet until I know what's going on back in England. What do you think?'

'I agree. Follow your instincts. You always make the right decisions when you do.'

'I hope so, but sometimes it's really difficult to know what to do for the best. I don't want to be accused of withholding evidence. I'll give you a call later and update you on everything. Antonia and Tom should be there soon so you'll have some company.'

'OK. *Ciao* for now then.'

'*Ciao, bella.*'

I sent Sally the following text message:

Hi Sally. Hope all is well. Haven't heard from you. Was wondering how Isabelle is? What's the news? Let me know. I'm in Melbourne now. Alicia

I finished my coffee and pastry and embarked on a tour of Carlton itself. After several hours traipsing around the blocks between Queensberry and Elgin Street, I headed off to Carlton Gardens. I walked up to the Victoria Street entrance because the guidebook said that the view from there up the central avenue to the Royal Exhibition Building was dramatic. I spent a while wandering through the rambling gardens. It was beautiful weather and I was determined to make the most it.

Since it was such a lovely day I toyed up whether I should walk the length of Gertrude Street or just to the corner of Nicholson Street. From there I could pick up the City Circle Tram which would take me straight to the centre. I was curious to feel the atmosphere of Gertrude Street and there seemed no better way to do that but on foot. Jeremy had described it very well; and there was nothing exceptional to see, during the day at any rate, so I decided to go back. I noticed that it was on a tram route so I bought a Zone 1 ticket from a newsagent and hopped on a tram, dutifully validating my ticket in the little machine on board.

I managed to pick up another tram which took me to the eastern end of Collins Street which is supposed to be *the* smart Melbourne address. I only had to walk a little way along this tree-lined street to discover that it is an area of five-star hotels, chic designer shops, exclusive jewellers and home to some big corporations. I wanted to go down to the Rialto Towers building at the western end and take the lift up to the Observation Deck on the 55th floor because it boasts spectacular 360-degree views of Melbourne and the surrounding area. However, I decided to leave that trip until another day and to concentrate on the seven city arcades, the most opulent one of which is the L-shaped Block Arcade, built in the 1890s.

After completing my tour of the arcades, I paused momentarily at the Bourke Street end of Royal Arcade to look at my map, contemplating where to go next. Suddenly I heard someone call my name; the voice was female. Apart from Jeremy I did not know anyone in Melbourne. I turned around and, to my utter amazement, Luisa Bruneschi was standing in front of me. She wore her sunglasses back on her head and was dressed quite casually, as before, in black palazzo pants and a red linen sleeveless shirt.

'Hi,' she said, grinning broadly, bending down and greeting me with a kiss on each cheek. 'Talk about surprises. I didn't expect to see you here.'

'Likewise.'

'How are you?'

'I'm fine, thanks. I'm staying in Melbourne for a few days. You remember I said I was coming here?' She nodded. 'I'm doing the tourist thing. How about you? Back visiting family or on a shopping spree?'

'Neither. Worse luck, although I'll get some shopping in. Don't you worry about that. I'm here doing research for a piece I've got to write. Actually, do you fancy going for a coffee or something to eat?'

'Yes. I'd love to. I thought I might go up to China Town, explore around there and have lunch. Does that suit you or would you rather go somewhere else?'

'No. That sounds perfect. I've got a meeting at five, which is plenty of time,' she said, glancing at her watch. I glimpsed down at mine; it was just after three. 'Let's head up towards Lonsdale Street. There are some great little restaurants up there.'

'I see you know your way around.'

'Oh yeah, of course. I was born here as you know.'

'Yes, you did tell me.'

We headed east towards China Town which seemed the appropriate direction. As we walked we chatted. We climbed the hill and walked up Bourke Street passing numerous cafés and bars including Pellegrini's, which Luisa explained was Melbourne's first espresso bar. I was looking forward to sampling the delights of China Town.

'Mmm…all these smells are making my mouth water,' I said, breathing in the oriental aromas and spices wafting on the air.

'I know. How about this place?' she said, leading me into a small authentic establishment. I followed her in.

I ordered a bottle of sparkling mineral water and an exotic fruit cocktail – which subsequently arrived with what seemed like half the Caribbean in it.

'Tell me, what's this piece you're working on?' I asked, looking up from the menu.

'Oh, it's something very boring about the history of Melbourne. I'm actually doing a bit of personal research. You know, the Kiwi lawyer who was murdered here?'

'I did,' I nodded, observing her expression closely as I chewed the piece of pineapple from the side of my cocktail glass. I closed my menu. I had the feeling this was about to become a very interesting conversation.

'What do you mean, you did?' The waitress appeared and took our order.

'Oh, I met him once.' I paused. 'I'll have Shark's fin soup and Bok Choy, please,' I said, turning to the waitress.

'I'll have the same,' said Luisa. I sensed she was hungrier for information than food. 'You were saying?' she asked, leaning forward, elbows on the table.

'Well, he was a Partner at a firm in London one of my client's previously instructed,' I replied cautiously, not wishing to disclose too much information.

'You mean Isabelle's old firm, don't you? I know because Lucy e-mailed me yesterday. She also told me that Isabelle had taken an overdose. She asked me if I could find out anything this end. I was coming to Melbourne anyway and thought I'd see what I could dig up. Tell me more about John MacFadzean. What was he like?'

'There's nothing much to tell,' I replied casually. 'As I said I only met him once.' For a split second I thought about mentioning to her *how* I had met him, but then I would have to explain the ins and outs of everything, and besides, I had neither spoken to Isabelle about his murder yet, nor to the Victorian State Police. The last thing I needed was to divulge my theories on his murder to an investigative journalist. However, that did not stop me asking her what she knew about him and his murder. 'I suppose because I met him I'm curious about what happened to him. So what have *you* found about him so far?'

'That he wasn't quite what he seemed.'

'Which of us is?'

'Hmm... Well he certainly wasn't. He was leading a double life: clubs, bars, women, gambling. I've learnt that he was a serious gambler and had substantial debts which he couldn't repay. It's possible that someone he owed money to caught up with him and murdered him. We have proof he was playing Blackjack and Roulette on the night of his murder.'

'When was that exactly?'

'At the beginning of last week. Why?'

'I just wondered. So you don't think it was a mugging turned nasty?'

'I'd be surprised if it was.'

'Where would he go gambling here?'

'The Crown Entertainment Complex.'

'The one on the Southbank?'

'Yes. It isn't quite Las Vegas, but it's the largest Casino we've got. Have you been there?'

'I haven't been over to the Southbank yet. It's a tourist area, isn't it?'

'Oh yes. It's probably one of the most popular spots. Go there for dinner if you can. The riverside setting and fantastic views of the city skyline are what make it appealing. There are cafés and restaurants all the way along the promenade from the Southgate complex to the Crown Casino, so you're spoilt for choice. And if you're into art, then go to St Kilda Road. The Australian Ballet, Melbourne Symphony, The National Gallery of Victoria, the Victorian Arts Centre, Playbox Theatre and the Malthouse are all up there.'

'Not exactly a rough area then?'

'Not at all.'

'Do you think MacFadzean met someone at the Casino and then went back to Gertrude Street with them, or that he had a rendezvous there?'

'Quite possibly. That's what I'm trying to find out. I'll just have to keep digging.'

'Isn't that something the police are doing as part of the investigation? They must be checking out his life back in London as well. If he was such a compulsive gambler, he must have been gambling there too.' I really needed to speak with Isabelle about all this, but still had no word from Sally.

'Yes, I'm sure. Tell me what you've been up to since you arrived in Melbourne?' she asked, changing the subject. 'All this murder stuff is getting a bit depressing.'

'I'm staying in Carlton and I've explored quite a lot of the area around there. I've been to the gardens today and then for a look at the arcades. I might go to Fitzroy Gardens tomorrow and possibly the Royal Botanic Gardens.'

'Oh, you must go to the Royal Botanic Gardens. You'll have plenty to see there. As for Fitzroy Gardens you've got...' My mobile phone was on the table and it beeped twice indicating that I had received a text message. 'Are you going to get that?' she asked. It was a message from Alex:

Ciao, bella. Your sister and Tom have been in. All is well. Any more murders since we spoke? A x

I read his text and put my mobile in my handbag. I decided it was better to text him back later. 'Who's that from?' asked Luisa, leaning across the table.

'Nobody in particular.'

'From the look on your face I'd say it was.'

'Well, if you must know it's from a close friend. He was at my previous firm.'

'So what's the story with him then?'

'There isn't one. You were saying about Fitzroy Gardens?' I replied. It was my turn to change the subject.

'Oh yes. I think those are my favourite gardens. The floral displays are magnificent. It's worth going there for that but also for Cook's Cottage. It's amazing to think, isn't it, that his parents' house was transported here all the way from Yorkshire in 1934?'

'It is.'

After we finished our meal we walked down to Swanston Street.

'Where are you heading now?' she asked.

'Back to base, I think.'

'You can take the tram from here up to Carlton. I have to run to that meeting. It's been great,' she said, bending down to kiss me.

'Yes. It's been very interesting. *Ciao!*'

As I walked along the street I rummaged in my handbag for my mobile which, predictably, had slipped to the bottom. I intended to respond to Alex's text. The tram arrived and I jumped on board. When finally I retrieved my 'phone I discovered that I had received a text message from Sally. Obviously she must have sent it after I put it in my handbag at the restaurant as I had not heard it beep because of the hubbub all around me. It read:

Hi, Alicia. Thanks for the text. Isabelle discharged herself from hospital and now she's disappeared. She can't have gone far though as she hasn't taken her passport. Going to work. I'll call you from the office. Sally

Chapter 16

'Disappeared where?' I asked myself as the tram arrived at my stop. I would not have thought that she was well enough to travel. I ambled back to Jeremy's house and let myself in as he had not yet returned home. I freshened up, made myself a cup of tea and called Alex.

'You OK? You seem preoccupied. What's the matter?' He sounded concerned.

'Yes. I'm fine. How are you feeling?'

'Much better. I don't think you're fine. Tell me what's been going on? Did you get my text by the way?'

'Yes, thanks. Listen, Alex, the strangest thing happened. Guess who I bumped into, or should I say bumped into me, while I was wandering around the city centre.' There was a brief pause at the end of the line as if he was mulling that one over.

'I really have no idea. Who?'

'Luisa.'

'Not *the* Luisa?' He seemed genuinely astonished.

'Yes.'

'That's a coincidence and a half. What's she doing in Melbourne?'

'She said she's here for work, but taking the opportunity to see what she can dig up about John MacFadzean.'

'Really? Has she discovered anything and, if so, did she tell you what it is?' I relayed to Alex what Luisa had told me including her murder theory.

'The thing is, Alex, I don't know whether she's right or not, but

I'm not convinced that he was the victim of a brutal mugging either. I think there's more to it. Shall I tell you what my theory is?'

'Which one? You have several,' he quipped.

'Stop it! Are you interested or not?'

'Of course I am. I'm only teasing you.'

'His death must have something to do with Isabelle and the Latham estate.'

'Why?'

'Well, if he had gambling debts he would surely have been desperate for money. Say he found out something about the murderer and tried to blackmail him or her and asked for money to buy his silence.'

'You mean the murderer decided it was too expensive to pay him *ad infinitum* and decided to silence him permanently.'

'Yes.'

'But for the murderer to manage to fly between London and Australia within the time frame these murders took place would be some feat, Alicia.'

'But he or she wouldn't have needed to – not if there was an accomplice.'

'I'm finding it difficult to get my head around all this, but I have to concede that it is a possibility, improbable though it is. But you still have no evidence to support your theories. It's like stabbing in the dark.'

'That's what happened to John MacFadzean.'

'Hmm... Very droll.'

'I wasn't trying to be funny, Alex. This is really serious. I've been going over in my mind what John MacFadzean said to me. I wonder if I missed something but I can't for the life of me think what, except that maybe it has something to do with Jonathan Masterton and the Australian connection.'

'I don't follow.'

'John MacFadzean got his job at Holmwood & Hitchins through a friend he'd worked with in Australia, and I believe that the friend was Jonathan Masterton.'

'What makes you say that?'

'I think that Jonathan Masterton must have met John MacFadzean while he was working in Australia. When Masterton returned home he was offered the position at Holmwood & Hitchins, enabling John MacFadzean to come on board a few years down the line. This all fits in with what MacFadzean told me. Isabelle indicated that it was her grandfather who recommended Jonathan Masterton to Holmwood & Hitchins in the first place.'

'Really?'

'Yes. She gave me the impression that it was because her grandfather knew Masterton's father. There seems to be quite a connection between the two families.'

'It sounds like it.'

'The thing is, Isabelle doesn't seem that keen on Jonathan Masterton. She must have her reasons.'

'You're not suggesting that Jonathan Masterton has anything to do with the murders, are you?'

'No. Well, not at this stage anyway. I'm just bandying ideas about. Mind you, she says playing devil's advocate, he's pretty well-placed to know all the family business and for all we know he might have been aware of John MacFadzean's debts. Maybe John MacFadzean was on to him and tried to blackmail him and that's why Jonathan Masterton killed him. Then again, there's the question of motive and opportunity. As the family's lawyer he's not going to gain anything financially by murdering members of the family unless he's in to charging excessive legal fees to sort out all the probates!'

'Quite.'

'Oh, I know this all sounds ridiculous, but instinct tells me I'm on the right lines. I'm sure that there are skeletons in the Latham family closet we have yet to discover.'

'Talking of which, what's happened to Isabelle? Have you heard from Sally?'

'Yes. Isabelle's disappeared.'

'What? Disappeared in terms of abducted or of her own accord?'

'Apparently she discharged herself from hospital. I'm waiting for Sally to call me. I'll chat to you when I've spoken to her.'

'I look forward to it. *Ciao, bella.*'

'*Ciao, carino.*'

I switched on the television in my bedroom and lay down. I flicked through all the TV channels with the remote control. There was a game of Australian Rules football on one of them. I had read somewhere that in Melbourne Australian Rules football has been elevated almost to cult status, so I had to watch the game to see what the fascination with it is. I was actually getting quite engrossed in it when my mobile rang. It was Sally.

'Where are you?' she asked. I turned down the volume on the TV.

'I was watching telly. Thanks for calling.'

'How are you? How's Melbourne?'

'I'm well, thanks, and I like Melbourne very much. Don't keep me in suspense. When did Isabelle disappear?'

'Yesterday evening. Lucy said that she only found out because she couldn't make it in to the hospital to visit her last night and 'phoned to see how she was. When the ward sister informed her that Isabelle had left, Lucy went straight round to the flat but Isabelle wasn't there. She knew she had been home because the hand luggage bag she always uses for overnight or weekend trips was missing. She can't have gone far, however, because her passport is still in the top drawer of the desk where she always keeps it. Lucy keeps trying to call her, but she must have switched off her mobile. We're all desperately worried that she might do something drastic after the overdose and everything. Lucy contacted the police, but I don't know what they're doing.'

'I'm sure Isabelle will be fine.' I was not convinced that she had deliberately meant to harm herself. 'And she hasn't gone down to the West Country to her grandfather's house?'

'Well, if she did she hasn't arrived yet and she didn't drive there because her car's still parked in front of the house.'

'If, as you say, she's only taken an overnight bag and no passport then she may be back sooner than you think. Did anything happen yesterday to make her react like this?' There had to be some incident that had triggered Isabelle's disappearance.

'That I don't know.'

'Where would you like to go this evening?' asked Jeremy when he returned home.

'For a walk along the Southbank to the Crown Entertainment Complex.'

'I wouldn't have put you down as the gambling sort.'

'Unless the odds are in my favour… No, I'm not, only the odd flutter now and then. Actually, I gather that John MacFadzean was a compulsive gambler and was there the night of his murder; I'm curious to go and have a look at the place.'

'Ah, so that's the attraction. Well, for a gambler it's like all your birthdays coming at once. I think I read somewhere that it has about 350 gambling tables and 2500 machines and most of the complex is open twenty-four hours a day. But you can suss the place out for yourself and then I'll take you to dinner. There's a fantastic little Greek restaurant just off Russell Street where the service is particularly attentive and the food superb. Do you like Greek food?'

'Yes. That sounds perfect.'

'May I ask how you know MacFadzean was at the Casino the night he was murdered? Only it wasn't on the news or in any of the papers – unless I missed something.' We crossed the road from Flinders Street station and walked into Federation Square.

'I heard it from a reliable source.' Jeremy glanced sideways at me with a questioning look.

'Who?' he asked. We walked across the square in the direction of the Yarra River and towards Princes Bridge.

'You remember the client I was telling you about?' He nodded. 'A friend of hers who works for the *Courier Mail* contacted me when I was in Brisbane. I bumped into her today while I was out shopping and that's when she told me. She's here doing some personal research on him.' We started to walk across the bridge to the Southbank.

'Tom has a friend who used to work at the *Courier Mail* as one of the subs. He has contacts on the paper. You probably met him at the wedding. His name's Paul Heddington.'

'Yes. I did. He gave me his card. We had a good chat.'

'You can contact him yourself if you want or I don't mind doing it. Tell you what, why don't I give him a call tomorrow?'

'OK. Whatever.'

'So what's the name of this journalist?'

'Luisa Bruneschi. Actually, I'd be interested in knowing a bit more about her myself. Perhaps Paul knows of her.'

'It sounds as if you're suspicious of her. May I ask why?' We had crossed the bridge and were now walking along the promenade to the complex which was bustling with activity.

'It isn't anything in particular and it's difficult to explain what it is about her that makes me feel wary. I mean, she's very pleasant and I'm probably doing her a terrible injustice, but I wouldn't say I completely trust her. Something isn't right – but I can't put my finger on it.'

'Let me see what I can find out about her,' he said as we arrived at the Casino. 'Welcome to Melbourne's answer to Las Vegas!'

We entered the Casino complex and I was immediately struck by the frenetic, feverish atmosphere, commotion and clamour, and quite dazzled by all the bright lights and vibrant colours. There were people rushing about everywhere, jostling each other at the gaming tables, vying to place their bets or transfixed to their slot machine screens waiting for that elusive row of symbols to appear and for the jangling sound of coins falling into the tray below. Jeremy and I walked through one room after another and the scene was almost the same in every one. We seemed to walk forever.

'Do you think John MacFadzean went off with someone from here or arranged to meet up with him or her later? The police must have CCTV footage of him in the Casino. I would have thought that if he'd met someone in here the police would have put that information in the public domain in the hope of witnesses stepping forward. On the other hand, none of the reports have referred to him gambling, so maybe they have an idea of who it is and don't want to alert their suspect.'

'Hmm... I suppose it is a possibility. Have you thought any more about going to the police yourself?'

'Yes, I have, but I still haven't spoken to my client and the thing is there's been a slight complication on that front.'

'Which is?'

'She's vanished.'

'I'm sure she'll turn up.'

'As long as it's not dead.'

Chapter 17

The next morning I left Jeremy's house early as I planned to walk through the University precincts and then to Royal Park via Royal Parade. I wanted to have a look at the memorial to the explorers Burke & Wills and then head for the zoo. I thought that later I would go to the shopping centre opposite Melbourne Central and, if I had time, go to Melbourne Gaol where the folk hero and bushranger Ned Kelly was hanged.

I was ambling through Royal Park when my mobile rang. I retrieved it from my pocket but the number came up as withheld so I answered it cautiously.

'Hello.'

'Alicia, is that you?'

'Isabelle?' This time I recognised her voice. 'I spoke to Sally. She said you'd disappeared. How are you? And where are you? What's going on?' I was relieved to hear her voice but anxious to find out what had happened to her.

'I'm OK. I'm at the airport. Are you still in Brisbane?' She sounded very flat.

'No. I'm in Melbourne. I've been here a couple of days. Why?'

'I was hoping you'd be there. Can you meet me?' Then it dawned on me that she was also in Melbourne. When she said she was at the airport I had thought she meant Heathrow.

'Of course I can. But how did you get here, only Sally told me you didn't take your passport?'

'Not my Australian one, no. It expired a couple of weeks back and I didn't see the point of renewing it until after the wedding as I'd only have had to change it again to my married name. Not that that applies now.' She sighed deeply. 'I'm using my British one.'

'Oh, I see.' Lucy must have seen the passport in the drawer and jumped to the wrong conclusion.

'Do you know the Rialto Towers Building?'

'Yes.'

'Good. You can take the tram there. All of the trams on Collins Street pass the Rialto Building. If you come on the City Circle Tram, jump off at the intersection of Spencer and Collins Street. Meet me on the Observation Deck, by the Information Booth in an hour. Can you make that?'

'OK. I'll be there.'

Within the hour I had arrived. I paid my entrance fee and took the lift to the 55th floor. I looked all around but I did not see Isabelle. I wandered out onto both the outdoor viewing balconies but there was no sign of her. I stood for a moment to look at the spectacular view.

'Fantastic, isn't it? It stretches about 60 kilometres to the horizon. I used to love coming up here. Michael hated it, but then he didn't like heights. We're 253 metres above the ground you know.'

'Isabelle!' I exclaimed, turning around to face her. She was hollow-eyed, her cheeks were sunken and she was visibly thinner than when I had last seen her. The navy linen jacket she was wearing simply hung on her. It was, in fact, quite a dramatic physiological change, but the shock of Drew's death and the 'overdose' had evidently taken their toll. 'Everyone's been really worried about you,' I said gently, putting my arms around her fleetingly.

'You mean because everyone thinks I tried to kill myself,' she replied blandly and staring at me hard. I noticed that she was carrying one small overnight bag, presumably the bag she had taken from the apartment the night she left.

'No, I meant that they're just concerned about your welfare, that's all.'

'The only thing is, I didn't. I don't want to die. I want to avenge Drew's death, and Michael's and Grandpa's and I can't do that if I'm dead myself, can I? Do you really think I'd try to kill myself?'

'No. I don't. But if you didn't try to overdose yourself, how did it happen?' I asked, lowering my voice to almost a whisper so that nobody would overhear our conversation. 'Was it an accident or are you saying someone tried to kill you?'

'Let's find somewhere quiet to chat. I'm sure I don't know why I suggested meeting here. Unless you particularly want to go to the Café Bar?'

'I'm not bothered.'

'We'll go to Caffè e Cucina in Chapel Street. Have you been there?' I shook my head. 'It's one of my favourite haunts. I generally go there when I've been shopping in Chapel Street itself or the Toorak Road. Anyway, it's on the way to Grandma Edie's.' We walked back to the lift.

'Does she know you're coming?'

'Yes. I 'phoned her when I arrived.'

'Does she know what's been happening?' I called the lift.

'She knows about Drew's death, but she doesn't know that I've been in hospital. I told Lucy not to tell her, because she'd only worry. I knew that Lucy wouldn't call Grandma when I disappeared as she wouldn't want to give her unnecessary stress. But I had to get away. If I'd spoken to her she'd have tried to dissuade me from flying over.' The lift arrived and fortunately we were alone and able to continue our conversation in private.

'I'm sure the doctors weren't too happy about you leaving.'

'They would have let me go the next morning anyway. As I said, I don't want to die. I wouldn't have discharged myself were there any danger of that. Before I was rushed to hospital I spoke to the police and they said it was OK for me to come out. They have my contact details here. The coroner hasn't released Drew's body and so there won't be a funeral for a while.' She paused and I could detect the emotion in her voice. 'Obviously I'll be there for that. His parents said they'd organise it.' There was another pause. 'I still can't believe he's dead,' she said, looking at me, her eyes welling up with tears.

'It must have been the most terrible shock for you. I am so very sorry,' I said, patting her arm lightly. 'I can't bring Drew back, but I promised to help you find his murderer and, if I can, I will. Tell me why you believe the deaths of your grandfather, brother and Drew are connected and why you think the murderer wanted to kill you and not Drew. You have to tell me all you know.' We reached the bottom of the lift.

'I will. Let's get a taxi. I'm feeling very tired all of a sudden.'

'I'm not surprised. You must be jet-lagged too!'

'Do you want to sit outside or inside?' Isabelle asked when we arrived at the café.

'Shall we try inside? Only there doesn't seem anywhere to sit out here and it looks more private inside,' I replied, peeking in.

'If we go inside we can either sit downstairs or upstairs, but upstairs is quieter.' Isabelle led the way. I was immediately struck by the superb aroma of coffee and the quintessential fragrances of Italian cuisine. It was like entering a traditional Italian café with its wood-panelled walls and intimate size. 'This is the menu,' she said, pointing to a large blackboard. 'As an Italian, the food should be right up your street.' One of the waiters, who clearly recognised Isabelle as a 'regular', came forward to greet her and ushered us to the quietest corner.

'What are you having?' she asked.

'I'll have the fettucine and a green salad,' I replied, looking up at the blackboard. 'You?'

'Risotto and a mixed salad.' Isabelle beckoned the waiter over and we ordered. We both passed on the wine and opted instead for some mineral water. I sensed that Isabelle felt slightly awkward about opening up to me.

'Talk to me, Isabelle. I can't help you otherwise.'

'I don't know where to start. There's so much.' She took a deep breath and sighed. The waiter arrived with our bottle of water and poured each of us a glass full. Isabelle swallowed a mouthful of hers and cleared her throat. 'OK,' she said, running her left hand back through her hair. I noticed she had removed her engagement ring. 'When Michael died two years ago everyone said it was an accident. I never believed that it was and I'm convinced that someone fixed his motorbike. Michael loved that bike and he was scrupulous about maintaining it, particularly as about one month before the accident he'd had a near-death experience on it when the engine cut out for no reason. To be honest, he was lucky to survive that accident without being injured.' The waiter returned with some bread.

'Surely you told the police all this and they would have followed it up? No?' I looked at her quizzically.

'Well, yes, but they informed me that they were satisfied there was nothing untoward about the accident and that it was mechanical failure.'

'Wouldn't they have had the bike examined as part of the investigation and checked all that out?'

'I'm not disputing that they did, nor am I disputing that the accident was caused by mechanical failure. But how that mechanical failure came about is another matter. I might have accepted their findings had it not been for something else.'

'What do you mean?'

'About six weeks before Michael died he received an anonymous note. He showed it to me and, although it wasn't exactly threatening, it worried me. I remember urging him to take it to the police but he said I was overreacting and it was probably some practical joke by one of his friends as it arrived around April Fool's Day. After the first accident I knew the note must be significant and I was convinced that someone was trying to kill him. I pestered Michael to report it to the police and he said he would but he obviously never did.'

'What did the note say?'

'To *"look to the past to see what the future holds and to make recompense for what those before you have done".'*

'What happened to it? Didn't you give it to the police?'

'I couldn't find it. After his death I did tell them about it, but it was never found. I guess Michael must have disposed of it. The police wouldn't listen to me and I think everyone thought I was hysterical and just looking for someone to blame for the accident, which wasn't true. Have some bread,' she said, picking up the pannier and offering it to me. 'You must be starving.'

'I'm fine, thanks,' I replied. 'I'll have some in a moment. You eat if you're hungry.' She put a crusty piece of bread on her side plate. 'Tell me about the note. What was it like?'

'One of those notes where the letters have been cut out from a newspaper and stuck on a sheet of card. Quite amateurish, I guess.'

'And what do you suppose whoever wrote this note meant? Do you think it has anything to do with something which happened in your family's past?' Alex's theory about a distant relative bumping everyone off no longer seemed so far-fetched.

'I don't know, but why kill Michael for it?'

'Maybe he was in the way.'

'In the way of what?'

'Well, what two things do people mostly kill for?'

'Love and money, I suppose.'

'Yes, and in your family there's certainly no shortage of the latter.'

'But that doesn't make sense. The only person who benefited from Michael's death was me...Oh, my God,' she gasped, leaning forward and putting her hands up to her chest. 'It's the same with Grandpa. I'm the one who benefited. You can't think that I have anything to do with their deaths?' I watched her scrutinize my face as if she was trying to read my mind.

'I could, but I don't.' I replied, shaking my head. 'I wouldn't be sitting here otherwise.' I had no reason to believe, at this juncture anyway, that she was telling me anything other than the truth, but I needed to know the sequence of events leading up to Drew's death. 'Tell me why you were so distressed that Friday morning when you came into my office to sign your Will?'

'Drew was in really good form all week. One of the commissions he had been hoping for came up and we planned to go out on the Thursday evening with a group of friends to a restaurant in Hampstead to celebrate, which we did. Drew was very relaxed and happy and we had a great time. We all went to the pub first for a drink and then on to the restaurant. The next morning I remember Drew saying he couldn't find his mobile. He said he had probably mislaid it and he thought he might have left it at the studio as the last time he had used it was when he was there. He was in a bit of a rush, but as he was going out the door he told me to meet him in Covent Garden at six o'clock and said he'd speak to me later. I was running late for our meeting and I was on my way out the door when the post arrived. I didn't have time to open it so I just put it on the hall table for later.'

'That doesn't really explain why you were upset when you came into the office.'

'When I opened the front door there was a bouquet of flowers on my step. They were white lilies and a red rose. You know what that means, don't you?'

'I have no idea.' Flower arranging was not one of my strengths.

'You never put red and white flowers together like that. It signifies death,' she said.

'But whoever put them there must have done that between Drew leaving and you leaving and ran the risk of being seen. That's freaky.'

'I know. But all that week I felt uneasy. Call it my sixth sense.'

'Did you tell the police?'

'Subsequently. But there was no card or anything with them'. The waiter arrived with our side salads and main courses and Isabelle paused for a moment while he served us. I moved the bottle of water and my glass to make way for the dishes.

'I wish you had told me,' I said as I scooped a heaped teaspoon of Parmesan cheese from the little squat metal pot on the table and sprinkled it over my fettucine before passing it to Isabelle.

'Thanks,' she said, taking it from me and shaking a couple of teaspoons of Parmesan on to her risotto. 'What could you have done?' she said, shrugging her shoulders.

'Black pepper?' I asked, with the pepper mill poised in my hand ready to grind it over her food.

'Not for me, thanks. Anyway, I suppose you want to know what happened after I left you.'

'Yes,' I replied as I poured some olive oil and vinegar from the bottles on the table onto my green salad and mixed it in with my fork.

'I spent most of the day with Lucy because the night before she mentioned that she wanted me to go shopping with her. We met up in Selfridges, browsed around for a while and then had lunch. I received a text message from Drew about two o'clock to say he had found his mobile, that he would see me at six o'clock at the studio, and to let myself in if he wasn't there. Since he'd told me to meet him in Covent Garden I thought I would call him to double-check in case he had forgotten our earlier arrangement, but there was no reply so I sent him a text message to say I'd come to the studio instead. I subsequently received another text from him saying he had a big surprise for me so I mustn't be late. It didn't occur to me that anything might be wrong.'

'Well, you wouldn't, not from those exchanges anyway,' I replied, clearing my throat. While Isabelle had been talking I had been eating. 'What happened then?' I asked taking several sips of water.

'There were delays on the tube and I was very late. When I came out of the tube there was one missed call on my mobile and it was Drew saying he was running late but would be there as soon as he could. He'd left the message about five-thirty. I didn't mind because I had the key to the studio anyway, and I didn't suppose he could be much longer. But as I turned into the road I saw that the building was on fire. I couldn't see anything else because there was so much smoke. I tried to get nearer but one of the policemen held me back. I guess I became hysterical and I was shouting at him that my fiancé was in the building and they had to get him out. I asked him what had happened and he said that there had been an explosion.

'He took my details and Drew's and told me that one of the WPC's would stay with me while the fire brigade worked to tackle the blaze and rescue anyone who might still be inside and injured. He said that if Drew was in there, they would find him. But somehow I knew that if he was inside the studio he could not have survived the blast. When the police told me he was dead I must have blacked out or something, as the next thing I remember was one of the paramedics leaning over me.'

'I really don't want to press you,' I said, putting down my fork, 'as I know it's painful for you to talk about this, but when did you become suspicious about his death? Only, when you called me the following Tuesday you seemed convinced that the murders were connected?'

'At first I thought it was an accident. Then the police confirmed that it was murder because someone had deliberately planted a device in the studio to trigger the explosion which started the fire.'

'What sort of device?'

'Whoever set this up knew exactly what they were doing, Alicia. According to the police the explosion was caused by taking the thermostat out of a Teasmaid, filling it with petrol, setting the timer and then waiting for it to overheat and blow. Apparently, that would cause a significant blast and with all the chemicals, white-spirit, turpentine and paints in Drew's studio....' She stopped for a moment and put her head in her hands and took a deep breath. 'It doesn't bear thinking about.' She pushed her plate away. 'I don't think I have any appetite for that now.' She had barely touched her risotto. 'Anyway, after receiving the news that he was dead, I was in such state that the doctor prescribed me something to help me sleep. I think that I was operating on automatic pilot that weekend. I kept asking myself why anybody would want to kill Drew and nothing made any sense.'

'I can imagine. Tell me what happened between then and the time you called me?'

'Lucy stayed with me all weekend, but on the Monday morning she said that she had some errands to run but would come back later. After she left I started to look through Drew's things, but all of sudden I felt really claustrophobic inside the house and needed some fresh air. I always leave my keys on the hall table, and I went to pick them up and I saw a pile of post. I remembered that in my haste to leave to get to you on the Friday I had not opened that day's post. Lucy must have put the post from Saturday and Monday morning there as well. I sifted through it and put everything addressed to Drew aside. Amongst the post for me was a small hard-backed envelope with a typed address label and an Edinburgh postmark. I ripped it open and pulled out the contents. I couldn't believe what I was reading. It was a note just like the one Michael received before his accident two years ago.'

'Really?'

'Yes. And the words were exactly the same as those on his note telling me *"to look to the past to see what the future holds and to make recompense for what those before you have done".* I started to shake like a leaf, my chest felt tight, I couldn't breathe and I felt myself coming out in a cold sweat. I was in a complete panic. I decided to take the note to the police. Now perhaps someone might believe what I have always said about Michael receiving such a note, even though it was never found. The fact that I had received the same note had to mean something. What I couldn't fathom was how Drew fitted in to all this, and then it occurred to me that maybe the murderer intended to kill me and not Drew and somehow the plan went wrong, but how I didn't know.

'But what about the postmark? Do you know anyone in Edinburgh?'

'No. Do you think the fact that it was posted from there is relevant?'

'It could be.'

'On my way out I bumped into my neighbour, William Cole. He's a retired Lieutenant Colonel in the army and looks after the house for me when I'm not there. He was really sympathetic about Drew. He saw that I was in a bit of a state and asked me in. He told me he saw Drew outside the house at about five-thirty on the evening he died. He said Drew told him he was in a bit of a rush because he was meeting me in Covent Garden at six and was running late, that he'd bought some paints and was going to drop them off at the studio, but had stopped off at home first because he'd mislaid his mobile and thought it was there. He even made some joke about hoping I wouldn't be annoyed with him for being late.'

'I thought you said that Drew had sent you two text messages earlier arranging to meet you at the studio instead of Covent Garden, but if he didn't have his mobile then...'

'He couldn't have sent them,' she said, interrupting me and finishing my sentence. 'The call he made to me when he left the voice message on my mobile was from home and that fits in with everything William said. For a split second after William told me all this my mind went completely blank, and then I realized that whoever it was who sent those texts didn't intend to kill Drew at all. They wanted to kill me, which ties in with the note that I received.'

'Did you go to the police?'

'Yes. William came with me. He made a statement.' The waiter cleared our plates and enquired if we wished to have dessert. 'Do you want anything else?' she asked. I shook my head. 'Coffee then?'

'Yes. That'd be good. A doppio espresso for me, please,' I said, turning to the waiter.

'And a flat white for me,' she said, addressing him and then turning back to me said, 'Fortunately, I hadn't deleted the texts that were sent from Drew's mobile or his voice message, so the police have all that to work with.'

'And what about the note? What did they say about that?'

'I think they're taking it seriously. This evidence has put a completely different spin on the murder investigation.'

'I'm sure it has. I mean, it can't fail to have done.' The waiter arrived with our coffee. I waited until he was out of earshot before asking any further questions. 'Tell me about the overdose,' I said, looking up at her as I stirred my coffee.

'It wasn't an overdose,' she said, placing her glass of coffee firmly down on the table almost to emphasise her point. 'That evening I took the pills the doctor had prescribed just as I had every evening of the previous week. But this time soon after taking them I started to feel really strange.'

'What do you mean?'

'Woozy, I suppose. I went to fetch myself a glass of water but my coordination was poor, I dropped the glass, I felt short of breath and I must have lost consciousness as the next thing I remember was coming round in hospital. I was lucky that Lucy came back when she did.'

'Are you sure you didn't take extra tablets by mistake?'

'I don't think so. I know that the paramedics took the tablets away and the doctor at the hospital said that there were a few tablets missing but that, with the type of drug I was taking, I'd have to have taken significantly more to have the effects that I did.'

'So you must have taken something else?'

'I'll come back to that point in a moment. The drug I was prescribed was Diazepam. My understanding is that it's an anxiolytic drug, which means, among other things, it's used to treat anxiety and to help you sleep. It's one of the benzodiazepine tranquillisers which apparently are much safer in the event of an overdose, because you have to take a much higher dose for it to be lethal. I gather interaction with other drugs or alcohol could enhance the effects and precipitate an overdose that might not otherwise have happened.'

'Did the doctor tell you all this?' I finished my coffee.

'I asked him, and also I'm one of those boring people who always read the label or the leaflet inside before taking any tablets to see what the side effects might be. Like not being able to drink alcohol while on the medication, for example.'

'That's not boring. That's sensible. So what caused you to collapse if you didn't take too many tablets or any alcohol or other drugs?'

'A supplement.'

'What kind of supplement?'

'Valerian. Apparently it interacts badly with the drug I was taking and can cause excessive drowsiness or a collapse just like I had.'

'So you did take something?'

'No. It was in my blood stream, but I didn't put it there.'

'But how did it get into your system? There has to be a logical explanation.'

'I don't know. I told the doctor that I've never taken it, but I'm sure they think I'm just saying that. At least they don't feel I'm a case for a psychiatrist.' She beckoned the waiter over for the bill.

'What do you mean?'

'Because if nothing else, they don't believe I wanted to overdose and that it was an accident because I forgot I was taking valerian!'

'Oh, I see.'

'I know it's hard to believe, Alicia, but I swear I didn't knowingly taken valerian. The way I look at it, whoever it was who failed to kill me the first time tried again a second time and is not going to give up until I'm dead. Let's hope it's *not* third time lucky.'

Chapter 18

'What are your plans, Alicia?' asked Isabelle as we walked out on to Chapel Street. 'Only, do you fancy coming with me to meet my grandmother? I know there's much more we need to talk about, but I really need a bit of a rest first. You could stay and chill by the pool and have dinner with us if you like.' I sensed she really wanted me to say 'yes' and I was curious to meet Grandma Edie, but I was not sure how she felt about strangers descending on her unexpectedly.

'That's very kind, but I wouldn't want to impose.'

'You wouldn't be. She thrives on company. Please come. I'd really like it if you did.' I felt I could not disappoint her.

'OK. I'd love to.' By agreeing to come I now had the opportunity to talk to Grandma Edie about Grandpa Jam, the family background and particularly his marriage to Diane Latham. I was eager to ask Isabelle about John MacFadzean, Lucy, and Luisa, but I did not want to push too hard as I knew that she must have found talking about Drew's death emotionally draining.

'Have you been to South Yarra before today?' I shook my head. 'Well, if you like fashion it's the best place to be. Chapel Street is the main drag. You've got trendy shops and very chic cafés like the one we've just been to. Toorak Road is equally fantastic with its designer boutiques.' As we continued our journey to Glen Iris Isabelle chattered on about shopping and travel and places of interest to visit in Melbourne. It was as if she wanted to talk about anything apart from the murders. I was amazed how calm and collected she was given the circumstances. She appeared to be trying to black out everything horrid.

Grandma Edie's house was set well back from the road and we walked down the long leafy drive to the front terrace. I could smell the exotic fragrance of the frangipani trees bordering the drive.

'Grandma's particularly fond of her oleanders. Aren't they lovely?' said Isabelle, pointing to some red and pink ones. 'She also has the white and yellow varieties.'

'They're very beautiful; but aren't they poisonous?'

'Yes, incredibly. The whole plant is. The toxins cause heart failure. Not so long ago somebody died after drinking herbal tea made by boiling oleander leaves which they mistook for eucalyptus, and skewers of oleander wood used in cooking meat have led to fatal poisoning. I suppose I should be careful what I eat in case the murderer is following me.'

'That isn't something to joke about, Isabelle!'

'I wasn't intending to be funny. I'm being perfectly serious. Oh, look,' she said, changing the subject, 'Grandma must have seen us. She's coming out.' I observed a tall, wiry, silver-haired figure in a floral print dress approaching us from the other end of the drive and I sensed a slight limp in her walk. Isabelle quickened her pace until we were almost running down the drive. 'Gran,' she said, dropping her bag, flinging her arms around her and giving her an enormous hug before bursting into tears. I stood back feeling rather awkward as if I was intruding on this moment of shared grief.

'Hello, my darling,' she said, holding Isabelle tightly. 'It's all right. Let it all out.' I noticed that her eyes, which were bright blue, were filled with tears. 'You will get through this,' she added, rubbing Isabelle's back with one hand while continuing to keep the other arm around her. We must have stood for about five minutes while Isabelle sobbed her heart out on her grandmother's shoulder. At some point, I suppose, she would have to have released all that pent-up emotion. 'Come on, dry your tears,' said her grandmother. 'Let's go in.'

'Do you have a handkerchief?' asked Isabelle, lifting her head off her grandmother's shoulder, glancing over to me and sniffing as she rummaged in her coat pocket. Her face was tear-stained from all that crying. 'I don't seem to have one.'

'I have some tissues,' I replied, pulling out a small packet of Kleenex from my handbag. 'Here,' I said, handing them to her. 'Take these.'

'Thanks.' She took one out of the packet, wiped her eyes and blew her nose.

'Aren't you going to introduce me to your friend?' asked Grandma Edie, addressing Isabelle but looking at me intently.

'Oh, of course. I'm sorry, Alicia; you must think me very rude,' she said, giving her nose another blow. 'Gran, this is Alicia Allen. She's the lawyer I told you about.'

'How do you do?' I extended my hand.

'How do I do, indeed? I'm doing just fine.' She grasped my hand with both of hers. 'Please come on in. You are staying to dinner, aren't you?' she added as she picked up Isabelle's bag and we walked up the steps to the front terrace.

'I really don't want to put you out.'

'You're not. Besides I enjoy young company.'

'See. I told you,' said Isabelle, smiling.

'You don't work for the estate lawyers, do you?' asked Grandma Edie. We were sitting on the terrace drinking Lemon, Lime and Bitters. Isabelle had gone to her room to rest as she was evidently exhausted both emotionally and physically by recent events.

'No. Isabelle instructed me to make her a Will. She came to me because she wanted to do that independently from Holmwood & Hitchins. I have nothing to do with the Probate of her grandfather's estate. They are still dealing with that for her.'

'I didn't think there was the remotest possibility that you could be connected with that firm.'

'What makes you say that?' I was slightly perplexed.

'She trusts you. She would not have brought you here to meet me otherwise.'

'May I talk plainly with you, Mrs Parker?' I wanted to ask her some questions and from what Grandma Edie had already said I felt that she would be amenable to answering them.

'Of course,' she replied, offering me a slice of her home-made carrot cake. I took a piece and placed it on my plate. 'And please call me Edie.'

'Thank you. I'm not quite sure how I should put this as there is no easy way of saying what I have to say.' I put a forkful of carrot cake into my mouth. It was delicious, particularly the topping, and simply melted on my tongue.

'What is it? It sounds serious.' I cleared my throat.

'I don't wish to alarm you but you need to be aware that Isabelle is in grave danger. Drew was not killed in an accident. The police now have evidence that he was murdered and...'

'Oh, my God!' she said, putting her hands up to her face. 'Murdered? Drew? But why? It doesn't make any sense.'

'No, it doesn't, but that's because Drew wasn't the intended victim. We believe that whoever killed him actually intended to kill Isabelle, which is why she's in danger.' I watched her turn pale. 'There is a possibility that the murderer of Drew and her brother is one and the same.' I sensed that she was listening to me intently.

'But Michael died two years ago. The police concluded it was an accident. I know that Isabelle believes he was murdered, but there was no evidence to substantiate it and of course the note was never found.' Evidently she was fully apprised of those details.

'And what do you believe?'

'I had my doubts, but I admit that I tried to put Isabelle off pursuing her case with the police at the time.'

'Why?'

'Because I felt that she was banging her head against a brick wall, and it was hurting her more. How can you be so sure that the murders are connected?' She was sitting in the chair opposite me and leaned directly forward as she asked the question.

'Because Isabelle received a note too.'

'What?' She sounded incredulous. 'But when?'

'It arrived on the morning of Drew's murder, only she was in a hurry to leave home and left her post unopened. What with Drew's death and everything, she didn't get around to opening it for a few days. Tell me, did you speak to Isabelle last week?' I had no intention of mentioning the 'overdose' and I did not think it necessary in the context of our conversation. It was the time leading up to it in which I was interested.

'Well, yes, a couple of times, but all she would say was that the police were investigating what had happened to Drew. I presumed she didn't want to talk about it. I was anxious to go over to London but she said the journey would be too much for me and, anyway, there was no point because she intended to come out here. You see I had a car accident a few months back, broke my hip and had to have a replacement. I'm absolutely fine, but she worries about me travelling.' Hence the slight limp I had noticed earlier.

'Isabelle has asked me to help her find the murderer. The problem is I know very little about her family background and from what she has told me I don't think she knows very much about it herself. I was wondering if you could fill me in on some details.' I looked at her expectantly.

'I'd be happy to help you – especially if it takes you any further forward in catching whoever is responsible – but my knowledge of the family back in the UK is fairly patchy. What do you want to know?'

'Tell me about James Latham. What sort of a man was he?'

'What do you mean?'

'What was he like? The reason why I ask is that Isabelle believes that his death last year wasn't accidental either. I suppose what I'm asking is if you think he was the sort of man who would have had enemies. I don't expect you really know much about his life because you've lived out here all these years, but how did you rate him personally?'

'He was quite autocratic. I first met him just after Matthew, that's my son, and James' daughter, Mary, became engaged. I don't think he ever warmed to Matt. I always felt he was a little too possessive of Mary and he certainly didn't want the marriage to proceed.' That corroborated what Isabelle had already told me.

'Do you think that was because he lost his first wife, and then his second wife and daughter died, and so it wasn't that he was possessive of Mary, just that she was very precious to him?' To me that seemed a perfectly logical explanation for his behaviour.

'Yes, but he was quite a dominant person. He was somewhat controlling towards Mary. Perhaps, Alicia, I'm not the best person to ask. My judgement is slightly coloured. You have to remember that he blamed my son for the boat accident and death of his daughter and then had nothing to do with Michael and Isabelle for several years. I don't say too much to Isabelle. She was very fond of her grandfather and in later years he was very good to her but, in the beginning, it was extremely difficult. After my husband and I brought the children to live in Melbourne I went to enormous lengths to try and persuade him to be a part of their lives. I think when he finally came out here I had almost given up.'

'Well, it's to your credit that you persevered and brought them together. Do you know anything about Mary's stepmother Diane Latham?'

'Very little. She died many years before I met James. What makes you ask?'

'When Isabelle first came to see me, she mentioned something which you had told her about her grandfather's second marriage.' She leaned forward and furrowed her brow as if she was trying to recollect what that might be. 'How did you know that Diane ran off with their daughter, that they were both killed in a car accident and James blamed himself for what happened?'

'Ah, yes,' she replied. 'Before Mary and Matt were married we stayed at Stowick House and the housekeeper showed me around the estate. Naturally, the tour started in the mansion and I recall there was a magnificent portrait of Diane in the library. I don't know whether it's still there. Anyway, we were talking and I remember saying what a tragedy for someone so young and beautiful to lose her life. She told me that James had never got over her death and the loss of Frances, their daughter. She said that he had been enormously proud of Diane, but he could be quite possessive of her. If I'm absolutely honest, Alicia, I can't exactly remember what she told me because this conversation took place nearly thirty years ago. But I'm sure she made some comment that James was jealous over Diane's association with any other men. She said that James never spoke about what happened.'

'Why do you think she told you this?'

'Because she felt sorry for him and wanted me to understand a little more about him and the family into which my son was marrying.'

'Who was the housekeeper?' I wondered whether this was the one to whom James Latham had left £20,000 in his Will.

'Mrs Banks. I remember her distinctly because she reminded me of my drama teacher when I was a child.'

'Do you know what happened to her? Only she doesn't work there now.'

'No, I don't suppose she does,' she replied, and let out a half-chuckle. 'She seemed pretty near retirement age then. If she's still alive she would be even older than me.' It occurred to me that if Dorothy's friend Emily knew Diane she might also have known the housekeeper who would probably be a great source of information.

Everything Grandma Edie was telling me was building up a rather negative picture of Grandpa Jam. Nonetheless, I did not believe that he had anything directly to do with Diane's death, nor was I convinced by Alex's theory that he murdered her. Indirectly, of course, his jealousy could have destroyed their relationship and ultimately make her want to flee from him – which was perhaps why he blamed himself for her death and had never forgiven himself for what had happened to her. I was interested in Grandma Edie's views on the subject.

'Do you think he might have killed her?' I asked her straight out.

'And risk killing his child? No. I believe it was an accident. Why do you ask?'

'I'm just trying to ascertain whether there's reason for anyone to hold a grudge against the Latham family. If I could establish the motive then that would help.'

'Do you think that it is to do with the inheritance?'

'It's a strong possibility. I'm sure money has something to do with it. Tell me, from what you said earlier I had the impression that you weren't very keen on Holmwood & Hitchins either. Have you had any dealings with Isabelle's trustees?'

'My husband used to deal with all the legal things, but I know who they are if that's what you're asking.'

'Then you'll know who John MacFadzean is?'

'Yes.'

'And that he's been murdered?'

'I saw it on the news. It was quite a shock actually. I haven't had a chance to talk to Isabelle about what's happened. Do you think his murder has something to do with the other ones?'

'Quite possibly. Why do you think Isabelle doesn't trust the firm?'

'She disliked the way her trustees treated her after Michael died. I think there were problems over administration of the trust fund and advancing money to her.'

'I see…how well do you know Lucy Winters?' I asked, moving slightly away from the subject.

'She's a lovely girl and she's been a very good friend to Isabelle. After Michael died she really supported her through some of her most difficult moments. They've known each other since university. Lucy's also very artistic, so they have a lot in common. They've always been close, more like sisters than friends.'

'But what do you know about her family background?'

'Not much. She's actually a Sydney girl. You'll have to ask Isabelle. What makes you ask?'

'I'm trying to find out about anyone who's close to Isabelle or who has benefited by knowing her or has befriended her recently. How much do you really know about any of Isabelle's friends?'

'Oh, I see your point. But surely you're not suggesting that Lucy has anything to do with these murders?' She seemed genuinely aghast that I might. I did not have a chance to respond because Isabelle walked out on to the terrace. It bothered me that she might have heard what I had just said to her grandmother because, although I intended to ask her about Lucy anyway, that would be a brutal way of doing it. Fortunately, she did not seem to have overheard our conversation.

'You talking about me?' She pulled up a chair and sat down at the table.

'How are you feeling, darling? Did you manage to rest?' replied Grandma Edie, ignoring Isabelle's question.

'A little. What have you two been chatting about?' She helped herself to a piece of her grandmother's home-made carrot cake. 'Do you want some more?' she asked, with the knife poised to cut me another piece.

'No, thanks. I haven't finished this piece yet. Your grandmother has been trying to help me shed light on what's been happening.' Isabelle looked over to her grandmother and back at me expectantly. I sensed she was hoping that her grandmother had come out with some revelation which would bring resolution to the matter and give her peace of mind. I wished I could tell her that was the case.

'I'm sorry, darling,' said Grandma Edie. 'I don't think that the murders are going to be solved on anything I have to say. I'm going to make a start on dinner.' She got up from the table, collected the dirty plates and glasses and put them on the tray. 'I know you two have a lot to talk about. You are still staying to dinner?' she added, addressing me.

'Yes,' I replied, looking at my watch. 'But I should call Jeremy and let him know that I'll be back late.'

'Jeremy?' quizzed her grandmother.

'He's the friend I'm staying with in Melbourne.'

'Why don't you stay the night,' said Isabelle. 'There's plenty of room and I can lend you anything you might need. We look as if we're the same size. It would be a lot easier, and then you don't have to worry about the time or getting back tonight.'

'Well, only if you're sure,' I answered, looking at her grandmother for confirmation.

'No problem at all,' she said, smiling at me. 'You can stay in the room next to Isabelle's.' She disappeared into the house with the tray.

'Why don't you call Jeremy now,' said Isabelle. I had turned my mobile off after I met up with Isabelle that morning. It beeped when I switched it on. There was a text message from Alex:

How's it going? Any news on the whereabouts of IP yet? Call me when you have a moment. Your A

I wondered what Alex would make of all this. I decided to text him or, preferably, give him a call later when I was alone. By then I might have gleaned a little more information.

'Somebody's popular,' said Isabelle.

'I don't know about that. That was a text from a former colleague who also went to my friend's wedding in Brisbane. He had to have an emergency appendectomy last weekend. He's in hospital in Nambour.'

'The poor thing. At least he can recuperate in the sunshine.'

'Yes. There is that.'

'I'll leave you to make your call.' Isabelle stood up.

'Oh, you don't have to leave on my account.'

'I need something to drink,' she said as she walked across the terrace to the door of the house. 'Can I bring you anything?'

'I'm fine, thanks.' Isabelle disappeared inside and I 'phoned Jeremy. There was no response on his landline so I called his mobile.

'Hi, Alicia. How's your day going?' It sounded as if he was walking along the street because I could hear traffic in the background and I strained to hear him.

'Eventful.'

'What do you mean?'

'Isabelle turned up this morning. She's here in Melbourne. She called me and I've spent most of the day with her. I'm now at her grandmother's house in Glen Iris and they've asked me to stay the night. You don't mind?'

'Of course not. I appreciate you letting me know. You must have been relieved to hear from Isabelle. I know you were worried about her.'

'Yes. I still am.'

'Have you've managed to talk to her about what happened to her fiancé and John MacFadzean?'

'Only the former. We haven't got around to discussing the latter yet, but I hope to.'

'Good. Fingers crossed you make some progress. Listen, while you're on the 'phone, I spoke to Paul about Luisa Bruneschi.'

'Oh really. What did he say?'

'She's worked at the *Courier Mail* for a couple of years. She's very good at her job apparently and at getting results. He said she's ambitious so she'll probably move on before long.'

'Nothing extraordinary then?' I suppose I had not really expected him to turn up anything shady about her. I began to question my instincts.

'No. But at least you know. Have a productive night. I'll see you tomorrow.'

'Thanks Jeremy.' Isabelle returned with a plate of nibbles but not her drink.

'Grandma thought you might want something to pick at before dinner. Would you like a glass of wine? You can have anything you like. You just have to ask.'

'Wine's fine. Doesn't your grandmother want any help in the kitchen? I can't just sit here and do nothing. There must be something I can help with?'

'You are helping by being here. Red or white?'
'Red, thanks.'

While Isabelle went to fetch the wine I sent a quick text message to Alex:

With IP. Long story. Hope u r OK. Speak later. A x

'Grandma thought you might like to try some wine from the Victoria region,' said Isabelle, taking the glass of red wine off a tray and putting it down on the table. I noticed that she was drinking fruit juice. 'It's a Rutherglen Durif. The Durif is unique to Australia. I hope you like it. Help yourself to something to eat,' she added, passing me the plate of nibbles. The olives looked particularly inviting.

'Thanks.' I took a couple.

'I love it here.' She sat down and looked out into the garden. 'It's so peaceful and restful. I suppose,' she said, taking a deep sigh and turning towards me, 'we should talk.'

'We are talking,' I replied, trying to make light of the situation. I knew perfectly well what she meant. 'I appreciate it's really difficult for you, Isabelle, to talk about recent events. You've been through so much, but there's still so much I need to know. Why did you discharge yourself from hospital the other night? Did something happen to make you want to leave?'

'I had a visit from Jonathan Masterton that afternoon. You remember I told you that his children Timothy and Mark used to come and play with Michael and me up at the house?' I recalled that she had.

'You never mentioned their names before. Is that the Timothy who brought Lucy back to the apartment the night of your 'alleged' overdose?'

'Yes, but how do you know that?'

'Sally Hamilton told me. She's the one who called to tell me that

Drew had been killed. When you mentioned his name I presumed that he must be the same Timothy. I'm just trying to figure out where everyone fits in. Sally said he was a friend of Lucy's. Is that correct?'

'He met her through me. It must be about seven years ago now. I think it was the first Christmas she and I were at university together. She came to the UK with me. She's got family over there you see. Anyway, he and Lucy hit it off as soon as they met. He came out to Australia for a year or so a few years back and travelled all over the country. He stayed with Lucy's family in Sydney. I think he has a bit of a soft spot for her. He looks on her like a little sister.'

'Really? What's he like?'

'Quiet. I've always thought that he never has much to say for himself. I prefer Mark, the younger brother. He has more of a personality. Lucy disagrees. She likes Timothy a lot.'

'Is he a lawyer as well?'

'No. I think he's some sort of academic. Now you ask me I'm not sure what he does. You'd have to ask Lucy that. She'd know for sure.'

'I see. Sorry, Isabelle, I interrupted you when you were talking about Jonathan Masterton coming to see you in hospital.' I intended to ask her a little more about the Masterton children but we could come back to that. I was also interested in finding out more about Lucy's family background, particularly now that Isabelle had mentioned she had family in the UK.

'Yes. He came to tell me about John MacFadzean's murder and that they've discovered that he had been withdrawing money from the trust – to cover his gambling debts, no doubt. They think that he owed someone an awful lot of money, couldn't repay it and that's why he was murdered.'

'Who do you mean by 'they'? The police, his fellow trustees or both?'

'I presumed both. Why are you looking at me like that, Alicia?'

'What do you mean?'

'As if you know something I don't.'

'Well, maybe I do. Let me explain.'

'I wish you would. I don't know what's going on. It's bad enough trying to keep a grip on my life right now without trying to second guess everything.'

'I'm sorry, Isabelle. What I'm about to tell you may sound bizarre but is absolutely true. I met John MacFadzean on the plane on the way to Singapore.' She did not say a word but I could tell she was listening to me intently because she was looking at me hard and barely blinking. 'He chatted about his background and work. He said he got the job at Holmwood & Hitchins through a friend he'd worked with in Australia. That friend has to be Jonathan Masterton, don't you think?'

'Yes,' she said, nodding in agreement, 'that makes sense because Jonathan did live in Australia for a while.'

'Anyway, I didn't think any more about John MacFadzean and then, of course, he was stabbed to death. Having heard the news of Drew's murder, your suspected overdose and John MacFadzean's demise my mind was racing. I'm sure that MacFadzean's murder is linked with these other events.'

'But how?'

'I had some initial thoughts and then I met your friend Luisa and she told me her theory on MacFadzean's murder.'

'Luisa. She contacted you?' I nodded. 'So what's *her* theory?'

'The same as Jonathan Masterton's.'

'And what do *you* think, Alicia? Do you agree?'

'It's a very good theory and is a possible explanation for his murder, but I'm not convinced that's what happened.'

'You mean because it doesn't deal with your point about his death being connected to what's been happening in my family?'

'Exactly. Maybe he found out who the killer is and tried to squeeze him or her for cash.'

'Blackmail then?'

'Yes. But unfortunately for him it backfired. The thing is, Isabelle, there is something else you need to be aware of. If what you've told me about the overdose is true, then whoever it was who tried to kill you must be close to you, or in a position to get close to you. How else would they be able to administer the valerian to you or engineer a way of you taking it?'

'You mean one of my friends?' She swallowed hard.

'I can't swear to that Isabelle. That's what we have to find out. I know it seems improbable, but it is definitely not impossible. And what about the loss of Drew's mobile? The likelihood is that it was stolen from him the night before he was murdered, either when you were both in the pub or the restaurant. Don't forget, whoever took it sent you those messages pretending to be Drew. It has to be someone closely connected to one or both of you.'

'I'm trying to remember who was there. There were a lot of people and quite a few of them were associated with Drew through his art, so I don't really know them. If I knew who to trust I could find out about them.'

'The trouble is, Isabelle, I don't think you can afford to trust anyone right now.'

Chapter 19

'At least I have you. You are the only person I can trust,' she said. I felt the weight of emotional responsibility resting heavily on my shoulders and I was slightly uneasy about it. 'Will you come with me to the police?'

'The Victorian State Police, you mean?' I was quite happy to talk to the British police too, if that was what she wanted.

'Yes. You haven't spoken to them yet, have you?'

'No. I decided to wait until we'd discussed it. I'm sure what I have to say won't add much to the investigation though.'

'Well, it might if you tell them your theory about John MacFadzean's murder.'

'It's worth a shot I suppose. But what about the police back in the UK? I'm really surprised that they aren't treating the overdose as suspicious, especially as they now know that you were the intended victim at the studio and not Drew and have the note you received.' I had my suspicions that they were running a covert investigation.

'Is that what Sally told you?' I looked at her quizzically. 'About the overdose, I mean?' I nodded. 'Good. That's exactly what the police want everyone to believe.' So the police were proceeding just as I thought. 'Apart from you, I haven't told anyone what's going on.'

'Not even Lucy?'

'Especially Lucy! She'd never be able to keep up the pretence. If I tell my friends the truth they'll start behaving oddly around me – which is precisely what the police don't want.'

'Of course. You seem to have more confidence in the police investigation than you had the night you asked for my help.'

'Well, yes, but only because they now believe what I've been telling them and are taking some action. I'm glad I asked you to help me. I feel reassured talking to you. I don't know what I'd do without your continued support. You have incredible insight and a way of analysing what you've gleaned and making sense of it.' I did not feel that I was currently making sense of anything despite her flattering remarks.

'I'm only telling you what I think, that's all. How do the police say they will handle the investigation?'

'They're hoping that their smokescreen will lull the murderer into a false sense of security and he or she'll get careless.'

'And what about your safety in the meantime? If John MacFadzean's murder is connected with Drew's, then Melbourne may not be the safe haven you think it to be.'

'That thought has crossed my mind. But to be honest with you I don't feel safe anywhere right now. What puzzles me, however, is how the murderer managed to kill Drew and then get out here to kill MacFadzean unless...' She rolled her eyes up as if she was mulling something over.

'Unless what, Isabelle?'

'Drew's murderer had an accomplice. It's a possibility, don't you think?'

'Yes. Definitely.' It was good to know she was on my wavelength. 'But apart from the fact that it would be more practical for the murderer to have an accomplice out here, we have nothing to substantiate our assertions.'

'You know something, Alicia.'

'What?'

'I can't hope thinking we're wrong, because if we're right whoever it is might be out here now. In which case I'm glad you're with me.' I shifted uneasily in my seat.

'Let's see what the police have to say tomorrow.'

'Yes. OK.'

'Do you intend to 'phone Lucy? Only she'll be worried sick because she hasn't heard from you.' If Lucy was involved, calling her might be a risk but I felt it was one Isabelle should take.

'I picked up her voice mail messages when I arrived. I knew she'd be worried so I sent her a text message to let her know I'm safe. She responded asking where I am but I haven't got back to her yet. I'll give her a call after dinner.'

'What are you going to do about Holmwood & Hitchins?' I asked, changing the subject. 'Jonathan Masterton must be worried about the stolen trust funds.'

'He is. He wants my reassurance that he won't be held liable for what John MacFadzean did. I couldn't give it to him. I need to find out what his liability is as a trustee first. There's also another trustee, Christopher Berkeley – but I've never had much to do with him. Are they liable, Alicia?' I was not surprised that Jonathan Masterton was *very* concerned about his position. In his shoes I would have felt the same.

'Well, without the full facts I can't really advise you, but I can give you some general guidance if that helps.'

'Please.'

'By misappropriating trust funds John MacFadzean breached his position as trustee. The question is whether the remaining trustees, who are each equally responsible for the administration of the trust fund, should be held liable for any loss suffered as a result of John MacFadzean's actions. I suspect that Masterton and Berkeley will argue that they shouldn't be held personally liable for the stolen funds, because that was down to the fraudulent actions of John MacFadzean and something about which they had no knowledge and over which they had no control.

'Equally, as co-trustees, they could be held liable if it is found they wrongly permitted John MacFadzean to have control of the trust fund thereby enabling him to take the money. It depends on the circumstances, but you can see why Jonathan Masterton is very anxious right now.'

'Yes, but this just gets worse.' Isabelle furrowed her brow.

'Do you trust Jonathan Masterton, Isabelle?'

'I did, but after everything you've just told me I'm not sure what to think anymore, Alicia. I'm scared and I don't know which way to turn. I want to wake up and for this nightmare to be over.'

'I know. But your grandfather must have thought highly of Jonathan Masterton as he recommended him to the firm and continued to instruct him up to his death.'

'I suppose he must have done, and don't forget he knew Jonathan Masterton's father so I think that had something to do with it.'

'Do you know how he knew him?' This connection was niggling at me.

'I remember asking Grandpa about his association with Jonathan's father, but he said it didn't matter how he knew him and got a bit testy with me. When I pressed him on the point he mentioned something about the father knowing Diane and doing him a favour.'

'Are you certain that's what your grandfather said? It sounds a bit ambiguous. I mean, who was doing who the favour?' Finally, I felt that we might have touched upon something of significance.

'I can't tell you for sure. Do you think that it's important?'

'Yes, I do.'

'How do you mean?' Isabelle sounded completely confused.

'Well, whoever was doing who the favour, there is clearly some link between the Masterton family and yours dating back to the time your grandfather was married to Diane. Your grandfather isn't alive, so we can't ask him. Do you know if Jonathan Masterton's father is still alive?'

'Yes he is.'

'Good. If we can reach him we have a chance of uncovering what ties the two families together.' That was presupposing he would talk to us, of course. It was certainly worth pursuing.

'I felt that Jonathan Masterton was embarrassed to have to tell me about John MacFadzean because he was his friend. Having met John MacFadzean I wouldn't have put him down as someone who was corrupt. It just goes to show what a poor judge of character I am.'

'I'm sure Jonathan Masterton is mortified; but don't forget he's also trying to fend off a potential claim against him and probably hopes that, because of the long-standing relationship with your grandfather, you'd view him more favourably,' I replied cynically. It seemed to me that Jonathan Masterton was only interested in saving his own skin. 'As for John MacFadzean, you had no reason to think him dishonest. I certainly didn't when I met him. I took him on face value. I'd very much like to meet Jonathan Masterton though. I'm curious about him.'

'Well, you can. I'll have to see him when I go back due to all this business with the trust, but I have decided to disinstruct the firm in any event and move my affairs elsewhere. I would like to instruct your firm, but in the circumstances understand if you felt you could not act for me now. I have asked too much of you already and certainly beyond the bounds of a solicitor and client relationship. Please do not feel obligated in any way.'

'I'm sure we can work something out,' I replied, slightly sidestepping the question and changing the subject. 'Are you certain your grandmother doesn't need a hand? She's been in there for ages and I feel bad sitting out here.'

'She's fine. She knows we need to talk.' I sat back and savoured a sip of my red wine. I had been so engrossed in our conversation that I had not touched it. 'She'll call us when dinner's ready.'

'Whatever she's preparing the smells coming from the kitchen are giving me quite an appetite. Now what was I going to ask you,' I said, toying with the rim of my wine glass, 'Oh yes. Whereabouts in the UK is Lucy's family based?'

'Why?'

'I'm interested.'

'Hampshire. The relatives are on her grandfather's side. She goes to stay with his brother's branch of the family. She was down there the night of the 'overdose'.'

'Really? Only I thought she was seeing friends that night in Hampshire.'

'She could have been. They are probably friends of the family or something. What makes you ask?' Poor Isabelle must have felt as if I was interrogating her.

'I just wondered. So, if Lucy's family are originally from the UK, how did she come to live in Australia? Did her parents emigrate or move out here to work?'

'Her grandparents emigrated to Sydney back in the early 1960s, I think. Lucy's mother was two when they moved, so to all intents and purposes she's an Australian like me. She doesn't remember her life in the UK at all.'

'She wouldn't. Not at that age. Do you know her well?'

'Oh yes, and I suppose I've grown quite close to her. She's the mother I've never had. It's quite apt I suppose that I should think of her as a mother figure because Lucy and I are like sisters in so many ways.'

'What do you mean?'

'She treats me like a daughter. I feel like part of her family. I don't exactly have much family of my own, so it means a lot to me. I have Grandma Edie, of course, and she's a wonderful grandmother but...

'You miss having a mother?' I said, finishing her sentence.

'Yes. Lucy's grandmother's a real sweetie as well. She was widowed a few years back and now lives in the granny flat they built for her at the back of the main house. She's very arthritic but she likes to be independent.'

'Why did she and her husband emigrate to Australia?'

'Apart from Claire, that's Lucy's mother, they had another daughter. She was a bit older than Claire but she died from leukaemia. I think Lucy's grandmother had a breakdown after she died and they decided to make a fresh start completely away from everything and everyone.'

'They couldn't have moved much further than Australia.

Whereabouts in Sydney do they live?'

'On the North Shore. Lavender Bay. It's a stunning location and only a ferry ride across the harbour to the city. All the surrounding area around is fantastic and has a great atmosphere. You haven't been to Sydney yet, have you?'

'No. I hoped to but I'm running out of time on this trip. I have to return to London next week.'

'Oh, that's heaps of time yet. Why don't you come with me to Sydney tomorrow or the day after? I could show you around and you can meet Lucy's family and judge them for yourself.' That was a tempting proposition because, apart from John MacFadzean, Luisa and Grandma Edie, I had not met any of the people associated with Isabelle who were possibly 'in the frame'. I had based virtually all my suppositions on what I had heard third hand and not what I had been told in person. If I could glean anything out of this trip it was worth taking.

'OK. I'd love to come with you. It's a shame I won't meet Lucy.'

'Yes, I know, but you can do that when we get back.'

'Have you ever met her family in the UK?'

'Yes. Once. A couple of years ago. I stayed with Toby and his wife Gemma. I liked him a lot, but can't say I was keen on *her.*'

'Oh, I see. Why don't you like her?'

'I think it's more a case of her not liking me. I certainly haven't done anything to make her dislike me, not wittingly anyway. Oh, I don't know. It's probably one of those things.'

'So, how are Toby and Gemma related to Lucy?'

'Toby's her mum's first cousin. So he's Lucy's grandfather's brother's son. I think that's right.' She rolled her eyes upwards as if she was thinking about it. 'Yes. It is. Why do you ask?'

'I'm trying to build up a picture of all the people who are close to you.'

'You can't believe that Lucy has anything to do with this can you? I mean she's my best friend. She has never been anything other than good to me.'

'You said earlier that Timothy Masterton came out to Australia,' I replied, avoiding the question. She nodded. 'I suppose he must have contacts here through his father.'

'I guess he does, but I don't know anything about that. I...' She paused momentarily and looked straight ahead but I could tell from the concentrated expression on her face that she was thinking very hard about something.

'What is it Isabelle?'

'I was trying to remember what Timothy told me about his grandfather's background. I thought it might help us work out what the connexion is between the two families. I'm sure he said that his grandparents moved out to Sydney when his father was a teenager, but they never really settled well there and the whole family returned home ten years later.'

'Interesting. How old is Jonathan Masterton? We can easily find out, but do you have any idea?'

'Mid-fifties I would say. Why?'

'Because that would mean his parents also emigrated to Australia in the 1960s, just like Lucy's.'

'But that's coincidental surely. What are you suggesting?'

'I'm not sure, but don't you think it's strange that they all came out here around the same time and not long after Diane's death?'

'I think you have a point regarding the Mastertons, but not Lucy's family. There was no connection with her family and mine back then.'

'So far as we know, Isabelle.'

'I'm more interested in Jonathan's father,' she replied, sweeping aside my comment. 'If you're right and he didn't move out to Australia until the 1960s he would have been living in the UK before that and around the time Grandpa married Diane.'

'Well, yes. That would tie in with what your grandfather told you.'

'Do you think Grandpa had anything to do with Diane's death, Alicia? It has crossed my mind that he did and that all these murders in the Latham family are being carried out by someone with a vendetta against us.'

'And psychopathic tendencies, Isabelle.'

'Hmm... The thing is I don't know if Diane's death was an accident, but I have to find out. Grandma Edie only knows what she's been told. It's very frustrating.'

'It is. Right now I have no idea whether your grandfather was involved or not. But my instinct and everything you have told me point towards the fact that Diane is the key to these murders. That's why we need to find out more about her.'

'I've all Grandpa's personal papers back in London. He used to keep them in his study at Stowick House. When I went through them I don't recall seeing anything, but it was only a cursory look. To be honest with you, I've been remiss about the house. I just arranged for it to be closed up after Grandpa died. It was all too upsetting for me to go there. But it's probably time I did. Maybe you would like to come with me when I come back to the UK.'

'Of course I will.'

'You know, Alicia, if Grandpa did kill Diane then I have to accept that,' she said, returning to the point. 'Then I'd be able to deal with it. It's the not knowing that I find hard to cope with. What else can I tell you?' Isabelle sounded exhausted and I was conscious that she had been answering my questions all day.

'I was going to ask you about Luisa, but that can wait until another time.'

'No, it's OK. My mind's a bit overloaded with all of this, that's all. What do you want to know? You've met her, so I'd say you'd have formed your own opinion of her.'

'What makes you say that?'

'By the way you analyse everybody and everything.'

'I suppose I have a view, but I'm keen to hear what you have to say about her.'

'I've known her a few years. She bumped into me at the Melbourne International Arts Festival – literally.'

'Yes. She told me.' That corroborated what Luisa had said.

'She's great to be around.'

'Would you categorize her as a close friend?'

'Well, she's a good friend, but we're not close like Lucy and me, no. We generally catch up when I'm over in Australia although she was in the UK a few weeks ago. That's when I told her about you.'

'She was very interested in your legal affairs. She asked me a lot of questions.'

'I don't think you should read too much into that, Alicia. She always does. I think it's part of her make-up and what makes her a top journalist.'

'Hmm…'

'You don't sound convinced. She's got a heart of gold, honestly. She'd do anything to help you if you were in trouble.'

'Maybe I'm naturally suspicious. What about Timothy Masterton? I suppose she knows him through Lucy?'

'No, I don't think so. I'm pretty certain they've never met.'

'And of course you know Sally Hamilton.'

'Yes, she's a chatty one. I don't see her that much as she works such long hours. I'm so glad she recommended you. I have every confidence in you, Alicia.' I wished I shared her faith in my own abilities to help her bring the murderers to justice. I felt myself coming out in a cold sweat at the prospect of fulfilling her expectations – and of the danger ahead.

Chapter 20

'I can't hear what you're saying, Alicia. Can you speak up?' I was lying on top of the bed in the room next to Isabelle's speaking to Alex. Isabelle and I had not continued our discussion over her grandmother's delicious roast dinner and she had disappeared, I presumed, to call Lucy and then gone to bed. This was the first opportunity I had had to 'phone to Alex all day. I was pleased he was feeling much better, the visit from Antonia and Tom had gone well and that he was leaving hospital in the morning.

'I'm sorry, Alex. I can't talk any louder,' I replied softly, almost in a whisper, 'but I thought I heard Isabelle open her bedroom door and I don't want her to know I'm calling you. I haven't told her about you yet.' I had spent almost twenty minutes relaying to Alex everything I had discussed with her and Grandma Edie during the day.

'That's OK. You must be tired of repeating it all anyway. Sounds like you've had a day of it. At least Isabelle's all right.'

'But what worries me is that she isn't. Apart from all the emotional trauma, I have serious concerns about her personal safety. Don't forget the murderer has already tried to kill her twice.' Isabelle's comment about 'third time lucky' preyed on my mind.

'And you believe that whoever it is will strike again?'

'Yes, I do. The more I think about it the more I'm sure we're looking for a psychopath.'

'Hmm… I've been thinking about all these murders.'

'And?'

'Have you considered why Michael was murdered two years ago, Grandpa Jam six months ago, Drew a few weeks back and John MacFadzean last week?'

'No. I suppose the murderer could have made plans to kill them and then waited for the right opportunity to execute them.'

'Great turn of phrase, but I don't agree, Alicia. Why murder Michael two years ago and then wait to kill the others?'

'You don't think Michael was murdered by someone else, do you?'

'No. That's not what I'm suggesting. Besides, if what Isabelle has told you about the note is correct, and we have no reason to doubt at this stage that she would be lying, then Michael's murder bears the same pre-murder hallmarks as Drew's.'

'What *are* you suggesting?' I replied, stifling a yawn. I was feeling exhausted and overloaded with murder theories. I had almost passed the stage where I could take on board anything else, for one evening at least.

'Was anything significant due to happen around the time each murder took place?'

'I don't know.' I had not thought to discuss that with Isabelle. I had been more concerned to ascertain what she knew about the murders themselves.

'Well, it's something you might want to look into. I may be completely on the wrong track, but I was thinking about this today and it struck me as an avenue to follow. You can blame me if it turns out to be a dead end.' Bearing in mind we had very few leads I was grateful for Alex's input nonetheless. He was an invaluable support and I found it beneficial to be able to swap ideas with him. I had every intention of following up on his suggestion.

'Everything is like a maze, right now I feel as if there are a lot of false turns; and that I've got about one hundredth of a jigsaw puzzle.'

'Which one hundredth might that be?' Alex was laughing.

'It's not funny. Isabelle is relying on me. I can't believe what I've got myself into, and don't say "I told you so"!' I said, all in one breath without giving Alex the chance to speak.

'I wouldn't dream of it. Just make sure you tell me where you're going.' I presumed he meant physically and not with the case itself.

'You mean in the event I disappear?'

'In the circumstances it's only sensible for someone to know where you are. I think you're right about the link with Diane Latham, and the connection between the Lathams and the Mastertons needs further investigation. Are you going to Sydney with Isabelle?'

'I will, because I want to meet Lucy's family in the hope of discovering something that links them to Isabelle's.'

'Hmm… How long do you think you'll be there?'

'I'm not sure yet. I don't know what Isabelle wants to do.'

'When are you flying back to London?'

'Next week. I have no idea what Isabelle's plans are. She might want to stay on here, although I have the feeling that she is eager to return to London and sort out all the trust business with Jonathan Masterton, and for me to go with her to Stowick House.'

'That will be interesting for you, to meet Jonathan Masterton, I mean. Actually that reminds me, what's happening with Dorothy's friend?'

'I need to chase that up, but thanks to Grandma Edie we now have the name of the housekeeper so we can make some enquiries. Anyway, enough about Isabelle. How about you? How long are you going to stay at the Sunshine Coast?' I could not help thinking what a pity it was that our trip had been cut short, but I had been focusing so much on Isabelle that I really had not had time to take stock of my own life.

'For a few days, but it isn't going to be much fun for me up there alone and I can't go surfing right now, so we'll see. I think I'll try and leave for London as soon as I feel well enough to make the trip. We probably won't see each other until we're both home, which is a shame. But if I get back first I'll do some research for you. Do you still want me to find out about Drew's background?'

'I'm not sure whether you need to, now that we know he wasn't the intended victim. Although it might be worth finding out if there was anyone hanging around Drew trying to get close to Isabelle. That's another possibility. It would really help me, however, if you could do the research we discussed before.'

'Consider it done. Just give me the details and I'll see what I can dig up. When are you going to the Victorian State Police?'

'Tomorrow. Goodness knows what they'll make of my theory about John MacFadzean's murder.'

'You might be pleasantly surprised.'

'Now wouldn't that make a change?'

'OK. *Ciao, bella!*'

'*Buona notte, carino.*'

After Isabelle and I had arrived at the police station and given our name and address details and reason for being there, we were ushered into an interview room by one of the police officers. He told us that the detective in charge of the investigation was on a call, but would be with us shortly. We sat and waited and waited. Isabelle was very restless and started to fidget.

'What's taking him so long?' she said, standing up and pacing the floor. 'This place gives me the creeps. I feel like a criminal coming in here. It's horrible.'

'I'm sure they only put us in this room to give us some privacy. I don't think we'll have to wait much longer.' Indeed, a few minutes later the door opened and a stern looking woman with shiny brown hair swept back into a sleek pony-tail and wearing a navy blue trouser suit and a crisp white shirt entered the room. She was carrying a clipboard.

'Sorry to keep you,' she said, glancing first at Isabelle who was standing by the window and then at me, but clearly taking us both in as she sat down opposite me. Isabelle came to sit in the chair next to mine. I sensed she was pleasantly surprised that the investigating officer was female. 'I'm Detective Inspector Morris. I understand you have some information on the murder of John MacFadzean.'

'Yes. I'm Alicia Allen,' I replied, extending my hand which she took.

'And you must be Isabelle Parker,' she said, turning to Isabelle. 'If what it says on this sheet is correct,' she added blandly, looking down at the piece of paper attached to the clipboard.

'Yes, that's right.'

'You're English,' said DI Morris addressing me. 'What is your connection?' she asked.

'Well, I…'

'Let me explain the background details,' replied Isabelle, interrupting me and putting her hand out to stop me talking. 'Then it will make sense why we're here.'

'Please. Go ahead.' DI Morris sat back in her seat looking slightly bemused.

'You are probably aware through your investigations that John MacFadzean was a Partner at the London firm of Holmwood & Hitchins. But what you may not know is that the firm is dealing with the estate of my grandfather, James Latham, and that John MacFadzean was one of my trustees.' I was watching DI Morris's expression very closely but it certainly gave nothing away to suggest what she might be thinking.

'Please go on,' she said.

'I understand from one of his fellow Partners that John MacFadzean stole trust funds. It is believed that he was a compulsive gambler and had substantial debts. It has been suggested to me that he was murdered by someone he could not repay. But I note from the media reports here that it is alleged he was the victim of a terrible mugging and that this is the line of enquiry the police are following?' Isabelle paused for a moment, I assumed hoping for some response, but DI Morris did not comment. 'Only, it is our contention that neither of these hypotheses provides the motive for his murder,' she continued.

'I'm listening,' said DI Morris, leaning forward with her elbows on the table. Finally, Isabelle had grabbed her attention.

'A couple of weeks ago my fiancé was murdered in an explosion at his studio.' I noticed Isabelle swallowing hard. It was obvious she was finding it difficult to talk about Drew's death. She took a sharp intake of breath. 'I won't waste your time with all the details, but you can check with the police back in London,' she said, opening her handbag, taking out an envelope and putting it on the table. 'These are the details of the police dealing with the enquiry,' she added, pushing the envelope towards DI Morris. 'The bottom line, Detective Inspector, is that the police now believe I was the intended victim, not my fiancé.'

'I am very sorry to hear what you are telling me, Miss Parker,' said DI Morris opening the envelope and quickly scanning the contents, 'and it is evident that you have been through a great deal of trauma. But how is the murder of your fiancé connected to the murder of John MacFadzean – apart from the fact that they both knew you? I fail to see how what you have told me takes us further forward.'

'Maybe I can assist,' I replied, stepping in. I felt slightly frustrated by DI Morris's attitude, particularly as I could see Isabelle was becoming distressed. It appeared that she might burst into tears any moment. 'In my opinion, John MacFadzean could have been murdered due to his connection with Isabelle's family.'

'And how are you qualified to give an opinion?' She was dismissive.

'Alicia is a solicitor and has been advising me. I wanted to be independent from Holmwood & Hitchins and Alicia was recommended to me. She knows all about my family background.'

'I see. So what do *you* think is the motive for John MacFadzean's murder, Miss Allen?'

'We believe he discovered who the murderer is and tried to blackmail him/her. That would give the murderer a motive to kill him.'

'And you have evidence of this?'

'Not yet, no, but…' DI Morris raised her eyebrows.

'Look, I don't mean to be rude, but I have another appointment,' she said, looking pointedly at her watch. 'So, unless there's anything else?' She peered first at me and then at Isabelle.

'There is actually,' I replied. 'By some strange twist of fate I met John MacFadzean on my flight here. It was when I heard that he had been murdered that I began to think there was a link between the murders in Isabelle's family and his murder. Although, I don't believe he was killed for the same reason they were.'

'What do you mean murders? I thought it was only your fiancé who was murdered?' asked DI Morris, addressing Isabelle. I was encouraged that she had been paying attention to what Isabelle and I had been telling her.

'My brother was killed two years ago. I believed he was murdered, but some of the evidence went missing. It's all a bit complicated but there are pre-murder similarities with the murder of Drew and my brother. I also believe that my grandfather was murdered.' DI Morris looked incredulous.

'It is our contention that the killer is someone close to the Latham family, has strong ties with Australia and may have an accomplice here,' I said, continuing the conversation on Isabelle's behalf. 'We did not come here today to waste your time. We came because, whether you follow up what we have told you or not, we decided that you should be aware of us, Isabelle's connection with John MacFadzean, and the fact that she may be in danger here in Australia. I'm sure you will appreciate that.'

'I have your details, so I can contact you if there are any developments. How long will you be in Melbourne, only we might need you to make statements?'

'We're intending to travel to Sydney tomorrow for a couple of days,' said Isabelle. 'I may return to Melbourne but I think I ought to go back to London. I have affairs to attend to there.'

'And you, Miss Allen?'

'I'm flying back to London next week as I have to return to work. I may come back to Melbourne before I do, but if it makes things easier I'd be quite happy to make a statement now. I'm sure Isabelle would too,' I added, glancing at her. She nodded in affirmation. 'So, if you want us to do that, we'll stay on.'

'OK. That would be helpful. I have to make a move but I'll get that arranged on my way out. Do you guys want a cup of tea or something?' I sensed that she was mellowing towards us.

'Water for me, please,' said Isabelle.

'A cup of tea, milk no sugar for me, thanks,' I said.

'Well, thank you for coming in.' DI Morris stood up and offered her hand to each of us in turn. 'I'll be in touch if I need to ask you any more questions,' she added with a faint hint of a smile.

By the time Isabelle and I left the police station it was mid-afternoon and we had nearly spent most of the day there. I felt drained and Isabelle looked it. It was a relief to be outside in the fresh air. We found a lovely open-air café and ordered some tea.

'Do you think DI Morris thinks we're crazy?' said Isabelle, picking up her teacup. 'Do you fancy a cake or anything?' she asked, looking over at the adjacent table. 'That cheesecake looks particularly divine.' I shook my head.

'She was a bit frosty at first, but I thought she warmed to us *eventually*. I'm sure she'll mull over what we've told her. Bearing in mind the police here already knew John MacFadzean worked in London, I can't believe that she hasn't been liaising with the UK police. I felt she was simply playing her cards close to the chest. So, no, I'm sure she doesn't think we're crazy – well, not completely anyway. Actually, I felt quite embarrassed when she asked me what evidence I had, but I half expected her to raise her eyebrows when I told her I didn't have any. We didn't get around to asking for protection for you. Let's hope she follows up on what she's heard. Did you speak to Lucy last night?' I asked, digressing slightly.

'Yes. Sorry, I clean forgot to tell you.'

'That's all right. Did you tell her where you are?'

'Yes. I think she was relieved to hear from me. She seemed quite surprised that I've come to Melbourne. I didn't mention that you were with me though.'

'But she's in contact with Sally who, as you know, has been keeping me informed about what's been happening. And don't forget, you originally asked Sally for my number and then for her to pass on a message for me to call you urgently. She'll probably think that you've tried to get in touch with me. I haven't spoken to her since she sent me a text to say that you'd discharged yourself from hospital and had disappeared. It's likely she'll 'phone or text me.'

'Yes, that's a point.'

'In any case, as we're going to Sydney to see Lucy's family, she'll soon find out that I'm with you. I presume you mentioned the trip to her?'

'Well, I said I intended to go there, yes. I was tired when we spoke and wasn't really thinking straight. I thought it best to say as little as possible about you. I'm concerned that by getting involved with my affairs you will be endangered.'

'I'm already involved, and believe me I have already considered the dangers. I don't think it matters that any of them know we've seen each other. If Sally asks me awkward questions I can easily dodge them. I did that when Luisa probed. It isn't a problem. I think we could do with the assistance of someone independent. There is someone I have in mind.'

'Who?'

'You remember that former colleague I mentioned?'

'Yes. The one who's just had the appendectomy?' I nodded.

'His name's Alex Waterford. I know he'd be willing to help you if I asked him.'

'If you think he can, and he's trustworthy, I'm not going to object. I will of course pay him for his time and any expenses he incurs. But is he well enough after his operation? You'd have to fill him in on everything.'

'No problem.' Alex was familiar with most of the facts already so that was hardly an onerous task. 'He's staying on in Australia until he feels up to travelling home so you'll meet him when we return to London.'

'But we could see him when we come back from Sydney – or if you have to leave for London I don't mind going up to the Sunshine Coast alone.'

'OK. I'll give him a call later and we can take it from there.' Talking about Alex reminded me of the remark he had made the night before. 'I have another question I'd like to ask you following on from our discussions yesterday.'

'Go on.'

'Was anything significant due to happen around the time each murder took place?'

'Michael's twenty-fifth birthday was coming up a few weeks after he died and that's the only thing I can think of.'

'What about when Grandpa Jam died?'

'Nothing to speak of. Is that your mobile or mine?' she asked, delving into her handbag.

'It's yours,' I replied. She retrieved her mobile.

'It's Luisa,' she said, scanning the screen. 'Hello... What...? Were you...? She is.' Isabelle looked at me and smiled, so I presumed Luisa was asking about me. Obviously I could only hear Isabelle's side of the conversation. 'Meet up...? What now...?' Isabelle glanced at her watch. 'Oh, OK. See you in Federation Square in half an hour. Bye.' She put her 'phone down on the table. 'I'm sure you caught most of that?'

'Yes. Did Luisa know I was with you?' I assumed that she must have guessed, or was checking because she knew I was in Melbourne.

'No. She asked if you were with me. Lucy told her I was here. She was berating me for not calling her and wants to meet us...'

'Yes, I heard the last bit of the conversation. I suppose we'd better start making tracks soon,' I said, picking up my cup and finishing my tea.

'Isabelle,' exclaimed Luisa rushing towards her as we walked up the steps from the embankment and into the Square. She gave Isabelle a hug. 'How are you bearing up? I'm so sorry about Drew. I don't know what to say. Why didn't you tell me you were here? I can't believe I had to receive a call from Lucy to find out you're in Melbourne. We've been so worried about you.'

'It is fortunate, then, that all Isabelle's friends are so close that you keep each other informed as to her welfare and whereabouts,' I commented sarcastically.

'What have you two been up to today? Anything I can help with?' She ignored my comment, but I knew she had taken the point.

'We thought we'd go out for the day. Isabelle said she wanted a change of scene and needed to do some shopping.'

'It hasn't been a very successful day then as you haven't bought anything.'

'There was nothing I wanted to buy,' Isabelle swiftly replied. She was quick to follow my lead. 'Perhaps I wasn't really in the mood for shopping. I just wanted something to take my mind off things.'

'How did you two meet up then?' asked Luisa turning to me.

'I was in Melbourne as you know. My office rang and said that Isabelle had left a message for me to call her, so I did and here we are,' I replied nonchalantly.

'Yes. Here you are.' I had the strongest feeling that Luisa would have preferred it if I was not there because that she wanted to talk to Isabelle alone. I thought I might give her that opportunity. We had walked across Federation Square and up towards the main shopping area of the city.

'I'll just have a peek in this shoe shop,' I said, engineering it. 'You two carry on. I'll catch up with you.' I strolled inside the shop. I looked through the shop window and watched Isabelle and Luisa amble slowly up the street. One of the sales assistants distracted me for a second so I glanced away. The next thing I heard was an enormous thud and the screeching of brakes. 'What was that?' I asked the sales assistant who had spoken to me as she was rushing outside the shop.

'I think somebody's been hit by a tram,' she said, pausing momentarily in the doorway.

'What on earth? Oh, my God! Isabelle!' I exclaimed, charging out of the shop after her. I stood and looked up and down the street, but there was no sign of either Isabelle or Luisa. I could feel my heart pounding in my chest. As I dashed towards the front of the tram my view was obscured by a group of people who had gathered to see what the commotion was all about, but Isabelle was simply nowhere to be seen. Then much to my relief I espied her hunched over on the pavement on the other side of the road. A young man, whom I presumed to be a passer by and/or witness to what had occurred, had crouched down beside her and it appeared that he and the tram driver were talking to her. There were several other people hovering about as well. I could not see the young man's face clearly, but he had his arm on Isabelle's back and seemed to be comforting her. Luisa had vanished completely out of sight. I hastened across the road to Isabelle's side.

'Are you OK?' I asked gently, bending down. 'She's my friend,' I said, addressing the young man and the tram driver. The young man was clean-shaven and fresh-faced, probably in his late twenties or early thirties, and he was wearing a chic Italian suit. I assumed he was a young professional on his way home from work.

'I...I....I don't know what ha...pp...en...ed,' she stammered. 'One minute I was wa...wa...walking across the st...st...reet and the next thing the...the tram was there.' Clearly she was in shock. I noticed that the heel from one of her open-toed mules was missing and she was nursing her right wrist.

'I don't understand,' I said, looking up at the tram driver hoping for some kind of explanation. 'The last time I saw her she was walking up the road and not across it. Didn't you see her?'

'She was suddenly there in front of me. I slammed on the brakes.' The poor man sounded distraught. 'I've been a tram driver for nearly twenty years. Nothing like this has ever happened before,' he added, running his fingers back through his greying hair. 'I'll radio my supervisor but I have to wait for the police to come before I can move the tram.' He walked back across the road and climbed back into the driver's seat.

'How about you?' I said, turning to the young man. 'Did you witness what happened?'

'Not completely. I was on this side of the road. My office is only up the street,' he said, turning his head in the direction where his office must be. 'I noticed that there was a fairly large group of people at the stop. Somebody must have jostled her as she was walking passed and she stumbled into the path of the tram. I pulled her to safety across to this side of the road.' That must have been how she lost the heel of her shoe and hurt her wrist.

'Did any of you see anything?' I said, standing up and addressing the small group of people who had gathered around Isabelle. None of them seemed to have done. Maybe I was paranoid but I could not help but look at these people with suspicion. For all I knew, any one of them could have pushed Isabelle into the path of that tram. If the murderer was among them, I would never know. After the group of people dispersed, Isabelle and I were left with the young man.

'You saved my life,' said Isabelle weakly. 'I don't know what to say.'

'Yes. You did. That was some good deed,' I added, smiling at him.

'Oh, it was instinctive. I didn't have time to think about it. She's lucky she wasn't seriously hurt though,' he replied, returning my smile.

'So are you,' I said. 'You both could have been.'

'Don't you think you should go to the hospital? You've had a nasty shock and it looks like I bruised your wrist when I grabbed you,' he said to Isabelle.

'No. I'm all right. I just want to go home.'

'Can I help you at all?' he asked.

No. Thank you. You've done enough. But you could tell us your name so we can thank you properly.'

'Gerry.'

'Thank you, Gerry,' I said. He helped Isabelle up. I wanted to talk to him but I lost my chance because two policemen arrived on the scene wanting to talk to us. Isabelle reassured them that the injury to her wrist was minor and they seemed satisfied that she did not have to attend hospital. The last thing Isabelle needed was the trauma of attending the police station again. I explained that we had actually spent most of the day there providing information relating to the murder of John MacFadzean and had spoken to DI Morris. The policemen confirmed that they would probably need to question Isabelle, but that could wait until the morning.

'I want to make sure you're home safely,' I said as we sat in the back of the taxi on our return to Glen Iris, 'but I really need to go back to Jeremy's tonight. I'd like to pick up some fresh clothes for a start.'

'Oh, OK. Why don't you pack all your stuff because you may not have the chance to come back to Melbourne if we go up to see Alex when we leave Sydney. You are still coming with me to Sydney tomorrow, aren't you?' Tomorrow would be Saturday. It was incredible to think that it was almost a week since Kim's wedding. After the events of the past seven days that happy occasion seemed like a distant memory. By all accounts this had definitely been a memorable week, albeit not quite the one I would have envisaged when I first arrived in Australia.

'I guess you should wait until you've spoken to the police before making any definite plans for tomorrow, Isabelle. Don't misunderstand me. It makes no difference to me. I'm quite happy to fall in with you. I just need to know how the land lies.'

'I'll call you in the morning and let you know what's going on.'

'OK. Where did Luisa disappear to?' I asked, changing the subject.

'She said she had to go. She left me after you went into the shop.'

'That's a bit odd, don't you think? For her to rush off like that I mean, especially when she asked to meet up with you. Are you sure what happened back there was an accident, Isabelle?'

'Yes. I didn't deliberately try and throw myself under the tram.'

'That's not what I'm getting at. I know you didn't. Did somebody push you into the path of the tram?'

'There were a lot of people waiting at the stop. They did surge forward when they saw the tram coming. I felt somebody shove me but it all happened in a matter of seconds.'

'It could have been intentional. What if we were being followed and after I went into the shop and Luisa left, whoever it was took the opportunity to strike?'

'In the middle of a Melbourne street in broad daylight?'

'You can't afford to rule it out, Isabelle. You're lucky Gerry was there.'

'I'm aware of that. Where did he go?'

'I don't know. He vanished. He must have gone when the police were talking to us. I expect they have his details though because they'd have taken a statement from him. One thing's for sure. Your guardian angel was certainly watching over you today.'

Chapter 21

'Do you think Luisa did it?' asked Alex. 'Knowing what you think about her, I can't believe it hasn't crossed your mind that she saw an opportunity and took it.' It was now late evening, I had arrived back at Jeremy's house and just relayed to Alex the day's events – including Isabelle's unfortunate encounter with the tram. Alex had discharged himself from hospital and had returned to the apartment on the Sunshine Coast where he planned to stay for the next week or so.

'Instinct tells me that she isn't quite what she seems, but accusing her of attempted murder is a completely different matter altogether. I admit it did occur to me that she had something to do with it, but even if she did, she can't be involved in Drew's murder and the overdose incident because I'm pretty certain she wasn't in the UK on either occasion.'

'You'd need confirmation of that. What about your accomplice theory? She was in Australia when John MacFadzean was murdered. You met her for lunch in Brisbane the day before so you know she was there then. But *was* she actually there the night of his murder? For all we know she may have been in Melbourne. You should check that out. She could be the Australian connection.'

'Jeremy has a contact who used to work at the *Courier Mail* and knows Luisa.'

'Really?'

'Yes.'

'Maybe he can make a few discreet enquiries for you.'

'I hope so. I agree that we need to find out if she was in Melbourne the night MacFadzean died. She certainly knows a lot about what happened to him. After all she was the one who told me he was a gambler, and nothing about his habit was reported in the press.'

'Yes. But she'd know about it if she's involved in his murder or is working with someone in the UK, like Jonathan Masterton, for example. I bet he already knew about John MacFadzean's gambling. I think you could be right about MacFadzean discovering that Masterton is the murderer and blackmailing him?'

'Hmm… Possibly.'

'You sound doubtful. I thought you were convinced that Jonathan Masterton's involved. After all, Masterton knows about the family, he worked with MacFadzean, and he is connected to Australia.' Alex had evidently given great consideration to my comments since we had last spoken.

'I know what I said. It's just so bizarre. We haven't even met Jonathan Masterton and we've decided he's our prime suspect. As for Luisa, even if we establish that she had the opportunity to commit the murder, what about motive? Why would she do it?'

'That's what we need to find out. Perhaps somebody offered to make it worth her while. As for what happened today, I reckon that when Luisa saw Isabelle crossing the road and the tram approaching she grabbed her chance. It wasn't pre-meditated. It must have been a spur-of-the-moment thing. Let's face it. In the time between her leaving Isabelle and supposedly walking up the street, that crash would have been well within her earshot. Why didn't she come back?'

'It did strike me as odd that she seemed to have completely disappeared.'

'We work well as a team, don't you think?' asked Alex, going off at a tangent.

'I guess we do. Your input has been invaluable. I can't tell you how grateful I am.'

'Maybe you can tell me in person quite soon. I have no objection to you showing me either…' he added glibly, and then paused momentarily. 'Any chance you'll make it back up here before you fly home?'

'There is, actually. Isabelle wants to meet you. I hope you don't mind but I told her you might be able to assist us. I should have run it by you first. I'm sorry, Alex.'

'You don't need to apologise. I'm happy to help.'

'Thanks. I need all the help I can get.'

'When does she want to meet?'

'She suggested that we fly straight from Sydney to you. What do you think?'

'Fine by me. I would have preferred to get you on your own, but if it means I get to spend some time with you, I'm happy. Let me know when you're likely to be here.'

'The police are coming to interview Isabelle tomorrow morning about the tram incident and her intention is that we fly across to Sydney in the afternoon. I expect we'll stay there for a couple of days. We'll probably be with you on Monday or Tuesday. I was planning to fly back to London next Saturday, so that I'm home on Sunday ready for work the following Monday.'

'Perhaps we can all fly back together. I'll feel up to facing the plane journey by then. Did you ask her about the time of each of the murders?'

'Yes, I did.'

'And?'

'She couldn't think of anything significant.'

'That's disappointing. I was sure we'd get somewhere on that. Oh well, it was worth a shot. Call me when you get to Sydney. Take care. *Ciao, bella.*'

'How's Alex?' asked Jeremy, looking up at me over his reading glasses as I walked into the family room where he was reading a newspaper.

'He's good. He's much better, especially now that he's out of hospital.'

'Yes. Tom called earlier. He sends his love. Antonia's on her way back to London, of course. He said that Alex was in very good form when he and Antonia saw him but was missing you, I understand,' he said, with a glint in his eye. 'You've been having an eventful time by all accounts. Anyway, tell me how you are? Are you making any progress? Did you go to the police?'

'In answer to your questions: fine, sort of and yes.'

'How did you get on with the police?'

'The Detective Inspector was a bit brusque to begin with but I think, at least I hope, she's going to follow up what we told her. As for the investigation itself I'm quite frustrated. We have all these theories but nothing definite.'

'Is there anything I could help you with?'

'Yes, there is actually. You could do me a favour.'

'I will if I can.'

'Paul gave me his card, but I can't find it and I want to get in touch with him. Could you give me his details?' He nodded. 'I need to ask him something else. I'm trying to ascertain whether Luisa was in Brisbane on 4 March when John MacFadzean was murdered.'

'As opposed to Melbourne you mean?' he replied knowingly.

'Exactly.'

'I take it that you suspect her of being involved with John MacFadzean's murder then?'

'That's the general idea, yes.'

'I'm more than happy to call him again because you've got enough on your plate.'

'Thanks, Jeremy. I really appreciate it.'

'No worries. What are your plans? You know you can stay on here as long as you like.'

'I'd love to. I really like this city. The thing is Isabelle has asked me to go with her to Sydney for a few days and then up to the Sunshine Coast to meet Alex. He's agreed to help us.'

'That's good of him. Well, you do what you have to. At this rate you'll have to come back to Australia for another holiday. I don't suppose you've had much time to relax?'

'I did in Brisbane and I managed to get to the beach at Alexandra Headland. I've really enjoyed my stay in Melbourne and at least I've seen some of the city. If I get to see the sites of Sydney, I won't have done too badly. I'll certainly remember this holiday though.'

'I'm sure you will. Listen, I'll call you when I've spoken to Paul. You look tired. Try and get a good night's sleep. By the sound of it you're going to have a busy time in Sydney. I hope the trip is worthwhile for you.'

'So do I. Goodnight, Jeremy.'

Although I was keen to visit Sydney I was itching to return to London and start my research. In the space of the two weeks since I had left London, so much had happened most of which seemed unreal. I could never have imagined that I would become embroiled in a murder investigation which would involve sleuthing on the other side of the world.

Jeremy was right; I was exhausted and needed sleep. I had only slept fitfully the night before because my head was spinning with thoughts about the murders especially after everything Isabelle had relayed to me. Fortunately, I had been able to discuss the matter with Alex, bounce ideas off him and obtain his input. I felt relieved and reassured that I had his support and assistance.

The next morning I received the anticipated text message from Sally. It read as follows:

Lucy says she spoke to Isabelle and that you're with her in Melbourne. Glad that she's safe and well. Catch you later. Take care. Sally

I sent the following message in reply:

Hi Sally. Thanks for the text. All is well here. Home next weekend. A

Isabelle told me that she had not mentioned to Lucy that I was with

her, so I deduced that Lucy must have received that information
from Luisa on the 'friends' network. Lucy would have passed on the
news to Sally, hence the latter's text message to me. Lucy and Luisa
were evidently close; at least that was how it appeared. The more I
mulled over recent events the more I was drawn to the conclusion
that Luisa was somehow connected to the murder of John
MacFadzean. Luisa might only be friendly with Lucy in order to
retain her confidence and obtain details of Isabelle's life.
Alternatively, and more alarmingly, she and Lucy could be in league
together. After all, Lucy was close enough to Isabelle to administer
the overdose.

Isabelle 'phoned me just after nine to say the police would be
with her around ten. She had booked us on an afternoon flight to
Sydney and insisted on paying for my flight despite my protestations. She had also spoken to Lucy's mother who was expecting us
for dinner. Since I had packed earlier I set out for Glen Iris straight
away. By the time I arrived at Grandma Edie's house the police had
already left, but Isabelle was in good spirits and I presumed the
interview with the police had proceeded smoothly.

'How did it go?' I asked.

'Fine. I told them what I told you. I was just grateful that Gerry
was there and I didn't end up under the tram. I asked for his details
so that I can send him something by way of a thank you. He liked
you, you know.'

'What makes you say that?'

'The way he was looking at you when he was talking to me. He
didn't take his eyes off you.'

'I think you're mistaken. He was just concerned about you.
Talking of which, how are you feeling? I mean you look quite cheery
but...'

'I'm bearing up. I spoke to Drew's parents last night. I wanted to
know what was happening about the funeral. It won't be for a couple
of weeks but I'm not going to stay on here. I'll come back to London
with you. I still can't believe I won't see him again.' She took a deep

breath and sighed. 'Did you manage to speak to Alex?'

'Yes. I called him last night. He's more than happy to help. He's expecting us after we've finished in Sydney.'

'Oh good. I don't suppose you had time to fill him in on everything.'

'He has the general picture, but I think it will be mutually beneficial for you to meet. Have you heard from Luisa today?'

'No. Why?'

'I just wondered. I had a text from Sally.'

'You said you'd hear from her. What did she say?'

'That Lucy told her you were here.' I did not mention that she knew Isabelle was with me, and my theories vis-à-vis Luisa and Lucy. Rather than make an adverse comment about Lucy, and bearing in mind we were about to meet Lucy's family, I refrained from saying anything at all. This trip to Sydney might provide the answer to some of my questions about Lucy's background.

We arrived in Sydney at around four-thirty that afternoon. I was disappointed that we did not fly in over the Harbour Bridge and the Opera House as I was looking forward to an aerial view of those famous city sights. We caught the train from the airport into the city. It only took about fifteen minutes to Central Station and then a few minutes more from City Circle to Circular Quay.

'We're staying in Kent Street, near the historical Rocks area,' said Isabelle as we stepped off the train. 'I thought you might appreciate that. And before we fall out over this, I'm paying for your accommodation. It's the least I can do bearing in mind you are here at my behest. Let's take a taxi up to the hotel. I don't fancy the hike in this boiling sunshine and with these bags,' she said, looking down at the luggage at her feet. 'I thought we could settle in and then walk back down here. I'm sure you'd like to wander around Circular Quay and have a look at the Harbour Bridge and Opera House.'

'Yes. Well, since I'm here it would be a pity not to do a little bit of sightseeing. What time are we expected for dinner?'

'Not until after eight. So there's plenty of time. The ferry goes from Wharf 5 to McMahons Point. You'll get a great view of the harbour during the crossing.'

'I'm looking forward to meeting Lucy's mother and grandmother, especially since you speak so highly of them,' I said to Isabelle as we sat drinking our iced coffees at an Opera Quays Café overlooking the impressively large natural harbour. I had a direct view of the Harbour Bridge – known to Australians as 'the coathanger' so Isabelle reliably informed me – looming majestically over everything. It was a glorious summer's evening, and the whole area in and around Circular Quay was bustling with people. There was no shortage of tourists milling about, and Sydneysiders making their way home across the harbour or en route to a rendezvous with friends. It was still stiflingly hot and I was grateful to be sitting out of the sun.

'Talking of which we should be making a move,' said Isabelle, looking at her watch. We walked down to Wharf 5, bought some ferry tickets and, by the time we returned, the ferry – a double-decker with a green-painted hull – had arrived. We proceeded through the ticket barrier and made our way on board. I decided to sit on the front deck, enjoy the view and take advantage of the cooling sea breeze and the slight spray off the water. The first stop was Milsons Point. As the ferry pulled away from the wharf Isabelle pointed out the Olympic pool and the vividly painted face of the clown marking the entrance to Luna Park on the way over to our stop, McMahons Point.

'Oh, look,' said Isabelle as we stepped off the ferry and walked from the landing stage up on to the road. 'There's Claire, Lucy's mum. How sweet of her to come and collect us.' She quickened her step in the direction of the silver Mercedes estate parked on the other side of the road and I hurried along after her. Isabelle opened the front passenger door and popped her head inside. 'Claire. It's great to see you.' She clambered in and extended her right arm around Claire in a semi-hug. I climbed in at the back.

'You too, darling.' She hugged her back and clasped her tightly. I sensed that she truly cared about Isabelle. 'I'm so sorry about Drew,' she said softly. 'It's such a tragedy. None of us have words to express how much we feel for you. If there's anything we can do, you know you only have to ask. Lucy's been worried sick about you.' There was real emotion in her voice and I detected nothing other than genuine concern for Isabelle.

'Thank you. That means everything to me. I'm just happy to be here. You know how much I value you all.' Isabelle then turned to me and said, 'Claire, this is my lawyer friend, Alicia, the one I mentioned to you on the 'phone.'

'It's a pleasure to meet you, Alicia,' said Claire, swivelling around in her seat to shake my hand. 'Any friend of Isabelle's is always welcome.'

'Thank you. I'm very pleased to meet you too, Mrs Winters.'

'Oh, please. Call me Claire.' I sat quietly in the back listening to her conversation with Isabelle as she drove home. 'Gran's looking forward to seeing you,' she said, addressing Isabelle.

'How's she been?'

'Her arthritis is making her life progressively more difficult, but she's not letting it get in the way of her independence. Lucy called this morning. It's such a shame she's not here, but I understand that you decided to make the trip out on the spur-of-the-moment,' she added, glancing sideways at her fleetingly. 'I suppose you had to get away.'

'Something like that. I needed to leave London and I wanted to see Grandma Edie.'

'How is she?' How's her hip?'

'She's fine. Her hip's good.' It was evident that Isabelle had a close relationship with Lucy's mother from the easy relaxed manner between them. We turned into a tree-lined residential road and parked outside a fairly sizeable late-nineteenth or turn-of-the-twentieth century Federation house with a green picket fence. We walked along the path towards the front door. There were a few steps up to a gate leading on to a veranda which ran all the way around the front of the house. The screen door and front door were both open as if whoever it was inside the house was expecting our arrival imminently.

'Claire, is that you?' a woman called out. There was a slight quaver in the voice. I presumed this was Lucy's grandmother. Then I heard the tapping sound that a stick makes on a wooden floor as somebody walks across it.

'Yes, Mum, we're home,' replied Claire as we all walked in to the hallway where the frail figure of Lucy's grandmother was waiting for us. She reminded me immediately of Dorothy, physically at least. 'You shouldn't have come out, Mum. Isabelle didn't expect it.'

'Hello, Gran,' said Isabelle, stepping forward and giving her a hug.

'Hello, my darling,' she replied warmly. Again I saw nothing other than genuine affection for Isabelle. Maybe my theory was way off the mark, but then I had not had the benefit of meeting Lucy, so I was not in a position to assess her. Mind you, if she was anything as caring towards Isabelle as her mother and grandmother were, then it seemed inconceivable that she would want to do anything to harm her. Although Isabelle had left Lucy one million pounds in her Will, which would give her a motive to kill Isabelle had she known about it, it certainly did not explain the other deaths in the family for which she appeared to have no motive either – or the death of John MacFadzean.

'Alicia,' said Isabelle, turning to me, 'Let me introduce you to my surrogate grandmother, Granny Whiteley.' I shook her hand.

Claire ushered me into the living room and I looked around while I waited for her to return. Nobody had mentioned a Mr Winters, and on scanning the room I observed there were a number of framed photographs but mostly of Lucy. I was curious and thought I might discreetly ask about him over dinner. What I did notice on a side table were three framed photographs of three young women whom I presumed to be Gran, Claire and Lucy taken when they were all of similar age. On returning to the room Claire must have seen me scrutinizing them.

'Each of those photographs was taken when we were aged twenty-one respectively. What do you think?'

'I haven't met Lucy, but she looks very like you, at least you have the same colouring and set of the eyes.' From the photographs I noted that Lucy was dark-haired just like her mother, although Claire's hair was more salt-and-pepper now. It was strange because I had imagined Lucy to be blonde for some unknown reason. 'Do you take after your father?'

'What makes you say that?'

'Only that you look very different from your mother.'

'Well, I don't think I look like either of my parents. It's always been a standing joke in the family that I'm a throwback or something.'

'You should research your family background. I believe we need to know where we come from to know where we're going. I've always been very interested in my family history.' I was interested to see what reaction I would elicit from her.

'I've never really thought about it, to be honest. I suppose I'm quite happy with my lot and besides I've never had the time.'

'Aren't you curious about your roots in the UK? Isabelle said your parents emigrated to Australia in the 1960s when you were two.'

'It was 1960 in fact. There are some photographs of me on the boat with my parents. If you're interested, I'll dig the box out. It's only upstairs.'

'Yes. I am. I'd like that. I enjoy looking at old photographs.' I was, especially if I could glean something from them that would assist me with this investigation. 'I think Isabelle feels a lot of empathy with you because she came out here when she was three, not that either of you can remember your life back in England.'

'Well, yes. That's right. Mum doesn't talk about it much, unfortunately. You see my elder sister died from leukaemia and she associates a lot of painful memories with the place. I guess that's why she's never been back. I went once with my husband before we were married. In case you were wondering, Josh and I divorced when Lucy was ten. It was all rather acrimonious, so the least said about that the better.' That answered my question concerning the absence of Mr Winters.

'Whereabouts in England did your parents live? Only, I understand from Isabelle that you have a cousin in Hampshire.'

'Somerset. Oh...I'm terribly sorry, Alicia, but I can't believe how inhospitable I'm being. I haven't even offered you a drink. Let's go into the kitchen. I need to check on dinner anyway.'

'OK. Where have Isabelle and Gran gone?' I asked, following her. They had disappeared soon after we had arrived at the house.

'Into the family room for a chat I expect.'

'Something smells good,' I said as she opened the oven door.

'It's just a simple roast; lamb with rosemary, roast potatoes, roasted sweet potatoes, pumpkin and carrot.' She took the roasting dish out of the oven and basted the meat. 'I hope you like lamb. You're not vegetarian or anything, are you? I should have asked. If so, I can make you something else.'

'No I'm not. It looks delicious. I can't wait to eat it.'

'Great. Now, what would you like to drink? A glass of wine or a beer? I don't know what you prefer.'

'Wine, please.'

'I've got a fine red I've been waiting for a special occasion to open. I'll go and get it. I'll only be two ticks.' It seemed like an age until Claire returned, but when she did she was carrying a brown box and no wine.

'Is everything OK?'

'Yes, thanks. I thought I'd get you that box of photographs. I was looking through it trying to find the ones of me on the ship. Have a look.' She took off the lid, pulled out a bundle of photographs and handed them to me. 'Mum's very meticulous. You'll see that she has written on the back of every photo.' They were black and white but very clear. There were pictures of Claire with her parents and inscribed as she had said. Claire then disappeared again and I was pouring over the photographs when Isabelle and Gran came into the kitchen.

'What do you think you're doing?' Gran snapped.

'Claire was just showing me some old photographs from your trip over in 1960.'

'She had no business to,' she said tersely. 'Those are family photographs.'

'I'm sorry,' I replied, putting them back into the box. 'But Claire…'

'What's going on?' Claire had returned with the wine and immediately picked up on the tense atmosphere.

'Why are you showing *her* those photographs?' said Gran, casting a disparaging look at me.

'Oh, for goodness sake, Mum, what's the big deal? They're only old photographs.'

'Look,' I said, stepping in, 'I'm very sorry about the confusion, Mrs Whiteley. I was talking to your daughter about your family and she asked me if I'd like to see the photographs. It certainly wasn't my intention to cause any offence.'

'None taken,' said Claire, attempting to diffuse the situation. 'Mum, I'll bring your dinner through to you on a tray. Isabelle, why don't you go and sit with Gran.' Isabelle took the hint and they both left the room. 'I really must apologise for Mum's behaviour, Alicia, but those bad memories about our life before we moved out here make her overly sensitive at times.'

I was not convinced by Claire's explanation for her mother's extraordinary outburst. My instinctive feeling was that there was something in Mrs Whiteley's background that she did not want disclosed, and it could be to do with the photographs, but what it was eluded me. So, when Claire left the room, I purloined one of her and her parents on the ship and slipped it into my handbag. Although Claire was very pleasant to me over dinner, needless to say, after the incident I did not feel overly welcome at the Winters' household and I was relieved when Isabelle and I left.

'I might have a lie in tomorrow,' said Isabelle as we stood waiting for the return ferry to Circular Quay. 'I need to have my haircut and do some shopping but that can wait 'til later. Would you mind amusing yourself for a few hours?'

'Not at all. I'll get up early and explore the city. Will you be OK on your own?'

'Oh yeah. I'm not pretending that I'm happy with my situation right now but I can't let my life be ruled by fear. You might as well make the most of your time here. Why don't you meet me at Westfield Centrepoint at two o'clock. It's on the corner of Market and Pitt Street. We could do some shopping and then go to Darling Harbour together, if you'd like that.'

'Well, I want to visit the Aquarium and the Chinese Garden anyway so that sounds perfect. It would be good to have some company. Isabelle, why do you think Gran was so upset over those photographs?' I thought perhaps she might be able to enlighten me.

'I don't know. It was a bit weird. I've never seen her like that before. Mind you, she doesn't like talking about her past. I remember Lucy telling me to avoid asking her any questions about it. Maybe it's too painful for her to be reminded of certain things. She hardly said anything to me after she barked at you.'

I felt it was better to keep my thoughts on Lucy's grandmother to myself for the time being. I was determined to find out more about her past, but until I had anything concrete there seemed little point in discussing it further with Isabelle.

Chapter 22

The next morning I left the hotel just after seven-thirty. It was already quite balmy but the forecast was for another swelteringly hot day. I had bought myself a Sydney City map from the Rocks Visitors Centre on my way down to Circular Quay from the hotel the day before. I decided to take a better look at the Opera House. From a distance the sail-like structures making up the roof look white and smooth, just like the sails of an old cutter, but as I approached I could see that they are actually made up of thousands of individual tiles more beige than white. I wandered up the steps to the Opera House and took in the view across the harbour of the city skyscrapers disappearing in the blue heat haze.

From the Opera House it was only a moments walk to the lush and manicured Royal Botanic Gardens. If I followed the path through the gardens I could walk straight to the Art Gallery of New South Wales taking in a number of tourist attractions on my way including Government House, Mrs Macquarie's Chair, and the Andrew (Boy) Charlton pool. It turned out to be a very scenic route and I thoroughly enjoyed the walk. I finally arrived at the Art Gallery, sat on a bench outside in the grounds, surrounded by palm trees, and called Alex to update him on the latest developments.

'Don't you think it was bizarre for Lucy's grandmother to react the way she did over a box of photographs?'

'It does seem a bit extreme, yes.'

'I don't buy all that stuff about not wanting to rake up the past because it's too distressing. I reckon she's probably got something to hide.'

'Hmm… Well, if she hasn't, why the overreaction? What did Isabelle say?'

'Not much.'

'Where is she anyway?'

'She had a few things to do. I'm supposed to be meeting her later.'

'Where are you now?'

'Outside the Art Gallery.'

'Have you been in there yet?'

'Just about to. Why?'

'Have a look at the Canaletto. They've got one of *Piazzo di San Marco*. By the way, have you told Isabelle you've spoken to me about coming on board?'

'Yes. She's very happy about that. I think she's keen to meet you. I'll let you know when to expect us. I'll speak to you later.'

'I look forward to it.'

'Anch'io, carino.'

'Ciao, bella.'

'Baci. Ciao.'

I spent a couple of hours in the blissfully air-conditioned Art Gallery wandering around. I enjoyed looking at the Australian art, particularly the Yiribana Gallery of Aboriginal and Torres Strait Islander Art, and the modern works of Tom Roberts, Sir Sidney Nolan and Brett Whiteley. But, my favourite painting in the Gallery was the classical painting by Carlo Cignani called *The Five Senses* even though it reminded me that, when it came to this investigation, what I desperately required was a sixth one.

After a much-needed cup of coffee in the restaurant, I left the Gallery and headed in the direction of Westfield Centrepoint. I walked through the Domain to St Mary's Cathedral, then over into Hyde Park and down the shady central path to the Pool of Reflection and the Anzac War Memorial. I paused there for a while before continuing on my way. It was just after two when I arrived at Westfield Centrepoint and called Isabelle on her mobile.

'Where are you?'

'Right behind you,' she said, tapping me on the shoulder. I spun around to face her.

'Isabelle!' I exclaimed. 'Where did you spring from? And your hair!'

'I've been here for ages. You don't think my hair's too short, do you?' she asked, smoothing down the back of her honey-blonde hair with her hand slightly self-consciously. 'I wanted a complete change.'

'It looks fantastic. It really suits you. Very gamine. Have you had a good day? You didn't find anything to buy then?' She was not carrying any shopping bags.

'I only got up at ten-thirty. It's the first time I've slept properly these past few weeks. I had my hair cut, but I wasn't really in the mood for shopping. Luisa called earlier. She'd heard we're in Sydney from Lucy. She wanted to know if I was going back to Melbourne, but I told her I haven't decided yet.' I imagined that Luisa was very keen to know Isabelle's plans and I was not at all surprised to learn that she and Lucy had been in contact.

'Did you tell her about your near miss with the tram?'

'Yes. She seemed totally amazed.' I found that hard to believe, but her reaction was the one I expected.

'Hmm... So what are you going to do?'

'Go and see Alex with you and then fly back to London. I told you!'

'Yes. I know. I meant about Luisa.'

'I didn't tell her about Alex and our trip to see him, if that's what you mean. I thought about what you said and, as much as I hate to think it, I agree that Luisa could be involved. On that basis I'm proceeding on your 'trust no-one' policy.'

'You can't afford to trust blindly, Isabelle. It's better to be cautious.'

'And while I can't believe that Lucy is involved, I have taken on board your comments.'

'Good. They come from concern for you. When do you want to leave for the Sunshine Coast.'

'Early tomorrow. Alex is expecting us, isn't he?'

'I'll give him a call later to let him know.'

'I'm looking forward to meeting him. Do you still want to go to Darling Harbour?' I nodded. 'And what would you like to do this evening?'

'What do you suggest?'

'We could take the harbour lights cruise. It's only an hour and a half trip. Then for dinner, I thought Doyles at Watsons Bay. It has fantastic seafood and the views across the harbour are stunning. You might as well enjoy the remainder of your visit to Sydney even though it's been a flying one.'

Alex looked remarkably well considering his recent surgery and he was a much better colour, but seemed very thin considering these past weeks of illness. He was moving slightly awkwardly and it was obvious he was still in some discomfort. Isabelle and I had arrived at the Sunshine Coast mid-afternoon and it was now after midnight. The three of us had talked non-stop and we were all exhausted.

'I'm very grateful to you for agreeing to assist,' said Isabelle, addressing Alex as she stood up to go to bed. 'Alicia recommended you and I have every confidence in her judgment.'

'I will have to endeavour to live up to her expectations then.' He turned to me and smiled.

'There is something I would like to ask of you though, Alex,' she said.

'Which is?'

'Would you mind staying at the house with me?' Her tone was plaintive. 'It's best that Lucy doesn't stay now, but I don't want to be alone. With the way things are, I would feel safer having a man around. I could say that you're a university friend of Michael's then nobody would suspect anything. I wouldn't ask, but there isn't anyone else I can trust.'

'I can see you've already thought about it.' Alex glanced at me I felt for some sign as to whether he should agree or not.

'It's probably a good idea for you to stay close to Isabelle. I think it's a very practical solution.'

'You do?' he said, sounding rather surprised.

'Yes. I do.'

'OK. If it would make you feel better, I could do that, but I need to make a few arrangements first.'

'Thank you so much. I really appreciate it. I'm going to bed. Don't stay up the whole night talking. Goodnight.'

'What was all that about?' asked Alex after Isabelle had disappeared. 'I was rather hoping to stay close to you.' He moved from the armchair, sat down next to me and ran his arm along the back of the sofa behind me.

'You will be, now that we're working together again,' I replied, edging away from him.

'What's the matter, Alicia?' he said, scanning my face. 'You're very distant. Is everything OK between us? Have I done something to offend you? If I have tell me so I can make it right.' He reached out to take my hand.

'Oh, Alex, it isn't anything you've done,' I replied, pulling my hand away and standing up. 'I just think that we need to keep everything on a purely professional footing for Isabelle's sake.'

'I don't follow. Why does us working together on this investigation have to be a problem?' He stood up and gently took hold of my shoulders. 'I thought that's what you wanted.' I sensed disappointment in his voice.

'I do.'

'What is it then? I'm really trying to understand. You just don't trust me, do you?' He seemed very hurt.

'I suppose I was really surprised when you told me how you felt.

Until now I haven't had time to stop still and consider my own feelings because of everything that's happened with Isabelle, and then I saw you this evening and I…oh, I don't know how to explain. It isn't you. It's me.'

'But when you came to see me that afternoon before you left for Melbourne I thought you felt the same. What's changed?'

'It's complicated,' I replied, looking down.

'Clearly.' He let go of my shoulders. From his pained expression I knew that I had wounded him deeply.

'I'm sorry, Alex. I can't…'

'Don't!' he said interrupting me. 'Forget it. It's very late, we're both tired and I really don't want to say anything to you that I might regret tomorrow. I'm going to bed. I'll see you in the morning. Goodnight, Alicia.'

Although I was not planning to take the flight back to London until the following Saturday, Isabelle was eager to return. I did not object to leaving sooner because it would give me a few extra days with her before I returned to work when my time would be more limited. Alex was not opposed to taking an earlier flight either. There was probably no incentive for him to stay now. Since our conversation on the Monday evening he had not mentioned another word to me about it. In fact, he was behaving as if nothing had happened which slightly perplexed me. If anything, I was feeling rather awkward about the situation. Isabelle took on the responsibility of organising our flights and we arranged to take one on Wednesday afternoon which meant we would arrive back in London very early on Thursday.

On the Wednesday morning all three of us were sitting out on the deck when Isabelle received a call. 'You'll never guess who that was, Alicia.'

'I've no idea.'

'It was one of the policemen who came to see me the other day. He gave me Gerry's details.'

'Oh, good.'

'Gerry?' asked Alex, looking up from his newspaper.

'He's the one that pulled me across the road to safety and out of the path of the tram when we were in Melbourne. I'll get in touch with him. Do you have a message for him, Alicia?'

'No.'

'Only I'm sure he'd be very happy to hear from you. I thought he was quite keen.'

'What's this?' asked Alex, putting his newspaper down.

'It's nothing,' I swiftly responded. I did not want Alex to think that I was throwing him over because I was interested in someone else. Nothing could be further from the truth.

'I think he really liked Alicia,' Isabelle continued innocently. 'Anyway, I'll leave you two to it. I need to finish packing.' I waited until Isabelle was out of earshot before speaking to Alex.

'It's not what you think. Isabelle's mistaken.'

'It really isn't any of my business. What you do or who you see is your own affair,' he said in an unconcerned, carefree tone as he picked up his paper.

We agreed that Isabelle would spend our first night back in London with me because Alex had some personal matters to attend to and could not stay at her house until the following night. This would also give her breathing space before she contacted Lucy, and all of us would be able to catch up on some sleep. We arrived in London on the Thursday morning but I was far more jet-lagged than when I flew out to Australia. After Isabelle had settled in, I hopped out for some fresh milk and dropped in on Dorothy as I had a few little presents from Australia to give her.

I suspected that she might have seen the taxi pull up outside the house, but I knew she was far too considerate to disturb me so soon after my return. I, on the other hand, was itching to see her and keen to find out if she had heard from her friend Emily Middleton. I picked up my bag of presents, ran downstairs and knocked on her door.

'Alicia!' she said, opening it. She was wearing her outdoor coat and I noticed a bag of shopping in the hallway and I presumed she had just returned. 'What a lovely surprise! I wasn't expecting you back until the weekend. Come in.' I gave her a hug.

'How are you? You look well.'

'I am, and all the better for seeing you. When did you get back?' She took off her coat, hung it on the coat rack in the hall and walked through to the kitchen. I picked up her bag of shopping and followed her into the kitchen.

'About an hour ago. I thought you might have heard us come back.'

'No. I was out. It's such a beautiful spring day today that I thought I would take advantage of it, go for a walk and pick up some groceries.' She started to unpack her shopping. 'The weather here has been so wet these past few weeks and I really haven't felt like leaving the flat at all. Mind you, we did need the rain. The garden was so dry. You must be very tired after that long flight.' She paused and looked at me hard.

'I am a bit, but I was on my way out and thought I'd pop in, say hello and give you this.' I handed her the bag of presents. 'It's just a few things I picked up on my way.'

'Oh, thank you.' She opened the bag and pulled out a packet of Macadamia nut shortbread, a pot of honey and two linen tea towels, one of an Aboriginal design and the other of the native animals of Australia.

'How is everything?'

'Fine. As it happens I have some good news for you. I expect you've been wondering if I've heard from Emily?' I nodded. 'It's so strange that you should come back today because I had it in mind to 'phone you. I received a call from her last night. What do you want to drink? Tea or coffee?'

'A cup of tea, please.' I sat down at Dorothy's kitchen table. 'What did she say?' Dorothy flicked on the electric switch to boil the kettle and put a couple of teaspoons of leaf tea into her blue china teapot. She then took two cups and saucers out of the cupboard.

'That she knew Diane for about four years from the time of her engagement up until her death. They became quite well-acquainted and she went to the house a number of times.'

'Really?' I presumed she meant to Stowick House in which case she probably had met the housekeeper Mrs Banks.

'Yes. She asked me what you wanted to know and I told her that it would be better if you spoke to her yourself. I didn't mention that you're advising James Latham's granddaughter. I thought it best to leave it up to you to decide what you want to tell her.' How discreet and intelligent of Dorothy, as always. The kettle boiled and she poured hot water over the tea-leaves. She stirred the pot, put on the lid and placed the teapot on the table. I stood up and reached for the cups and saucers.

'Actually, she's upstairs right now. So I can't stay long.'

'Oh, I see. I thought you said 'us' but I wasn't sure whether I had misheard you.' She walked to the fridge, took out the milk and poured some into a small jug. Dorothy never missed a thing. 'Is everything all right, Alicia?' she asked, with that knowing look of hers, as she sat down at the table.

'I can't go into detail, Dorothy, but suffice to say there have been some major developments concerning Isabelle Parker since I last saw you, including several failed attempts on her life, one of which resulted in her fiancé being blown up. One of her trustees has also been murdered. I'm sure the murderer will strike again.'

'What a scenario.'

'Yes it is.'

'And do you have any leads, dear?' Dorothy poured the tea. I helped myself to milk.

'Well, the thing is, Dorothy, my gut feeling is that recent events are somehow connected to what happened to Diane Latham all those years ago, which is why I'm keen to speak to Emily. Do you think she would meet me?' I sipped my tea.

'I was coming to that. She'd be very happy to, but she's not really up to making the journey down to London, so you'd have to go up to Skipton.'

'I wouldn't expect her to. Did she leave a number?'

'Yes. It's here.' She tore off the top piece of paper from a jotter pad on the work surface next to the fridge and handed it to me.

'Thank you very much for your help,' I replied, taking it and smiling at her.

'I haven't done anything.'

'If I go up to see her, why don't you come with me? I'm sure it would be lovely for you two to see each other again.'

'That's very thoughtful of you, dear. How are you going to get there?'

'By train, I think, from Kings Cross, unless you come, in which case I'll drive.'

'All right. I'll think about it. Apart from all this nasty business, how was Australia? Did you enjoy the wedding?' It was strange because although the purpose of my trip had been to attend Kim's wedding and to do some sightseeing, somehow subsequent events had overshadowed it.

'I did manage to see a fair bit of the country in the two and half weeks I was there. The wedding was lovely. I took a lot of photographs. I'll upload them on to my computer so you can have a look. I think you'd have approved of Kim's dress. It was very elegant. I'm sorry, Dorothy, I'd love to stay and chat but I'd better run. Isabelle will be wondering where I've gone. I'll come back and see you later,' I said, standing up to leave.

'Yes. Let me know how you get on with Emily.'

'Of course.' I kissed her on the cheek. 'Thanks, Dorothy.' I let myself out.

'Isabelle, I have some news for you,' I cried out as I burst through the front door. I rushed through the hall and into the living room where Isabelle was watching television.

'What is it? You've been ages,' she replied, turning around. 'I was getting worried. You seemed an awfully long time gone just for a litre of skinny milk. Hope you don't mind by the way but I was feeling hungry and took a tube of Pringles out of your store cupboard.' I noticed the open tube of Salt and Vinegar Pringles on my coffee table. 'You must really like them. You've got six tubes in there.'

'Help yourself. I'm a bit of a Pringles addict, as you've probably guessed. Sorry I've been a while, but I popped in to see my neighbour Dorothy and we got chatting. I presume you still want to find out whether Grandpa Jam was involved in Diane's death?' I walked through to the kitchen and put the milk in the fridge.

'Yes,' she replied, following me. 'I need to know. Why? Have you found out something?'

'Not exactly, but I may have found *someone* who can give us some information.'

'Really?' Isabelle sounded intrigued. We returned to the living room and she sat down on the sofa.

'I was intrigued by what you told me about Diane and I did some research on the internet. Anyway, I came across this piece,' I said, opening the second drawer of my desk, taking out the three-paged article I had shown to Dorothy a few weeks back and handing the stapled document to Isabelle. I watched her flick through the article. 'See the caption under the photograph of Diane on the second page.' She nodded. 'Dorothy used to work at Norman Hartnell and was there in Diane's era. It turns out she has a friend, Emily, who knew Diane very well and has agreed to meet me.'

'Then you thought that there was something strange about Diane's death from the start and even before I asked you to help me?'

'Well, yes. I suppose I did.'

'Why?'

'Just a feeling. Will you come with me to see Emily?'

'Yes. If she knows anything which could shed light on what happened back then I'd like to hear it first hand.'

'That's settled then. I'll give her a call and find out if it's worth us going all the way up there. She might be able to tell us everything we need to know over the 'phone. Or, if she can't help, as least we'll save ourselves a wasted trip.'

'Where does she live?'

'Yorkshire.'

'Right. If you decide to go, when will that be?'

'At the weekend?'

'Oh, that's OK. I'm planning to see Jonathan Masterton tomorrow. I'll call him in the morning. He doesn't know I'm back so that will put him on the spot. Do you still want to meet him?'

'Yes. Very much. What are you going to do about Lucy?'

'I'll speak to her tomorrow.'

'And when do you want to go to Stowick House?'

'Perhaps we can take a trip to Devon next weekend? It's too much to drive there and back in one day so I'll sort out a hotel. The house is all shut up and it hardly seems worth opening it up for one night. I'll need to contact Keith Millard so that he knows we're coming.'

'Who's he?'

'Grandpa's Estate Manager. He's been looking after the place for me these past few months. Do you think Alex would come with us?'

'I don't see why not. Ask him.'

'OK. When are you going to call Emily?'

'No time like the present. Why don't you listen in on the extension in my bedroom?'

'Good idea.'

Emily told me that she first met Diane after her engagement to James Latham and when she was Miss Diane Gordon. Diane originally consulted Hartnell's because she wanted them to design her wedding dress, but she continued to use them as her couturier thereafter. Emily described her as a delightful person, full of energy and vitality and clearly excited about her forthcoming marriage. She also remembered the great affection with which she spoke of her step-daughter Mary from James's first marriage. Emily confirmed that over the four years she knew Diane she was a fairly frequent visitor at the house and became well-acquainted with the housekeeper. Any information about that interested me greatly.

'Was that Mrs Banks?'

'Yes. But how do you know?'

'I met Mary Latham's Australian mother-in-law recently and she mentioned meeting her at the time Mary and her son were engaged. Although that would have been in the early seventies so much later than you're time.'

'Yes, very much later.'

'Are you still in touch with Mrs Banks, only I really want to make contact with her?' If Mrs Banks had openly discussed with Grandma Edie details of Grandpa Jam's relationship with Diane, then it was likely that she would talk to us. As housekeeper she would have been privy to almost everything that went on in that household and there must have been things that she saw or heard that might lead us somewhere.

'I was, but she died a couple of years ago.'

'Oh, I see,' I replied, feeling slightly dispirited. It had occurred to me that she might have died, but I had hoped otherwise.

'Well, Phyllida was in her late eighties. She was a few years younger than me. I was only saying to Dorothy last night, that none of us is getting any younger. But she does have a daughter. *She* might be able to help you. I have her details if you want to get in touch with her. She actually doesn't live far from Stowick House.'

'That's very kind of you, but I don't see how she can help me. I mean it's not as if she was around the family like her mother.'

'Oh, I'm sorry. I should have explained. Phyllida's husband was a manager on the estate. The whole family lived there, so Bridget knew the Lathams very well.'

'Really? But wouldn't she have been a little girl at that time?' I was trying to work out the arithmetic in my head as we spoke.

'I suppose she was about ten when I first met her. She used to play with Mary; I can see the two of them together now. Why don't you get in touch with her? You have nothing to lose.'

'Yes, you're right. What are her details?' I grabbed a pen and scribbled them down on the back of an envelope, which was the first thing to hand. She lived at Newton Abbot, not that far from Buckfastleigh and Stowick House. 'Thank you so much. I really appreciate you responding to Dorothy's letter and taking the time to talk to me today.'

'You're most welcome, dear. Dorothy spoke very highly of you. Maybe one of these days you'll bring her up to see me.'

'I will. Thank you again.'

'My pleasure. Goodbye and good luck with your research.'

'Thank you. Goodbye.'

Isabelle emerged from the bedroom looking pleasantly surprised.

'What a lovely lady.'

'Yes. That changes our plans, doesn't it?' I said. Isabelle looked slightly perplexed. 'Now that we don't have to go up to Yorkshire this weekend, we're free to go down to Stowick House. We might as well try and get to see Bridget Ward at the same time. She might know something about what happened between your grandfather and Diane.'

'I hope so. I just want to know the truth.'

'Believe me Isabelle, so do I.'

Chapter 23

'You did what?' scolded Antonia. *'Sei pazza!'* Isabelle was still asleep so I had 'phoned Antonia to find out how she was, because we had barely seen each other in Australia and not spoken for almost two weeks. Unfortunately, our friendly sisterly catch-up turned into a somewhat heated conversation with Antonia berating me over my behaviour towards Alex.

'Don't mix yourself in, Antonia. This isn't anything to do with you. *Non sono affari tuoi!'*

'Che assurdità! You're my sister, and I care about you. I think you're making a big mistake. I can't believe you told him you weren't interested. I thought this is what you wanted. Tom and I were only saying last night how keen he is on you. Maybe you can patch things up especially now he's coming back to London.'

'He's already here.'

'Well, you've got the perfect opportunity to make a go of things then.'

'I think it's too late for that. I just don't think we're meant to be together.'

'Santo cielo! Take a reality check. I thought I was supposed to be the impetuous one of the family. You're throwing away something good. I know he hurt you before, but he's doing everything he can to make it up to you and prove how sincere he is. How have you left it with him anyway?'

'He's got three months garden leave and he's helping me with some research.'

'At least that means you'll have to see each other. *Mi dispiace.* I don't mean to go on, but please make sure you don't do anything thing you might come to regret.'

'I already have,' I mumbled under my breath.

'What was that?'

'*Va bene,* OK.'

'Why don't you come over for dinner tonight and we can have a proper chat?'

'I can't. I've a dinner with a client.'

'But I thought you were still on holiday.'

'I am; but this is something I can't get out of.'

'How about you come round some time over the weekend then?'

'I can't do that either, sorry. I'm going away.'

'Where? You've only just come home.'

'I know, but I have to make a trip down to Devon in relation to a case I'm working on. I need to visit the family estate.'

'*In nome del cielo!* I thought I had to work all the time. I hope they're paying you well at CFP & Co. You wouldn't catch me giving up my weekends for nothing.'

'I'll see you next week. I've got to go,' I replied, avoiding answering her question. 'I must call Mamma and then I have to go out.'

'OK. *Ciao, carina.*'

'*Ciao, ciao.*'

I had the distinct impression that Antonia thought I was making excuses not to see her because I was peeved she had remonstrated with me over Alex. Although I dearly wanted to vindicate myself, I was not prepared to divulge to her the nature of my involvement with Isabelle. No doubt she would have taken issue with me over that too. I managed to speak to Mamma before Isabelle woke up. She was pleased that I had arrived home safe and sound, but was disappointed when I explained to her that I had to work the coming weekend and I could not make it down to see her until the following one.

'Good morning,' said Isabelle, walking in to the room. 'You're up early. Couldn't you sleep?' It was just after eight-thirty.

'Yes I did, but I went to bed earlier than you and I thought I might as well get up when I woke as I had things to do. Do you want any breakfast? There's raisin bread in the freezer if you'd like that. I'll make some coffee.'

'Thanks. I appreciate you letting me stay here.'

'You're very welcome,' I replied, opening the jar of ground coffee beans. 'Are you sure you want to see Jonathan Masterton today?'

'Yes. I'll call him after breakfast. Have you spoken to Alex? I hope he's still OK about staying at the house. He seemed a bit preoccupied yesterday.' I had a feeling that was my fault.

'I haven't heard from him, no, but he might still be asleep. Why don't you fix up a time for us to see Masterton and we can work the rest of the day around that.'

After some initial reluctance on the part of Jonathan Masterton to meet with us before the weekend due to his being heavily engaged on other pressing matters, Isabelle arranged an appointment with him at two o'clock. I tried to call Alex but there was no answer on his mobile, so I left a message to let him know that we would be with Jonathan Masterton from approximately two to three. We arrived at the offices of Holmwood & Hitchins five minutes before our appointment. We pressed the intercom button next to the highly polished brass name plaque on the door, Isabelle announced who we were, the door clicked open and we walked inside.

We proceeded up the narrow red-carpeted staircase to an oak-panelled reception area where a rather po-faced receptionist with a bland voice told us to take a seat. We had barely sat down when a striking-looking man probably in his late fifties appeared. I presumed this must be Jonathan Masterton. It was hard to pinpoint his exact age for whilst his hair was grey he seemed remarkably youthful. I put that down to his regular features. He seemed slightly taken aback when he saw me sitting with Isabelle as evidently he had expected Isabelle to attend unaccompanied, or at least, hoped that she would.

'Isabelle, how are you?' he asked in a concerned manner and in a broader Australian accent than I would have imagined.

'I'm doing well…in the circumstances,' she replied, dropping her voice and looking at him hard. 'I know you're very busy, but I do have some extremely important issues to discuss with you following on from our conversation early last week when I was in hospital. They really couldn't wait until after the weekend.'

'No, no, of course.' His tone was obsequious. 'Fortunately, I managed to clear my diary, so no problem at all. Shall we?' He indicated with his arm for Isabelle and me to follow him through to his office. We both stood up.

'Oh, Jonathan, let me introduce you to Alicia Allen. She's also a Private Client lawyer. I've brought her along as I thought it was important for me to be clear on the legal issues. She's here with me on an informal basis.' I watched his grey eyes narrow and his back stiffen. Clearly my presence made him feel uncomfortable.

'How do you do?' I said, extending my hand.

'How do you do?' he replied, taking it perfunctorily. He led us through to his office. We sat down in front of his enormous desk. I noticed that he had some framed photographs on one side of it. I could not see them clearly because of the angle at which I was sitting, so I swivelled my chair around hoping for a better look. There was one of a woman – whom I presumed to be his wife – and two young men, who were no doubt the Masterton children. I wondered which one was Timothy and which one was Mark.

'I won't beat around the bush,' said Isabelle, 'but I have serious concerns about the way my affairs have been handled by this firm. John MacFadzean's misappropriation of trust funds is a highly serious issue and while I do not wish to believe that you personally had any involvement or knowledge of his dealings, you will understand that I find myself no longer able to instruct your firm. I have had no alternative but to put this into the hands of independent lawyers to investigate the matter further.' I watched Jonathan Masterton swallowing hard.

'I appreciate your frankness, Isabelle, and the courtesy you have extended to me by coming to tell me in person.' He remained very cool, composed and charming – which I thought no mean feat given the awkward and highly embarrassing situation in which he found himself.

'Off the record, I would like you to know that it is extremely difficult for me to talk to you in this vein. My grandfather had nothing but respect for you. It is out of respect for his judgment in recommending you to this firm, appreciation for the work you did for him over the years, and for his long-standing connection with your *father* and family that I have come here today.' As Isabelle emphasised the word father she glanced at me. It was that connection with his father and Isabelle's grandfather that we desperately needed to ascertain.

'Thank you. It is very good of you to say so.'

'My grandfather always spoke so highly of your father. How is he?'

'In good health, considering his age. He has angina, but his condition is manageable.'

'It must be a worry, though, with him living so far away.' He wrinkled his brow and looked slightly baffled by her comment or perhaps, despite the current situation, by her friendliness toward him.

'He used to live in Somerset, but he's lived near us in Wimbledon for a few years now. After my mother died it seemed sensible for him to move closer.' He seemed surprised that Isabelle was not aware of this. I was interested to hear that his father used to live in Somerset because that was where Lucy's grandmother came from. I took my opportunity to ask him a question about the timing of his parent's move to Australia.

'When did your parents move to Sydney? Only I understand that you qualified as a lawyer out there before returning to the UK.'

'Yes, we went in 1960 and came back in 1972. I met John MacFadzean while I was doing my training and we became good friends. It grieves me that our friendship has led to this.' He sounded as if he was trying to justify his position.

'When was the last time you saw my grandfather?' Isabelle asked, changing the subject.

'He called me the week he died. He said he wanted to talk about his Will, but of course he died before I met with him.'

'Really? Did he say what he wanted you to do, only it did occur to me that his Will was made in 1969 and I have wondered why he did not update it?' Again she glanced at me.

'That I can't tell you. I'm sorry.'

'I see. Thank you for meeting me at such short notice today.' Isabelle stood up and extended her hand to him. 'Goodbye, Jonathan.'

'Goodbye, Isabelle,' he said, taking it. He very courteously shook my hand and we left.

'What did you think of him?' she asked as we opened the door and walked out on to the street and straight into a young man who looked remarkably like Jonathan Masterton.

'Isabelle!' he exclaimed, giving her a hug. 'It's wonderful to see you. How are you?'

'I'm OK, thanks,' she replied in a bland tone of voice. I had the feeling he was the last person she wanted to have a conversation with right now.

'Have you just been to see Dad? This business over John MacFadzean is so awful. I hope you guys can sort it out.' Isabelle did not respond. I had been right about his physical resemblance to his father and he had that same charm. It must be hereditary. 'Aren't you going to introduce me to your friend?' He smiled broadly at me.

'Yes, of course. This is Alicia Allen.' Her tone of voice was still bland.

'How do you do? I'm Timothy Masterton.'

'How do you do?' I shook his hand.

'What are you guys up to this evening?'

'Hmm…' Isabelle glanced at me.

'Why don't you come out to dinner?' he said enthusiastically.

'That's very kind of you, but a friend of Michael's from university is coming to stay with me and we've made other arrangements, sorry.'

'Which friend?'

'Oh, you don't know him,' she replied casually.

'Right. Oh well. I'd better go and see Dad. I'll catch you two later. Good to meet you, Alicia. See you again. Bye.'

'That was embarrassing,' said Isabelle as we walked along the street. 'I *would* have to bump in to him after telling his father I'm disinstructing his firm and especially when I haven't even called Lucy yet. Let's get a taxi to your place.' She hailed one, we settled into the back and resumed our conversation.

'I would have thought that it was more embarrassing for Timothy, bearing in mind he is aware of the John MacFadzean situation. Also, I thought you said he was quiet. He seemed quite loquacious to me.'

'He was very chatty today. He's not normally like that I can assure you.'

'Maybe it's because he's anxious about things. People often talk nineteen-to-the-dozen when they're nervy.'

'I was worried he'd ask loads of questions about Alex, but we managed to avoid that one. I'd better give Lucy a call and we need to speak to Alex too. Has he left any messages on your mobile?' My mobile had been switched off since we went into the meeting with Jonathan Masterton. I turned it on but there were none.

'I'll call him when we get back to the flat.'

'So what did you think of Jonathan Masterton?'

'I'm not quite sure what to make of him to be honest. He's very smooth and he doesn't get ruffled, but I think you had him quite perplexed. One minute you were talking about disinstructing his firm and then you launched into a friendly chat about his family. He looked slightly bewildered.'

'Well, I wanted to find out where his father is.'

'Yes. It's interesting what he said about your grandfather contacting him to change his Will.'

'Do you think it's significant?'

'Not necessarily, but I did wonder why he never updated it.'

'Hmm... Why did you ask Jonathan when his parents moved to Sydney?'

'We already suspected that they went there around the time of Diane's death and now we know for certain that it was the same year.' Lucy's grandparents also moved out to Sydney in 1960. The increasing number of similarities between these two families' move to Australia only served to strengthen my conviction that Lucy's family was connected to what happened to Diane all those years before.

'Yes. You're right. Let's hope that Bridget Ward can fill in the gaps for us. Would you mind if I 'phoned her rather than you?'

'No. Of course not. I'll give you her number when we get home.'

'Great. I'll call and make sure she can see us tomorrow. I wouldn't want us to have a wasted journey.'

We arrived at my flat just after four. We had been home only about quarter of an hour, and Isabelle was on the 'phone to Bridget Ward when there was a knock at the front door. I thought it must be someone from inside the building because anybody else would have to gain access via the video Entryphone security system. I looked through my spyhole and saw Alex waiting outside complete with his small backpack.

'Alex! Where did you spring from?' I asked, opening the door to let him in.

'I bumped into Dorothy,' he answered, wiping his feet on the mat before stepping inside. 'We had a little chat and she let me into the building.'

'Oh, right.' That was all I needed as Dorothy was bound to mention him to me when next I saw her. 'Are you OK? You look very tired. You shouldn't overdo it.'

'I am a bit,' he replied, taking off his jacket and dropping his bag in the hall. I took his jacket from him and hung it up in the hall cupboard. 'I've been rushing around today but with good reason. I'll tell you about that in a minute. You ought to be careful yourself.' I gave him a questioning look. 'You sound as if you *almost* care about me. You wouldn't want to give people the wrong impression would you now?'

'I...' I did not have the chance to respond as Isabelle hurried out into the hall from the living room.

'Bridget says to call her when we get to Newton Abbot. Hi, Alex, I thought I heard your voice. How are you?'

'Good, thanks. Who's Bridget?' he asked, following Isabelle and me into the living room. He sat down at one end of the sofa and Isabelle sat at the other.

'Tell him, Alicia.'

'No, you tell him. I'm going to make some tea.' I slipped away into the kitchen. I could not hear very well because the kitchen was around the corner and when the kettle boiled it made such a noise that it obliterated the sound of anything else. I made the tea, cut up some home-made fruit cake which I had stored in a tin before leaving for Australia, placed the crockery, cutlery and paper napkins on a tray with the teapot and cake and carried it through to the living room. I put the tray down on the coffee table and handed them both a plate and napkin.

'It sounds like Dorothy has come up trumps again,' said Alex.

'Well, as you know, I think she's marvellous anyway. Cake?' I picked up the plate of sliced fruit cake and offered it first to Isabelle and then to Alex. They both took a piece. 'It was good of Dorothy to write to Emily Middleton. Emily was lovely too. I'm hoping that Bridget Ward can help.'

'So you're going down to Stowick House tomorrow?'

'Yes. Do you feel up to coming with us? I don't mind driving if we leave really early.' I poured the tea and handed each of them a cup. 'There's sugar here if you want it.'

'Actually, Alicia,' said Isabelle, reaching for the sugar, 'I think we should take my car. It could do with a good run. Since Alex will be staying with me, we can come and pick you up in the morning.'

'Fine. I'll drive you back to Hampstead this evening though.'

'Don't worry about that. We can grab a cab.' Isabelle's 'phone started to ring. 'It's Lucy,' she said, looking at the screen. 'I should have called her. I'd better take it. I'll go into the other room.' She walked through to the second bedroom and shut the door leaving me alone with Alex. A good minute passed before he spoke.

'Delicious cake,' he said, breaking the awkward silence as he finished off the piece on his plate.

'Thanks.'

'So what did you think of Jonathan Masterton?'

'He's very charming, but he could be involved for all the reasons we've discussed before. What perplexes me though is where Lucy fits in.'

'That business with her grandmother over the photographs really got to you, didn't it?'

'It's not just that. Look at it logically. Jonathan Masterton's parents went out to Sydney in 1960 too.'

'How do you know that?'

'Masterton confirmed it.'

'I see.'

'What if Lucy has known Jonathan for years and she's working with him now? After all, it would help him to have a spy in the Latham camp. We've already discussed that Luisa could be the Australian connection and she's friends with both Lucy and Isabelle. How do we know that Luisa bumping into Isabelle at the Melbourne International Arts Festival wasn't contrived?'

'You've got it all worked out, haven't you?'

'No, not really, and we still have to prove it.'

'We?'

'Unless you're no longer interested.'

'Believe me, I'm still very interested. Alicia, I...' He stopped short because Isabelle walked back into the room.

'Lucy's looking forward to meeting you, Alex. She wanted to come and see me this evening and I felt I couldn't refuse. I hope you don't mind. Timothy called and told her I was back, so it was all a bit difficult.'

'No. Not at all.'

'You didn't say where you'd been today.'

'I've been doing some research. I went up to Colindale Avenue.' Isabelle looked confused. 'The British Library Newspapers Catalogue is based there. I went to the Reading Room. I thought it would be worth looking for any articles covering Diane's accident.'

'Oh, of course. No wonder you're tired. Did you find anything?' I asked.

'A couple of articles in the *Western Evening Herald* and *Western Evening News*, Cornwall edition and the *South Devon Chronicle*, South Devon edition.'

'And?' Isabelle said eagerly.

'The second article I came across in the *South Devon Chronicle* mentioned the inquest and there was reference to Diane having an elder brother called Philip. Time I went to the Family Records Office, don't you think?'

'Yes, I think a visit there is long overdue,' I replied. 'I'd go with you but I'm back at work on Monday.'

'I know. You might want to come with me though, Isabelle. You never know what we might find.' I had the feeling that finally a few skeletons were about to fall out of the Latham family closet.

Chapter 24

Stowick House was hidden away in the depths of the Devon countryside off a meandering country lane. Although it was supposed to
be three miles from Buckfastleigh, I suspected that was 'as the crow
flies' because it seemed considerably further. It felt as if we had been
driving forever before Isabelle finally turned off the lane and we
stopped a short distance from an early nineteenth-century sandstone
lodge with 'Gothick' windows. There was a Range Rover parked
outside.

'I won't be a moment,' she said, unfastening her seat belt and
opening the car door. 'I'll just let Keith know we're here and going
up to the house.' She stepped out of the car, ambled along the path
to the lodge and knocked on the door. A burly looking man
appeared, she spoke to him momentarily and he disappeared back
inside. Isabelle returned to the car. 'Keith will join us in about five
minutes. We might as well go on ahead.'

The winding drive finally led to an open gravelled area in front
of the main house which was set in extensive grounds. It was no
surprise that James Latham had needed the services of a housekeeper
and an estate manager. Nobody could manage that estate alone.
However, I was surprised that he had stayed in the house by himself.
It was too remote for my liking. Isabelle parked her silver Golf GTi
close to the main entrance.

'It's a beautiful house,' commented Alex, climbing out of the
back seat and looking up at the pale yellow stucco-fronted Regency
villa.

'Yes. I think it's lovely. The house was built in the early 1800s and enlarged and renovated in the early 1900s. The gardens were also altered then. There's a fantastic walled rose garden but March isn't the time to see it at its best! Grandpa was very fond of his herbaceous borders as well. All the formal lawns are near the main house. It's a bit cold, otherwise I'd suggest we go for a walk around.'

'There's a lot of land. How many acres are there?' asked Alex.

'The gardens are about thirty, but the whole estate must be twelve hundred. Keith will be able to tell you.'

'How long has he worked here?' I asked.

'For about twenty years. He's very trustworthy. Grandpa said he was probably the best estate manager he'd had.' Keith then arrived in his Range Rover. Isabelle introduced him to Alex and me, and he opened up the house for us. 'Thanks, Keith. Do you mind waiting? We shouldn't be very long. My friends want to have a quick look around and I'd like to talk to you about the garden.'

'No problem at all,' he replied. I could detect the hint of a West Country accent.

'Feel free to wander about,' Isabelle called out before disappearing with Keith into the garden.'

'This place must be worth a fortune,' whispered Alex as we strolled inside. He opened a door in the grand hall. 'Just take a look at what's on the walls in here alone. There're a couple of Gainsboroughs over there and a rather flashy Lawrence through that doorway.'

'But James Latham was a connoisseur of the arts, wasn't he, and his first wife loved art as well? I imagine he was an avid collector but I expect a lot of the possessions in this house must have been passed down from generation to generation. I wonder if there are any family portraits.'

'Well, if there are, check for a resemblance to anyone you suspect of being the murderer.'

'Alex, what are you talking about?'

'*The Hound of the Baskervilles*, my dear Miss Allen. We are on the edge of Dartmoor are we not, and it was a relative who was responsible for all those family murders.'

'Hmm… How did it go with Lucy last night?' I asked, changing the subject. I had desperately wanted to ask him about her, but the opportunity had not arisen because Isabelle had been with us the whole time since we left London. As I had not met Lucy I was curious. 'Only, neither you nor Isabelle have mentioned her and I was wondering what you thought of her.'

'Whether she makes murderer material you mean?' he teased.

'And does she?'

'Her friendship with Isabelle seems genuine enough, although I had the distinct impression that she doesn't really like me being around.'

'Don't you think that might be because she's involved with these murders and needs to keep close to Isabelle? With you there that's more difficult.'

'Possibly, but it could just be that she's feeling sidelined. Don't forget she's used to Isabelle confiding in her and these past few weeks she hasn't done that. Isabelle flew off to Melbourne without letting her know and didn't call her straightaway when she came back. Lucy made a point of telling me that if she hadn't spoken to Luisa she wouldn't have found out that Isabelle was in Melbourne at all. It was only because Timothy Masterton called her yesterday that she knew Isabelle was back. She was very intrigued about your involvement with Isabelle though, and asked her a lot of questions.'

'About what? She already knows I've been advising Isabelle on legal matters.'

'She wanted to know about the time you spent with Isabelle in Australia. She wondered why you were with her so much.'

'What did Isabelle say?'

'She insisted that you were assisting her in a professional capacity.'

'Does Lucy know we're down here today?'

'Yes, because she asked Isabelle what we had planned for the weekend and Isabelle told her. She was angling for an invitation and when it wasn't forthcoming she seemed very put-out.'

'I suppose she would be. What was she like?'

'Very striking. A bit taller than you, I'd say, long nut-brown hair, dark eyes. Now which part of the house do you want to see first? Any particular preference or is it going to be a mystery tour?'

'Where's the study do you think?'

'This way.' He walked off down the hallway.

'How do you know?' I was slightly puzzled that he should.

'Because Isabelle showed me some plans of the house last night! Come on.'

As we opened the double doors of the study I noticed a silver-framed photograph on top of James Latham's desk. I could not see the people in it clearly so I walked nearer to take a closer look. It was a photograph of James, Diane and two little girls. I presumed that the elder fair-haired one was Mary and the younger dark-haired one was Frances. Only it could not be her because the little girl in *this* photograph was the spitting image of the one in the photograph I had removed from Claire's box in Sydney. Realizing what I had discovered, I spun around to tell Alex, but he had left the room. I rushed out through the double doors into the hall and careered straight into him. He winced in pain and clutched his stomach.

'Oh, Alex, I'm so sorry,' I said apologetically. 'Are you OK? It was my fault. I wasn't looking where I was going.' I hoped I had not hurt him.

'I'll survive,' he said, rubbing his side. 'But what on earth's the matter? You look as if you've seen a ghost.'

'Did you see the photograph in the study?'

'Which one? There are several.'

'The one on the desk.'

'No.'

'Come and look.' He followed me back into the study and scrutinised it.

'What's so remarkable about it?'

'See the younger child in the photograph?'

'Yes. That's Frances, isn't it? Diane and James's daughter.'

'Yes.'

'I don't understand what you're getting at. What are you saying?'

'Frances is the spitting image of the little girl in the photograph I took from Claire's house in Sydney.'

'What? Which photograph? You didn't say you'd taken any photographs.'

'Well, I did – when Claire wasn't looking; one of Lucy's grandmother, her husband and Claire on the ship when they emigrated to Australia. I swear that the little girl in my photograph and this one here,' I said, picking up the framed photograph, 'is one and the same. Which means that...'

'Claire is Frances?'

'Yes.'

'But how?'

'I don't know exactly, but I think I have a pretty good idea. You need to look at the photograph I have.'

'Do you have it with you?' I nodded.

'I've been carrying it around in my bag for the past few days. Isabelle doesn't know I have it. Tell me what you think.' I took it out of my handbag and handed it to him. I observed him as he compared the two photographs closely. He turned my one over and read the words on the back: *Nicholas & Christine with Claire July 1960.*

'There is a striking resemblance, I'll give you that, but if you're right how did Frances become Claire and end up on the other side of the world? And who are Christine and Nicholas Whiteley and how did they pass themselves off as her parents?'

'I'm not sure. I didn't think Claire bore any resemblance to Mrs Whiteley when I saw the photographs, and according to Claire she doesn't take after Mr Whiteley either. I realize that children don't always inherit their parents features, but Claire certainly wouldn't look like them if they're not her parents, would she? What if Frances didn't die in the car accident with Diane? How do we know she was actually in the car with her? After all, their bodies were never recovered. Think about it. If Diane was planning to leave James she might have arranged for Frances to be safely out of the way first. In which case she probably took her to the home of a close friend or family member.'

'Why do you say that?'

'Because I don't think she would have entrusted her daughter to a stranger, and whoever it was would have to be completely trust-worthy because they would be complicit in Diane's plan. Perhaps Diane was hoping to slip away without James knowing and to pick up Frances later but, of course, the plan went wrong.'

'I suppose it's possible, even though it seems incredible. But if Claire *is* Frances, how do you think she ended up in Australia?'

'The only thing I can think of is that Mr and Mrs Whiteley were emigrating to Australia anyway and agreed to pass off Frances as their daughter. They'd already lost their own daughter from leukaemia so probably jumped at the chance of having another child and a fresh start. Who knows?'

'If what you say is correct, Alicia, then your point about them not being total strangers makes sense. My bet would be that the 'parents' are in some way related to Diane themselves. What if the husband was actually Diane's brother Philip? We don't know anything about him at all.'

'No. We don't.'

'So we can't rule him out.'

'But Lucy's grandmother's surname is Whiteley not Gordon.'

'Her married name, yes, but what's her maiden name? I'd be interested to know what it is. It looks like I need to check a few more records than I thought.'

'You don't have their full names but you should have enough information to look for their marriage certificate and see if a Christine Gordon married a Nicholas Whiteley.'

'Exactly. One thing does puzzle me, though, which could throw out our theory.'

'What's that?'

'For Frances to become Claire somebody must have created a new identity for her. I wonder how they managed it.'

'I have no idea how easy it would have been to create, but I'm sure that Claire and Frances are one and the same. Claire is the exact age Frances would be now. She was two when the Whiteley's emigrated to Australia in 1960 and Frances was two at the time of Diane's accident in 1960. You're going to have a busy time at the Family Records Office on Monday.'

'Yes, well let's hope it's worth it. Have you told Isabelle any of this?'

'No. I've only just discovered it, remember. I won't say anything to her yet. But if Claire is Frances, this has huge implications for Lucy as she's also James Latham's grandchild and fully entitled to a share of the estate under his Will on exactly the same terms as Isabelle. Now that would give her reason to kill, don't you think?'

'But even if she could have committed all these murders, wouldn't it be simpler for her to prove who she is rather than bumping everyone off?'

'You tell me. I'm not a criminal psychologist, but the more I think about this the more I feel we're looking for a psychopath,' I replied, feeling slightly frustrated.

'You have good instincts, so let's follow them. Since we're going to see Bridget Ward later why don't you show her that photograph and ask her if she knows anything about the people in it. She might even recognize Frances. She's certainly old enough to remember her. Let's be positive. I feel as if finally we're getting somewhere.'

'I hope so.' I sighed. 'Alex, what were you going to say to me yesterday when Isabelle came in?' That was something else I had been waiting to ask him.

'Isabelle said there's a portrait of Diane in the library. Let's take a look.' If he was going to ignore my question, I was not going to pursue it.

'You can lead the way since you seem to know where everything is. I wonder where Isabelle's got to. She should be back by now.'

'I'm right here.' I turned around and she was behind us. 'I'm sorry I've been so long. Have you had a good look at everything?'

'I'm keen to see the portrait of Diane,' I replied as we walked along the corridor and followed Alex into the library. The portrait, which was smaller than I had imagined, hung over the fireplace. 'Who's it by?'

'Sir Gerald Kelly. It was painted around the time of her marriage to Grandpa. She was very pretty, wasn't she?'

'I thought that when I saw her photograph. That's a beautiful gold locket she's wearing.' I approached the portrait to take a closer look and noticed the entwined initials on it. 'I wonder whose initials those are. I can't make them out. Do you know what happened to the locket, Isabelle?'

'I can't say I've ever seen it,' she said, scrutinising the portrait.

'What time is Bridget Ward expecting us?' asked Alex.

'I suppose we'd better start making a move,' she replied, looking at her watch. 'If you want to grab a bite to eat before we see her we should leave now. It's after one now and I told her that we'd be there mid-afternoon.'

'Good idea,' said Alex enthusiastically. 'I'm absolutely starving. We left at the crack of dawn this morning and I didn't have time for breakfast.'

'OK. Let's find somewhere on the way.'

Bridget Ward lived on the outskirts of Newton Abbot, off the A380 Newton Abbot Road, in a small village called Coffinswell. Isabelle said she knew exactly where it was because she had been with her grandfather to a fourteenth-century thatched inn called the Linny Inn a few years back. We arrived at Bridget Ward's house about three-thirty. It was a chalet style bungalow, set back off the road and very private with an established hedge across the front of the property. Bridget was clearly expecting us because she was standing in the doorway as we walked up the front path. She was of middling height and build, and wore her fading blonde hair swept back loosely in a chignon. Her skin was pale but she had the brightest grey/blue eyes. She smiled broadly as we approached.

'Mrs Ward,' said Isabelle, extending her hand, 'thank you so much for seeing us today. I really appreciate it.'

'You're very welcome, dear,' she replied, grabbing Isabelle's hand with both of hers. She did not have a West Country accent and sounded as if she came from the Home Counties. 'I remember your grandfather well. My parents must have worked for him for nearly thirty years. I used to play with your mother as a girl, although she was a few years younger than me, and I remember her marriage to your father. It's a pleasure to meet you.'

'Thank you. Likewise. These are my friends, Alex and Alicia.' Isabelle turned to introduce us.

'Hello,' said Bridget, addressing us both. 'Please come in.' She led us through to a living room at the back of the house which opened on to the most magnificent secluded garden. Just outside the French doors there was a decked area and beyond that a lawned garden and what looked like a raised pond feature to the side. Although the garden was private, it was surrounded by rolling countryside and the views from the window were stunning. I noticed that the round table in the alcove was set for tea and that there were scones, jam and a cake in the centre of it.

'What a wonderful garden,' I said enthusiastically. 'You also have a fantastic landscape to look out on to.'

'Yes. Isn't it? Having grown up on such a large estate, I like open spaces. I don't think I could live without my garden. Mind you, it's a lot of work. Fortunately, my husband is retired and we both love gardening. I'm sorry he's not here. He had to go into Torquay.' She indicated for us to sit down.

'We've just come from Stowick House,' said Isabelle. 'My friends wanted to see it.'

'Oh, how is the old place? I haven't been there for years.'

'You must come and see it the next time I'm down.'

'That would be lovely. I'd like that very much. Now, you are staying for tea, aren't you? I hope you like scones and cake.' Alex seemed delighted about the prospect of having a Devonshire cream tea.

'Oh, that sounds wonderful,' he said.

'But we didn't expect anything,' I added. 'We didn't want to put you to any trouble.'

'You haven't. I made the scones this morning knowing you were coming, and I always have plenty of cake so everything's prepared. I only need to make the tea. It won't take a moment.' She disappeared into the kitchen and five minutes later returned with the teapot and a large bowl of clotted cream. 'Please help yourselves to scones,' she said, indicating for us to sit at the table and starting to pour the tea. Alex sat on one side of me, and Isabelle on the other, so I was sitting opposite Bridget. 'There's plenty more jam and cream if you need it.' Alex and I both helped ourselves to scones. 'Now, if I understand you correctly, Isabelle, you're trying to find out some information about your grandfather's second wife Diane.' She handed each of us a cup of tea.

'Yes. As I explained on the 'phone, Alicia obtained your details from an old friend of your mother's, Emily Middleton. Emily said you might be able to help me because you lived on the estate with your parents when you were a little girl.'

'Yes, that's right. What do you want to know?'

'I'm not sure how old you were when my grandfather was married to Diane but what do you remember about her? Were she and my grandfather happy? You see I'm trying to find out what really happened the day of the accident. I need to know how my grandfather was involved.'

'I was only about five when my parents started to work for your grandfather in the early fifties. I think I'm right in saying that your grandmother was still alive then – but I don't remember her at all. By the time he married Diane I would have been about eleven. I'd been going up to the house to play with Mary ever since we'd moved to the estate, and that continued after he married Diane. She used to take Mary out and sometimes I went too. I wasn't aware of what when on in the household. To be honest with you most of what I know about Diane and your grandfather is what my mother told me.'

'That doesn't matter. I'm just interested to hear what you do know and I don't care if what you have to tell me is bad.'

'According to my mother, your grandfather met Diane at a charity art function, and by all accounts it was a whirlwind romance. He was simply captivated by her and she was certainly fond of him. Although he loved her he became very possessive of her and he even accused her of having an affair and that's when the trouble in their marriage began.' I was intrigued to hear that previously unknown piece of information as that could put a completely different complexion on things.

'But why would he do that?' asked Isabelle. 'He must have had good reason to be suspicious. Something must have happened to make him suspect her.' Although Isabelle had told me she wanted to learn the truth whether it condemned her grandfather or not, I could tell that she desperately wanted him to be innocent. I was worried that hearing anything adverse might just tip her over the edge, so to speak, after what she had been through in recent weeks.

'All I know is that, after their daughter was born, the marriage had near broken down and Diane confided in my mother that she wanted to leave him, but she was frightened that he'd never let her go. According to her, his unfounded jealousy had destroyed their marriage.' I was interested to hear what Bridget had to say because this essentially corroborated what Grandma Edie had said Bridget's mother had told her about him being possessive.

'If that's the case, he did cause her to die because she was trying to get away from him…'

'But it was an accident, Isabelle.' I sensed she was already distressed.

'Talking of which,' said Bridget, 'you've reminded me of something. A couple of months before Diane died, an American ex-serviceman was killed in an horrendous motorbike accident not far from Stowick House. The police came to interview Diane because one of the villagers in Buckfastleigh told them that they had seen him with her in her car on several occasions. According to my mother Diane denied ever having met this man, but I think James didn't believe her, and this heightened his suspicions over her having an affair.'

'Then he did have justification,' said Isabelle. She was becoming more emotional so I decided to step in.

'Who was the American?' I asked.

'I don't remember his name,' replied Bridget.

'It doesn't matter,' said Alex reassuringly, putting down the scone he was eating. 'We'll find out. We can look up details of the accident.'

'Did your mother ever talk to you about the events leading up to Diane's death?' I asked.

'Unfortunately, on the day of the accident my mother was not at the house because it was her day off, so she did not witness what happened. But she was surprised when she heard that James had returned home as she thought he was still in London on business. You see he only left the day before and wasn't expected back for a few days.' This would fit in with my theory that Diane was planning to leave in his absence. With him away, it would have been so easy for her to make her escape.

'How did they know that Diane and Frances were in the car?' I asked. 'After all, they didn't find their bodies.'

'But Diane was driving.'

'Sorry. What I meant was, how did they know Frances was actually in the car?' Isabelle looked a little confused and Bridget was becoming flustered.

'I don't know. They found her dolly, and clothes from a suitcase which were thrown out of the car. They presumed...' I cut her short.

'What? That she was in the car because some of her possessions were. What if Diane put all those things in the car to make it look as if Frances was with her?'

'What are you saying?' she asked.

'Yes, what on earth are you talking about?' said Isabelle. She sounded distressed. 'Diane and Frances died in that accident. Grandpa chased them in the car. Isn't that what the newspaper articles said, Alex?' she asked, turning to him for confirmation.

'It was reported that they both died. At the inquest your grandfather told them that he saw Frances' favourite doll on the rear shelf and he believed she was in the car because she'd never go anywhere without that doll. But at no time did he ever say he saw her in the car.'

'But my mother said that Frances was at the house the day before,' said Bridget questioningly.

'I'm sure she was, but Diane may have taken her somewhere else early in the morning or someone could have picked her up from the house. We know she had a brother called Philip. Do you ever recall him visiting her there?'

'I didn't even know she had a brother. She had lots of visitors, but I don't know who they were.'

'Would you be able to remember any of them if you saw them in a photograph?'

'I can try, but bearing in mind we are talking about events of nearly fifty years ago, I can't make any promises,' she replied, with some reluctance.

'I have a photograph I'd like you to look at, Bridget.' I pulled the photograph, which I had shown to Alex earlier, out of my handbag.

'What's that?' asked Isabelle, leaning across me.

'I'll show it to you in a moment. I just want Bridget to look at it first.' I passed it across the table to her. 'Do you recognize any of the people in this photograph?' She put her reading glasses, which hung from a chain around her neck, up on to her nose and studied it.

'The little girl's Frances.'

'Are you sure about that?' I glanced over to Alex. He looked very serious.

'Positive. I remember her distinctly.'

'What about the adults with her?'

'I don't recognize either of them. I'm sorry.' She handed the photograph back to me.

'Do the names Nicholas and Christine Whiteley mean anything to you?' She shook her head. 'Their names are on the back.'

'Whiteley?' Isabelle sounded surprised. 'That's Lucy's grandmother's surname. Let me look at that photograph,' she said, snatching it from me. 'Where did you get this?' she asked, scanning it, turning it over and looking at the back.

'From Claire's box of photographs. It's Claire and her parents, only it's not. It's Frances.' Isabelle was visibly shocked.

'What? You must have made a mistake. That can't be right. Claire is the name written on here.'

'There's no mistake, Isabelle. This photograph is dated July 1960. The accident in which Frances was supposed to have died was May 1960. Only she didn't die. She became Claire, and Claire doesn't know that she's actually Frances.'

'I can hardly believe what I'm hearing,' said Bridget. 'I wish my mother was here. She might have known how the Whiteley's were connected with Frances.' Isabelle was staring at the photograph.

'It's incredible. I can hardly take any of this in. But if Claire is Frances she's Grandpa's daughter which means that Lucy is also his...'

'...granddaughter,' I said, finishing her sentence.

Chapter 25

Understandably these latest revelations came as an enormous blow to Isabelle and she was in a state of shock. She was convinced that Lucy had no idea of her true identity or that they were related. Any suggestion by either Alex or me that Lucy was a possible suspect was met with a quick rebuff, and she would not be persuaded by any arguments to the contrary.

We decided not to stay in Devon for the night and arrived back in London late on Saturday evening. I was worried about Isabelle's safety, so Alex agreed he would continue to stay with her in Hampstead.

By the time I reached home I was really exhausted but could not sleep and sat up into the early hours churning over the facts of the case. Although we were making positive progress and piecing the puzzle together, vital parts were still missing and finding them was taking too long. I had an awful sense of foreboding that time was running out for Isabelle.

On Sunday morning I 'phoned Sally to ask her if she was free for lunch. We had not spoken since my return to London and it seemed a good opportunity for us to catch up. There was no answer on her landline so I called her mobile, but there was no response on that either. I left a message saying I was back from Australia and hoped we could meet some time during the week.

I did not want to see Antonia because I was not in the mood for another post-mortem discussion about my relationship with Alex. I decided to spend the day alone, reading the Sunday newspapers and catching up on a few household chores. On my way out to buy a paper I noticed Dorothy's front door was ajar. I wanted to speak to her but I knew she had spoken with Alex on Friday afternoon and I anticipated the fallout from that conversation.

'Dorothy,' I called out as I pushed the door open. 'Are you there?' She hobbled out into the hall. 'Are you OK?' I asked, noticing that she was a little unsteady on her feet.

'Yes. I've just been bending down in the garden and my knees are a bit stiff.'

'You should take it easy. You push yourself too hard.'

'So do you,' she said, touching my cheek, 'You're looking tired. How did it go with Emily?'

'She was very helpful. She put us in touch with the housekeeper's daughter in Devon. That's why I'm tired. We came back late last night.'

'Oh, my word, that was a bit of a trek for one day. So it was you going out at the crack of dawn yesterday. I hope the trip was productive.'

'It was. She gave us some useful information.' I filled Dorothy in on the details we had discovered.

'This is utterly incredible. What an extraordinary state of affairs. But I hope you're not taking any risks with all this digging around for information.'

'I'm trying not to. Anyway, Alex is helping us.'

'Oh, I see. How is he? When I saw him the other day he said that he'd just had his appendix out. I thought he was looking a bit peaky. I must admit I had high hopes that you were together. It's such a shame you're not.'

'Why does everyone think we should be?'

'I thought you were very fond of him.'

'I was. I am, only he let me down. He can't expect me to fall at his feet because he tells me he loves me and now is the right time in his life to have a relationship.'

'Hmm... Well make sure you turn him down for the right reason, not because you think he has to pay for hurting you. Leave it too long and it might be too late. You don't want to turn around one day and find nobody there.'

'But...'

'No buts. Don't throw everything away for a whim or some point of principle.'

Suitably admonished by Dorothy, I returned upstairs with my tail between my legs. Deep down I knew I had been too harsh on Alex and that Dorothy was right. Antonia had a point too and I had let my impetuosity and that stubborn streak of mine colour my judgment yet again. I raided my store cupboard for sufficient supplies of Pringles and sat down to watch a DVD of *Breakfast at Tiffany's* to take my mind off everything.

I had neglected to check my e-mails all day, so I logged on before I went to bed. As I trawled through the e-mails in my inbox I noticed there was one from Jeremy Brown. It had completely slipped my mind that he was going to ask Paul if he could find out whether Luisa had taken any time off work around the time John MacFadzean was murdered. Paul had discovered from a source at the *Courier Mail* that she had called in to the paper late in the evening of Sunday 4 March to say that her mother had been taken sick on the Friday night and that she had flown home to Melbourne. She said she would get the first flight back to Brisbane on Monday morning but would be late in to work. That all tied in as Monday 5 March was the day she left the note for me and I met her on 6 March. She then flew back to Melbourne the following week, on 14 March, which was the day I bumped into her in the city so that sounded right.

I responded to Jeremy's e-mail immediately. I very much appreciated his help and I was sorry that my stay in Melbourne had been curtailed but I hoped to see him again very soon. Jeremy had provided me with Paul's e-mail address so I e-mailed him to thank him for the information about Luisa.

On Monday morning, had it not been for my alarm clock ringing loudly in my ears, I probably would have slept until noon. I could not have felt less like returning to work – that was the last thing on my mind. Armed with a double shot of caffeine in my regular caffè latte, which I picked up from the Italian café on my way to the office, I braced myself for the day. Fortunately, everything seemed to be under control, Graham had monitored my files in my absence and there was no significant backlog of work.

This was just as well because I was like a cat on hot bricks all morning hoping for news from Alex and was unable to concentrate. As I was being preternaturally unproductive I decided to take an early lunch and a leisurely stroll across the park. On returning I was greeted by a beaming Danielle coming out of my office.

'There's been a delivery for you,' she said. 'I've put it on your desk.'

'What is it?' I replied, thinking that it was probably my new *Trusts & Estates Law Handbook* ordered weeks ago.

'Someone has sent you some flowers. I think you must have an admirer,' she said in an airy tone, following me in to the office. 'But I didn't see a card. I wondered who they could be from…' She hovered for a moment waiting for me to comment. Danielle was not exactly subtle.

'*Mamma mia!*' I exclaimed, seeing the flowers. They were chrysanthemums. 'Who would send me these? Do you know what they signify?'

'I'm not sure I follow your questions.' Danielle looked at me blankly.

'To an Italian, chrysanthemums signify death. It's customary to send them when someone has died.'

'Who's dead? I didn't know anyone in your family had died.'

'They haven't.' At least I sincerely hoped not. I had the strongest feeling that whoever sent them knew I would pick up on their importance and intended to unnerve me.

'I'm sure it was just an innocent mistake, Alicia. I certainly didn't know about the Italian custom. When I saw the chrysanthemums I thought, "what a romantic gesture it was for someone to send them." I always associate flowers with joy and I thought it was a good sign.' Danielle meant well, but since I could not reveal the real reasons for my negative reaction, I simply did not engage in any further conversation on the subject.

I felt that receiving the flowers was particularly significant and that I was being given an augury of what might happen if I persisted with my involvement in Isabelle's affairs and the investigation into the murders. To be given a warning like this, I knew that I must be close to discovering the truth. In a curious sort of way it was both terrifying and exhilarating, but admittedly more the former than the latter.

For one fleeting second when Danielle told me there was no card, and before I saw that they were chrysanthemums, I did think that they might have come from Alex – but it was obvious that Alex was not responsible. Besides, it was highly unlikely he would buy me flowers after what I had said to him. But with no florist's card there was no way of knowing whom they were from. It was all very frustrating and bizarre.

The rest of Monday passed uneventfully and I did not hear from either Alex or Isabelle. I did not read anything untoward into that because I knew Isabelle was with Alex, and he would let me know the results of his research in early course.

On Tuesday I immersed myself in work. I put my phone on 'DND' (do not disturb), reviewed my files and worked through the notes Graham had left for me. There were one or two matters I needed to discuss with him, but he was out of the office for a few days so they would have to wait. It was after five-thirty and I was marking up a trust document when I was startled by someone opening the door to my office and looked up from my work. Danielle had already left so I knew it could not be her unless she had forgotten something and returned. To my surprise it was Alex and he was alone. I was pleased because I had been giving some particularly serious consideration to Dorothy's comments and this was my opportunity to revisit that last conversation we had had on the Sunshine Coast.

'I saw Danielle on her way out. She said you were still here and to come straight up,' he said, popping his head around the door and smiling at me. 'I didn't somehow think you would have left for the day.' He pushed the door wide open and stepped in to the office. 'May I...' He glanced at the chair opposite my desk.

'Of course.' I signalled for him to sit and smiled back with my brightest smile. 'You don't have to ask.' He literally sank down into the chair, dropping his soft tan leather briefcase by his side. 'Are you OK? I really appreciate you doing all this running around for me, but if you're not up to it you must say so.'

'I'm fine. I'm more tired than usual and still a bit sore, but well on the mend. It's just been one hell of a day. What lovely flowers,' he said, espying the vase of chrysanthemums on my desk. Danielle had insisted she put them there despite my protestations that they were unlucky.

'They arrived yesterday. I think they were sent as a forewarning.' He looked at me vaguely. 'Italians don't send chrysanthemums unless someone has died. It's what the flowers represent that's relevant here. I'm sure of it.'

'Then I think it's rather sinister, Alicia.' He sounded serious. 'I don't mean to alarm you, but I see it as more of a personal threat. You need to be very vigilant from now on.'

'Don't freak me out, Alex!'

'I'm genuinely concerned, that's all. If we're talking about safety issues then I have to say I'm worried about yours. Why do you always jump down my throat?'

'I'm sorry. I didn't mean it like that. I guess I am on edge. Anyway, what's happened with you? Why have you had such a bad day and where's Isabelle? I thought she'd be with you. Nothing's happened to her, has it?' I was anxious about her whereabouts.

'Don't panic,' he said calmly, undoing his suede jacket and leaning back in the chair. 'She's quite safe. She's with Drew's parents in Hertfordshire. She spoke to them on Sunday night because she hadn't heard anything further on the funeral arrangements. They asked her if she wanted to go and stay with them for a few days. They want to organize a posthumous exhibition of Drew's work and to discuss that with her.'

'Yes. I know. She mentioned it to me when we were in Australia.'

'She was reluctant to go at first because she's desperate to be here in case there are any developments and she wanted to come to the Family Records Office with me. It took a little bit of persuasion, but she left yesterday morning, and before you ask she called me to say she had arrived safely.'

'Well, as long as she's OK. I can't help worrying.'

'Yes, I realize that. Drew's parents will keep an eye on her though. There's no point staying at her place tonight so I'm going to go back to my apartment.'

'I thought a friend of yours is there.'

'He is, but he knew it was always going to be a temporary arrangement. I'm quite happy for him to stay until he finds somewhere else. Anyway, the reason why I dropped by is to tell you what I've found out so far.' He bent down to pick up his briefcase and put it on his lap. He unfastened its two buckles and pulled out an A4 sized clear plastic folder containing some papers. 'We don't have all the answers, but I think you'll be pleased with what we do have.'

'Any answers would be a start. Don't keep me in suspense. What have you discovered?' I leaned forward across the desk.

'OK. The first thing I looked for was Diane's birth certificate, but I couldn't find it.'

'What do you mean?' I was puzzled.

'What I say. Not under the name of Gordon anyhow.'

'I don't follow?'

'I'm trying to explain.' Poor Alex seemed a little frustrated by my impatience. 'I decided to check out her marriage to James Latham. That was easy to find and I think you'll agree it is somewhat revealing,' he said, handing the certified copy of the marriage certificate to me. I scanned down each column…date of marriage, name and surname, age, marital status, rank or profession, residence at the time of the marriage until I reached the seventh column where details of the father's name and surname are provided. I could hardly believe the four words I was reading: Paul Richard Masterton (Deceased).

Chapter 26

'Oh, Alex, this is amazing,' I said enthusiastically. 'So Diane was a Masterton. I can hardly believe it; although it fits that one of her family might want to avenge her. But where does the Gordon come in? Did she change her name perhaps? She wasn't married before because it says spinster on the certificate.' I glanced at it again and noticed that the maiden name recorded was Gordon. 'Maybe her mother remarried and what about her brother Philip? Was he older or younger and a Masterton or a Gordon?' I looked over at Alex. 'What else did you discover? Only I can see quite a few more certified copies in that plastic folder of yours,' I said with intense curiosity.

'With the details from Diane's marriage certificate I was able to find her birth certificate.' He pulled it out of the plastic folder and passed it across the desk to me. 'So now we have both her parents' details.' Her mother was Lillian Mary Masterton and her maiden name was Pierce.' The fact that Gordon was not her mother's maiden name reinforced my belief that she had married again.

'It says here that Diane was born in Somerset.' I held up the certificate and pointed to column one. 'That's where Lucy's so-called grandmother came from. That means that she and her husband could have known Diane's parents. I wonder if Diane's mother is still alive. I don't suppose she is. Oh, no she can't be,' I said, picking up her marriage certificate to Paul Masterton. 'They were married in May 1918 and she was twenty then.'

'She isn't. I checked. She died in 1965. What I was trying to find out was when Diane's brother was born. We know from her birth certificate that Diane was born in October 1930. I thought it was more likely that if Lillian married in 1918 that Philip was older than Diane, but then again, by my reckoning Lillian could have had him in her forties, so I thought I might have to check the period from 1919 up until the early 1940s.

Then there was the added problem of whether he was a Masterton or a Gordon. I decided the best thing would be to find out when Diane's mother married Mr Gordon as in that way, if it was much later, I could rule out having to check under the Gordon surname because she'd be beyond child-bearing age by then. As you can see, Mrs Lillian Masterton, the widow, married Mr Charles Duncan Gordon in January 1946,' he said, passing me a certified copy of her second marriage.

'Then Philip must be a child of the first marriage.'

'Yes. Here's his birth certificate.' He held it up and waved it at me. 'Do you want to look at it?'

'Yes, please.' I reached across the table, took it from him and reviewed it. Philip Richard Masterton was born in February 1920 and was over ten years older than Diane. He was also born in Frome, Somerset, at the same address as Diane, and therefore their parents must have lived there for quite a while. 'I wonder why Diane changed her name from Masterton to Gordon?' I said, thinking out loud.

'I suppose when her mother remarried Diane who was only fifteen at the time, wanted to be known by the same name as her mother and step-father. It's understandable. Philip was older so it wouldn't have affected him in the same way.'

'That's possible. You've done a fantastic job, Alex. I'm really grateful. You must have been at the Family Records Office all day yesterday.'

'I was and I was back there today. But I haven't finished yet. I have more documents for you including a certified copy of both Frances' birth and death certificates and Diane's.' He put them on the table. 'I was on a roll. I thought I might as well find out as much information as I could while I was there.'

'You've certainly done that. I know we've established that Diane and Philip are both Mastertons, but what I want to know is how they are related to Jonathan Masterton. Is it possible, do you think, that Philip is Jonathan's father?' I continued, without pausing long enough to give Alex a chance to speak. 'Because if it is him, we know he's still alive and living in Wimbledon. He was closely connected to Isabelle's grandfather and someone I'd very much like to meet. We need to check that.'

'Bearing in mind his potential significance to the case, I did just that and searched for Jonathan's birth certificate. I remembered when we discussed him that you mentioned something about him being circa mid-fifties. I knew he was born here so I checked against all the dates when I thought he could have been born and I found him. He's actually a bit older. So, here's another certificate to add to your pile.' He placed it on the desk. I neatly stacked it with the other certificates. 'Jonathan *is* Philip's son.' I ran my eye over the document. I noticed that he was born in Frome as well – in October 1946. His mother was Annette Rosemary Thompson. 'And here's another one.' Alex handed me a certified copy of Philip and Annette's marriage certificate. 'I figured if Philip was born in 1920 and Jonathan was born a year or so after the War that they either married during the War or soon after. You'll see that they married in September 1945.'

'Yes. That means Diane was Jonathan's aunt, which suggests he's related to Lucy. It would make sense if they're working together.'

'Keeping it in the family and all that?' He raised his eyebrows and gave me a winsome smile.

'Hmm... It seems like it. I know I initially dismissed your "long lost relative of Diane" theory, but I've been thinking about it for some time and agree that everything points that way.'

'Yes. But why would Luisa murder John MacFadzean for Jonathan or Lucy? What's in it for her? Unless she's some long lost relative too, although I think that's unlikely. Mind you, they keep popping up out of the woodwork, don't they?'

'Maybe we should check out her records too.'

'If needs be the police in Australia can do that very easily. It's more probable that Jonathan offered to make it worth her while. MacFadzean must have got in Jonathan's way. It's very convenient that he had gambling debts and supposedly raided the trust as everyone thinks he's the bad guy, which takes the onus off Jonathan. What if MacFadzean was framed and didn't take money from the trust at all?'

'That's a very interesting point, Alex. And it's a possibility. Talking about Luisa, Paul Heddington has come up with some interesting information.'

'Which is?'

'We know that MacFadzean was murdered on 4 March. Well, she went to Melbourne on 2 March and didn't return to Brisbane until 5 March. It puts her in the right place at the right time, doesn't it?'

'Yes it does.'

'Do you know if Isabelle has heard from the police here?'

'On Sunday afternoon.'

'And?' I was hoping the Australian police had been liaising with them and he had some positive feedback for me.

'They came round to the house. It seems that DI Morris did take you seriously after all, because she has followed up on what you and Isabelle told her about John MacFadzean. She's been working with the British police all along so you were right about that. According to DI Evans, the Victorian State Police are giving weight to your murder theory and no longer investigating a mugging. Actually, I'm surprised you haven't heard from DI Evans yet. He seemed very keen to hear all your views on the case.'

'Hmm... Nobody from the police has contacted me. They are still proceeding as if they are investigating the intended murder of Drew rather than Isabelle.'

'Yes, it's part of DI Evans' strategy. I think that he's very interested in reopening the investigation into Michael's accident – but not Grandpa Jam's death, although Isabelle insists he was murdered. Apart from Isabelle, none of us is convinced he was.'

'What have you told them about what *we've* discovered?'

'Nothing. Simply that I met Isabelle through you and that we've been looking out for her. I didn't want to disclose any details without talking to you first, and Isabelle is adamant that we don't tell them anything yet. She wants us to have strong evidence before we approach the police with it and would rather we take control of things for now.'

'Hmm… That's all very well, Alex. It's a shame Jo and Will aren't here especially as Will is good at handling the police with all his contacts from his CID days.' Unfortunately, they were still in the South of France and not expected back for a while. 'I don't want to be accused of withholding evidence which could help with the investigation. I think that we should tell DI Evans what we know. That's the reason why I went to the police in Melbourne. Our theories might help solve the case and there's no reason for us not to work in conjunction with him.'

'I take your point. I think Isabelle is slightly reluctant because of Lucy. She's convinced herself that Lucy can't be involved and doesn't want us to say anything to the police, which suggests she is. Maybe you and she should have a chat about that. Which reminds me; I'll pick up Nicholas and Christine's marriage certificate tomorrow. I ran out of time yesterday and when I went back to collect the other certificates today I requested it. I can't tell you how many hours I've spent trawling through everything and it wasn't as straightforward as it sounds. I had to search through more entries in the registers than I care to tell you to obtain all this information.'

'I know what it's like, Alex. I'm not expecting you to perform miracles. It can take hours, days or even weeks in there sometimes, especially when you don't have the full details and have to order up quite a few certificates until you find the right one. At least we can get certificates within twenty-four hours even though it costs an absolute fortune.'

'Well, there was no point in ordering them and then waiting to receive them through the post because we need the information as a matter of urgency. I'll see you tomorrow then.' He lifted up the flap of his briefcase and slipped the plastic folder inside. 'Do you want those certified copies or shall I take them back?' he asked, pointing to them.

'I'll keep them if you don't mind. I'd like to take them home,' I replied, pushing them into the side pocket of my briefcase.

'OK. No problem.' He proceeded to do up the buckles of his briefcase. 'I thought that after I've been back to Islington, I'll go up to Colindale again and look for some details about that American ex-serviceman who was killed just before Diane had her accident. I'm not quite sure what you want to do about getting to Philip Masterton. Have a think about it. Well, I think I'll head home now.' He stood up and fastened his jacket.

'I'll come with you. It's time I made tracks.' If I was going to try and talk to him it might as well be now. I picked up my briefcase, took my raincoat off the hook on the door, flung it over the back of my arm, switched off the lights and followed him out. We walked down the corridor to the lift in silence. I called the lift and as we waited for it to arrive I put on my raincoat.

'You're very quiet, Alex,' I remarked, doing up the buttons. 'What are your thoughts?'

'On what? The case or generally?'

'The case.'

'Let's see what tomorrow brings.' The lift arrived and we stepped inside. I pressed the button for the ground floor. I was bursting to say something but for some reason found myself tongue-tied.

'It's a very modern building,' he commented. 'It makes a change from your previous firms, doesn't it?' I nodded. We reached the ground floor, the lift opened and we walked out into the main foyer. I said goodnight to the security guard as we passed the front desk and we proceeded through the revolving doors into the street outside. If I did not speak to him now I would lose my chance.

'Talk to you tomorrow then. Goodnight, Alicia.' He was about to walk off but I caught hold of his arm.

'Do you need to go?' I gave him a long and lingering look. 'I thought you might like to come back for dinner,' I said casually, trying not to seem too eager.

'I'm very tempted and I appreciate the offer, but I don't think I should.' He sounded matter of fact and distant.

'Why not? Can't we be friends?' I felt my opportunity to make things up with him rapidly slipping away.

'We are friends but… I don't want to be *just* friends,' he said flatly, removing my arms from his and looking at me hard. 'I would be lying to both of us if I told you otherwise. *You* on the other hand have made it perfectly clear that's all *you* want, so I think it's best we leave things as they are. You put things on a professional footing and that's what you've got.' He turned on his heel and started to walk from me.

'Alex! Don't go,' I called out in a plaintive voice. He stopped walking and spun around.

'Goodnight, Alicia,' he repeated. 'I'll speak to you in the morning.' And he carried on down the street leaving me standing watching him until he disappeared from view.

Chapter 27

I arrived home a few minutes after seven, starving and not in the best of moods. As I walked by the railings at the front of the building I glimpsed Dorothy at the window below drawing her curtains. She saw me too and waved. I waved back, but I decided not to pop downstairs to see her. I could not face chatting tonight to the all-too-knowing Dorothy. With my keys ready I hastened up the front steps, let myself in through the main front door and bolted up the stairs to my flat.

There were two messages on my answerphone. The first was from Antonia hoping that my day had gone well and inviting me to dinner with her and Tom on Friday. The second was from Isabelle asking me to 'phone her because she understood the police would be interviewing me and she wanted to discuss a couple of points with me before they did. I wondered if she had spoken to Alex. I returned Antonia's call immediately but neither she nor Tom was home. I left a message that all was well and dinner on Friday would be lovely.

Before I 'phoned Isabelle I made a start on dinner. I decided to have some penne all'arrabbiata – appropriate, considering my state of mind. I put a large pan of salted water on the hob to boil, took a packet of penne and a clove of garlic out of the cupboard and a smallish chilli pepper from the fridge. I picked up my cordless handset, which I had put down on one of the work surfaces, and dialled the number Isabelle left for me.

'Mrs Hyde-Dowler?' I presumed that the lady who answered the 'phone was Drew's mother.

'Speaking.'

'Oh, good evening. My name's Alicia Allen. Isabelle left a message for me to call her. Is she there?'

'Yes. Just one moment, please.' I could hear voices in the background and then the sound of footsteps on what sounded like either a wooden or tiled floor as Isabelle came to the 'phone.

'Hi, Alicia, thanks for getting back to me.'

'No problem,' I said, taking the frying pan out of the lower kitchen cupboard and putting it on the hob. 'What do you want to talk to me about?' I balanced the 'phone between ear and chin as I opened a bottle of olive oil and poured some into the frying pan.

'What are you going to tell the police?'

'Well, that rather depends upon what they ask me,' I replied, standing on tiptoes and reaching for a tin of chopped Italian tomatoes at the back of the cupboard.

'I meant about Lucy.' I picked up the can-opener and opened the tin of tomatoes. 'I realize you want to be frank with them, but could you please not tell them your theories about Lucy's involvement until Alex has more information on the Whiteleys? I briefly spoke to him this evening. I can't believe what he's found out. I'm still trying to take it all in. It's remarkable.' While she was talking I turned on the gas under the frying pan to heat the olive oil and took a knife and my garlic squeezer out of the kitchen drawer next to the oven.

'Yes, it is. Listen, Isabelle, I know that you've been friends with Lucy for quite a few years now,' I said, putting the garlic clove into the squeezer and pressing the handles together hard. I dropped the crushed pieces of garlic into the frying pan, 'and your loyalty is admirable, but if she's innocent, why do you need to protect her?' I chopped a couple of small pieces off the chilli pepper. That would be more than enough to flavour the dish without making it too hot. 'Surely your concern is unfounded?' I threw the pieces of chilli pepper into the frying pan of olive oil and garlic causing it to sizzle.

'What's that sound Alicia? Where are you?'

'I'm in the kitchen preparing dinner. What is it you want me to do?' I asked, pressing the point. The water was boiling so I shot the penne into the saucepan. There was a pause at the end of the line. 'Isabelle, are you still there?' I stirred the pasta and then tipped the contents from the tin of tomatoes into the frying pan and added some seasoning. 'Isabelle?'

'Yes. I'm here.'

'You didn't answer my question. Why are you so concerned?' I mixed in the tomatoes, put the lid on the frying pan and turned the gas down to simmer. I checked on the pasta, gave it another stir around, perched on my kitchen stool and waited for Isabelle to respond.

'Call it an instinct thing. Mine tells me to hold off for a little longer. Please wait until Alex completes his research.'

'All right. I won't say anything...for now. But it *is* against my better judgment.' Although I agreed to Isabelle's request I was reluctant so to do because I had an awful sense of foreboding about it.

'Thank you, Alicia. Let me know how it goes with the police.'

'OK. I'll speak to you later.'

'Thanks again. Bye.'

'Bye.'

After clearing away the dishes I settled down to check my e-mails. I was about to e-mail Kim to find out how the newly-weds were doing, when my video Entryphone buzzer rang. I walked from the living room into the hall to answer it. On the video screen I could make out a man with a stocky build standing on the front step. There seemed to be another man hovering behind him but more than that I could not tell.

'Hello,' I said, over the intercom.

'Miss Allen?'

'Speaking.'

'I'm Detective Inspector Evans,' he said, holding up his ID. I

thought I could hear a slight Welsh accent. 'And this is Detective
Sergeant Mitchell,' he added, moving aside to allow the younger
man to hold up his ID. All I could see of him was his arm. The DS
then moved out of the way and DI Evans continued to speak. 'We're
investigating the murder of Andrew Hyde-Dowler and we'd like to
ask you a few questions, if it's convenient.' I was correct; that was a
Welsh accent. There was no point in putting off the evil moment so
I might as well speak to them there and then.

'OK,' I responded, pressing the door release button. 'Please come
up. I'm on the first floor.' I heard them walk into the hall and the
front door click shut behind them. I put my door on the latch and
waited at the top of the stairs for the two policemen. It was only a
minute or two before they rounded the stairwell and bounded up
the stairs towards me. They both looked up on seeing me standing
there.

'Good evening,' I said, extending my hand first to DI Evans and
then to DS Mitchell. I estimated that DI Evans was in his late
forties. He was of middling height and quite thick set with dark
wavy hair, which was greying at the temples. He half-smiled at me
when he saw me; he had rather a pleasant countenance. DS Mitchell
was probably in his early thirties. He was taller and leaner, with light
cropped brown hair and regular features. His expression was more
serious; I could detect not even the trace of a smile. I led them into
the hall and indicated for them to walk through to the living room
and take a seat. I shut the front door and followed them in. They
both sat on the sofa.

'Could I offer either of you a drink?' I asked, remaining standing.
DS Mitchell shook his head.

'Thank you, no,' replied DI Evans. I sat down in my armchair.
'I'll get straight to the point,' he continued, clearing his throat. 'Miss
Allen I understand that Isabelle Parker is your client and that she
asked you to help with the investigation into the murder of her
fiancé Andrew Hyde-Dowler? How long have you acted for her?' I
presumed he knew that we did not have a long-standing professional

relationship and was wondering why she would confide in me.

'Isabelle only recently instructed my firm. I was recommended to her by a mutual acquaintance. I made her a Will, as I'm sure you already know.'

'Yes. My point is, didn't you think it strange that she instructed you to make it rather than Holmwood & Hitchins, especially as they were already dealing with the probate of her grandfather's estate?'

'Isn't that something you should be asking Isabelle?'

'I will ask her, but I'd like to hear what you have to say about it.'

'There's nothing much to say except that she didn't seem at all keen on her trustees and I felt she wanted to break away from the firm.'

'Did she mention John MacFadzean?'

'No. Only Jonathan Masterton.'

'In what context? That she didn't like him?'

'His name came up in conversation because he was one of her trustees, her grandfather's solicitor and also a personal friend of his. But she neither said that she liked or disliked him.' He was starting to irritate me already.

'I understand from the Victorian State Police that you believe John MacFadzean was murdered because of his connection to the Latham family. What made you think that?'

'I take it you've read a copy of the detailed statement I gave them?'

'Yes.'

'Then why do you need to ask me any more questions about him?'

'Because it is helpful if I hear it directly from you,' replied DI Evans, undeterred by my robust riposte. 'What did you think of him?'

'He was pleasant enough, but beyond that I can't say. If you want to know whether he came across as the sort who would misappropriate trust funds I can't answer that.' DS Mitchell caught my eye and smiled, animating his whole face. What a contrast from when he first walked in. 'I really don't mean to sound unhelpful. Believe me I want this matter resolved as much as you do.'

'Are you sure there's nothing else you can tell us?'

'There is another point you might want to think about,' I said, remembering Alex's suggestion that John MacFadzean could have been framed.

'Which is?'

'Have you considered the possibility that it wasn't John MacFadzean who stole from the trust and that someone else made it look like he did, knowing that people would jump to the immediate conclusion that he was culpable because of his debts. His initials are the same as Jonathan Masterton's. Who's to say he didn't do it?' I wanted to draw the police and ascertain whether Jonathan Masterton was on their list of suspects.

'Are you suggesting that Jonathan Masterton is the murderer?' asked DS Mitchell who seemed surprised that I might.

'Well, not of John MacFadzean, no.'

'Only he couldn't have done it because he was in London when John MacFadzean was murdered,' he said smugly.

'Yes, but he could have committed the other murders. He knows everything about the Latham family.' I refrained from mentioning my accomplice theory just yet.

'But what would he gain?' asked DI Evans.

'I don't think it's about money. It's about avenging the death of his aunt.'

'His aunt?' He looked befuddled.

'Diane Latham. James Latham's second wife. Alex Waterford did some research for me,' I said, standing up and walking into the hall to retrieve my briefcase.

'Where are you going?'

'I want to show you something,' I called out from the hall. I pulled the copy certificates out of the side pocket of my briefcase and returned to the living room.

'What do you have there?'

'Take a look at these,' I said, passing the certificates to him. He handed them to DS Mitchell who started to scan through them. 'You'll see that Diane Latham was born Diane Masterton. Her mother remarried, after her father's death, to a Mr Gordon and she took his name. Philip Masterton's her brother and the father of Jonathan Masterton. Now he's someone you should really interview, Philip Masterton that is. It is my understanding that they were problems in the Latham marriage, Diane was unhappy and she planned to leave her husband. She was killed in a car accident trying to get away. Maybe the Masterton family blames Isabelle's grandfather, hence the killings.'

'An interesting theory,' he said. I was beginning to feel rather frustrated that neither of them appeared to be taking me seriously.

'Forgive me, but you don't seem to be making much progress in catching the killer, unless there's something you're not telling me,' I retorted. I looked at both of them but their facial expressions gave nothing away. 'Here's another theory for you. What if Jonathan Masterton isn't working alone and has at least one accomplice?'

'What do you mean at least one? How many do you think he has?' asked DS Mitchell, furrowing his brow and knitting his eyebrows in the process. I was thinking of Luisa and Lucy but I wanted to steer clear of any discussion about Lucy and needed to think quickly on my feet.

'I meant, he must have an accomplice because, as you have confirmed, he was not in Melbourne and could not have committed MacFadzean's murder. I'm probably sticking my neck out here, but I believe that the person responsible is an Australian journalist who happens to be a friend of Isabelle's called Luisa Bruneschi.'

'You don't mention this in the statement you gave to the Victorian State Police. Why not?' asked DI Evans.

'I hope you're not suggesting anything by that comment,' I snapped. He raised his eyebrows.

'Not at all. Only as someone who seems very certain of her

complicity I am surprised that you made no reference to her. That's all.

'At the time I made my statement I was less certain. You see, although there was something about her I mistrusted when we first met and I had my suspicions, it wasn't until after the tram incident that I felt she must be involved.'

'But Isabelle told the Victorian State Police that was an accident.'

'Yes, she did.'

'Evidently you don't think it was. Perhaps you'd like to explain why you suspect her.'

'I met Luisa on two occasions prior to the incident in Melbourne. The first time was in Brisbane, before MacFadzean's murder, but after the death of Isabelle's fiancé. She struck me as overly interested in Isabelle's legal affairs and *only* that to be honest. The second time was when I bumped into her in Melbourne a week after MacFadzean's murder. She seemed to know all about his gambling debts and that he was in the Crown Casino the night he was killed. Later I heard that the police hadn't disclosed any of those details and I thought it was odd she knew so much. Again, she was fishing for information on Isabelle's affairs. For someone who is not a *really* close friend I felt it was too much.

'On the afternoon of the tram incident the three of us were walking along the road together. I went into a shop and Isabelle and Luisa carried on walking although Luisa left Isabelle moments before the accident, apparently. It seems incredible to me that she didn't hear it. Call me suspicious, but her movements around that time don't add up unless she was involved. She was in the right place and she had the opportunity to push Isabelle under that tram.'

'Why didn't you tell the Melbourne police any of this?'

'Because I didn't witness the incident. This is my opinion based on my dealings with her. I'm only telling *you* because *you* asked me to explain why I'm suspicious of her. As for John MacFadzean's murder, I've found out that Luisa was in Melbourne that night, as I'm sure the Victorian State Police can confirm if they check.'

'I see,' said DI Evans. 'But what would her motive be?'

'That I don't know. Perhaps the police out there should make some enquiries about her. I don't suppose she's been interviewed because she probably isn't even in the frame. But at least it's an option.'

'No. It's not. Not any more. Which is extremely unfortunate bearing in mind what you have just told us,' he said, sounding slightly despondent.

'Why not? What do you mean?'

'Because Luisa Bruneschi is dead, Miss Allen. She was found in her hotel room in Russell Square yesterday evening.'

'What?' I exclaimed, holding my hands up to my face in astonishment. 'When? How? I didn't even know she was in London.' My mind boggled.

'We'll have to wait for the results of the autopsy, but early indications would suggest that she haemorrhaged to death.'

'How? Was it an accident?' I already anticipated his response.

'No. It was murder,' he replied.

'And a brutal one at that,' added DS Mitchell.

Chapter 28

'We will need to speak to Isabelle about her friendship with Luisa Bruneschi,' said DI Evans as I accompanied him and DS Mitchell to the door.

'I hope you're not intending to call her tonight,' I replied curtly as I opened it to let them out. 'Only, in recent weeks she has sustained quite a few shocks. I don't think she can take much more.'

'We intend to tell her personally…in the morning,' said DI Mitchell, turning to DI Evans for confirmation.

'Yes. That's right. However, in the circumstances we would rather you did not make contact with her until after you have heard from us.'

'I have to go to work early and I doubt I'll have a chance to speak to her until later anyway.'

'Good. Well, thank you very much for your time,' said DI Evans as they strode out the door. 'Here's my card. *If* you think of anything else we should know about,' he added, handing it to me, 'give me a call. But we'll be in touch.' He started to make his way down the stairs. 'Goodnight, Miss Allen.' I shut the door and returned to the living room.

I would have called Alex to discuss this latest unexpected twist in the investigation, but after the way I left him earlier that evening I felt I could not 'phone him. I would just have to be patient and wait to speak to him until the next day, after he had been back to the Family Records Office for his research on Lucy's 'grandparents'. As for my interview with the police, my experiences with the Victorian State Police had taught me that they always wanted me to divulge what I knew. It would never be an exchange of information on a reciprocal basis.

I retired to bed early, but was again wakeful. At one o'clock I decided to e-mail Jeremy and Paul and alert them to the news about Luisa. On checking my inbox I noticed that I had actually received an e-mail from Paul, presumably in response to my e-mail to him of Sunday evening. It was, of course, now Wednesday morning in Australia. His e-mail read as follows:

Hi Alicia
Great to hear from you. Glad to be of assistance. I'm more than happy to help a friend. Have some more news for you. I understand that Luisa wasn't in work on Monday and she didn't turn up yesterday either and nobody has heard from her. Apparently she isn't at home and she isn't answering her mobile, but one of the neighbours in the block of units where she lives says she saw her leaving with a bag on Sunday evening. She seemed to be in a rush and didn't stop to chat. I'll see what else I can find out.
Cheers
Paul

Obviously, the news of Luisa's death had not yet filtered back to her work colleagues. The time difference would have caused a slight delay as it would have been night-time (Monday) in Australia when the murderer struck in London. She must have taken the evening flight from Brisbane to London on Sunday, arriving at Heathrow early Monday morning, which suggested she had not been in London for one day before she was murdered. It was not a work-related trip otherwise her colleagues would know where she was. I wondered where Jonathan Masterton was on Monday afternoon.

Then there was the question of the chrysanthemums I had

received after I returned from lunch. Perhaps they had come from her, or maybe they had been sent to me by her murderer. I had thought it was a warning but possibly it was a sign. Luisa after all was Italian, so sending chrysanthemums would be an appropriate way of announcing her death to another Italian. I responded to Paul's e-mail immediately:

Dear Paul
Thanks for your e-mail. I guess the news hasn't reached you yet. I had a visit from the police tonight. They told me that Luisa was in London. From what you say she must have arrived on Monday morning (my time). She's dead; found murdered in her hotel room yesterday evening. It was a shock to me I can tell you. The police wouldn't say much, but it all sounds pretty horrific. Somebody wanted rid of her that's for sure. Hear from you soon I hope.
Very best
Alicia

I sent a similar e-mail to Jeremy to let him know the state of play and returned to bed. First thing on Wednesday morning before I left for work I 'phoned Alex to fill him in on my visit from the police and Luisa's murder. I decided that it was ridiculous to delay talking to him and besides I was far too impatient to wait until the end of the day. He made no mention of my outburst the previous evening.

'What did Isabelle say?' he asked as soon as I finished relaying to him what the police had told me and what I had heard from Paul.

'She doesn't know yet. They're going up to see her this morning. At Isabelle's request I said nothing to the police about my theory that Lucy is involved. But I feel most uncomfortable about agreeing not to, especially now that Luisa has been murdered.'

'I'm with you. I'll do my best to obtain the information today, but Luisa's murder puts a different spin on things. If she's the accomplice then the murderer must have decided to dispose of her either because she had out-served her usefulness or had become a nuisance factor. I can't help thinking that another attempt on Isabelle's life is imminent. I'd better dash. I'll call you later, OK? I'll probably be out of contact for most of the day, but if anything happens send me a text.'

'OK. Will do. Bye, Alex.'

'Bye.'

I noted that Alex did not refer to the murderer by name – as if he was not entirely convinced that the murderer and Jonathan Masterton were one and the same. Quite probably I was reading more into what Alex had said than I ought to. On the other hand, if it was not Jonathan Masterton, then I had no clue who it might be, and that was a very sobering and terrifying thought.

I was having a particularly bad day in the office because Danielle was off sick, my mind was not on work, and she was not there to assist. I was standing outside my office trying to deal with a photocopier jam when Rachel Piper, the P in CFP & Co. came to speak to me.

'I think it must be that section there,' she said, pointing to the red area flashing on the front of the photocopier and pulling open a section at the back. 'No, it isn't,' she continued, closing it. 'Marvellous things these photocopiers, aren't they, when they work?' she added with a smile of resignation. I opened a section at the side and finally found the offending piece of paper, pulled it out, scrunched it up and threw it in the bin next to the photocopier. I slammed the front section shut in my irritation.

'Sorry, Rachel, did you need to speak to me about anything in particular?' I asked, pushing a hair out of my face and looking up at her.

'No. I wanted to tell you something. You'll never guess who I met on a course on Monday.'

'I have no idea,' I responded, slightly disinterestedly.

'Jonathan Masterton. He's from that former firm of your client Isabelle Parker, Holmwood & Hitchins, isn't he?'

'Yes.' She had now engaged my interest. 'Do you know him? Only it sounds as if you might.'

'I met him a couple of years back. I feel a bit sorry for him about what's happened with that fellow trustee to be honest. He seemed genuinely distraught by it all.'

'Was the course only Monday morning?' I was thinking about the timing of Luisa's murder.

'No, it was all day. Why? What's the matter, Alicia? Are you OK?' she said, putting her arm around my shoulder. That 'sobering and terrifying thought' I had had earlier about Jonathan Masterton *not* being the murderer was becoming a reality. I felt physically sick.

'I feel a bit faint,' I replied, staggering through to my office and sitting down.

'I'll get you some water.' A few minutes later Rachel appeared with a glass full. 'How are you feeling?' she asked, handing it to me.

'Better, thanks. I'm just tired. Was Jonathan Masterton there for the *whole* course?' I saw no purpose in sharing my concerns with her.

'Yes. I think so. Why?'

'Because I thought something was happening on Monday in relation to Isabelle's affairs and he was involved with it,' I replied evasively.

'Oh, right. Well, he was definitely there until after lunch and I'm sure I saw him later. Are you OK?' she repeated.

'Yes, thanks. I'll be fine. Out of interest, where was the course?'

'At the Café Royal.'

Now I was in a complete quandary. If Jonathan was at the course all day, that would provide him with the perfect alibi for Luisa's murder. On the other hand, there was the possibility that he might have slipped out for a while and it was easy to get from Regent Street to Russell Square. If Lucy was involved, I did not believe that she was acting alone. Mind you, her whereabouts for the previous afternoon were still unknown. I was pondering over this when my direct line rang causing me to start. It was Isabelle.

'Oh, Alicia, thank goodness you're there.' By the agitation in her voice it was evident she had received a visit from DI Evans and DS Mitchell. 'They told me about Luisa being murdered. I can't believe it. They wouldn't actually tell me what happened to her. They said they visited you last night. Did they tell you?'

'No. Only that she bled to death. I'm not sure I want to know any more than that. It sounds all too gruesome as it is. Listen Isabelle, have you heard from Lucy these past few days?' I asked, slightly changing the subject. For Isabelle's sake I was hoping to eliminate Lucy as a suspect.

'No. I haven't. I don't know where she is. It's really unusual for her not to have called me. I hope she's OK. You didn't mention anything to the police about her did you?'

'Not one word, but now Luisa's dead we should tell the police what we know. If Lucy isn't guilty the truth can't hurt her.'

'Just hold off until you hear from Alex.'

'OK.' I sighed.

Rather than send Alex a text, I thought I might as well wait until I saw him before announcing that my fantastic theory about Jonathan Masterton had fallen flat. I buried myself in work to take my mind off the subject. It must have been around four-thirty when I received a call from Susannah, our receptionist.

'Sorry to bother you, Alicia,' she said in a low voice, 'but there's a young lady in reception who wants to see you. She doesn't have an appointment and as Danielle's away I didn't know what to do. She says it's urgent and insists on speaking to you. What shall I say to her?'

'Who is she?'

'She says her name's Lucy Winters.' She was the last person I expected to walk into my office. It seemed like today was going to be full of surprises. Finally, I was going to meet her.

'I'll come out. Tell her I'll see her. Thanks, Susannah.'

Lucy was waiting for me by the reception desk. She was standing with her back to me as I walked towards her so I could not see her face. The long nut-brown hair which Alex had described was pulled back with a metal clasp.

'Miss Winters,' I said, approaching her. She spun around and as soon as I saw her face she reminded me of her mother, except Lucy's eyes were dark and her mother's were hazel. She looked apprehensive.

'Thank you for agreeing to see me,' she said, slightly breathlessly. 'I'm sorry to burst in on you like this, but I really do need to speak with you.' I detected a sense of urgency in her voice.

'No problem at all. Let's go to my office. Do you want tea or coffee or something else?' I asked as we walked down the corridor.

'I'm fine, thanks,' she replied, shaking her head. 'I've wanted to meet you. My mother spoke very highly of you.'

'But not your grandmother, I'm sure,' I said with a touch of irony, ushering her inside my office and indicating for her to sit down as I walked around to my side of the desk.

'I'm sorry about that. She's a bit oversensitive about certain issues.'

'Indeed. Enough said. How can I help you?' I sat down in my swivel chair and switched my 'phone to DND. Now was definitely not the time to be disturbed by calls.

'I'm very concerned about Isabelle.'

'Aren't we all.'

'No, you don't understand.'

'Try me.'

'I've been away these past few days. I wasn't feeling well and I went down to Hampshire to visit my family you see.'

'Right. Are you better now?'

'Yes, thanks. I think it was just a bug. I came back this morning and I made a shocking discovery which I felt you must know about immediately.' I assumed – as it happens mistakenly – that she was referring to the murder of Luisa. 'It's Alex.'

'What about him?' He was the last person I expected her to mention.

'He's an impostor.'

'What are you talking about?' I asked cautiously, gathering my thoughts.

'Apparently, he isn't a friend of Michael's at all. I must admit that when Isabelle introduced him to me as such I was a little surprised because I thought I knew most of their close friends and I'd never seen him before.'

'How do you know this?' I quizzed.

'I spoke to Timothy this morning. He said that he bumped into an old university friend of Michael over the weekend who told him that Michael never had a friend called Alex. Theirs was a long-standing friendship and he pretty much knew all Michael's other friends.'

'I see,' I replied, keeping my cool. 'Have you spoken to Isabelle about this? I mean, if this Alex is a fake then we should tell the police?' I continued, bluffing.

'I thought perhaps he might be involved in what's been happening. That's why I'm so worried. It's pretty strange that he turns up out of the blue, don't you think? How do *you* find him? You met him, didn't you, when you all went down to Stowick House?'

'So many questions,' I replied, attempting to avoid answering any of them. 'Leave it with me. I'll talk to the police. It's better that they deal with it.'

'What about Isabelle?'

'She isn't back in London yet. She's still staying with Drew's parents and isn't in any immediate danger from him. But I'll get on to the police straightaway so that they're alerted and she's kept safe.'

'Oh, thank you. I appreciate that.'

'You should call her. She was concerned not to hear from you.'

'I will, but I thought she might want to be left in peace for a few days with Drew's parents.'

'You do know about Luisa Bruneschi, don't you?'

'Know what?' I was observing her facial expression and body language especially closely and either she was a very good actress or she genuinely did not know what had happened to her.

'I'm sorry to have to tell you this, Lucy, as I know she was a friend of yours, but...'

'What do you mean 'was'?' she said, interrupting me.

'Luisa was found dead in her hotel room on Monday evening. She was murdered.'

'What? Oh, my God!' she said, gasping and raising her hands to her face in surprise.' She seemed truly shocked at the news. 'Does Isabelle know? This is all she needs.'

'Yes. The police told her this morning.'

'What happened to Luisa?'

'I don't have the details.'

'Do you think that Alex was involved? He could be, couldn't he?'

'I don't know. Let's leave it to the police to find out.'

'OK. Here's my number,' she said, taking a yellow Post-it note off the pad on my desk, grabbing a pen from the pot and scribbling it down before handing it to me. 'Please call me if you have any news.' She stood up to leave.

'Where are you going now?'

'Home. I rushed from the station to see you and I have a million-and-one things to do. Thank you for seeing me,' she said, shaking my hand. I walked her to the lifts, and bade her goodbye.

Although Lucy's arrival that afternoon was unforeseen I do not know why I was so surprised by it. After all, it is when you least expect something to happen that inevitably it does and this seemed to be the pattern when it came to this case.

Chapter 29

Lucy could have been gone no more than a few minutes when Alex burst through the door causing me nearly to jump out of my skin.

'Great news,' he beamed, striding into my office enthusiastically and sitting down in the chair opposite my desk. He was carrying a small folder. 'What's the matter? You look as white as a sheet?'

'Lucy's been here. I can't believe you missed her. I hope she didn't see you. She must have gone down in one lift as you came up in the other,' I replied in almost one breath.

'I did try to call you to let you know I was on my way but your 'phone diverted to Danielle's and I understand she's not here today; and your mobile was switched off.'

'Oh, of course,' I said, taking my 'phone off DND.

'You seem agitated over Lucy's visit. What's the problem? Why do you hope she didn't see me coming in?'

'She thinks you're an impostor, a probable murderer and that we need to warn Isabelle about you and tell the police. And another thing, Jonathan Masterton was on a course with Rachel Piper on Monday, which means he couldn't have murdered Luisa. However, she couldn't state categorically that he was there all day, so there's still the possibility that he did it,' I continued, gabbling away.

'Wow! Slow down. You're going too fast. What do you mean, Lucy thinks I'm an impostor?' Alex wrinkled his brow in puzzlement.

'Timothy said he met a good friend of Michael's from university who does not recall an 'Alex' among his friends. It's because of that she thinks you might be involved. But I told her I'd speak to the police about you and that seemed to satisfy her.'

'Wise move. What did you think of her?'

'She came across as genuine, like you said. She seemed totally shocked when I told her about Luisa.'

'Hmm… So where has she been these past few days?'

'Down with her family in Hampshire.'

'Well, that can be checked out very easily. Now what's this about Jonathan Masterton having an alibi for Monday?'

'He attended the same course as Rachel in Regent Street.'

'But she can't swear to it that he was there all day.'

'Yes, but she's pretty sure. It's just that, if he was, then…'

'…he's in the clear,' said Alex, finishing my sentence. 'Let's be constructive about this. There's no point in panicking. We need to clarify where he was at the time Luisa was murdered and take it from there. Do you want to know what I've discovered?' he said enthusiastically.

'Of course I do.'

'I have the promised marriage certificate for Lucy's grandparents,' he said, opening the folder and taking out the green certified copy and handing it to me. 'Nicholas John Whiteley married Christine Marie Gordon in April 1952.'

'Gordon? Could she be related to Diane through her stepfather?'

'If you look at the marriage certificate you'll see that Christine's father's full name was Robert Duncan Gordon, which is the name of the father on the marriage certificate of Charles Gordon, Diane's stepfather.'

'Then Christine is Charles Gordon's sister and Diane's step-aunt?' I replied, scanning the certificate.

'She's his younger sister to be precise. I looked up both his and her birth certificates to double check that I was not mistaken. They share the same parents: Robert Duncan Gordon and Margaret Mary Gordon, née MacDonald, so I think it's pretty conclusive.'

'You're amazing, Alex. This is absolutely fantastic,' I said with zeal. 'It's lucky for us that Christine inscribed the back of her photographs as it made your search easier. How did the Whiteleys get away with all the paperwork though?'

'I didn't tell you, but while I was searching yesterday I decided to look up Claire's birth certificate.'

'But she can't have one if Claire is actually Frances.'

'She can if one was created for her. Claire Louise Whiteley – who as it happens was born on exactly the same date as Frances Latham – was registered, guess when?'

'I don't know.'

'June 1960. One month after the accident and one month before the Whiteleys left for Australia. I was amazed because I thought births had to be registered within six weeks.'

'They are supposed to be, but registrations do take place sometimes years later provided the people wanting to make the registration have the right documentation.'

'That's what the very helpful man at the information desk said.'

'I don't know why I didn't think of that before. It explains a lot.'

'It does.'

'Except how they obtained the necessary documentation. Somebody must have provided it. Christine Whiteley has a lot of questions to answer. What shall we do about Isabelle? I suppose we should call her and tell her the results of your research. Hopefully we can persuade her that she can't put off informing the police about Lucy any longer.'

'There's no need. The police already know.'

'What do you mean?'

'After you called this morning and told me that Luisa had been murdered, I thought it was ridiculous that the police hadn't been told about Lucy's family. As soon as I had this information about the Whiteleys,' he said, waving the folder at me, 'I took it upon myself to call DI Evans and went to see him. Effectively, therefore, the decision has been taken out of Isabelle's hands. If you're mad with me it's just too bad,' he added, shrugging his shoulders. 'I think you'll agree, though, it's for the best.'

'Absolutely. I've been trying to persuade Isabelle to let me tell the police about Lucy's background. What did DI Evans say?'

'I filled him in on all the details and gave him my research material. He's certainly taking it seriously. I'm not sure whether the police are going to send someone out to Australia or just liaise with the police over there, but somebody will be interviewing Christine Whiteley in the immediate future that's for sure.'

'What did you say to him about us not mentioning this to the police before?'

'I explained we had our suspicions but didn't want to waste police time unless we felt we had some concrete evidence. I thought that would spare you and Isabelle from being extensively questioned on the subject.'

'Thank you. Do you think he believed you?'

'I had the impression that he felt you knew more than you were letting on. He seems to think you're quite spirited. I can't understand how he could possibly get that impression,' he said with a mischievous grin and rolling his eyes upwards. 'He'll be paying Isabelle another visit. Don't be surprised if he extends you the same courtesy.'

'Not quite my choice of word,' I replied sarcastically. 'But I'm not going to wait for him to contact me. I'll call him. I have to talk to him as Lucy's expecting me to report back to her once I've spoken to the police about her impostor theory. I need to find out what to do about that. And then there's Isabelle; I should speak to her, tell her about Lucy's visit and warn her that the police know who Lucy is.'

'Fair enough, but the police may have beaten you to it. I had the feeling they were going to see her straightaway. Now, about the American ex-serviceman who died a few months before Diane's accident.'

'Oh, him. Did you manage to find out anything?'

'Yes. After I left the police station I went up to Colindale again to see if anything was reported in the papers about the accident. There were a couple of pieces. I discovered that his name was Larry Tierney. He'd only been over here a few weeks when he was killed. Apparently he was in the UK towards the end of the war and was stationed down in the West Country. One article refers to a sister back home in Alabama. I'm going to see what else I can dig up.'

'There must be police records of the accident. Maybe you should speak to DI Evans about that. He'd know his way around. Do you know what I think is most interesting about what you've told me?'

'No,' he replied, shaking his head and looking slightly bemused.

'The Gordons, Lathams and Whiteleys are all connected to the West Country. Now you tell me this Larry Tierney was stationed there as well. Maybe it's significant. Bridget told us that someone in the village of Buckfastleigh saw him in the car with Diane on several occasions. Diane told the police that this witness was mistaken and she did not know him, but what if she did?'

'You mean from when he was stationed here during the War?'

'Yes. Knowing how suspicious James was about her friendships with any other man, she wouldn't have wanted him to know about Larry. But James might have found out about him and jumped to the conclusion that they were having an affair and had Larry murdered.'

'It's possible, I guess,' said Alex, sounding rather flat.

'You don't sound very convinced.'

'It's not that. I'm just thinking about other scenarios. What if he was a former lover who came back? That would really set the cat among the pigeons, wouldn't it?'

'Hmm... That certainly puts a different spin on things. Maybe she decided to go off with him, James found out and had him bumped him off or she wanted to get rid of him and she was the one to arrange his accident. It's quite intriguing.'

'That's what I think. I thought you'd be interested. I'll keep you posted. Are you going to call Isabelle now?' he asked, standing up to leave.

'Yes,' I replied, remaining seated behind my desk. 'Then the police. Where are you off to?' I said as he walked towards the door.

'I'm going to pick up my scooter. There was something wrong with the brake and I had to get it fixed.'

'Are you sure you should be riding it so soon after your operation?'

'I'm fine, but thanks for your concern. I'll catch you later, OK? Good luck with Isabelle and the police.'

'Thanks, Alex.'

'*Ciao*,' he said, shutting the door behind him on his way out.

Isabelle's mobile was switched off and the landline number at Drew's parents' home was permanently engaged so I was unable to give her advance notice of what the police might ask her. But as Alex had pointed out, I might be too late anyway. I dialled the number DI Evans had given me, but I was told he was unavailable and would call me back later.

By the time I left the office I had neither spoken to Isabelle nor the police, which was very frustrating. I was just turning the corner into my street when somebody tooted me from a car. I glanced behind me and saw DI Evans and DS Mitchell pull up in a dark navy Audi. They must have followed me up the road from the tube station. I walked back to where they had parked and waited for them to get out of the car.

'Did you receive my message?' I asked DI Evans as he shut the car door and turned to me. DS Mitchell walked around from the passenger side and joined us on the pavement.

'Yes. We were out this way so thought we'd might as well come and speak to you personally,' he replied, locking the car with the remote control device causing the car to beep several times.

'You'd better come in then,' I responded. 'You were lucky to catch me,' I continued, leading them up the front steps and unlocking the main front door. We clambered up the stairs to my flat in silence. 'I'm going to make myself some tea,' I said, letting them into the flat. 'Do you want some?' They both nodded. I dropped my briefcase in the hall and hung my raincoat in the hall cupboard and walked through to the kitchen. They sat waiting in the living room while I made the tea. I carried in the tray of tea and some plain chocolate biscuits.

'What is it you wanted to talk to me about?' asked DI Evans as I handed him his cup of tea.

'Please help yourselves to sugar and biscuits,' I said, passing DS Mitchell his tea before picking up mine and settling back into my armchair. 'I received an unexpected visit from Lucy Winters today. I know that Alex Waterford met with you this morning and provided you with some critical information about her background...' I paused for a moment hoping for a response to that comment but none was forthcoming, 'but this visit was over a completely separate issue.'

'Go on,' said DI Evans. I observed DS Mitchell dunking his biscuit in his tea.

'As I believe you're aware, Isabelle made out that Alex was a university friend of her brother Michael. Well, Lucy found out through Timothy Masterton that there was no such friend called Alex, and she thinks that Alex is an impostor and a possible suspect and asked me to tell you. When you talk to Lucy about her friendship with Luisa Bruneschi I expect she will mention all this to you. And in case you were wondering, she told me that she was staying with her family in Hampshire yesterday and only returned this morning.'

'I see. Thanks for letting us know. I do intend to ask her some questions about Luisa Bruneschi. I'll tell her we've spoken to you and are dealing with the Alex matter so you don't need to concern yourself with that.'

'Have another biscuit,' I said, offering the plate to DS Mitchell. He smiled at me. 'I tried to speak to Isabelle this afternoon,' I continued, turning to DI Evans. 'Have you spoken to her about Lucy? Only they're very close and I think she'd be terribly upset if there was any implication that Lucy was a suspect,' I said, fishing for information.

'We saw her this morning. She took the news remarkably well I thought,' he replied, with a characteristic raise of his eyebrows.

'Oh, right. I suppose you're following up what I told you about Luisa yesterday; and of course Christine Whiteley has to be interviewed now,' I said, presuming that they must be checking out Alex's information.

'Yes. That is in hand. I don't have anything to tell you on that front yet.'

'Not even in relation to Luisa? You don't have any clues as to what happened?' To me that seemed incredible.

'We believe she was murdered between two and four on Monday afternoon.'

'Oh, I see,' I replied. 'There is something else I must tell you. You recall I strongly suspected that Jonathan Masterton is responsible for these murders?'

'Yes.'

'Only I'm not as sure as I was when I told you yesterday.'

'What do you mean?' DI Evans finished his tea and placed the cup and saucer back on the tray.

'A work colleague, one of the Partners in my firm in fact, told me this morning that she was on a course with Jonathan Masterton on Monday at the Café Royal and was pretty sure he was there for the whole day. He was certainly there at lunchtime.'

'I see.'

'I thought you should know.'

'Thank you. Anything else you want to tell us?'

'No. Last night I gave you my views on the murders. On the basis of all the information you now have, surely you must know who committed them? Do you at least have a prime suspect?'

'Yes, but it is a question of proof. We'll be in touch.' DI Evans stood up and cut the conversation dead. DS Mitchell followed suit. 'Thank you for the tea and biscuits,' he said as he walked out.

Despite being a solicitor, and effectively discussing with the police one of my clients, they were giving very little away.

After they left I rang Isabelle. Mrs Hyde-Dowler answered the 'phone.

'Is Isabelle there? Only I tried to call her on and off this afternoon and the 'phone was permanently engaged?'

'Our 'phone line was down I'm afraid. I'll call Isabelle for you.' Again I heard the sound of her footsteps as she traipsed to the 'phone.

'Hello, Alicia.'

'Is everything OK? Drew's mother told me that the landline was out of order but your mobile was off, so I was worried about you. I was hoping to speak to you before the police turned up.'

'I can't make or receive any calls. There's something wrong with the handset. I'll get a new mobile tomorrow. The police were here at lunchtime. They asked me some questions about Luisa and also told me that some new information had come to light.'

'You mean about Lucy being related to you?'

'Yes. I twigged that either you or Alex must have told them. I know it was the right thing to do. I'm sorry I stopped you doing it before. Anyway, I understand the police are sending someone out to Australia to interview Grandma Whiteley.'

'Yes, or at least they're liaising with the police out there.'

'Lucy called about twenty minutes ago. She'd been trying to get hold of me as well. She told me that she'd been to see you in the office and about her suspicions in respect of Alex. Obviously I didn't let on who he is. She said you would speak to the police on her behalf.'

'I couldn't tell her the truth about him, could I? The police turned up here this evening and I filled them in. They're going to interview her about Luisa so they'll deal with it then. When are you coming back to London?'

'On Friday I think. Drew's parents have been really fantastic.

They asked me to stay on and I've enjoyed being with them. I'll sort out my mobile and if I don't speak to you before then I'll text you when I'm back in London.'

'OK. Goodnight, Isabelle.'

'Goodnight, Alicia. Thanks for everything.'

I logged on to check my e-mails hoping for a response from Jeremy and Paul. There was no reply from Jeremy but the one from Paul was most intriguing:

Hi Alicia

I could hardly believe my eyes when I read your e-mail. I had a chat with a few of my former colleagues. Apparently there is a rumour flying around that Luisa had a boyfriend over there. Maybe they had a lover's tiff and he did her in! It's probably a load of rubbish but I thought you'd like to know.

Hope you're OK.

Hear from you soon.

Regards.

Paul

I called Isabelle back as I was sure she, more than anyone, would have a better idea whether what Paul had told me was true.

'Hi, Alicia. I didn't expect to hear from you again tonight. What's happened? Is anything the matter?' She sounded concerned.

'No, no, everything's fine. I have a question for you about Luisa, that's all.'

'Ask away.'

'Did she have a boyfriend over here?'

'Not that I know of; but then she never really talked much about herself. What makes you ask?'

'I just wondered.'

'Actually, now I come to think of it, I do recall having a conversation with her not long after we met about a relationship she was having with someone from London. I'm sure they met when he was travelling around Australia. She never mentioned it again so I don't suppose it's significant, but I had the impression that he was a student as she talked about helping him with his research. It's probably totally irrelevant. As I say, I didn't think she had a boyfriend currently.'

'Food for thought though,' I replied. At that moment the Entryphone buzzer rang. 'I'll have to go, Isabelle. There's somebody at the door.'

'Oh, OK. I'll speak to you later?'

'You will.'

'Bye, Alicia.'

'Bye.

I walked into the hall and peeked at the video entry screen. It was Alex. He was holding his crash helmet so he must have ridden over on his scooter.

'Do you have a minute?' he asked over the intercom.

'Yes, of course. Come up.' I pressed the door release button, left the door ajar and went back to my computer. I heard him come into the hall, drop his bag and take off his shoes.

'Hello?' he called out.

'I'm in here.' He walked through to the living room. 'Do you want anything to eat?' I asked, standing up. I hoped I might be able to persuade him to stay.

'I'm fine, thanks. I can't stop as I'm on my way out to dinner.' I tried not to show my disappointment. 'I dropped by because I've discovered something from the police I thought you'd really like to know about.'

'Then you're more fortunate than I.' He looked at me quizzically. 'DI Evans and DS Mitchell were here but they disclosed nothing to me as usual.'

'It's actually a contact in forensics whom I've just been speaking to.'

'About Luisa?'

'Yes.'

'What did he tell you?'

'You mean she.'

'She? That fits. Charmed it out of her, did you?'

'That remark is unworthy of you, Alicia. Do you want to know what she told me or not?'

'Yes.'

'You'll never guess.'

'I really don't know, Alex.'

'Luisa was pregnant.'

Chapter 30

'Pregnant? So that rumour about Luisa having a boyfriend over here could be true,' I mumbled under my breath. 'It's incredible.'

'What rumour, Alicia? What are you talking about?' Alex was slightly flummoxed.

'Sorry, Alex. Have a read of the e-mail I received from Paul this evening,' I said, walking over to my computer which was still on, and printing it out and handing it to him. He scanned it.

'Very interesting,' he said.

'I called Isabelle, but she says as far as she knows Luisa doesn't have a boyfriend here – not that she'd necessarily have told her.'

'I guess she wouldn't if it was Jonathan Masterton, would she?'

'But that's presupposing he *is* the murderer which could be in doubt.'

'Well, let's say he is.'

'Do you think they could have been lovers then?'

'Oh, I don't know, Alicia. Perhaps she found out she was pregnant and came back to tell him in person. A pregnant accomplice would be the last thing he would want I should imagine.'

'Maybe she was madly in love with him and he milked it for what it's worth, so much so that she agreed to kill John MacFadzean for him.'

'Possibly. Listen, I'm sorry, but I must go.' He walked to the door and put on his shoes. 'I just dropped by to let you know that.'

'Enjoy your evening,' I said wistfully, standing in the doorway as he started to walk down the stairs.

'Thanks. I'll call you tomorrow. *Ciao, bella!*' he called out as he disappeared.

As it happens I heard from Alex early on Thursday morning, when, for the third time that week, he arrived unexpectedly at the office.

'This is becoming quite a habit,' I joked on seeing him.

'I know, but some habits are hard to break,' he swiftly replied. 'Have you spoken to the police today?'

'No. Why?'

'Then you haven't heard.'

'Heard what?'

'Unofficially, Jonathan Masterton's about to be arrested.'

'What? So the police do think he's guilty? Which means that he couldn't have been on the course at the Café Royal all day then? But how do you know?'

'DS Mitchell told me when I spoke to him first thing.'

'You'd better tell me what you found out, Alex Waterford,' I said, wagging my finger at him. 'What's happened?'

'He wouldn't give me any other details about the arrest but he did tell me that Christine Whiteley has been interviewed in Sydney. You remember that locket Diane's wearing in the portrait which hangs in the library at Stowick House?'

'Yes; the gold one with the initials on it. The one Isabelle said she thought had gone missing or something.'

'Well, apparently Christine has this locket. She told the police that Diane's mother had it and gave it to her when she and her husband left for Australia with Frances. It has a picture of Diane with Frances inside it. She was supposed to pass it on to Frances but never felt she could because then she would have had to tell her the truth. She insists that neither Claire nor Lucy know who they really are.'

'But what is the truth?'

'According to Christine, Philip was fiercely protective of his younger sister and would have done anything for her. After the accident it was agreed that Christine and her husband would take Frances and bring her up as their own daughter.'

'Who agreed though? If Diane's mother had the locket her whole family were probably in on it. After all, Christine was Diane's step-aunt. They must all have really hated James Latham to take his daughter away from him. He may not have been a good husband, but he sounds as if he was a doting father. No wonder he never got over what happened. Imagine letting him think his daughter was dead. It's cruel and so tragic.'

'I expect they thought it was Diane's intention to run off with Frances and they were merely following through with her wishes.'

'But with Diane dead, that changed everything, Alex. I find it hard to accept that they could really think they were acting in Frances' best interests by taking her away from her natural father. What they did would be revenge enough I would have thought.'

'Well, personal opinions aside, all I can tell you is what has been relayed to me. Philip arranged all their documents. He was quite a prominent civil servant apparently. I do recall that on Jonathan's marriage certificate Philip's occupation is stated as such.'

'But I thought he was a civil engineer. I'm sure that's what's on his own marriage certificate, although I suppose the War came along and he changed careers afterwards.' I was a little confused. 'Sorry, I digress as usual. You were saying that he arranged all their papers.'

'Yes. According to Christine, Philip was absolutely devastated after Diane's death and he did not want to stay in England. He and his wife Annette decided to emigrate to Australia because he wanted to be near to Frances as she grew up but soon realized that that arrangement would be unworkable if their secret was to remain hidden. So they agreed that they could not stay in touch and, even though Philip and Annette still emigrated, Christine says she didn't see them. Subsequently of course Philip and Annette moved back to England.' I felt that there was something odd about this.

'About twelve years later, Alex. Did she say anything about Philip's feelings towards James Latham? I mean, she said he was fiercely protective of his sister. He must have loathed him for making his sister miserable.'

'I guess that's a question for Philip to answer, Alicia.'

'I find it hard to believe that Philip and Annette had no contact with her after they came out to Australia. It all seems very strange, well to me anyway. And what about Jonathan? He would have been about fourteen when they emigrated so old enough to be very much aware of everything that was going on around him. Perhaps he's been harbouring knowledge of all this for years and waiting for his revenge. Do you think Christine's telling the truth?'

'I don't know.'

'And what about Philip Masterton? Have the police interviewed him yet? Surely they have? Christine's evidence does drop him in it rather.'

'They have spoken to him. They believe he's protecting Jonathan, but I don't know any more than that.'

'Did DS Mitchell say anything about Lucy?' Alex shook his head. 'Only I've been thinking about her and it's more probable that Isabelle's right and she isn't involved at all, save for her blood connection. When we discovered who she was I was suspicious but, as you pointed out, it would be so much easier for her to prove it than to go around murdering people.'

'Yes, I did. But we both had doubts about her and we can't rule her out yet.'

'I know. However, I think your "avenging Diane's death" theory has more appeal. Jonathan is better placed than anyone to discover the family's secrets and with the benefit of knowing how the entitlement works under the Will, if he wanted to avenge Diane's death and ensure her next of kin get hold of the money, he'd know who to kill.'

'You have given this a lot of thought, haven't you?'

'I wonder how Luisa met Jonathan Masterton though. In some ways I find it hard to believe they were lovers. Maybe that's a red herring and she was having someone else's child.'

'Well, it's a possibility.'

'I'd love to know what the police asked Philip Masterton. I wouldn't be surprised if he knows the truth about Larry Tierney as well, especially if he was as close to his sister as we are led to believe.'

'Yes, that's true. I imagine he knows a great deal.'

'Isabelle's going to be relieved to learn of Jonathan Masterton's imminent arrest. Did you find out when the police are going to tell her?'

'No, but it'll be in person and before any announcement about his arrest is made. She's still with Drew's parents, isn't she?' I nodded. 'When did you last speak to her?'

'Last night. As you were arriving.'

'Then you haven't told her about Luisa being pregnant?'

'No.' My direct line rang and I answered it. It was DI Evans. I mouthed as such to Alex. He made a funny face and sank back in his chair. 'You want to see me now,' I replied, looking at Alex. 'No, that's fine. I'm in the office all day. Actually, Alex Waterford is with me. I'm sure he'll be very interested to hear about any progress you have made on the investigation.'

'The thing is, Miss Allen,' said DI Evans, pacing the floor with his hands in his trouser pockets, having told us what Alex had already relayed to me about Christine Whiteley and Luisa's pregnancy, 'we have arrested Jonathan Masterton and news of his arrest will be announced today. More than that I cannot tell you. But we've seen Isabelle and she has been fully appraised of all the details.'

'I see. May I ask what you're doing about questioning Philip Masterton further?'

'Presently nothing.'

'What do you mean?'

'Philip Masterton collapsed this morning with a heart attack. He's currently in hospital on life support, and in no position to answer further questions.' Alex and I looked at each other gravely. 'At this stage we don't know whether he'll survive.'

Chapter 31

'What about Lucy Winters?' I asked, glancing at Alex.

'What about her?' replied DI Evans.

'Presumably you don't think she's involved, otherwise you would be arresting her as well?' I scrutinized his face but it gave nothing away.

'It isn't that simple.'

'I'm sorry. I don't follow. Why not?' I asked, pressing him for an answer.

'There are still a number of questions we need to put to her in relation to the investigation.' I knew from his evasive response that there was more to be gleaned.

'I suppose with her close connection to the Latham family and Luisa there are things she *might* know,' I said, hoping to draw him. 'She's going to have a lot on her plate though. Learning that she's James Latham's granddaughter and that the person she believed was her grandmother was complicit in a pact to take her mother away from him is going to come as a big shock. I can't imagine how I would feel to find out after twenty-five years that I'm not who I thought I was.'

'I'm sure discovering that you're actually an heiress might help soften the blow,' piped up Alex.

'Alex!' I scolded.

'Oh, come on Alicia, once she's over the initial shock I think the compensations from her new found identity will dull the pain,' he said somewhat stoically, his eyes moving heavenwards.

'Does she know yet, Detective Inspector?'

'No. We're arranging for her to return to Sydney. This has all been very traumatic for her mother and at her request we haven't told Lucy because she thinks it would be preferable for her to break the news.'

'Yes, of course, poor Frances, I mean Claire. For her it must almost be worse. At least she and Lucy are very close to Isabelle. Finding out that they are related to her rather than to a complete stranger will be of some comfort. Isabelle considers them family anyway. I assume you have discussed what is happening with her?'

'Of course. She is very concerned about Lucy and agreed that Lucy should return home to Sydney to be with her mother.'

'I suppose Claire will want to come over shortly. She must have so many unanswered questions about who she is and where she comes from.'

'Yes. I expect she does. Well, I really must be going,' said DI Evans, edging towards the door. 'There is still a great deal that needs to be done.'

'I'll walk down to the lifts with you,' said Alex, leaping out of his chair. 'I'll just be a minute,' he mouthed, turning back to me before disappearing out of the door after DI Evans.

'What was all that about?' I asked Alex when he returned.

'I wanted a quick word with him about Larry Tierney's file. It's a bit of a blow about Philip Masterton. The prognosis isn't good, is it?'

'No...you'll probably think I'm mad for saying this, but I just have a feeling that something's not quite right.'

'Not at all. I'm minded to agree with you.'

'Alex, I want to apologise about the other evening,' I blurted out, seizing the moment to say something on the matter. 'I shouldn't have put you on the spot like that and asked you to come over for dinner especially after what I said to you in Australia. I didn't mean to spoil things particularly as we make such a good team. I...'

'Yes, we do and no, you didn't. I'm sorry too. I overreacted. I admit I find you very frustrating sometimes, but if you weren't so damned...' Alex did not have a chance to finish his sentence because Rachel Piper burst into the room. Talk about bad timing.

'Jonathan Masterton's been arrested for the murder of Isabelle Parker's fiancé Andrew Hyde-Dowler,' she said, thrusting an open copy of the *Evening Standard* into my hand. 'I can't believe it. When I think I only saw him the other day on that course.'

'Does it say anything else?' I was wondering whether anyone was mentioned by name and in particular if there was a reference to Luisa Bruneschi.

'Read it,' she said, pointing to the relevant section. 'It doesn't say very much, but I thought you'd be interested.' I scanned the paragraph on page seven:

Detectives investigating the murder of Andrew Hyde-Dowler, a 31 year old artist, in an explosion at his studio in Hampstead on 2 March have today arrested Jonathan Masterton 59 on suspicion of his murder. It is also understood that Mr Masterton, who is a well-respected solicitor, is helping the police with their enquiries in relation to the murder of Luisa Bruneschi, a 29 year old Australian journalist, who was found dead in her hotel room on Monday 26 March.

'Alex,' I shrieked, looking up from the paper. 'Have a look at this.' I scanned the room for him but he seemed to have vanished. 'Where's Alex, Rachel?'

'I think he left. Why? Is there a problem?'

'Oh, no.' I rushed off to the lifts hoping to catch him up. Unfortunately, he had disappeared and, feeling disgruntled I traipsed back to my room.

'Are you all right, Alicia?' asked Danielle as I passed her desk.

'Yes. Perfectly thanks.'

'Only when you ran out of the room like that I thought you might be sick.'

'I wanted to ask Alex something that's all. But it'll have to wait.'

'Isabelle Parker 'phoned by the way. She'd like you to buzz her back.'

'OK. When did she call?'

'A minute ago. You just missed her. She'll be available here,' she said, handing me a piece of paper with a number on it, 'for about another hour. Otherwise you can reach her on her mobile.'

'OK. Thanks. I'll call her straight back,' I replied, opening the door to my office, walking inside and firmly shutting the door. I sent Alex a short text:

You rushed off. Are you OK? Hope all is well.

'Have the police spoken to you yet?' asked Isabelle. She sounded subdued, as if the news of the arrest had left her rather flat.

'Yes. DI Evans came in to the office this morning.'

'You know about Jonathan Masterton's arrest then?'

'Yes. And it's been reported in the early edition of the *Evening Standard*. How do you feel?'

'Not sure. Numb. Angry. Relieved. There are still so many things that remain unanswered. I think Drew's parents feel the same. I asked DS Mitchell whether Jonathan was going to be charged with Michael's murder, but he was non-committal which concerned me rather, and then there's Grandpa's death which needs to be accounted for…'

'Yes, I agree there are still quite a few loose ends, such as how he did it all! Alex is still trying to find out more on the American ex-serviceman. So far he's discovered that his name's Larry Tierney, he came from Alabama and was based down in the West Country during the War.'

'Then it's possible that he knew Diane. Maybe he was having an affair with her or that's what Grandpa thought. I don't suppose what happened back then is relevant to the case, but I'd like to know what went on between my grandfather and Diane. I guess I have to accept that I'm never going to.'

'I think Philip Masterton knows much more than he's disclosed to the police. Don't forget Christine Whiteley told them that he was very close to Diane and the one who organized everything. I think he would be able to answer quite a few of our outstanding questions. I've always felt his connection was important.'

'Why don't we ask him then?'

'We could – only he's had a heart attack. Didn't DS Mitchell tell you?'

'No. It didn't come up. How is he?'

'Critical. He mightn't survive. I guess he's a very old man and the strain of finding out that Jonathan is responsible for these murders was all too much for him. We'll just have to wait and see. Have you spoken to Lucy?'

'Yesterday. I told her I'm coming back to London tomorrow.'

'Is that definite now?'

'Yes. I don't feel unsafe anymore and I want to return home. I'll let you know when I'm back. Perhaps you'd come over tomorrow evening. I'd like to see you. You've been such a tower of strength these past few weeks. I don't know what I would have done without you. Are you free then?'

'Unfortunately not. My sister and her boyfriend are expecting me for dinner. Tell you what, why don't I drop by earlier. Is that OK?'

'Great.'

'I'll see you tomorrow then.'

'OK. Bye, Alicia.'

'*Ciao*, Bye.'

I had not spoken to Dorothy after she had berated me about Alex at the weekend and I felt slightly guilty, so on my way home from work on Thursday evening I called in to see her.

'It's funny you should pop down,' she said, opening the door. 'I spoke to Emily Middleton today.'

'Really?'

'Yes. She was wondering how you got on with the housekeeper's daughter. I told her I thought your meeting was productive. She was pleased. Do you want a cup of tea?' She indicated for me to come in. I remained hovering in the doorway.

'Thanks, but I can't stop. I just wanted to see if you were OK?'

'I'm fine. How are things with you?' She gave me a very penetrating look. It was most likely she had seen both the police and Alex arrive at the flat during the course of the week. If she was seated in her armchair by the window she had a perfect view of anyone entering or leaving the building.

'I'm OK. It's been an eventful week. The police made an arrest today on the case. It was in the *Evening Standard*. I don't know whether you've seen it?'

'No. I haven't been out to buy one.' I showed her the relevant paragraph in my paper. 'Do you think Jonathan Masterton's guilty, Alicia?'

'I thought there was a strong possibility that it was him and everything does point that way so I suppose he must be.'

'How's Alex?'

'He's good. We're still trying to solve the mystery of James and Diane Latham.'

'I meant, how are things between the two of you?' I knew that is what she had intended by her question but I was hoping to avoid answering it.

'Oh, you know. Still the same. I have to go. I'll see you later,' I said, pecking her on the cheek and then darting off upstairs.

I hated answering questions about Alex at the best of times and I knew I was bound to face a barrage of questions from Antonia at dinner on Friday night. We had not spoken since our exchange over Alex the previous week, but I had to call her to explain that I might be a little late for dinner because of my arrangement with Isabelle.

'No problem. Text me when you're on your way. We'll eat when you get here.'

'OK. I'll do that.'

'Bring Alex if you want.'

'Not an option.'

'Oh, Ally, why not?'

'You know why not. I'll see you tomorrow. *Baci, baci. Ciao,*' I replied, cutting her short and ringing off as quickly as possible.

Friday afternoon at about four o'clock I received a text message from Isabelle. Although I half-expected a text from her, I was waiting to receive one from Alex. So for that split second when my mobile beeped I hoped the message was from him. I was perplexed because he had not responded to my text from the previous afternoon. Her message read as follows:

Hi Alicia. I'm back in London. Come over as soon as you've finished work. Looking forward to seeing you.

I dialled her number but it went straight to voice mail so I sent a text back:

I'll be there as soon after six-thirty as I can make it. A

I thought no more about it. I left the office on time and made my way up to Hampstead by tube. I considered returning home to fetch my car, but I estimated that it was actually quicker to travel there straight from the office. I came out of the tube station and switched on my mobile. There was a voice message from Sally who must have called literally moments after I had gone down into the tube. My mind had been so taken up with everything else that I had forgotten that I had left a couple of 'phone messages for her at the weekend. I supposed that she was incredibly busy at work and had not had time to call. As I walked up the road from the tube station towards Isabelle's house I called her.

'Oh. Hi, Alicia. How are you? Thanks for your messages. I'm sorry I didn't get back to you sooner.'

'That's OK. I called you on Sunday as I was hoping you might be free to meet up for lunch and a chat.'

'Oh, what a pity I wasn't around. I was in Shropshire the whole weekend with my parents for their ruby wedding anniversary. All the family was there. Is everything OK with you?'

'Yes. I'm fine. Did you know the police have arrested Jonathan Masterton for Drew's murder?'

'What? No. I've been on a big case all week, working into the early hours of the morning. I haven't seen the news or read a paper these past couple of days. How's Isabelle? How's she taken the news? I haven't heard from her, though I've been really remiss these past few weeks.'

'She's bearing up very well considering everything she's been through. She's back in London. I'm on my way to see her now as it happens.'

'I thought it sounded as if you were walking along the street. Isn't Jonathan Masterton Isabelle's solicitor at Holmwood & Hitchins? Only when I last spoke to Lucy she told me that one of Isabelle's trustees at Holmwood & Hitchins is guilty of stealing trust funds. She said that it's a bit embarrassing because her friend Timothy is the son of one of the other trustees. Is Timothy Jonathan Masterton's son then?'

'Yes. He is. The trustee Lucy was talking about is John MacFadzean. He's the one who was murdered in Melbourne.'

'Oh, of course. How awful for Timothy Masterton knowing what his father has been accused of. 'Do you know Timothy?'

'Not exactly. I've only met him once, last week actually. I went with Isabelle for a meeting with his father about the missing trust funds. We bumped into him on our way out. What makes you ask?'

'I just wondered. I've only met him once myself, at an art exhibition. Isabelle couldn't go because she had 'flu, there was a ticket going spare and Luisa came in her place. I can't say I liked her that much.' I was puzzled because Isabelle had told me that Luisa and Timothy had never met. Obviously she was not aware that they had. I was slightly thrown by what Sally was telling me and stopped walking.

'You did say Luisa, didn't you?'

'Yes. Why?'

'Isabelle indicated that Timothy and Luisa didn't know each other. Were they there together?'

'I don't know, but I had the distinct impression they had definitely met before and knew each other well. You know how you can tell these things from people's body language. He didn't speak to me. We could always ask Luisa if you think it's important.'

'Luisa's dead, Sally. She was found murdered in her hotel room at the beginning of the week. The police think Jonathan Masterton did it.'

'What? Oh, I know I said I didn't like her, but I wouldn't wish her dead. How was she involved?'

'It's believed that she was Masterton's accomplice and murdered John MacFadzean for him.'

'I really have missed everything, haven't I? And on top of that I have to go now. Sorry! I'm supposed to be in a departmental meeting. I've lost track of the time as usual. We'll carry on this conversation later, yes?'

'OK.'

'Send my love to Isabelle.'

'Of course.'

'Bye, now.'

'Bye.'

I put my mobile back in my pocket, crossed the road and turned into Isabelle's street. My mind was racing with thoughts of my conversation with Sally and then it struck me that I had made a grave error. I had overlooked the clues that pointed to Timothy's involvement. I had convinced myself that Jonathan Masterton was a psychopath and the mastermind behind these murders and not considered that Timothy might be involved. After all, Timothy was as closely connected to the Lathams as his father. He had played at Stowick House with Isabelle and Michael when they were all children and knew them well.

Isabelle had told me that he had travelled around Australia for a year or so about five years ago, spending time with her and Lucy in Melbourne and even staying with Lucy's family in Sydney. It was therefore quite possible he could have met Luisa when he was in Australia. When I had originally asked Isabelle what his occupation was she said that he was an academic. Later, after I asked her if Luisa had a boyfriend here, she mentioned a relationship Luisa had told her about where she had undertaken some research on his behalf. It now occurred to me that they had probably become lovers and that he was the father of her unborn child.

I already suspected that Luisa's meeting with Isabelle and Lucy at the Melbourne International Arts Festival was contrived, but now I felt that this must have been at Timothy's instigation. By Luisa befriending Isabelle and Lucy she would be able to keep him informed. He himself was particularly friendly with Lucy, was at Isabelle's house the night of the alleged overdose, and the one who told Lucy Alex was an impostor.

If I was correct in my assumptions then Isabelle remained in mortal danger. I hotfooted it along the street to her house as there was no time to waste. I retrieved my mobile from my pocket to call DI Evans, but frustratingly I had left his card in my other handbag and did not have his numbers to hand. I called Alex instead but his 'phone diverted to voice mail. I left him a message:

Alex. I'm on my way to Isabelle's. I just realized Jonathan isn't the murderer. It's Timothy. No time to explain. Please call me.

Chapter 32

As I walked up the steps to Isabelle's house I noticed that the front door was ajar. I glanced at my watch; it was almost six-thirty so perhaps Isabelle was waiting for me and had opened the door in anticipation.

'Isabelle?' I called out on reaching the top step. No answer. I gently pushed open the heavy black-painted door. It creaked as I did so as if the hinges needed some oil. 'Isabelle?' I repeated, stepping into the hall. Again there was no answer. The door suddenly slammed shut behind me causing me to start. 'Isabelle,' I said, spinning around, 'there you are.' Only it was not Isabelle. 'Timothy?' I gasped, trying to catch my breath and slowly edging backwards and away from him. 'What are you doing here? Where's Isabelle?' I asked, glancing around me.

'You don't seem very pleased to see me, Alicia.' He shifted towards me menacingly. 'I thought it was time we had a little chat. Don't you?' he said, lunging forward and grabbing me by the wrists, and twisting me around with such force that he shoved me against the front door hitting the back of my head against the lock. I winced with the pain. I must have cut my head as I felt blood trickling down the side of my face.

'Let go of me,' I shouted, struggling and flailing about. He was too strong and I could not release his grip on me, and because he was pressing against me and pushing me back I could barely breathe.

'You responded to my message. You said you were coming to see me as near to six-thirty as you could make it. I thought you were looking forward to it. I've very much been looking forward to our meeting this evening.'

'I sent a message to Isabelle, not to you,' I replied, drawing on all the air in my lungs to respond.

'And there was me thinking you were intelligent. I sent the message to you on Isabelle's mobile just like I sent the messages to Isabelle on Drew's.'

'What have you done with Isabelle?' I said through gritted teeth.

'She's still alive…' he paused. 'For now,' he added sardonically. 'If that's what you're worried about; and I know how *much* you worry about her,' he mocked.

'You'll never get away with it. When I don't turn up for dinner my sister will wonder where I am.' I did not tell him that I had called Alex and left him a message telling him my whereabouts. I prayed that Alex would receive it.

'I've got away with everything else. I'm not going to let you spoil it. I've been working on this for years. You're coming with me,' he barked, dragging me by the arms along the hall and down towards the narrow back stairs with me trying to resist him all the way. My mobile started to ring in my pocket.

'Who is it?' he snarled.

'How do I know?' I retorted. He had to release my arm temporarily to allow me to retrieve it from my pocket.

'Give it to me!' he shouted.

'Here you are!' I squealed, pressing the answer button on the handset and hurling it down the hall towards the front door. I hoped that whoever it was at the end of the line would be able to hear the commotion my end. It was a long shot but worth a try.

'Now that wasn't very POLITE,' he bawled, pulling me by the hair and bending my right arm behind my back again, bringing tears of pain to my eyes as he pushed me onwards down the stairs into the kitchen. 'Do you know how easy it is for me to kill you? They say that once you've killed one person killing another is even easier. And I've already killed quite a few.'

'You're insane!' I cried, fighting to get away from him and trying to kick him. He must have hit me as I temporarily lost consciousness. When I opened my eyes everything was bleary, my head was pounding and I was in the kitchen roped to a sturdy old farmhouse-type wooden chair. My hands were fastened behind my back, and my feet were bound. Timothy was sitting in another chair observing me. I started to moan with the pain.

'Nobody can hear you,' he taunted, putting his hands over his ears and moving his head from side to side. 'There's no point in even trying to scream. Nobody's coming to save you, Alicia. There's going to be no happy ending for you. Alex Waterford is not coming to rescue you. I fixed his scooter,' he said, leaning forward with a quite manic expression, then throwing his head back and starting to laugh. 'The next time he goes for a ride it will be his last.'

'Is that...what you did...to Michael's...motorbike?' I stammered, trying to conceal my agitation, but I knew my voice was trembling. 'Fixed it?'

'Now wouldn't you like to know that?' he said, wagging his finger at me.

'I would. I'm interested,' I said, wheezing. The rope was pulled very tightly across my chest and impeding my breathing. 'Tell me...why you...killed him.'

'It's a long story and I'm not sure we've got the time or, more precisely, whether you have,' he answered, looking at his watch and then glancing at me sadistically.

'Please,' I implored.

'OK, since you ask so politely, it will be your final request. I was always interested in what happened to my Great Aunt Diane after seeing pictures of her in my grandfather's family albums. He told me how she was married to James Latham and that she and Frances had died in a car accident. I did think it slightly odd that although my father was friendly with James Latham my grandparents had nothing to do with him. My grandfather was always evasive when I asked him questions and it made me suspicious. Then I met Lucy

Winters and made a discovery.'

'About her background you mean?'

'Did I say you could ask questions?' he snapped, hitting his thighs with his hands and standing up. As he strutted over to the French windows I noticed a fairly sizeable can of petrol on the floor next to a pile of newspapers. 'I met Lucy for the first time six years ago when Isabelle brought her over to England during the Christmas holidays. I was enamoured by her from the moment I met her.' I did not suppose for one moment that Lucy reciprocated this passion. 'I decided to go out to Australia for a year and to take the opportunity to see as much of her as I could. I was staying at the house in Sydney around the time her grandmother moved there. Her grandmother asked me if I would move some packing boxes for her.

'There was one particular box she did not want me to open and became rather fraught when she thought I had, because it had 'family things' in it, as she put it. I was curious nonetheless, so when everyone was out I retrieved the box and went through it. Among the possessions was a green leather jewellery case with a locket in it. As you know, I had been to Stowick House often and I was familiar with the portrait of Diane which hangs in the library. I recognized the locket Christine Whiteley has as something very similar if not identical to the one worn in the portrait of Diane.

'Later when I saw Isabelle I asked her about it but she said it was mislaid. Lucy knew nothing about it, so I presumed she didn't know. I wondered how Christine had come to be in possession of it. I knew that the Whiteley's had emigrated to Australia from the UK and when I discovered that this was just after Diane's accident and they came from the same part of the country, I was intrigued. I thought perhaps Christine might be related to Diane or a close friend of hers.'

'So you...did some research?'

'I thought I told you NOT to speak,' he snapped, grabbing my jaw and pushing my chin up. 'Do you really want me to gag you?' I shook my head and he released his hold on my jaw. 'Anyway, my research took me back to the UK. I discovered, like you have, that Christine Whiteley's maiden name was Gordon. I thought there must be some family connection because my middle name, and that of my father, is Gordon. My grandfather Philip told me that Gordon was his and Diane's stepfather's name and the name she adopted. He did not want to reveal to me who Christine was at first, but through my research I found out that she was Diane's step-aunt.

'Under pressure, my grandfather disclosed that Lucy is Diane's granddaughter so, unlike you, I had the benefit of being told who she was. I must say I'm very impressed with how you worked it all out. I take my hat off to you. Your research skills and intuition are excellent, but maybe you've been a little *too* thorough for your own good this time,' he gibed. Perhaps that was his idea of a compliment. 'My grandfather told me that James was possessive of Diane and he was making her life a misery and she had decided to leave him. But it all went wrong and she died trying to get away from him. Effectively he drove her to her death. I knew it was possible to prove who Lucy is, but why should she share her inheritance with those who don't deserve it? She deserves to have it all and the only way that was possible was to kill off the Lathams one by one. What do you think?' He could hardly believe I was going to agree with his warped logic. Clearly he was more unhinged than I had at first thought.

'Is that why you sent the notes?' I asked, avoiding answering the question.

'Yes.'

'Where does Luisa fit in with all of this?'

'Ah yes. *La bella* Luisa. We met when I travelled out to Australia. We had an affair but I broke it off because she was too intense. But she was besotted with me and pursued me. I resisted for a while and then, after I discovered the truth about the Latham family, it occurred to me that Luisa might be useful. It was evident that she would do just about anything for me...'

'Including murder?' I interjected.

'Don't interrupt me when I'm speaking! But in answer to your question it would appear so, yes. At my instigation she befriended Isabelle. She deliberately attended the Melbourne International Arts Festival specifically to meet them. She pretended that she was there doing a piece on young exhibitors. She spilt red wine over Isabelle's dress and skilfully managed to wangle her way into Isabelle's set. I was so proud of her. By Luisa befriending Isabelle I was able to follow every move she made without having to ask her or Lucy and therefore remain as the unobtrusive friend in the background.'

'Then you never cared for her at all. You were using her?'

'I never heard her complaining. She did nothing she didn't agree to do,' he replied callously.

'You knew she'd do anything for you, even murder, and you exploited it. I can't believe she would have murdered John MacFadzean unless she thought it was also in her vested interest.'

'You're sharp, I'll give you that. Luisa believed we'd be together and she was doing it for us. It's rather romantic, don't you think?' He started to pull off sheets of newspaper and scrunch them into balls.

'Not from where I'm sitting, no. Why did you want John MacFadzean killed?'

'He was a nuisance. He started to become suspicious because I was always fishing around trying to find out things about the Latham family. Late one evening I had taken my father's keys and I was in the office rummaging through some files. I was on the 'phone to Luisa discussing what to do about Isabelle. I didn't know that John MacFadzean had come into the office and that he had overheard my conversation. We had a bit of a confrontation and although I bluffed my way out of it, I knew that I had to kill him when a few days later he tried to blackmail me.'

'He was a serious gambler, I understand.'

'He was and he owed money everywhere. I agreed to pay him money to keep him quiet but I didn't have the funds. Then it occurred to me how easy it would be to frame him by withdrawing funds from the trust and forging his signature. In that way I could kill two birds with one stone; give him the money and frame him at the same time. The opportunity to kill him arose when he said he was going to Australia, but had he not done so I would have killed him anyway.'

'How did Luisa lure him to Gertrude Street?' I observed him as he continued methodically to scrunch sheets of newspaper into balls.

'They met at the Casino. She was disguised, of course. She knew which buttons to press when it came to his gambling. She invited him back to Gertrude Street to continue the night's entertainment. He didn't need much encouragement. You know the rest.'

'But why did you kill Luisa?'

'I didn't actually intend to kill her when I went to the hotel room. I wanted her to help me kill Isabelle first. She tried in Melbourne, but failed.' So it had been Luisa who had pushed Isabelle into the path of the tram. My instinct about her had been right all along. 'My intention was to persuade her to get rid of the baby. I arranged for a romantic rendezvous at a hotel. She was ecstatic about having our child and would have none of my talk about her terminating the pregnancy. We had an argument. She fell onto the glass table and severed what I presumed was an artery in her leg. She was bleeding profusely from it anyway.'

'So it was an accident?'

'Yes, but I had some Warfarin tablets with me which my grand-father takes for his heart condition to thin his blood. You see, I was hoping to make her miscarry and lose the baby. Suddenly it all seemed perfect. I forced them down her one by one. I did stay with her until she died though. I felt I owed her that.'

'How did you fix Michael's bike?'

'It was easy. I acquired my passion for motorbikes from my grandfather. He was originally an engineer. I can strip down an engine with no problem at all. It was only a question of time and opportunity.' I prayed that he was bluffing about Alex's scooter.

'Did you kill James Latham?'

'I did break in to the house. I was looking for information about Diane. He had a weak heart anyway. I just helped him meet his Maker a little sooner, that's all. The shock of hearing that his daughter was alive and well in Sydney and that I had killed Michael was too much for him. He stumbled and fell, but I would have killed him if he hadn't. Drew's death was unfortunate because I rather liked his art. I managed to lift his mobile at the party the night before to enable me to send those messages to Isabelle.'

'And the overdose?'

'I bungled that. I mixed valerian with her sleeping tablets – but unfortunately the dosage wasn't enough to make it fatal. When I gave the tablets to the paramedics I had removed the valerian.'

'Why did you post the notes from Edinburgh?'

'I thought it was an interesting touch bearing in mind my second name is Gordon.'

'And the flowers I received?'

'They were from me, of course.' Timothy started to place the scrunched up newspaper on the floor. He picked up the can of petrol and had begun to douse the newspaper with it when the doorbell upstairs rang. 'Who on earth can that be?' he snarled, stopping in his tracks and sounding irritated. I presumed it was a rhetorical question and did not respond. At first I thought he was going to ignore it, but the doorbell rang again. 'I'll get rid of whoever it is,' he said, approaching the bottom of the stairs. 'Now is not a good time for visitors. Oh, and just in case you were thinking of screaming,' he added, 'I'm afraid I have to do this,' he said, turning back, taking a roll of carpet tape from a plastic bag on the floor, cutting a piece off with a pair of kitchen scissors and sticking it firmly across my mouth. He left the room, climbed the stairs and I heard the boards creak as he walked across the floor upstairs.

It was impossible to know who it was at the front door, even though I was straining to listen, but I thought it sounded like a man's voice. Whoever it was appeared to be keeping Timothy talking. All of a sudden I was startled by a light tap on the French windows. I turned my head as far as I could and saw Alex peering through them with a horrified look on his face. He must have picked up my message and realized something was seriously wrong. I wondered whether the call I had received when Timothy was attacking me had been from Alex. I could only hope Timothy had not picked up my mobile when he went to the front door as then he'd know that Alex had 'phoned me. Alex tried the door but it was locked. He mouthed something and pointed to the left of him but I could not understand what he meant. Then I heard Timothy's footsteps on the stairs.

'What was that?' he said, entering the kitchen. Obviously I could not respond because my mouth was taped. He pulled the tape off with such force that I felt he had taken half the skin around my mouth with it. 'Sorry about that,' he said, 'but I couldn't have you screaming and ruining things. Did you see anyone outside?' he said suspiciously, walking up to the French windows and scanning the garden area. I shook my head. He must have seen some shadow or movement. He picked up the can of petrol and continued to pour it all around me. The smell of petrol fumes was becoming over-whelming. I would have thought that whoever it was at the front door must have smelt petrol too.

'Who was at the door?' It hurt to move my lips as they were stinging. Evidently he had not picked up my mobile.

'Isabelle's neighbour or friendly neighbourhood watch, should I say.' I assumed he was referring to William Cole, the retired Lieutenant Colonel from next door. 'I couldn't get rid of him. He wanted to know where Isabelle was.' There was a crashing sound from outside as if someone had dropped a milk bottle on the ground. Again Timothy looked out onto the garden, but this time he pushed back the bolts at the top and bottom of the doors, reached for the key from on top of the work surface, put it in the lock, turned the key, pushed open the doors and stepped outside. He wandered into the garden. 'Strange,' he said, turning around. 'There's nobody there,' he continued, walking back inside.

At that moment Alex, who I presumed must have been hiding around the side of the house, leapt out and pounced on Timothy from behind knocking him to the floor. But Timothy was too strong and Alex who was obviously weakened by his abdominal operation could not keep him pinned down. Somehow Timothy managed to throw Alex off, causing him to fall sideways against the wall by the French doors. Alex slumped down to the floor. Tied to the chair I was totally helpless to come to his aid and all I could do was try to scream HELP. However, I was so tightly bound and hyperventilating to such a degree that, with the petrol fumes, I could hardly breathe to speak let alone shout. I started to sob uncontrollably.

'Shut up, bitch!' yelled Timothy, crouching down and feeling Alex's neck for a pulse. 'Don't worry. He's not dead. But you've asked for it now,' he bellowed, bending forward and grabbing the sides of my chair rocking it forcibly. 'You and lover boy have had it coming for a while,' he sneered venomously as he began to drag my chair over to where Alex was lying. Then he reached into his pocket and slowly pulled out a chrome cigarette lighter from within it. 'Now you see it, now you don't,' he taunted, holding the lighter in front of my face and flicking it on and off menacingly.

He turned away from me, picked up a piece of newspaper and rolled it up lengthwise. As he lit the end of it with the lighter a tall silver-haired man – whom I had never set eyes on, but presumed to be Isabelle's neighbour – burst into the kitchen through the open doors and forcibly whacked him across the back of his head with the double-handed thrust of a cricket bat. So great was the impact that it caused him to fall sideways on to the tiled floor banging his head. But as he fell he dropped the lighted piece of newspaper setting light to the petrol-soaked newspaper already lying on the floor. Within seconds the kitchen was ablaze and was filled with billowing blue smoke.

'We've got to get out,' said the stranger, dropping the bat and frantically pulling at the ropes binding me to the chair. 'This place is going to blow up any second.'

'You can't leave Alex,' I implored. Unable to rouse Alex, he slapped his face.

'Get up! Get up! You've got to move.' Alex remained unconscious.

'Let me get you out first,' he exclaimed, hauling the chair with me still tied to it out into the garden. He dragged me as far away from the back of the house as he could and turned the chair with me in it onto its side to shield my face. I heard him run back to the house. It seemed like forever before he returned, dragging something – I hoped it was Alex – with him. 'He's OK,' he said, quickly lying flat on the ground next to me, 'but only just conscious.'

Seconds later there was a huge explosion, shattering the French doors and blasting glass and debris everywhere. Suddenly time stood still and everything went silent. Then I heard the sound of police sirens in the distance. If Isabelle was still inside the house she must be dead.

Chapter 33

'How are you?' asked DI Evans.

It was the afternoon of the day following the explosion. I was still in the Royal Free Hospital but I had been discharged and I was sitting in the chair beside my bed waiting for Antonia to come and collect me. I was desperate for news of Isabelle and nobody had told me anything. When DI Evans appeared I was relieved to see him, but I was also anxious about the news that he would bring.

'I've been better.' I had a nasty cut to my head, some lacerations, rope burns, severe bruising and a broken arm. The doctors had insisted that I stay in hospital overnight because they were concerned with the effects of smoke inhalation. 'Timothy Masterton *is* dead, isn't he?' I asked, not that I believed he could possibly survive that explosion. He nodded. 'And what about Isabelle? Have you found her yet?'

'Yes.'

'Tell me she isn't dead,' I said nervously.

'She isn't.' I smiled weakly with relief.

'Is she all right?'

'Yes.'

'What did Timothy do with her?'

'She told us he met her at the station when she returned to London. He'd found out from Lucy that she was coming back. He made an excuse to accompany her home and once within the confines of her own walls tied her up and put her in the shed. He took her mobile, sent you the text and awaited your arrival.'

'Yes. He told me that.'

'Apparently he was planning to set fire to you both. From what Isabelle tells me, he certainly never had any intention of going up in flames himself.'

'I think that when Alex turned up he decided to kill all three of us together. When he was taunting me with the cigarette lighter I felt that he wouldn't set fire to the place unless he knew he could get out. But then the neighbour came in and thwacked him with the cricket bat. That caused the fire because Timothy was holding the lighted taper when he fell to the floor. Mind you, he would have killed us anyway, so thank God the neighbour was there to drag me out.'

'You were very lucky; Alex Waterford, too, by the sound of it. Lieutenant Colonel Cole is very agile. He said that Alex contacted him after he received your message. Isabelle introduced them when Alex was staying with her, so he knew who Alex was. Cole diverted Timothy by ringing the doorbell and Alex accessed the garden through Cole's and you know the rest.'

'How is Alex? I did ask, but they said he had been discharged already.'

'He suffered a rather nasty bump to the side of his head when he fell and inhaled some smoke but he's going to be fine.'

'Oh, that's excellent news,' I replied, perking up. 'I thought Timothy had killed him. I am still very concerned though, because Timothy told me he had fixed Alex's scooter. He said that the next time Alex rode it would be his last. I don't know whether he just said that to rile me, but I don't think we can take any of his threats for granted. On no account must Alex ride it.'

'Don't worry. We'll see to that. Now, when you're up to it, I would like to take a detailed statement from you about what happened at the house with Timothy.'

'How he confessed you mean? He confirmed that he was responsible for the murders of Michael, Drew, and Luisa. Luisa killed John MacFadzean for him. He was the one that broke into James Latham's house. He taunted him about Frances not being dead, but alive and well in Sydney, and told him he had killed Michael. He would have killed him if he hadn't died of natural causes.'

'I see.' DI Evans swallowed hard.

'No, you don't. He delighted in telling me how he murdered them all. He savoured every minute. He sat and waited for Luisa to bleed to death. Can you imagine doing that?' I began to feel rather traumatised by the previous days events. 'Anyway, I presume you've released Jonathan Masterton?' He nodded. 'What's the news on Philip Masterton? Has he regained consciousness yet?'

'Yes. He seems to have improved.'

'Do you think he'll talk to us?'

'We'll have to wait and see.'

About half an hour after DI Evans left Antonia arrived to collect me.

'*Ciao, carina. Come stai? Stai bene?*'

'*Così così,*' I replied.

'I don't know, the steps some people will take to avoid coming to dinner with their sister,' she chided.

'I'm sorry.' She laughed.

'Guess who I bumped into on my way in?' she said, bending down and kissing me on both cheeks. Alex appeared from around the corner carrying a big spray of spring flowers.

'Alex!' I exclaimed. He had a dressing on the side of his head and a rather black eye. 'How are you?'

'I'll be fine. You?' he asked, smiling at me.

'My head's a bit sore and my arm aches but I'm glad to be alive. Thanks for turning up when you did.'

'I picked up your voice message and I called you back. I knew there was something very wrong because you answered it and all I could hear was shouting in the background.'

'Timothy wanted my mobile so I just pressed the answer button and threw it across the floor hoping that whoever it was at the other end would hear what was going on.'

'I called Mamma,' said Antonia. 'Don't be cross. I know you didn't want me to, but I had to tell her.'

'I just didn't want to worry her.'

'Well, you'll never stop that. Come on; let's get you home. Why don't you come with us, Alex? I know you and Alicia must have a lot to talk about,' she said, glancing at him and then back at me.

We had barely arrived back at the flat when there was a call from DS Mitchell to say that he was sending a car to take us to St George's Hospital in Tooting which was where Philip Masterton was hospitalized. Philip had told the police he wanted to speak to Isabelle and she had requested that Alex and I be present and he had agreed. DS Mitchell and Isabelle greeted Alex and me at the entrance to the hospital.

'Are you both OK?' she said, with a worried expression on her face as soon as she saw us.

'We look worse than we feel,' said Alex. 'How are you?'

'Physically, I'm OK. I'm more of an emotional wreck than anything else. I don't think I can take much more of this.'

'Let's see what Philip Masterton has to say,' said DS Mitchell, leading us inside. Philip Masterton was in a side room off the ward. He had been moved from the high dependency unit. I thought he looked very frail in his hospital bed surrounded by monitors and machinery. The back of the bed was raised and he was propped up by pillows. He lifted his head on seeing us enter the room.

'Isabelle Parker?' he asked. I thought his breathing was quite laboured and shallow.

'Yes. That's me,' she replied, moving forward. 'This is Alex Waterford and Alicia Allen,' she said, introducing us. She pulled up a chair beside his bed and Alex and I sat on chairs at the end of the bed. DS Mitchell remained standing.

'I know about Timothy,' he said. His voice was very weak and I had to concentrate hard to hear what he was saying from where I sat. 'It's my entire fault. I should have told him the truth about himself.' Alex and I looked at each other.

'What do you mean? We know who he is,' said Isabelle.

'No. That's the thing. You all think you do, but you don't.'

'Please explain.' Isabelle looked confused, Alex seemed bewildered and I was totally perplexed.

'As you know, Diane was my younger sister. Our father died during World War II and just after the war our mother married Charles Gordon and Diane took his name.'

'Yes,' said Isabelle, nodding.

'But what you don't know is that she fell madly in love with an American airman called Larry Tierney who was stationed near us at the end of the war.' My ears pricked up. This was the American Alex had been trying to find out about. 'To cut a long story short, when she discovered she was pregnant he abandoned her and returned to the States. Apart from myself, my wife Annette and our mother and stepfather nobody knew of her pregnancy. She was only fifteen at the time and Annette and I had recently married so we decided to take the child and pass him off as our own son.'

'So Jonathan was Diane's son, not yours?' said Isabelle, sounding incredulous. This meant that Timothy was actually Diane's grandson. Something I would never have guessed.

'Yes. We thought that our secret was safe. Diane was introduced to your grandfather at a charity art function in the spring of 1955. He quickly took a shine to her and it was rather a whirlwind romance. They seemed like the perfect couple at first but he was very possessive and jealous of her spending time with other men, even accusing her of having an affair with one of his friends.'

'Was she having an affair?' asked Isabelle.

'No. But after Frances was born the marriage deteriorated and Diane confided in me that she wanted to leave him. She knew that if she tried to divorce him he would fight her through the courts and there was Frances to consider. It came to me that in order for Diane and Frances to get away from him we would have to feign their deaths and create a new identity for them. The original plan was to send them to Canada.'

'So why didn't they go?' she asked.

'Something unexpected happened. Larry Tierney turned up trying to blackmail her. Back in the US he saw a picture of Diane with James Latham at a charity function in a society magazine: *Town & Country* or the *New Yorker*. I can't remember which. But he realized that she had married into money and returned to England. He demanded she pay for his silence. Diane refused, but he said he would tell your grandfather about her past if she didn't pay him.' It was unsurprising Diane had told the police she did not know him. No doubt the day the witness saw him in her car she was trying to persuade him to leave her be. 'He also wanted to know what had happened to their child. She told him that she had miscarried, but he did not believe her, although he could find no birth certificate as Jonathan had been registered as my child. Diane was behaving rather strangely so this encouraged James to think she was having an affair. Although Larry had no evidence to substantiate his claims, with James the way he was, the risk of him telling him was too great.'

'So what did she do?' asked Isabelle.

'I told Diane to arrange to meet Larry in a remote place late at night, supposedly to pay him some money. The idea was that I would come with her and warn him off. When he turned up on a motorbike I saw an opportunity to get rid of him. You see, before the war I had been training as an automobile engineer and knew what to do to fix his motorbike. While she was pleading with him I did just that. He had an accident and was killed.' Timothy had clearly learned his mechanical skills at Philip's knee.

'So you killed Jonathan's father and Timothy's grandfather?' I interrupted. That was indeed a revelation. I could hardly absorb what he was disclosing.

'Yes. I did it for Diane. I'd do it again. But after his death there were rumours that Diane was involved with Larry and, although Diane denied any connection with him, James became suspicious.'

'I think that's understandable,' said Isabelle. I thought she was taking all this remarkably calmly. 'So what happened next?'

'Diane planned to leave your grandfather when he was in London. Annette and I agreed to take Frances for her. Jonathan was away at school so he didn't know about it. Diane arranged to meet Annette and entrusted her with Frances. It was the housekeeper's day off so easier for Diane to make arrangements. She put Frances' things in the car with her favourite doll because she intended to collect her later. But James returned unexpectedly from London. He saw her driving off and chased her in his car thinking that she had taken Frances. When I heard the news that Diane had been killed, I knew we had to move her so we entrusted her to the care of Christine Whiteley and her husband Nicholas. As you know, Christine was my stepfather's sister. They were planning to emigrate to Australia and were more than happy for Frances to be passed off as their daughter. The one thing Christine kept for her was a locket belonging to Diane.'

'The one that she's wearing in the portrait Grandpa had painted of her,' said Isabelle.

'And the one Timothy saw in Christine's 'family' box,' I added.

'Yes,' he replied.

'How could you do that to my grandfather?' Isabelle interjected violently, losing her composure and breaking down. 'You took away his daughter and let him think she was dead,' she raged, but tears were pouring down her face. 'My grandfather thought he had killed his wife and daughter and never forgave himself. And because he felt guilty about your sister he recommended your son to a post at Holmwood & Hitchins. Perhaps if you'd told Timothy the truth none of this would have happened. But you didn't want to tell him that it was *you* who killed his real grandfather, did you? To think that all this time I thought my grandfather might have been guilty. I hate you,' she said, jumping out of her chair and running out of the room. 'You destroyed *my* family!'

'What do you think will happen now?' I asked Alex after we left the hospital and were making our way back to my flat.

'Isabelle will come to terms with it. She wanted to know the truth about what happened with her grandfather. Now she does.'

'I meant about Philip Masterton.'

'I don't suppose anything will happen. He's a very old man with a failing heart. I think he wanted to unburden himself before he dies. He did what he thought was for the best. Unfortunately, the consequences for his family were dire. I think he never thought the truth would be discovered, but the truth nearly always has a strange way of coming out…eventually. Not that I think if he had told Timothy the truth it would have made that much difference because Timothy was a psychopath anyway.'

'I suppose you're right. I can't believe I got it so wrong. I should have realized it was Timothy sooner.'

'You didn't get it wrong. *We* did. We're a team remember, although now our professional arrangement is at an end I'm not quite sure how that leaves things between us,' he said, looking wistfully at me.

'Dorothy thinks we should give it a go,' I replied, catching his arm.

'She does? Well, she's a remarkable woman. I've always valued her opinion,' he said whimsically. 'But what do you think? Is there a chance her goodwill towards me will ever rub off onto you?'

'You know when you were in the office and Rachel interrupted us?' He nodded. 'You never finished your sentence. You said that if only I wasn't so damned… So damned what?'

'Indecisive.'

'Hmm… *Così sono le donne. Tutto cambiare di parere.*'

'What are you talking about?' he asked, looking perplexed. 'You haven't answered my question?'

'Every chance.'

THE END

Read the first part of the trilogy…

ALICIA ALLEN INVESTIGATES 1

A MODEL MURDER

By Celia Conrad

Alicia Allen is a London solicitor about to discover she has
an unusual flair for solving crime. When her Australian
neighbour, Tamsin Brown, a model, is brutally raped and
beaten to death, her flatmate Kimberley Davies begs for
Alicia's help and she cannot easily refuse. After her
inquisitive elderly neighbour Dorothy Hammond is
savagely attacked, Alicia knows there's no turning back and
she soon becomes embroiled in the hunt for Tamsin's killer
and the sleazy world of hostess clubs. Meanwhile, having
accepted a new job at the firm of Wilson, Weil & Co.,
where Kimberley works as a secretary, she discovers that
nothing there is as it seems and that nobody can be trusted,
not even a Junior Partner called Alexander Waterford to
whom she is attracted. Alicia's tenacious investigations,
however, have life-threatening consequences for those drawn
into the evil web created by Tamsin's killer, who believes
there is such a thing as a model murder…

ISBN 978 09546233 26 (0 9546233 2 0)
PUBLISHED BY BARCHAM BOOKS
£10.99
ORDER YOUR COPY NOW

Read the final part of the trilogy…

ALICIA ALLEN INVESTIGATES 3

MURDER IN HAND

By Celia Conrad

Through her Uncle Vico, a New York attorney, Alicia Allen, a young London solicitor, is introduced to Fabio Angelino to deal with the Probate of his mother's English estate. Fabio's father once worked with Vico at the New York firm of Scarpetti, Steiglitz & Co., but sixteen years earlier disappeared in Sicily, the Italian police concluding that he was murdered by the Mafia. After a trip to the Amalfi Coast, Fabio tells Alicia someone has tried to kill him. When Fabio's sister, Giulia, is found callously murdered, Alicia investigates their father's disappearance, and is convinced that Giulia's research on the Angelino family background in Lucca holds the key to the mystery. Finding evidence of massive corruption in both London and Italy, Alicia determines to expose the criminals. But in her bid to entrap them, has Alicia taken on malevolent forces too great, and will this be her last investigation?

ISBN 978 09546233 4 0 (0 9546233 4 7)
PUBLISHED BY BARCHAM BOOKS
£10.99
ORDER YOUR COPY NOW

Celia Conrad was educated at King's College at the
University of London and now lives and writes in London.